THE SHIP

Stefán Máni grew up in Ólafsvík, a small village on the west coast of Iceland. He left school at an early age and became a fisherman, which meant a hard and often violent life at sea. Over time Stefán realised he wanted something else from life, especially as many of his friends ended up in prison – or worse. Sixteen years and several books later, he wrote *Skipið*, which won the 2007 Drop of Blood prize for best Icelandic crime novel. *The Ship* has been translated into many European languages and at last is now available in English. Stefán lives in Reykjavík.

THE SHIP

STEFÁN MÁNI

Translated by Wincie Jóhansdottir

PIER 9

Published for the first time in the English language by Pier 9, an imprint of Murdoch Books Australia Pty Limited, 2012

Murdoch Books Australia
Pier 8/9
23 Hickson Road
Millers Point NSW 2000
Phone: +61 (0) 2 8220 2000
Fax: +61 (0) 2 8220 2558
www.murdochbooks.com.au
info@murdochbooks.com.au

Copyright © Stefán Máni 2007

Title of the original Icelandic edition: *Skipið*
Published by agreement with Forlagið, www.forlagid.is.
English translation copyright © Wincie Jóhansdottir 2012

The moral right of the author has been asserted.

All rights reserved. No part of this publication may be reproduced, stored in a retrieval system or transmitted in any form or by any means, electronic, mechanical, photocopying, recording or otherwise, without the prior written permission of the publisher.

National Library of Australia
Cataloguing-in-Publication entry:

Author: Mani, Stefan.

Title: The ship / Stefan Mani.

ISBN: 9781742661919 (pbk.).

Subjects: Crime--Fiction.
Suspense fiction.

Dewey Number: A823.4

Cover design by Madacin Creative
Cover images by Malcolm Fife / © Alamy (ship); Kim Westerskov / © Getty Images (sea); Maga / © Shutterstock (lightning)
Author picture courtesy of Jóhann Páll Valdimarsson
Printed in Australia by Griffin Press

 The paper this book is printed on is certified against the Forest Stewardship Council® Standards. Griffin Press holds FSC chain of custody certification SGS-COC-005088. FSC promotes environmentally responsible, socially beneficial and economically viable management of the world's forests.

The rusty brown hull rests on underwater crags, sloping five degrees to port and thirty astern. Its prow pierces the ice at a sharp angle and the stern juts out over a murky fissure, causing the six-storey wheelhouse to lean over the abyss like a haunted house, the empty windows of the bridge staring at nothing. During the day, bluish light filters through the ice into the depths, where curious seals swim around the wreck, which quickens occasionally in the ocean currents, producing a long, drawn-out screech, heavy thumps and a thick oil slick, green, pink and purple in the weak light that floats up under the ice like liquid aurora borealis.

That which sleeps forever is not dead.

I

Monday, 10 September 2001

It's four minutes to eight in the narrow kitchen of the Old Town house where a young family of three is eating cabbage and meatballs with melted butter and new potatoes.

Outside the window is the cold and dark of autumn; inside the kitchen it is warm and bright.

'I'd have liked to have something a little better for your dinner, Sæli love,' says his partner as she cuts up a meatball for their three-year-old son.

'This is just what I wanted, Lára, my sweet,' says Sæli, smiling as he helps himself to more food. 'I'll be getting nothing but cream soups, roast meat and gravy for the next month.'

'Poor you!' says Lára with a grin.

'Come on, you know what I mean,' Sæli says, gently pinching her waist.

Sæli is first seaman on a freighter and Lára works as a hairdresser in 101 Reykjavík, the heart of the city.

'Did I show you that flat on Framnes Road?' asks Lára, wiping most of the tomato sauce off her son's face. 'There were pictures of it in today's paper.'

'Yes. No … I didn't see it,' mutters Sæli with a sigh. 'I thought we weren't going to look at flats just yet?'

'There's no harm in keeping our eyes open,' says Lára, irritated.

'Yes, I know ... I just ...' Sæli puts his right hand over her left. 'It's just that there are enough payments as things stand, and ...'

'We can't stay here forever,' says Lára with a maternal smile for her son, who is guzzling water from a sticky glass. 'Not now that – you know?'

'I know,' Sæli says under his breath. He carries on eating, though his appetite is gone.

'We'll look into it when you get back, okay?' says Lára, affectionate now.

'Yes, we will.' Sæli looks tenderly into the eyes of the woman he loves, then the distracting sound of his mobile phone, ringing out in the hall, suddenly makes him tense.

'Do you have to answer it?' says Lára.

'I'll be quick,' says Sæli, bolting from the table. He fishes the phone out of the inside pocket of his jacket and looks at the lit-up screen.

Name withheld

'Hello?'
'This is Satan.'

Sæli has no idea of the real name of this man, who introduced himself that way when he phoned the first time, a few days ago.

'Yes, hello,' says Sæli, then continues in a lower voice: 'I'll phone you back in a while ... Don't phone again. I'll phone, all right?'

'Listen to me,' says the cold, calm voice on the phone.

'No, you listen to —'

'I'm in the neighbourhood,' says Satan firmly. 'Would you rather invite me in?'

'No, I ...' Sæli glances into the kitchen, where Lára is pretending to not watch or listen. 'What do you want?'

Sæli slips to the front door and peers out the window beside it. He sees a maroon BMW 750 parked halfway up on the footpath across the street. The car is purring in neutral and at the wheel sits a young man the size of a full-grown bear.

'You owe money,' says the caller.

'I know, I know,' responds Sæli, scratching his head as he speaks. 'And I intend to …'

'Nobody forced you to play poker with those guys,' says the voice, still flat, calm and as cold as before.

'No, I —'

'You're about to sail, aren't you?' says Satan without waiting for an answer. 'My client has connections in Colombia. His people will take a package addressed to you to the harbour down there. They know the name of your ship and when it's expected to arrive. You are to bring that package home. Do you understand what I'm saying?'

'Smuggling?' whispers Sæli, so dry mouthed he's hoarse.

'First instalment on your debt,' says Satan calmly.

'First instalment?' whispers Sæli fiercely, going red to the roots of his hair. '*I could land in jail.* Who … How … What's in this …?'

'You sail, you collect the package. That's it,' says Satan icily. 'I'll make sure nothing happens to your wife and son while you're away. Understand?'

'If you … Don't you dare –'

'You bring the package,' Satan interjects with the conviction of one who's in control. 'I look after the family. That's it.'

'What … Hello?' says Sæli, but there's no one on the line, just silence and the echo of his own heartbeat. He again looks out the window, in time to see the BMW roll down off the footpath and disappear around the corner, its exhaust streaming behind it like a tail.

'I wonder what it costs to have a man killed?' Sæli asks himself softly as he returns his mobile phone to his jacket pocket.

Sæli has already been in touch with a friend of his cousin's who has some knowledge of the underworld; Sæli told him about this problem when Satan first called, in the hope that the friend could give him some good advice or even sort out the mess for him. That guy was pretty tough himself, but when he heard the name 'Satan' he just wished Sæli good luck and hung up.

What should he do, Sæli wonders now. What *can* he do?

Sæli tries to swallow but feels as if he has a potato stuck in his throat. Then he tries to rid himself of all worries and ugly thoughts before turning back to the kitchen and his family.

'Who …?' asks Lára, giving her partner the look of a woman who suspects there's another woman in the picture. After all, he often disappears for hours on end when he's on shore leave. What's she supposed to think?

'It was just Rúnar,' says Sæli, clearing his throat as he resumes his place at the table. Then he forces a smile and pats his son's head, before he fleetingly looks at his partner, who is trying to rid herself of her suspicions.

'Is everything all right?' asks Lára cautiously.

'Yes, it's just …' Sæli sighs. The bosun, Rúnar, had phoned him earlier and asked him to meet him and three other crew members before they joined the ship. 'He was just reminding me of that meeting I told you about.'

'Oh … I see.' Lára smiles crookedly.

An hour or so later Sæli is sitting by his son's bed, reading him a fairytale by lamplight.

'You know Daddy has to leave later on?' says Sæli when the story is finished.

'On the ship?' the boy says with a sigh.

'Yes.'

'Can I come too?' asks the boy eagerly but without much conviction.

'No, lad,' says his father, smiling despite all his worries and the pain of parting. 'You have to look after Mummy for me.'

'I know,' the boy mutters, pulling his doona up to his chin.

'Daddy will be thinking about you,' says Sæli, kissing the

boy on the forehead and turning off the light. 'Your daddy loves you.'

'Egill loves his daddy,' says the boy in the dark. As Sæli squeezes the little hand his stomach knots up and salty tears run down his cheeks.

Once the boy is asleep, Sæli joins Lára on the couch. She pulls a blanket over the two of them and snuggles up to him.

Candles glow in the living room; incense smokes on top of the darkened television set and the soundtrack of *Fire Walk with Me* sounds softly from the CD player.

Sæli stares at the flames and absentmindedly fiddles with Lára's hair, which flows down her back like silk.

'You remember I've got to meet Rúnar and the others,' says Sæli softly and he feels how Lára stiffens under the blanket.

'Why?'

'I don't know,' says Sæli with a sigh. 'Something to do with work.'

'Can't it wait?' she asks, irritated.

'Apparently not,' mutters Sæli with another sigh.

'Don't you let them get you into any trouble,' Lára says, sitting up to look him in the eye.

'No, of course not.' Sæli is anxious now and somewhat uncomfortable. 'There just seems to be something they need to talk about.'

'Will you be back?'

'No,' answers Sæli, his stomach clenching. 'We'll take a cab out to the ship after.'

'I'm going to miss you,' says Lára with an empty look. 'I mean, like, more than usual … you know.'

'I understand.' Sæli says, placing his left palm on her stomach, which has a tiny life swimming in its warm sea. 'You might have a bulge by the time I get back?'

'Maybe.' Lára smiles faintly. 'When should we tell Egill?'

'When I get back,' says Sæli firmly. 'Then we'll tell him together.'

'All right,' Lára murmurs, dreamy-eyed. She leans forward and kisses her man, who pulls her down on top of him and rolls her carefully onto the floor. 'Am I the one and only?' she whispers between kisses.

'Absolutely the one and only.'

Outside the wind is coming up from the west, the curtains twitch, the candle flames flicker and fat raindrops burst against the dark windowpanes in tune to wet kisses, wild hearts and the sombre music. The flames hiss, sputter and go out, the glow dies and the blue smoke swims like a fish into the dark, disappearing into the deep.

Evil lasts forever and nothing good is eternal.

II

The dark in the double garage is absolute, then ceiling lights flicker and come on one after another. Footsteps echo from wall to wall as a young woman wearing high-heeled leather boots strides quickly across the concrete floor. She is dressed in a short skirt, thin blouse and high-heeled leather boots, and carries her two-year-old daughter under one arm.

'Mummy's car,' says the little girl as her mother walks past a two-door Mercedes-Benz convertible.

'Daddy's car,' she says when her mother unlocks a silver Range Rover Vogue with a smart key.

'Yeah, yeah, keep still,' says the mother impatiently as she secures her daughter in the car seat in the back of the four-wheel drive, which smells of leather polish, rubber and cleaning fluids, like the new car that it is.

The eight-cylinder petrol engine purrs as the garage doors open and the woman backs out the car, past two concrete lions and onto the street. The garage is under a two-storey villa which is all lit up in the cold and dark of the autumn night, its windows like the red eyes of a wary sphinx. The garage doors close, the engine note rises and the Range Rover disappears into the dark of the suburb of Staðahverfi, one of the most thinly populated areas of Reykjavík.

'Where are we going?' asks the child in the back seat. She is dressed in pyjamas and woollen socks, and she'd been sound asleep just a few minutes earlier.

'To Granny's,' her mother answers briskly as she puts even more pressure on the accelerator.

Three minutes later she pulls up in front of a block of flats in the suburb of Rimahverfi.

'Can I come in?' asks the little girl, rubbing her eyes.

'No, just wait. I won't be a minute,' says her mother without turning around. She hops out of the car, leaving it running in the dark car park.

'Mummy,' says the little girl softly as she watches her mother run towards the building and disappear through an open ground-floor window.

An old lady wakes up when someone turns on the light in her bedroom. On a dark shelf by her bed stands a seven-branched gold candlestick and on the edge of the shelf a highly polished copper plaque proclaims:

Hear, O Israel: the Lord our God is one Lord!

'Where's the case?' demands the woman's daughter-in-law, standing at the end of the bed.

'Lilja?' says the old lady, sitting up in bed. She is slim and healthy looking, brown-eyed and olive-skinned. 'What are you doing?' she continues in her strong German accent. 'Is something wrong? How did you get in? Where is Jon Karl?'

'Where is the case?' says Lilja again, grinding her teeth. 'He sent me to fetch the case. Where is it?'

'The case? What case, dear?' The woman slips out of bed and puts on a bathrobe over her nightgown. She moves like a ballerina.

'The red case. The suitcase,' Lilja hisses. 'The case he asked you to keep for him.'

'Oh, *that* case,' mutters the old lady, studying her daughter-in-law with a look of doubt and suspicion. 'I almost decided to just take it to the recycling. Don't care to keep something I don't know what it is. And then you come to fetch it in the middle of the night! I haven't seen you for over a week and then you just wake me up like …'

'The case. *Now!*' Lilja spits out and clenches her fists. 'I haven't got all night!'

'What in the world?' says the woman in her accented Icelandic, pulling her bathrobe tighter. 'I'm woken suddenly from a deep sleep and then you just insult me and —'

'Listen! None of that!' says Lilja, grabbing the old lady's shoulder. 'Little Sara is waiting in the car. Do you want her to be kidnapped or something?'

'Is the baby out in the car?' the woman says, gasping. 'Is something the matter with you, woman? Why are you gadding about with the child in the middle of the night? Why did you not bring her inside? Is something wrong? Where is Jon Karl?'

'*Where is the fucking case?*' screams Lilja and yanks her mother-in-law's shoulder so hard that the sleeve rips off her bathrobe.

'In the laundry room. Don't …' says the old lady weakly, but she stops speaking when her daughter-in-law lets go of her.

'Where?' asks Lilja, turning on the laundry-room light.

'Under the table. Behind the laundry basket.' The old lady has followed her into the hall.

'Here it is,' mutters Lilja. She pulls out a red suitcase which she attempts to open, but it's locked and she doesn't know the combination.

'Where is Jon Karl?' the woman says again, following her daughter-in-law to the front door. 'Where is my son? Is he in trouble?'

'Mind your own business,' is Lilja's answer. Then Lilja strides out into the night, both hands locked round the suitcase handle.

Lilja opens the back of the Range Rover, lifts the case in, secures it and closes the door.

'Granny!' shouts the girl in the car.

'My sweetheart!' says her grandmother, on the verge of tears. With trembling fingers she taps the window in front of the child's face.

'Bugger off!' says Lilja, shoving her mother-in-law into a flowerbed before getting into the car. She backs out of the parking lot at speed, brakes sharply and burns rubber along the tarmac.

'Where's Granny?' asks her child from the back seat.

'She just went back to sleep,' says her mother dryly as she lights a cigarette.

'Mummy, it's not allowed to smoke in —'

'Mind your own business,' her mother spits out as she cracks open the driver's window a little.

In another two minutes or so they are back in Staðahverfi, where the houses all look alike as the growling car rushes past them in the dark.

When their house comes into sight, however, we recognise it right away: the concrete lions eternally on guard by the driveway and the horizontal windows flaming like the eyes of a creature neither old nor young, real nor imagined.

Lilja parks the Range Rover partly up on the footpath in front of the stairs leading to the front door, puts it into neutral and considers whether she should honk the horn. But the night is too electric, too silent. She doesn't honk.

'Mummy …'

'Hush!' says Lilja, staring at the house. She bites her lower lip and taps the ash from her cigarette out of the open window.

Then she glances at the clock in the instrument panel.

01:13

Suddenly the house goes dark. Less than fifteen seconds later three shots blast a hole in the fragile silence. The gunpowder flashes light up the house, one of the living-room windows shatters and shards of glass rain down on the driveway.

Lilja throws her cigarette out the window, shoves the car into gear and floors the accelerator. The Range Rover bounds away, roars down off the footpath and disappears into the night.

'Mummy,' whimpers the little girl when they are halfway

to the town of Mosfellsbær. 'Where are we going?'

'To the summer house,' mutters her mother as, with shaking hands, she lights another cigarette. She turns on the wipers; a few raindrops hit the windscreen.

There aren't many cars around and the dark Westland Highway merges with the cold night.

'Where's Daddy?' asks the child as she stares out the window.

'He's coming later,' her mother replies, forcing a smile in the rear-view mirror. 'Just try to sleep, my love.'

'Yes,' says the girl, watching the lights as the car zooms through Mosfellsbær doing well over 100 kilometres an hour.

Near the Thingvellir turn-off the Range Rover hits something hard and swerves back and forth until Lilja regains control.

'Mummy?' asks the girl, waking suddenly from her nap.

'It's nothing,' says her mother, her slim fingers clenched round the steering wheel.

The right headlight is broken and there's a long crack in the windscreen, which has dark red streaks of blood running across it.

Lilja presses a button that squirts lemon-scented fluid onto the windscreen and then speeds up the wipers. They mix the blood with the rain and spread it around until it can hardly be seen any more.

'Oh, my God,' says Lilja under her breath as she blinks away the tears, but instead of slowing down or stopping, she accelerates, hurtling into the rainy night at almost 200 kilometres an hour.

Lilja stares ahead as if in a trance, but the only thing she sees is the face of the man she hit. Frozen in a single moment. After he appeared in the lights and just before the car hit him. An ash-grey face. Paper thin.

A death mask.

Engraved on her mind.

III

Heavy blues music, the clamour of voices and a cloud of bitter smoke are pierced by the loud peal of a bell, as if from a ship lost in fog near the shore of some strange land.

The sound creates ripples on the dark surface of the regulars' subconscious, and a cold sweat on their backs.

Déjà vu.

'Fifteen minutes to closing!' the bartender shouts, letting go of the cord that hangs from the clapper of the old brass bell that once served a Dutch freighter.

On the ground floor of the bar customers are smoking and drinking at the tables; some are playing chess or whist, others talking with their neighbours and others still are sitting alone at the bar, intent on their own wretchedness and the oblivion of drink.

Like the guy in denim who looks glassy eyed at the last sip in a greasy beer glass and then at his watch, which tells him it's fifteen minutes to one in the morning on Tuesday.

00:45

He finishes the last of his beer, puts out his half-smoked cigarette and gets down off the high bar stool. Then he weaves his way over to a circular table, where five men sit drinking. He claps the two nearest on the back, leans forward between them and smiles ingratiatingly through his untrimmed beard.

'D'you think you could lend me a ten-coin, lads?' he asks, clearing his throat. 'I haven't got any change and I have to make a call.'

'Leave us alone, man!' says one of the men he's leaning on, poking an elbow in the drunk's stomach and pushing him away from the table.

The drunk takes two steps back then stops to gain his balance, freezes in that position and stares straight ahead, as though in a trance.

It's as if his soul has gone to sleep, as if his personality has abandoned his drunken body. His eyes go dark and sink into his head, his mouth gapes and for just a moment there is literally no sign of life in his deathly pale face, which is little more than a skin-covered skull. He is lifeless – he has turned into a ghost or a zombie – but only for that single moment.

Then it's as if an invisible hand seizes a silver thread in a dusky dream. His lungs draw breath, his eyes swell back out of their sockets, his fingers twitch and his tongue moves in his gaping mouth.

His soul has awakened, his heart beats and a character, of sorts, flickers like candlelight behind his glassy eyes.

'Five, five, five … ship,' the drunken man mumbles. He regains his balance on the floorboards, then clutches the stair rail and trudges up to the second floor of the bar.

'Do you suppose that guy realises he's walking on dry land?' says the one who had pushed him. His mates laugh at this. But their laughter is neither long nor loud. They happen to be discussing serious matters. And they don't have all night.

'Anyway, getting back to those capitalists,' one of them says, curling his huge hand around a small shot glass of whiskey. 'I have dependable sources inside the shipping company who say they're about to cancel the flag-state contract on our ship.'

The speaker is the self-appointed socialist leader 'Big' John Pétursson, chief engineer on a large freighter that was built in China ten years ago and now belongs to a Malaysian investor, is registered in Monrovia and has been chartered by the Icelandic shipping company Polar Ships for the past five years.

'What's a flag-state contract?' says Ási, the cook, as he lights a cigarette.

'That means the chartering company pays for everything,' answers the bosun, Rúnar Hallgrímsson.

'Insurance, repairs, the lot?' asks Ási.

'I'm telling you,' says Rúnar, who had pushed the drunk away from the table.

'And then what?' asks Ársæll 'Sæli' Egilsson.

'They're planning to get a new ship, those capitalist princes,' says Big John, squinting like a sleepy bear. 'And a new crew.'

'Enough with the griping about capitalists!' says Methúsalem Sigurðsson, chief mate, and the only one of this gang of five who comes from 'upstairs' – that is, from the bridge. 'This matter is above politics and factions.'

'What crew?' asks Sæli, whose mouth is dry and head aching with the worry of everything that's going on in his simple life.

'The crew will come with the ship,' says Big John calmly.

'Some scabs with a one-year contract,' says Methúsalem, his right hand fiddling with the heavy gold Freemason's ring that fits loosely on the middle finger of his left hand, 'who'll be sent home at the end of the year and replaced by another lot of the same kind.'

'Have you ever heard anything like it?' says Rúnar, softly beating the table with his clenched fist.

'We're a dying breed, boys,' responds Big John, finishing his whiskey. 'The dodo birds of Icelandic sailors.'

'It would serve them right if ...' says Sæli, sighing.

'We should stick together and refuse to sail tonight!' declares Ási, violently crushing his cigarette in the ashtray. 'Make those pen-pushers sit up and take notice!'

'Hear, hear!' says Sæli.

'No. That's just what they want,' says Big John, ever the stoic. 'That would give them a reason to sack the lot of us and save the expense of our severance pay. Besides, all our rights would be called into question.'

'What do you suggest?' asks Ási, who starts chewing on a match.

'Why did you call us together?' Sæli says. 'And how come only us?'

'I don't trust the other four,' says Big John, leaning forward. 'Simple as that.'

'John, Rúnar and me had already got together,' says Methúsalem, 'and we felt we could count on your support.'

'I'd have thought that Jónas could be trusted,' says Ási of the second mate.

'That's what I'd have thought, too,' Sæli says, nodding.

'I'm not taking any chances. Jónas isn't entirely trustworthy, in my opinion. And don't forget that the new deckhand is his brother-in-law,' says Big John. 'We don't know a thing about him!'

'That's true,' mutters Sæli.

'As far as I remember,' says Methúsalem, 'Jónas has pretty much stood by those penny-pinchers over the years, like that time they decided to cut the crew by four. Have you forgotten that?'

'No,' Sæli and Ási respond quietly.

'He's always sucked up to the Old Man and done everything he's told. And the Old Man is just the shipping company's mouthpiece,' says Big John. 'Whether those two have been told what's happening and been promised other jobs, I don't know. But this I do know: the Old Man knows everything the office knows, so he's going to try to have a majority of the crew on his side, in case word gets out about the management's capitalistic plot.'

'No politics!' says Methúsalem, waving an imperious finger.

'Unless it suits you conservatives, is that it?' says Big John, his bearded face going as red as the old Soviet flag. 'Goddamn fascist bullshit all the time!'

'What did we agree on?' says the bosun, slamming the table. 'No bloody bickering. United we stand!'

'What about Stoker?' asks Ási, chewing on his match and casting a sideways glance at Big John. The man they call Stoker is named Óli Johnsen. He works under Big John.

'Stoker shovels coal for the Devil himself and no one else,' Big John answers with a faint grin, earning a laugh from his mates. 'But while I'm chief engineer is doesn't matter what the assistant engineer says or does, as long as he does what I tell him to do.'

'Hear, hear,' says Ási and he crunches his match between rotting molars.

'There's five of us, like the fingers on a clenched fist,' says Sæli. 'That's the majority in a nine-man crew.'

'Exactly,' says Big John with a faint smile. 'This is their payback for cutting the crew.'

'By fair means or foul,' says Rúnar, who clears his throat and nudges Methúsalem.

'Take it easy,' Methúsalem mutters, surreptitiously clasping his bag.

'What do you think we should do?' Ási asks Big John.

'Speak up, man!' says Sæli with an anxious look. 'The clock's ticking and I want to know everything about possible actions or protests before we cast off.'

'We're vulnerable on land,' says Big John, clasping his huge hands on the table. 'If we speak our minds before the ship sails they'll simply put us ashore and give our jobs to other guys. There are plenty of unemployed seamen on this island, that's for sure. But at sea we hold the reins. The engine and the wheel, in other words. After one week's sailing we'll be halfway between here and our destination. Then it'll be too late for the Old Man to turn around or send for help. That's when I suggest we make a move.'

'What do you want us to do?' murmurs Sæli. 'I'm not taking part in any mutiny – just so I make that clear.'

'Not exactly a mutiny,' says Big John and he takes a deep breath. 'But the engine could maybe fail.'

'And then what?' says Ási.

'We could make the Old Man understand that the only thing that could get the engine going again would be a fax from the management of the shipping company making it clear that they had abandoned all plans to cancel the contract and lay off the crew,' says Big John. 'Signed by every member of the board and the director.'

'So that's it,' Ási says, spitting out what's left of the match.

'That's nothing but mutiny, John,' says Sæli with a sigh. 'And I just —'

'It is and it isn't,' Big John says, lighting a cigar. 'But what the company's planning to do is nothing but the misuse of power, ruthlessness and an attack on the Icelandic sailor.'

'Hear, hear!' says Rúnar. 'I'm in. There's nothing wrong with this, guys!'

'Do you think it'll work?' asks Ási.

'I'm telling you,' says Rúnar, 'they'll do anything to get the ship back on schedule. The last thing they want to do is to disappoint that aluminium giant. If the bauxite doesn't arrive when it's supposed to be smelted, they'll lose their contract.'

'Exactly,' says Big John, puffing on his cigar.

'It's a simple question of independence,' says Methúsalem. 'A question of our right as individuals to —'

'Work together for the good of the whole,' Big John finishes for him with a deep laugh.

'You guys are terrible,' Sæli says somewhat darkly. 'You can hardly imagine what it'll be like up in the bridge if this actually happens. Methúsalem?'

'The bridge is my problem,' Methúsalem answers calmly, running his fingers through his fair, well-cut hair. 'You think about your part, I'll think about mine. That's how we'll come out on top.'

'We don't have any other choice, do we?' says Sæli, looking

at his companions one by one. 'I don't know about you, but this is not the best time for me to lose my job. But I've got to finish this trip and —'

'We have to decide right here and now,' Big John interjects, laying down his cigar. 'On behalf of the engine room, I endorse this plan.'

'The kitchen's in if Rúnar's in,' says Ási, looking at the bosun.

'The bosun guarantees the deckhands,' says Rúnar, most senior of the ordinary seamen, foreman on board and contact person between the bridge and the rest of the crew. 'We're in.'

'All right then,' mutters Sæli.

'That leaves just the bridge,' Big John says, looking towards Methúsalem.

'Independence above all!' says the chief mate, straightening his long back. 'It's not my style to turn my back on my mates.'

'Good for you!' says Rúnar and slaps him on the back.

'Fine,' says Big John, smiling faintly. 'Then we won't talk about this any more for the time being, but we'll try to find the chance to get together after we've sailed.'

'Agreed,' says Rúnar, polishing off his beer. 'So, shall we order a taxi and get our arses to the ship's berth?'

'Yeah, let's go,' says Methúsalem, then takes out his mobile phone and rings for a taxi.

'Last call!' cries the bartender and he rings the old copper bell three times, filling the smoky bar with its clamour.

A few minutes later the five men load themselves and their duffel bags into a seven-passenger taxi outside the bar, which is in a side street in the middle of Reykjavík.

'Where to?' asks the driver once they're all settled.

'The harbour at Grundartangi,' says Methúsalem, who is sitting in the front.

'Grundartangi,' the driver echoes and pulls away.

Apart from the caterwauling of some symphony on the car radio, which is tuned to the classical channel, silence reigns in the taxi. The five men sit still and stare out the windows at cars, houses and the lights of the city rushing past. After just a few hours, and then for the next fortnight, the endless ocean will be the only thing they'll see. They know this; it's why they're soaking up everything they see on the way to the harbour. They are collecting simple memories that will eventually be precious to them. Little images to remind them of their homeland and the people who wait there.

As they drive through Mosfellsbær it starts to rain. The odd drop hitting the windscreen to begin with, then the rain building up so that by the time they are on the last roundabout the rhythm of the windscreen wipers has become fast and regular.

'Look!' says Methúsalem suddenly, pointing at a man in dark clothes who is walking backwards along the verge, thumb raised in the manner of hitchhikers. 'Isn't that the guy from the bar?'

'The one who was scrounging change?' Ási asks from the back seat.

'Yeah,' answers Methúsalem, getting a momentary look at the soaking-wet man out the side window as the car rushes past him. 'Maybe we should give him a ride?'

'What?' says the driver and slows down.

'No way,' says Rúnar, signalling the driver to keep going. 'He's just a bloody scrounger. Nothing but trouble.'

'What was it he said again?' says Sæli, peering out the back window. 'Something about a ship. Five men on a ship. What was it?'

'He's just a drunk,' Rúnar mutters, irritated. 'Let's forget him!'

'Yeah, let's forget him,' says Methúsalem, peering into the passenger-side mirror, but there is nothing to be seen but the wet roadside, fading into the darkness.

Little by little the lights and houses grow more scarce. By the time they reach the mouth of the Hvalfjörður fjord there is nothing to be seen but the rain-laden night.

'Take the tunnel, mate,' says Big John, his great paw clapping the driver on his right shoulder. 'We'll pay the toll.'

'Yeah, sure,' the driver nods.

From the radio come the soft A-major chords of the lyrical Adagio Cantabile movement of Beethoven's eighth piano sonata, the *Pathétique*. The chords dissolve into monotonous static as the car plunges into the deep, dark tunnel under Hvalfjörður.

IV

A black telephone rings. It sits on a crocheted doily on the telephone table in the hall in the home of Jónas Bjarni Jónasson, second mate on the freighter *Per se*. Jónas lives in a fairly new semi-detached house in the Lendur district in Mosfellsbær. It's ten to one in the morning and the ring sounds uncomfortably loud in the house. The lights are on in most of the rooms and the curtains carefully drawn over all the windows.

Jónas stands utterly still, wearing only his underpants, and stares at the phone as if hypnotised, as if he is unsure whether the ringing is real or just in his imagination.

Nearly a minute passes before Jónas lays a sticky sledgehammer on the telephone table and picks up the receiver with bloody fingers.

'Hello?'

'Jónas, ish 'at you?' asks a thick-tongued voice in a place where the heavy beat of music must be shaking the walls as it blends with the sound of loud chatter.

'Who is it?'

'Ish your brother-in-law, Kalli.'

'What do you want?' asks Jónas quietly.

'Listen! Gonna gimme a lift later on?'

'No. Can't you just take a cab?' says Jónas, looking at himself in the mirror above the telephone, covered with blood from his chest halfway down his calves. Blood that isn't his. Blood that is turning black and starting to clot.

'I don' have enough money,' says Kalli. 'Can't I take a cab to your place an' just go along with you, eh?'

'If I've already left, just thumb a lift. Okay?' says Jónas.

'You in some kinda hurry?'

'No,' says Jónas, clearing his throat. 'But I have to go now.'

'Where's my sister?' Kalli asks cheerfully.

'She … She's just lying down,' says Jónas softly.

'I get you! Listen, I just —' But Jónas hangs up before Kalli can finish the sentence.

Jónas picks up the phone again, waits for the dial tone, punches in a number.

'Hello?'

'Mum? It's Jonni,' he says when his aged mother answers.

'Jonni dear, is everything all right?' his mother asks, her voice weak.

'I'm sorry, Mum. I didn't mean to wake you,' says Jónas. He coughs a little. 'I just wanted to let you know that María won't be able to fetch the kids tomorrow.'

'Oh? Why not?'

'Just … something came up,' says Jónas, taking a deep breath. 'She's going to be away for a few days. A week, even.'

'A week?' asks his mother, sounding bewildered. 'But your father and I are leaving for the Canaries in three days. We can't …'

'*Mum!* I'm about to be late! I haven't got time for this!' says Jónas, his voice shaking. 'I'll explain it all later. I … can't …'

Jónas hangs up and pulls the phone cord out of the wall. Then he wipes the sweat off his forehead, smearing blood across his face.

On the floor in the bedroom, María's naked body lies on a tarpaulin. She's on her back in a sticky puddle of blood, staring empty-eyed at the ceiling.

Jónas pulls off the stained bedding and uses it to hide his wife's cooling body. There is a bloodstain the size of a dinner plate on her side of the mattress. She had been asleep when he'd struck her in the head with the sledgehammer.

Jónas fetches a clean towel and places it over the bloodstain. Then he wraps the tarp around the body and the bedding and ties it all up with the cords on the tarp that have special loops for tent pegs.

After washing off all the blood in a hot shower, and drying himself carefully from head to toe, Jónas makes up the double bed with clean linen. Then in one bag he collects everything that clearly or just possibly has come into contact with his newly deceased wife's blood: the hammer, the phone, the doily from the telephone table, the soap from the shower and the towels with which he dried himself. He wets a cloth in hot water and wipes invisible fingerprints and imaginary bloodstains off doorknobs, doorframes, walls and floors, bedside tables and the bedstead. The cloth then follows the hammer and the other stuff into the bag. He ties a knot in the bag, sticks it into another bag and knots it as well. Then he puts on a shirt, trousers and a windcheater before wrestling the body out to his four-wheel drive.

The vehicle is a ten-year-old Jeep Cherokee, white with fog lights on the front and a ski rack on the roof. Jónas backs out of the carport by his house, looking around his peaceful neighbourhood. Not a light to be seen in any window, no people up and about.

Jónas puts the automatic shift into drive and starts slowly down the street. Suddenly he slams on the brakes, goes into reverse and returns to the front of the house. On the rear-view mirror hangs a rosary with a wooden crucifix that swings back and forth.

Did he definitely turn off all the lights?

Yes. It is dark behind the curtains in all the windows. But did he remember to lock the door? *What the fuck does it matter!* Jónas sighs and drives off again, turns once left and twice right, and then he's out on the Westland Highway, National Highway Number One.

It starts raining as he drives past the turn-off to Mosfellsdalur and Thingvellir. First there's only a few drops on the dirty windscreen, then the rain becomes heavier. Jónas turns on the windscreen wipers, whose worn blades spread the raindrops and mix them with the month-old dirt on the glass. Jónas tries to spray washer fluid on the windscreen, but the fluid tank is empty. This makes him check the gauge of the 100-litre petrol tank. The needle has reached the red part of the dial, but Jónas knows from experience that there are then about 20 litres left in the tank – more than enough to get him to the bottom of Hvalfjörður. By the time he signals right and turns east the rain has turned into a downpour. The wipers whip back and forth, and the heavy, ice-cold rain has washed away most of the dirt. Jónas clenches his hands on the steering wheel, the engine purrs under the hood, the wipers beat a steady rhythm, the heater blows warm air and his sleepless eyes stare into the gloom that sucks in the Jeep like a black hole.

After making his way along the shore by the old whaling station, Jónas gets out a shovel and in the light of the Jeep's spotlights digs his wife a damp grave in the black sand. Steam rises off him as he struggles against the collapsing sand and flowing water. In the distance waves collapse with a heavy thud, stirring up the pebbles and seaweed. Within just a few hours the ocean will hide this grave that deepens so slowly and fills so quickly with seawater and rain.

Jónas tosses aside the shovel and runs to get the body. The body is hard to handle and heavy, heavier with every step he takes. His feet sink in the soft sand and the rain pounds on the rumpled tarpaulin.

When Jónas lets his burden fall into its grave, water splashes all around it. He piles large beach stones on top of the body before shovelling sand over it. Huge sand mites wave their legs and antennae. They are deathly white, waxy insects that live off dead flesh – the ever-hungry descendants of the millions of sand mites that thrived in the time of Icelandic whaling.

Jónas leans on his shovel and vomits warm beer and poison-green digestive juices over the shallow grave. Then he walks, soaking wet, to the car, which is still revving in neutral up on the gravel ridge.

When he reaches the turn-off for Grundartangi on the north shore of the fjord it's seven minutes to three. The petrol light starts to flash a warning just as he signals left and turns into the road, which leads downhill. He sails his Jeep down this road like it's a little boat sailing along a river to its wide-open mouth.

He drives out onto the jetty where the lit-up ship lies along the quay. Rúnar and Sæli are waiting at the gangway and wave him to come near.

'Is something wrong?' asks Jónas after rolling down his window. His heart beats madly and his bloodless hands clench the wheel.

'Isn't your brother-in-law with you?' Rúnar says.

'Kalli – no,' says Jónas and clears his throat to squeeze out some saliva. 'Hasn't he arrived?'

'No,' Rúnar answers. 'We wouldn't be asking otherwise.'

'He probably thumbed a lift,' mutters Jónas, blinking.

'You've got to go find the guy!' says Rúnar, tossing his burning cigarette out into the dark. 'We're casting off in five minutes, whether he's here or not.'

'I have to get up to the bridge. My watch starts at four,' says Jónas. He puts the car in neutral, removes the rosary and crucifix from the mirror and takes them with him as he steps out of the car. 'Can you go look for him? I'm sure he's already set off walking from the highway.'

'All right,' says Rúnar in a disgruntled tone. He gets into the Jeep. 'So where do you want me to park this guzzler?'

'Wherever,' says Jónas with a shrug. 'I don't care.'

'Okay.'

Rúnar takes off.

'Has the Old Man arrived?' Jónas asks Sæli, lighting a cigarette.

'Of course,' says Sæli, zipping his parka up to his chin. The rain has stopped, but the night is still cold and damp.

'Yeah,' says Jónas distantly and he trots up the gangplank.

'Jónas!' Sæli calls after him, hands in his pockets, his hood pulled down to his eyes.

'Yeah, what?' Jónas turns around at the top of the gangplank.

'Haven't you got a duffel bag or some kind of luggage?' asks Sæli, hunching his shoulders inside his loose parka. 'You know. Clothes, cigarettes and stuff?'

'No,' Jónas answers slowly and looks up at the black sky, as if expecting something to come from it. 'I just … just forgot.'

'Forgot?' enquires Sæli with a grin.

'Yes,' says Jónas in a hollow tone. He jumps aboard the ship.

'Your problem! See you later!' Sæli calls out as the second mate disappears behind the wheelhouse. Sæli has the three-to-six night watch, so he will be Jónas's companion till early morning.

The wind is picking up from the west; the powerful ship does a slow dance, rhythmically pulling on the thick mooring ropes, which jerk tightly round the steel, spitting out drops of rain and old seawater.

One could almost think that this 100-metre-long, over 4000-tonne freighter was trying to break its chains.

V

Heavy blues music, the clamour of voices and a cloud of bitter smoke are pierced by the loud peal of a bell.

'Fifteen minutes to closing!' the bartender shouts, letting go of the cord that hangs from the clapper of the old brass bell that once served a Dutch freighter.

At the bar sits a man dressed in denim. He looks blearily at the last sip in a greasy beer glass and then at his watch, which tells him it's fifteen minutes to one in the morning on the eleventh day of the month. This is Karl Gudjónsson, an out-of-work joiner nearing forty who is on his way to his first trip as second seaman on a freighter that is moored in Grundartangi harbour, ready to cast off after two days of offloading, when the cargo was vacuumed out of the hold.

Fifteen minutes to closing.

Forever.

Déjà vu.

Karl finishes the last of his beer, puts out his half-smoked cigarette and gets down off the high bar stool. Then he weaves his way over to a circular table, where five men sit drinking. He claps the two nearest on the back, leans forward between them and smiles ingratiatingly through his untrimmed beard.

'D'you think you could lend me a ten-coin, lads?' he asks, clearing his throat. 'I haven't got any change and I have to make a call.'

'Leave us alone, man!' says one of the men he's leaning on.

He pokes an elbow in Karl's stomach and pushes him roughly away from the table.

Karl takes two steps back then freezes in that position while he tries to gain his balance – and succeeds.

He is filled with darkness and silence; inside his head cold winds are blowing and, for just one moment, it's as though he falls into a deep sleep. A sleep that is black as unending night, heavy as death and cold as eternal winter.

Empty as the echo in a bass drum.

Boom, boom, boom …

One moment, and it's over.

'Five, five, five … ship,' Karl mumbles and regains his balance on the floorboards, then he clutches the stair rail and trudges up to the second floor of the bar, where a middle-aged band is playing blues with a heavy beat for the depressed, bitter, sorry bunches of drunks sitting at tables or standing along the walls or at the bar, half invisible in the hot, thick clouds of smoke.

Got to get aboard the ship …

As a mournful guitar solo and lazy drum draw to a close, it seems that the band has lost its momentum, but just before the music fades away entirely the drummer gets back in gear with a gentle touch of the snare drum, the bass catches onto the beat, the guitar starts wailing again and the bearded singer hauls an emotional lyric from his soul's vale of tears: 'Before I sink into the big sleep, I want to hear the scream of the butterfly …'

On the worn wooden floor, ash and dirt gets ground into the spilled beer; cigarette butts, used chewing gum and peanuts are crushed underfoot. And here and there a crown or five-crown coin may be found. Even a fifty, brass-coloured with a crab on it.

Karl reaches for the fifty that is sliding around in a black puddle. He wipes the dirt off it then puts it in the slot of the payphone at the end of the downstairs bar.

From the pocket of his denim jacket he pulls a wrinkled piece of paper and checks the number that is written on it: 555-7547.

He punches in the number, pressing the receiver hard to his right ear and the palm of his left hand over his left ear.

'Hello?' says a suspicious voice at the other end of the line.

'Jónas, ish 'at you?' says Karl, pressing the receiver even tighter to his ear.

'Who is it?' asks the voice.

'Ish your brother-in-law, Kalli,' says Kalli, raising his voice.

'What do you want?' asks Jónas quietly.

'Listen! Gonna gimme a lift later on?' asks Kalli, who can hardly hear Jónas.

'No. Can't you just take a cab?'

'I don' have enough money,' says Kalli, watching his credit growing smaller and smaller on the phone's screen. 'Can't I take a cab to your place an' then just go along with you, eh?'

'If I've already left, just thumb a lift. Okay?' says Jónas, coldly.

'You in some kinda hurry?' asks Karl, smiling mirthlessly to himself.

'No,' says Jónas, clearing his throat in the emptiness inside the telephone. 'But I have to go now.'

'Where's my sister?' Kalli asks as cheerfully as he can.

'She ... She's just lying down,' says Jónas, so quietly that to Karl's ears it sounds like the scratching of mice.

'I get you! Listen, I just —' says Kalli as the phone's screen starts flashing. There is a click and the silence on the phone becomes somehow more real than it has been.

'Hello!' says Karl into the receiver. Then he removes it from his ear and looks at it uncomprehendingly, his eyes shiny with alcohol, before he hangs it up.

Karl stands by the phone and fishes his slim wallet out of his hip pocket, opens it and checks on the scanty contents. One bill of 1000, one of 500. Altogether 1500 crowns.

'Did you want something else?' the bartender says when Karl sits back down on the bar stool where he's spent the evening.

The bartender is big and fat, his shirt unbuttoned and the sleeves rolled up. On his hairy chest hangs a gold cross and chain. His smoothly shaven face is red and damp with sweat, his eyes are sunk into his bulging flesh and what is left of his dark hair is carefully combed over to the wrinkled back of his neck.

'Yeah, maybe a whiskey,' says Karl, feeling his crumpled pack of cigarettes before pulling out the third last one. 'And a pack of Camels.'

'Coming up,' says the bartender, filling a heavy shot glass with cheap whiskey.

Karl lights his cigarette and pulls the dirty ashtray nearer.

'So, could you pay your bill, then? says the bartender, peeling cellophane and silver paper off a fresh pack of Camels.

'How much is it?' says Karl, calm as can be.

'That makes …' The bartender adds the latest purchase to the evening's total. 'That makes seven thousand nine hundred crowns altogether.'

'Couldn't I just put it on a tab?' asks Karl, taking a careful sip of whiskey.

'Until when?' asks the bartender, slitting his bloodshot eyes.

'I'm off on a tour tonight, back in two weeks,' says Karl, inhaling the hot smoke and blowing it out through his nose.

'It would be better if you paid now,' says the bartender, putting his burly forearm on the bar in front of Karl – a forearm displaying a deep scar from elbow to wrist along with a mighty anchor, tattooed in blue ink, that long ago started to leak out under the weather-beaten skin.

'I see,' mutters Karl, tapping the ash off his cigarette and at the same time running his eyes over three framed photographs that hang, one below the other, under the brass bell.

The bottom photo is of the Steamship Company ship *Dettifoss*, which came new to Iceland in 1930 but was sunk by a German submarine off Ireland in 1945, with fifteen men lost.

In the middle is another Steamship Company *Dettifoss*, launched in 1949 and sold abroad twenty years later.

And the third photo is the third *Dettifoss*, which came to harbour in 1970 and served the Steamship Company for nineteen years, until it too was sold in 1989.

'Were you on the *Dettifoss*?' Karl asks, nodding towards the black-and-white photos.

'Yeah. Why?' says the bartender suspiciously.

'On the third one, was it?' Karl asks with interest.

'I was mate on the third one, yes,' the bartender says, glancing at the top photo. 'Second mate for a good while, but I was chief mate before they sold it.'

'And then what?' Karl sips his whiskey. 'Did you leave the sea?'

'What's with all the questions?' the bartender asks, looking accusingly at Karl, who shrugs innocently.

'My old dad was a sailor too,' says Karl after a short silence. 'Mate, like you. Mostly on fishing vessels. Then he left the sea in 1970. Bought a stake in a fishing company and started working ashore.'

'Good for him,' mutters the bartender, wiping ash of the bar with a wet cloth. 'But how about just paying your bill, mate, before I close up.'

'But working ashore didn't suit him,' says Karl, his mind elsewhere, taking a short drag on his smoke. 'And in early 1973 he went back to sea, after the company had virtually gone bankrupt.'

'Listen, mate!' says the bartender, putting his fists against the edge of the bar. 'I don't have time to listen to your dad's life story. Not now!'

'The boat he got a job on,' says Karl calmly, putting out his cigarette in the ashtray, 'was the *Seventh Star* from Keflavík.'

'The *Seventh Star*?' The bartender is all ears now. 'What year did you say, 1973?'

'Yep,' answers Karl coolly, nodding.

'Was he on board when they …?' The bartender trails off, leaning closer to Karl.

'When they left the Faroe Islands for Iceland on February eleventh, 1973?' says Karl, a faraway look in his eyes as he focuses on nothing behind the bartender's head. 'Yeah. He was on board then. The boat had been under repair and they were in a hurry to get home and to the fishing grounds.'

'I was on *Dettifoss* at the same time,' says the bartender, opening wide his world-weary eyes. 'We were on our way home from Leith in Scotland. I was up in the bridge when Captain Erlendur heard the emergency transmission. The *Seventh Star* was sunk by then, and the men were in the lifeboats.'

'Is that true?' Karl raises his eyebrows at the bartender, who wipes the sweat off his forehead.

'Yeah. I'll never forget it,' says the bartender, lighting a cigarette. 'After twenty minutes we heard the transmission again, but we couldn't make out the words. We tried to locate the castaways, but the weather was bad that night. A major storm and ten lives in immediate danger. I'll never forget that night. Never.'

'They only found one man,' says Karl, sighing. 'One corpse, I mean.'

'Yeah.' The bartender pours himself a shot of whiskey and fills Karl's glass up to the brim. 'Nineteen days later. After one of the most extensive searches in the history of accidents at sea. Did it turn out to be …?'

'Dad? No,' Karl says with a shake of his head. 'He was never found. May he rest in peace.'

'Cheers, pal!' says the bartender, lifting his glass. 'Here's to your dad!'

'Yeah. Cheers!' says Karl with a weak smile then they touch glasses and toss back the contents. Karl licks his lips and hopes the bartender won't ask him any more about that famous accident, which Karl only knows about from stories his brother-in-law Jónas has told him several times, during their numerous drinking sessions over the past years.

'So you're a seaman yourself?' says the bartender, taking

a drag of his cigarette.

'Yeah, I am,' mutters Karl. 'Against the will of my old man, who didn't intend ever to go back to sea himself.'

'That's how it goes,' murmurs the bartender, signalling to an impatient customer to wait. 'Listen, pal. I'll just keep your bill. You can just pay me next time you're ashore. Okay?'

'Thanks,' says Karl, smiling crookedly as he sticks the Camels in an inside pocket of his jacket. 'Could you maybe phone me a cab?'

'That I'll do!' The bartender waves his callused seaman's hand at Karl before turning to the last customer of the evening.

Karl walks to the exit, buttons up his duffel coat and turns up the collar before he walks out into the cold night.

'Last call before closing!' shouts the bartender and rings the old brass bell three times, so it resounds through the smoke-filled bar. Then the door closes behind Karl and the noisy hubbub immediately changes to a low rumble.

The taxi arrives and Karl asks the driver to take him to Mosfellsbær.

'The street was Hjarðarland, didn't you say?' the driver asks after a while.

'Huh? Yes,' says Karl, opening his eyes. He had fallen asleep in the softness of the back seat, with his head to the side. The cab is warm and Karl feels a bit sick waking up like that.

'Number what?' says the driver, slowing down.

'This is fine. I'll get out here,' says Karl after looking out the window and seeing his brother-in-law's house across the street.

'All right,' says the driver as he parks the car and turns on the inside light. 'That'll be fourteen-hundred crowns.'

'Keep the change,' says Karl, handing the man everything he's got.

'Thanks.' The driver takes the wrinkled bills. 'And goodnight.'

'Goodnight.' Karl closes the car door behind him.

His sister María's house is dark and no-one answers the

bell. Not even María. The garage is also dark, and Jónas's Jeep doesn't seem to be there.

'Damn,' says Karl under his breath, stepping down off the wheelbarrow he overturned by the garage to see in the window.

In front of the garage door is a white bag of rubbish that Karl picks up and shoves into the family garbage bin before strolling down to Highway One.

There aren't many cars on the road and drops of freezing rain are falling from the pitch-black heavens. Karl just misses a couple of transport trucks, and during the two minutes he's been huddled on the verge two saloon cars have shot past without even slowing down. The rain is getting denser and the cold drops slide in under the collar of his denim jacket, which is slowly getting soaked. Karl sets off walking east and turns around to stick his thumb in the air whenever he sees lights coming or hears an engine.

A seven-passenger taxi speeds past and then seems to slow down. Karl walks faster and waves at the taxi that lights up the dark of the Thingvellir turn-off with its bright red brakelights. He had seen a man's face through the passenger window. A face that seemed familiar. And he thought the passenger also recognised him. Karl has no idea where they might have met and it doesn't really matter. He runs after the taxi, which suddenly speeds up again and sails away into the rain-dark night.

Karl comes to a halt and catches his breath, freezing, wet and with a painful stitch in his chest from running.

The bar. That man had been in the bar earlier this evening. That guy in the taxi. The face in the car window.

'Doesn't matter,' he mutters. He stands by the road sign for Thingvellir, hunched over with his hands on his wet knees, the taste of blood in his mouth.

That's it, he thinks. *I'll never get to Grundartangi in time. The ship's going to sail without me.*

But then a cone of light appears on the bitumen, the deep roar of an engine approaches and wide radial tyres spurt water from under a silver Range Rover Vogue.

Karl straightens up, takes two steps onto the road, turns around, holds out his arm and points his blue-white thumb towards the sky.

The high-tech xenon lights blind him momentarily, then the big car kisses him on the cheek. Gives him a cold kiss. Breaks bones, tears flesh and mangles organs. All in a fraction of a second. It throws him onto the verge and rolls him face down into the ditch, where he jerks convulsively, half submerged in the mud of a brown puddle. Paralysed with shock. Unconscious.

The growling Range Rover hurtles on into the night with a broken headlight, a cracked windscreen and a streak of blood running from its front fender up to the roof.

No light but the creamy yellow of the streetlights. No noise but the pounding of the rain.

Nothing to see but a human form in a ditch.

Shoes on the side of the road.

And drops of blood on the wet bitumen.

VI

In a windowless basement, a naked man lies on a leather-covered bench, his hands gripping a bar that rests in the notches of steel uprights half a metre above his face. He tenses his chest and back, pushes the soles of his feet against the floor, keeps his buttocks just touching the bench and lifts the bar up out of its notches. He stares with concentration at the middle of the bar, fills his lungs with air and holds his breath as he allows the bar to sink to his chest. When the cold steel touches his straining muscles he lifts the bar off his chest and breathes out as the weight rises past the most difficult point. This he repeats four more times, slowly and deliberately but with increasing effort, higher blood pressure and shorter breaths. Eventually the bar slams back into the steel notches, so that both floor and walls shudder from the weight.

The heat in the room increases with every passing minute and the stagnant air smells of sour sweat and acrid testosterone.

The man sits up on the bench, closes his blue eyes and rolls his head clockwise and counterclockwise while he catches his breath. Apart from a Gothic 'S' on his right pectoral muscle, his tanned body is without tattoos. The scars, on the other hand, are of every length and depth, and so numerous that no-one has ever tried to count them. The same is true of his abrasions, old burns and pits from healed boils. Most of these are from motorcycle and car accidents, but unconventional sports, countless fist fights and several knife- and gun-fights have also marked his flesh. Besides these surface blemishes there are adhesions, scars and knobs on his skeleton, which is held together with a dozen steel pins, steel wires and two joint replacements. All his body hair has been removed with creams and wax, except for the hair around his genitals, which has been trimmed to three millimetres with clippers. On his head the hair is of even length and hangs down his back, dyed raven black with decorative red and blue highlights. The man wears no jewellery on his hands, nor round his neck, but in his earlobes he wears thick rings of engraved silver. They are snakes that have been folded together with pliers so their tails disappear into their open mouths, and these handmade ear decorations give his healthy-looking and otherwise confidence-inspiring face a sinister look.

This is Jón Karl Esrason, the twenty-six-year-old son of a fisherman, who deals in odd jobs and various rackets. He has an elaborate rap sheet, covering over a decade, with over thirty charges and a dozen sentences making up his curriculum vitae.

'Lilja?' says Jón Karl as he walks barefoot along the carpeted corridor, without really expecting or waiting for an answer. He knows Lilja is at home. And he knows that she knows that he knows she's at home. That's why she doesn't answer.

Jón Karl has now dressed in black athletic pants and pulled his hair back into an elastic band.

In the bright, roomy kitchen he mixes milk and a banana and strawberry-flavoured carbohydrate-and-protein powder in a large blender. He tosses a handful of vitamins and additives into his mouth and gulps down the tasty blend.

Jón Karl turns on the hot water tap in the kitchen sink, places the blender jug under the stream and looks out the window while it fills up. At the end of the street is the local school, beside which is a fenced basketball court where tall, spotty youths shoot at the netless basket way into the dark every evening. But now it's night and the court is without life. No movement. Just darkness. And a tiny glow by the windscreen of a parked car, as if someone inside were smoking on the driver's side.

Jón Karl moves fast and purposefully. He turns off the hot water and the kitchen lights. His pupils expand and so do his arteries, pectoral muscles and nostrils. He leans over the sink and lets the cold windowpane touch his right cheek and the curtain his left. In this position he stares sideways out the window without moving, like a lion sticking its nose through vegetation on the edge of the savannah. Now he can see better into the cold autumn night, deeply dark beyond the streetlights. There's a black van parked at the end of the basketball court, half up on the pavement. It might, of course, be brown, blue or dark green, but in the night it's black. There is, however, no glow to be seen inside the van – no movement, nothing. Had he been seeing things, or had whoever it was put out their smoke when he turned off the light? Is someone watching the house? Or is Jón Karl getting paranoid?

The laughter of two teenaged girls breaks the silence outside. They prance light-footed into his line of sight from the right, glide along the footpath on the other side of the street and cause Jón Karl to tear his intense gaze from the black van and direct his bestial attention to firm buttocks, slim legs and an innocent bearing.

He knows them, these two, both the individuals and their kind. They live in the next street to Jón Karl and his family; they live in the next street in all the neighbourhoods of all the cities in the world: not quite sixteen-year-old friends who have recently discovered drugs, head jobs and their own allure, and who exist in the wonderful delusion that youth is eternal, the shopping mall is the universe, their pussy is its centre and life is nothing but a pink bubblegum cloud they can keep blowing until it pops.

'Little cunts,' mutters Jón Karl, his breath clouding the window as the blood starts to flow into his member, which twists about like a snake in his sports pants until it finds the right pants leg.

Jón Karl pats his left pants pocket, finds a crumpled pack of cigarettes and pulls out the last one, which he lights and draws on until the ember crackles. He blows smoke through dilated nostrils and continues to stare at the girls while wondering what the hell he's waiting for. Instead of still standing there staring out the window like an old lady, he should be at the wheel of the Range Rover already backed into the street. Accelerate once and a hundred metres later he would pull up beside the girls.

'Where you off to, sweethearts?'

They might hesitate a bit, since their self-confidence is nothing but a shell made of fashionable clothes and make-up. They would glance at each other, giggle and blush, but before they could properly assess the situation Jón Karl would have ordered them into the car.

'I'll drop you off, sweethearts. Don't be silly!'

Maybe they wouldn't get in a car with a stranger, but Jón Karl is familiar to them. They've often seen him and they think he's pretty cool, even though he's awfully old and all that. And they've heard their parents talk about him. Talk badly about him. And a man that their parents *hate* and are *frightened* of – he just has to be really awesome! Even if he is *maybe* a dope dealer or a debt collector or a lowlife or something. And that's a cool car. Expensive and cool. Not like the stupid saloon cars their parents drive.

They'd head for the city centre, where Jón Karl rents a top-floor flat in the seaside tower blocks. There he would coke up the party and fuck those fillies until the cum is leaking out of their tear-filled eyes.

So why hasn't he got going? Getting too old? Tired? Can't be bothered any more? Grown out of it?

'Fuck!'

They have virtually disappeared into the blackness.

Jón Karl throws his cigarette into the sink and briefly turns on the tap. Then he glances quickly out the window, as if from a presentiment or just habit, and sees that the black van is no longer at the end of the basketball court.

The well-kept hairs on the back of Jón Karl's neck stand up and his hands go cold. It's as if the absence of this black van bothers him more than its presence did a moment earlier. Which may seem strange, even irrational, but isn't that at all. A woman who sees a spider in her house is uncomfortable because the spider should not be there. Then, when the spider disappears, fear comes instead of discomfort, because the woman doesn't know where the spider is, which means it may be *anywhere*, and that fact raises the disturbing question of what the spider is doing where nobody can see it. The spider that existed simply as an eight-legged bug in the informed world of conscious thought has become an intelligent monster in the darkness of the subconscious.

What black van was that? Who was in it? What were they doing? And now where is it?

'Lilja!'

Jón Karl strides back to the living room, cracking the joints of his neck and fingers. 'Stand up, woman! Take the girl, go to Mum's and collect the case.'

'What's wrong? What case?' says Lilja, standing up from the couch.

'Mum knows *what case*,' Jón says and pushes Lilja along, almost knocking her into the corridor.

'Our child's asleep, Jón!' says Lilja, with a confused look at the father of her child, who is in a state she knows he won't be shaken out of.

'Listen to me,' hisses Jón Karl, pushing her against the wall and holding her trapped while he is speaking. 'Take the girl and go to Mum's and collect the fucking case. Then come back and get me and we'll all go up to Skorra Valley. Do you understand what I'm saying?'

'Yes, I understand,' says Lilja, looking away from his burning stare. 'But why do we have to go up to Borgarfjörður? What's wrong? What case are —'

'No questions!' says Jon Karl, letting her go. 'Take the car and do as I say.'

'Yes, I —'

'And Lilja,' says Jón Karl, his eyes turning flinty.

'Yes?' Lilja whispers, her stomach lurching.

'If anything's not right when you come to get me ... if anything – just *anything* – is not as it should be ... then you go without me up to Borgarfjörður and stay there until you hear from me. Do you understand?'

'Yes.'

'No phone calls, no guests, no panic ... nothing. Okay?' Jón Karl's voice is so cold that Lilja shudders.

'Okay,' she says, half sobbing, and disappears into the darkened children's room where their two-year-old daughter is sleeping, while Jón Karl goes to their bedroom and pulls out underclothes, socks, T-shirts, shoes, a half-empty carton of Prince cigarettes and a green duffel bag from drawers and shelves in the big closet, throwing it all on the unmade bed. He puts on black socks, a black T-shirt and black army boots, which he laces right to the top. The rest of his clothes he shoves in the duffel bag. Through the window in the master bedroom he can see Lilja driving off into the night.

In the living room Jón Karl slides a big cupboard aside and punches a seven-number code into the electronic lock that's built into the concrete wall.

Inside the safe are one million crowns in new 5000-crown bills; a revolver in an ankle holster; a box of .38 calibre shells; the family's passports; a hunting knife in a leather sheath; stock and share certificates; various documents, and three bank deposit books from Switzerland and Luxembourg. The revolver is a 1970 model, .38 calibre, Smith & Wesson, short-barrelled, its cylinder holding five rounds. It fits tightly into the custom-made holster that Jón Karl fastens with Velcro around the top of his right boot. Then he shovels the rest of the safe's contents into his duffel bag and tightens the drawstring. Everything except the miscellaneous documents, which he throws in the fireplace before lighting them.

Jón Karl stands in front of the fireplace and watches the flames take hold of the paper, burn it and change it into thin black membranes that break, float up, keep burning and, little by little, become ashes and finally nothing at all. The smoke rises up the chimney, the fire sputters and the reddish light flickers, reflected in the wide-open eyes that stare into the dancing flames, into them and beyond to somewhere much further, much deeper.

Hypnotising fire. Like an open doorway. And a lurking shadow.

Crying wolf?

Jón Karl turns suddenly and looks towards the French windows that open onto the deck behind the house. There is nothing to be seen. No shadow, no movement, no sound.

But something is bothering him. Something that is close enough to ring warning bells in his subconscious.

In the distance he hears a soft creaking.

And a moment later the electricity goes off in the whole house.

Darkness – apart from the fire in the fireplace, that forms dancing shadows on walls, floor and ceiling.

The only thing Jón Karl is sure of at this moment is that time is short. The fact that something evil is around is not what matters the most. And what form or purpose that embodiment of evil has is completely irrelevant. First and foremost he must be ready for its arrival, whatever it might be.

Jón Karl bends down, releases the revolver from its holster with his right hand while feeling around in the duffel bag for the ammunition with his left hand. When his fingers find the box they tear it open and grab a fistful of shells, most of which fall onto the living-room carpet and roll under tables and chairs. His hands move with the assurance of long practice; Jón Karl pushes the cylinder to the side and loads it, chamber by chamber, shoves it back in place and pulls back the hammer, his finger utterly still on the highly sensitive trigger. This is done in less than ten seconds.

There is still one shell in the palm of his left hand, which Jón Karl rolls between clammy fingers as he listens. There is the low creak of door hinges out by the entrance hall and someone hurries along the carpeted corridor. Jón Karl throws the shell in the fire and creeps, bent over, into the darker side of the living room, where he shelters behind a leather armchair.

When the shell explodes an uninvited guest leaps into the living room, turns in a circle, aims a sawn-off shotgun in all directions and shouts, 'You're dead!'

Jón Karl aims and fires two shots, which silence the intruder, echo around the room and light it up.

The first shot misses and shatters the glass in one of the windows that faces the driveway, but the second hits the intruder in his right shoulder.

'Help!' he yells and falls to his knees. He grabs the wound with his left hand and tries to handle the shotgun with his right, but his trembling fingers give way and the gun falls to the floor.

Help? Are there more of them?

Jón Karl steps away from his hiding place and cocks the gun for the third time, tasting blood, crazed thoughts spinning in his head and an ice-cold glint in his purposeful stare.

'*Don't!*' the man cries, starting to crawl along the floor. He has a dark blue ski mask over his face and claws and kicks his way forward like a disabled bug, leaving bloodstains on the carpet.

'Who sent you?' asks Jón Karl, stepping on the intruder's right ankle. He peers round in the dark and listens with one ear for the sound of other people as he bends down, points his revolver at the man's abdomen and curls his left hand round the sawn-off shotgun.

'Nobody,' he answers hoarsely, staring at the master of the house with the fear of death in his bulging eyes.

'Who are you?' asks Jón Karl quietly and he shoves the revolver up under the man's ribcage, eliciting a cry of fear and pain.

'*Nobody,*' he answers again, now thoroughly wet with his own blood and panting with discomfort.

Jón Karl lets go of the sawn-off shotgun, smashes his knee deep into the abdomen of this uninvited guest and tears his mask off with his left hand.

At the same moment somebody bashes him heavily in the back of his head. Bones crunch, muscles soften and everything goes black.

★ ★ ★

Travel without consciousness is an amazing experience. Rolling back and forth as if in a swing, only more slowly, with the addition of uncomfortable sideways movements and always this funny feeling that the swing down is longer and deeper than the swing up, as if your limp body were falling over some kind of rim, shown in slow motion like a television replay, again and again.

It's rather soothing in some hypnotic way but first and foremost there is an unending feeling of numbness that seems more unreal the longer you float about in this oppressive void that smells of warm blood and is as large or small as your mind, as deep as the echoing in the slow drumbeat of the blow to your head.

Boom, boom, boom ...

The inside of the ambulance is black. Jón Karl, wearing a light-blue-and-white seaman's outfit, lies tied to the stretcher. The doctor sitting by him is an octopus man with an Albert Einstein mask over his face.

If I say, 'It begins well, then jogs along, really takes flight around the middle, but no-one understands the ending', what would I be talking about?

Is it a film?

Yeah, but I'm not talking about a film.

Is it maybe a book?

Yeah, but I'm not talking about a book.

Is it this boat trip?

Yes, but I'm talking about something more and greater than this boat trip.

The ambulance drives along a pitted road and the bumps echo inside a metal box the size of a ship's hold.

Boom, boom, boom …

The pain is almost overpowering but at the same time as sweet as honey, as warm and tender as a sunbeam. The pain is a consequence of consciousness and consciousness is entwined with life itself. Pain is life and life is pain.

Not dead yet, thinks Jón Karl behind closed eyes, broken bones and swollen flesh. He pretends continued unconsciousness while he attempts to work out the surroundings, the situation and the state of his own body.

He is sitting on a chair, tied hand and foot. His ankles are tied to the front legs of the chair, while his wrists are bound together behind the chair back. The chair is bolted to the floor in a cold, damp space, under a naked lightbulb. His eyes are swollen, his nose sore and his jaw badly bruised, even broken. His ribs are aflame and his left collarbone cracked or broken. The back of his neck is extremely sore, his innards mauled and most of his joints stretched and twisted. Jón Karl can smell blood, cigarette smoke and foul sweat. He can distinguish three voices, but he can't hear what they're saying because of the ringing in his ears. But since the men are neither whispering nor keeping their voices down, Jón Karl knows he is in a 'safe' place somewhere far from help and civilisation.

These guys are professionals.

'Wake up, shithead!' says one of the men and he strikes Jón Karl a blow with a rubber truncheon on his right thigh, just above the knee.

Jón Karl lifts his head and opens his eyes. He knows they won't stop beating him until he comes to and talks to them. He doesn't know what they want, but he knows they won't let him go until they've got what they want, whatever it is. If they're going to let him go at all. The only thing Jón Karl wants to find out is how the hell he can get out of this alive and, without telling them anything about anything, whether he knows something about something or not.

'Where's the gambling joint?'

Gambling joint? What fucking gambling joint?

The questioner is hidden in a whirling haze, standing wide-legged in front of Jón Karl, who narrows swollen eyes and waits for confused colours and wavering outlines to take on a clearer form.

'Where is it?' says the man in a growling bass voice, slapping Jón Karl with a hand the size of a bear's paw.

The slap that comes snaps through flesh and bone and resonates through Jón Karl's body like a copper gong, waking him from the stupor of the knockout blow. His blood fairly boils in his veins, his muscles swell and in his head flare the fires of evil, revenge and blood letting. The plastic bands tighten round his ankles and wrists; there is a creaking in the chair and the floor it is bolted to; he grinds his teeth and his bloodshot eyes bulge halfway out of their sockets.

'I'll kill the lot of you!' he spits, spraying blood and a tooth onto the unpainted wooden floor.

'You're not killing anyone today,' says the deep-voiced man lighting a cheap cigar.

The voice and the dim outline of the man are familiar to

Jón Karl. He stares into a thunder cloud through humming mist and tries to dig information from his confused brain, while little by little the dark cloud takes on the form of a man.

Black leather jacket, black hair and eyes like black holes in a face like a fierce guard dog.

This man is none other than Óðin R Elsuson, the thirty-five-year-old legend of the Reykjavík underground, by far the oldest of the hard guys and debt collectors who still have some power and the most dangerous of them all; a full-blooded lowlife and merciless thug who trusts nobody, fears nothing and lives according to the devil-inspired maxim 'Happy is the man who has dead bodies as friends and ghosts as enemies'.

Behind Óðin are the shapes of men who fade into the gloom and the dark walls.

'I thought I heard someone crying wolf,' Jón Karl whispers.

'What did you say?' asks Óðin coldly as he pulls Jón Karl's gun out of the pocket of his leather jacket.

'Nothing,' says Jón Karl, snuffling blood up his nose.

Óðin is muscular as a young bull, dark complexioned and so ugly as to be almost handsome. His hair is carefully combed to the back of his head and his brown eyes are widely spaced, lying deep in his coarse, big-boned face that is reminiscent of either a young beast or an old man, depending on the light.

Jón Karl keeps it hidden, but the minute he recognises the man he loses all hope, like a flame going out in his breast. In the shadow of hopelessness, though, evil awakes from a deep sleep, and it is not concerned about life or death. It feeds off itself and shoves all else aside. It lives and behaves like a fire that grows and grows until it becomes so huge and fierce that it consumes itself and ceases to be.

Evil takes possession of Jón Karl. It growls in his head, pumps black poison into his blood, permeates every nerve and has no aim but to grow and grow, open up and blossom like a hellish spirit in the flesh that encompasses it, whatever the consequences.

Evil is essentially eternal and so has nothing to lose and nothing to win.

'What a pea-shooter this is,' says Óðin, handling the gun like a professional. He chews on his burning cigar, spins the cylinder on the gun, stops it with the thumb of his right hand, pulls back the hammer, shoves the barrel against Jón Karl's knee and immediately pulls the trigger:

Click!

The hammer hits an empty chamber and nothing happens.

Jón Karl jerks, his heart misses a beat and then does a somersault in his breast; his muscles stiffen; his veins, nostrils and pupils dilate, and a hot sweat breaks out on his face and back.

'You have a reputation as a lucky bastard,' says Óðin, putting the gun down on a rusty oil barrel. He picks up Jón Karl's duffel bag, pours its contents on the floor and starts investigating them.

Salty sweat drips into Jón Karl's eyes. He blinks rapidly and studies the situation. There are three men: Óðin and two assistants, both dark clad and rather similar to each other. One is sitting bent over on a stool, holding his trembling right hand around his bloody right shoulder. This is the one Jón Karl shot in his living room. The other assistant is standing off to Óðin's side, holding a rubber truncheon. These lads are hardly more than twenty years old. The one he shot is somehow familiar to Jón Karl, but he can't remember who he is or what he's called, which says it all about the reputations of these punks. They're just some Heckle and Jeckle whom Óðin has lured with vague promises, or paid to follow him for a time. Nameless dopeheads who dream of fame and success in the underworld but are going to end up shot, cut and canvas-bagged in some building foundations, at the bottom of the sea or in a lava field where nobody will ever find them.

'Planning a trip?' says Óðin as he flips through the family's passports before tearing them up. 'I think not.'

'You can't break a man who won't be broken,' says Jón

Karl, and continues studying where he is while he has the time and freedom to do so.

He's in some kind of shed, an old hovel, garage or storeroom. The walls are plywood or corrugated iron on a wooden frame, insulated with rockwool. There is rockwool in the windows and on the inside of the door. There are tools in a wooden chest on the floor near the door. Every joint on the chair Jón Karl is sitting on is reinforced with metal, but the chair creaks anyway after repeated use. On the floor and walls are black drops, black splashes and black streaks – dried blood that bears ugly witness to this unappealing space.

'Keep your philosophy to yourself,' says Óðin as he takes the million crowns out of the envelope and furtively hides them in his clothes. 'It doesn't affect me.'

'I wasn't talking to you,' says Jón Karl. He is trying to breathe calmly, relax and think clearly, but all three activities are difficult to achieve in these surroundings and this company.

Jón Karl is barefoot and shirtless; the plastic bands cut into his ankles and wrists, and he knows from experience that it's almost impossible to break them without scraping away flesh and tendons.

What can he do?

'Well,' says Óðin as he takes Jón Karl's hunting knife and slices through the leg of his sports pants from his ankle to above his knee. 'We'd better get started.'

Óðin picks up a blue one-litre gas canister with a burner attached and opens the gas halfway.

'I'm going to fry your leg,' Óðin says, taking his burning cigar out of his mouth. 'The smell will be gross and the pain indescribable. But you can get out of it if you talk now. Where is the gambling joint?'

'South of heaven?' says Jón Karl, just to say something. He can't start bawling like some old woman just because they're going to barbecue his leg. He has to think of his reputation. Without a reputation, he's finished.

'Wrong answer.' Óðin puts his cigar to the spout of the burner. Nothing happens.

'That was a question, not an answer,' says Jón Karl through clenched teeth.

'Save the jokes,' says Óðin as he sniffs at the spout of the burner, then throws it to the floor. 'It's empty!'

'I didn't know ...' says Jeckle, stiff with fear.

'Shut up!' Óðin shoves him against the wall by the door. 'Hand me the fucking bore!'

'Here,' says Jeckle, giving his boss a battery-driven hand bore with a steel bit in the chuck.

'For fuck's sake!' says Óðin when he pulls the trigger on the bore; it groans and turns the blood-covered bit a few times before stopping altogether with a sorry-sounding squeal.

Óðin throws it on the floor and punches Jeckle so hard in the stomach that he collapses, unable to breathe.

'You guys wait here while I go and get a new gas canister,' says Óðin to Heckle, who is still sitting holding his gunshot wound.

'Can't we just use a knife or the gun?' asks Heckle. 'Or cut off some fingers or toes?'

'Tonight I'm going to fry,' Óðin responds calmly and pats Heckle's head.

'But I need to get to a doctor!' wails Heckle, showing his employer the bloody palm of his left hand.

'Not until I've extracted the bullet.' Óðin opens the door. 'Hang tough. I won't be long.'

Óðin slams and locks the door on the outside with a padlock. A moment later a car door slams, a starter motor turns, a fanbelt screeches and an eight-stroke engine roars in the dark outside. Gravel rattles under wide tyres and the thunder of an engine fades into the distance.

'Goddamn him!' groans Jeckle, who is lying doubled up on the floor. He's breathing in short gasps, his face a mask of pain.

'Shut up, man,' Heckle says tersely to his partner.

'Sorry!' says Jeckle, stumbling to his feet.

'He's not coming back,' says Jón Karl with a cold grin.

'Just shut your fucking mouth!' says Heckle, bunching his fist in Jón Karl's face. Heckle's face twists from the pain of this gesture.

'Yes, he will come back,' mutters Jeckle. He collapses onto the tool chest by the door. 'Of course he'll come!'

'Do you see that envelope there?' says Jón Karl, nodding towards the contents of his duffel bag that are scattered over the floor. At the top of the pile is a cream-coloured envelope, still swollen from the million crowns it contained.

'What about it?' Jeckle says, looking first at the envelope, then at Jón Karl.

'Don't listen to him!' says Heckle, stamping his foot.

'Smell the inside of it,' says Jón Karl, staring calmly into Jeckle's irresolute eyes.

'*Do not smell it*,' says Heckle, determined.

'I know,' Jeckle rejoins, giving Jón Karl a searching look.

'There were five million crowns in that envelope,' says Jón Karl, smiling through blood and bruises. 'Óðin stuck them in his jacket when you weren't looking. The envelope probably still smells of money. It was all new 5000-crown bills.'

'Why should we believe you?' Jeckle asks, narrowing his eyes.

'Why should I have an empty envelope?' Jón Karl leers.

'He's fucking with us, man. Don't listen to him!' Heckle says, then gives Jón Karl a dirty look and addresses him: 'If you don't shut up soon, we'll have to shut you up.'

'He's not coming back.' Jón Karl looks paternally into the face of Jeckle, who clearly no longer knows whom to believe. 'He's already got what he was looking for. There is no gambling joint. What gambling joint is it supposed to be? Do you know?'

'You know perfectly well what gambling joint!' says Heckle, his voice trembling with rage and doubt. 'You do the collecting for them.'

'No, I do not,' says Jón Karl, sounding upbeat. 'You have no idea what you're talking about.'

'Shut up!' Heckle looks at Jeckle, who shrugs and then reaches for the envelope, cautiously smelling it before bunching it up and tossing it away.

'What?' asks Heckle, sounding irritated.

'Smells of money,' Jeckle says softly, starting to rock to and fro.

'What did he promise you?' asks Jón Karl coolly.

'None of your business!' says Heckle.

'It doesn't matter,' mutters Jeckle, clearing his throat.

'No, it doesn't matter,' says Jón Karl with a sneer. ''Cause you're getting zilch, *nada*, diddly-squat, you idiots.'

'Make him shut up!' says Heckle to Jeckle.

'Should we wait for Óðin to come back?' Jeckle says uncertainly.

'Yes, we're waiting,' says Heckle, annoyed. 'I can't take the risk of believing this clown.'

'Christ, what a pair of pansies!' Jón Karl spits blood on the floor. 'That's what you are.'

'Shut the fucker up,' says Heckle, groaning with pain.

'Yeah,' says Jeckle, standing up with the rubber truncheon in one hand and a roll of duct tape in the other. 'It's about time.'

'Devil, Lucifer, Prince of Darkness,' Jón Karl says softly as he grits his teeth and stokes his inner fires of hate, anger and hellish thoughts. 'Combine in me!'

Jeckle gives Jón Karl such a blow to the face with the truncheon that blood spurts from Jón Karl's mouth. Jón Karl jerks, makes a rattling noise in his throat, rolls his eyes up and drops his head on his right shoulder. Jeckle puts down the truncheon and pulls out a good length of tape. He bends over Jón Karl and prepares to stick the silver tape across his mouth.

Just before the strong-smelling tape is about to touch his lips, Jón Karl opens wild eyes, throws his head forward with his mouth wide opens and fastens his teeth on Jeckle's left hand.

'*No! Help!*' screams Jeckle, dropping the tape and watching the bloody teeth sink into the back of his hand. He hits out with his right hand and jumps on Jón Karl, who snaps backward at the same moment.

'*No! No! No!*' screams Heckle, standing up to watch, horrified, as the chair collapses under the combined weight of Jón Karl and Jeckle.

Jón Karl lands on his back, lets go of the broken hand and manages to kick Jeckle up and over behind him. Then he forces his tied hands down below his butt and to the front of his bent legs and the broken chair legs. He leaps up and jumps on Jeckle, driving him into the floor. Jeckle's ribs break like uncooked spaghetti, his joints pull apart and his head is crushed so badly that only the bloodshot whites of his eyes can be seen.

When Jón Karl turns around he finds that Heckle has his revolver in his shaking and bloody right hand. Before he can manage to aim and shoot, Jón Karl head-butts him in the face, kicking him to the floor and taking the gun off him.

Devil, Lucifer, Prince of Darkness …

Jón Karl growls and twists around in a frenzy, snorting blood and mucus through flaring nostrils. He still sees only red, still hears the fire roaring in his head, smells ashes and blood. He continues kicking Heckle and Jeckle, has trouble calming himself down to think clearly.

Combine in me.

But once the firestorm calms in his head, Jón Karl starts cutting off the plastic bands with his hunting knife. When that's done he puts the army boots on his bare feet, fastens the ankle holster and gets himself, with difficulty, into his black T-shirt, which has a torn neckline and sleeve. He collects the torn passports and his extra clothes, and shoves his possessions back in the duffel bag – everything except the pistol, which he keeps in his right hand.

'Hey, idiot!' says Jón Karl, giving Heckle a blow to the head with the handle of his pistol. Heckle jumps, opens his eyes and crawls, snivelling, to a wall.

'What?' Heckle says tearfully, and then Jón Karl grabs the chance to shove the barrel into his mouth.

'Listen,' whispers Jón Karl and then puts his finger carefully on the trigger.

Jón Karl gets the bitter taste of blood in his mouth and the inside of his head heats up, his pupils expand and a buzzing high starts spreading through his veins – an ice-cold high that deadens the pain, fills his mind with a blue glow and cools all emotions.

But Heckle goes stiff as a corpse, makes a flat-sounding cry, drools down his chin and pisses his pants.

Click!

The hammer slams against an empty shell and nothing happens.

Jón Karl blinks and pulls the wet gun out of the mouth of Heckle, who is crying like a little child.

'That was enough for me,' says Jón Karl, closing his eyes and drawing a deep breath. He stands up, puts the duffel bag over his left shoulder, turns off the light by breaking the bulb and kicks open the door of the shed.

The padlock shoots out into the night as the door breaks in two.

Jón Karl stretches out his right arm, aims the gun at nothing, grits his teeth and walks swiftly out into the dark.

The shed is up beyond the Vatnsendi neighbourhood, in a dark marsh west of the horse stables. Jón Karl starts running towards the Seljahverfi suburb, all lit up beyond a low hill and gentle slope. He runs across moor, mire and gravel, climbs over a fence, sneaks down between two-storey houses, then walks quickly along a short cul-de-sac down to Jaðarsel Street. There he hides in a bus shelter, where he can catch his breath while keeping an eye on the empty street.

After a few minutes a car appears to the south. It is going fast and, judging by the loud engine and heavy bass beat, this is a well-equipped sportscar.

Jón Karl steps into the street, right arm extended. The driver slams on the brakes and stares open mouthed through the windscreen, first at the bloody, swollen face of the black-clad man who is in his way, then at the revolver that same man holds in his right hand, aimed at him.

'Out!' orders Jón Karl, stepping to the right without taking his eyes off the driver. He opens the driver's door with his left hand and waits for the deathly pale yuppie to step out of his souped-up Impreza.

'I, I ...' stammers the man, trying to loosen his seatbelt with a trembling hand.

'*Out* – NOW!' yells Jón Karl, shoving the barrel of the gun into the left ear of the driver, who starts and manages to loosen his seatbelt.

Jón Karl grabs the driver's shoulder with his left hand and pulls him out of the car and onto the other side of the road.

'Don't steal ... don't,' whines the Impreza's owner, getting up on his hands and knees.

'*Shut up*,' says Jón Karl, tossing his duffel bag into the car before sitting in the driver's seat and slamming the door. He puts the gun in the passenger seat, turns off the music, steps on the clutch and puts the car in first. Just as he's about to drive off he hears a deep engine that he recognises immediately and which makes the hairs on the back of his painful neck stand on end.

He looks in the rear-view mirror and sees a black van appear, like death itself, and approaching at the speed of a tornado.

'Damn!' Jón Karl shouts and floors the Impreza, spinning the low-profile tyres. He's hardly started off when the van slams into the back of the car. The Impreza skids, lights break, shards of paint and plastic fly in all directions, blue burnt-rubber smoke swirls and engines scream at each other.

Jón Karl gains control of the sportscar and races towards Breiðholt Road with the black van – a one-eyed mass of dents from the collision – almost glued to his back bumper. He takes a right into Breiðholt Road and reaches 200 kmh before he gets to the South Highway roundabout. The van falls slightly behind, but Jón Karl would prefer to see the ghostly single headlight disappear entirely from his rear-view mirror. It's uncanny how fast and confidently Óðin is driving that 400-horsepower black box.

The Impreza speeds counterclockwise through the roundabout and then north along the South Highway, again reaching 200 kmh down the hill towards the Westland Highway. The hard tyres scream at every turn and the brake shoes are glowing behind the open aluminium wheel rims.

There's hardly any traffic and nothing to delay Jón Karl. He gains the Westland Highway and floors the sportscar on the wet road, reaching 135 kmh by the Keldur Research Station and keeping that speed right to the first roundabout in Mosfellsbær town.

Under the bonnet the engine screams at 6000 revolutions; the wipers beat in rhythm with blinking eyes as they battle the icy rain that hammers the windscreen; bloody hands clutch the wheel; the headlights slam into the solid wall of rain as if the car were plummeting at terrifying speed into a bottomless pit; his pupils dilate like black holes in his wide-open eyes, and the rear-view mirror shows only darkness.

On the north side of Kolla Fjord, Jón Karl gets stuck behind a semitrailer that is creeping forwards at legal speed, dousing the sportscar with dirty rainwater. There are a few cars coming the other way, and when Jón Karl can finally overtake the semi his mirror shows him a single headlight driving at speed over the bridge at the bottom of the fjord.

'The motherfucker,' mutters Jón Karl, forcing the engine to 7000 revolutions before shifting back up to fifth gear. A moment later he glances at the petrol gauge and sees that the tank is as good as empty.

'I don't believe this,' he says, slamming his fist into the

instrument panel as he soars at almost 200 kmh down into the mouth of the Whale Fjord tunnel. There the traffic, narrowness and speed cameras force him to slow down.

When Jón Karl drives up out of the tunnel at the north end the rain has almost stopped. He stops behind a pick-up truck, waits while the driver pays the toll and takes the receipt handed to him from the lit-up toll booth. Then he drives through without paying, overtakes the pick-up, runs quickly through the Impreza's gears and races east along the Whale Fjord coast. The toll collector will have phoned the police, who will immediately send a car towards him from the next town. If the petrol lasts Jón Karl should, with any luck, still be able to reach the turn-off to Skorra Valley before the police reach him.

But after driving only three minutes along the dark Whale Fjord coast, the engine starts to sputter, the car loses speed and, about a hundred metres further on, stalls.

'This is incredible,' says Jón Karl, letting the Impreza roll a few metres onto the verge. He turns off the lights, sticks his gun in the ankle holster, puts the car in neutral, grabs his duffel bag and gets out of the car, which then keeps rolling gently off the verge and sticks its nose in the ditch.

Jón Karl tosses the bag onto his left shoulder and heads east. He keeps looking over his shoulder, ready to run and hide if the one-eyed car shows up. The excitement of the car chase slowly leaves him, which brings the pain back from its temporary absence. Jón Karl is badly bruised; maybe even has broken bones. His body is on fire with pain, tendons twitching, muscles cramping, bones broadcasting nerve messages and joints grating like rusty iron.

And the icy wind pushes against him, burning his hands and face like a chill blue flame.

Suddenly Jón Karl is blinded by a car's high beams. He shades his eyes and steps onto the verge. A white Jeep approaches from the east, slows down and seems to be stopping. Jón Karl's heart skips a beat and he expects to see flashing lights at any moment, but when the driver turns off the high beams he sees that this is not a police car but a tired old Cherokee with fog lights and a ski rack on the roof.

'Karl?' calls the driver, sticking his face and an elbow out the open window.

'Yes?' answers Jón Karl, staring at the man, who he has never seen before.

'I'm Rúnar, the bosun!' says the driver, motions Jón Karl to get in. 'Hop in, man! We're already late!'

Too late for what-the-fuck?

Jón Karl doesn't know quite what to do or what to think about this stranger who wants him to get in his car, but when he notices a ghostly light approaching from the west, the man's strange request seems like a great offer.

'I'm coming,' says Jón Karl, limping across the road and getting into the Jeep, which smells as if it's been used to transport dead animals.

'What in the world happened, man?' asks Rúnar when he sees the swollen, blood-covered face of Jón Karl, who grits his teeth and dries the sweat from his forehead while Rúnar turns the Jeep around. The one-eyed van is approaching fast and Jón Karl is about to freeze up with pain.

Hurry, hurry, thinks Jón Karl, leaning up against the passenger door.

'I ... just ...' he starts, only to say something, because he has no idea what to really say to this stranger who acts as if he knows him.

'Is that your car?' asks Rúnar, stopping the Jeep right across the road.

In the glare of the high beams they can just see the crumpled back end of the Impreza sticking up out of the deep ditch.

'Yes, it is,' says Jón Karl, tensing up. The black van is still nearing them at speed, only about half a kilometre away now. 'Shouldn't we get a move on? Didn't you say we were late?'

'Yeah, very late,' answers Rúnar and drives off to the east.

'What happened? Did someone tail-end you?'

'No, I just … went off the road,' says Jón Karl quietly, watching the van in the side mirror.

'And are you okay?' asks Rúnar, signalling right. 'I mean, are you well enough to sail?'

What? Sail?

'I'm fine really,' says Jón Karl, who can see in the mirror that the van stops beside the Impreza. Damn! He'd been hoping Óðin wouldn't notice the sportscar and would just drive on. Now he's likely to put two and two together and follow the white Jeep.

But when Rúnar suddenly slows and turns down the side road towards the ferrosilicon and aluminium plants at Grundartangi, Jón Karl is filled with new worries and doubts.

'What, here … where to?' says Jón Karl, sure that Óðin will follow them here and get him, because this road almost certainly ends at the lit-up factories which glow under a cloud of yellow smoke like nightmare castles in the pitch-black night.

'They're waiting for us on the quay,' says Rúnar, turning right down a steep slope.

On the quay? Well enough to sail? Very late?

Jón Karl stares through the windscreen and sees a gloomy-looking freighter rocking ponderously alongside a long quay down by the dark shore. The ship's bridge is lit by yellow searchlights, the wind is wailing in the masts and aerials and a greyish layer of salt wreathes the scene in a ghastly aura. And in the side mirror the ghostly headlight draws nearer.

There are still two shells in his revolver, but Jón Karl is stiff now, confused and exhausted by pain, and Óðin has the reputation of being literally unkillable. Obviously nobody is unkillable, biologically, but when it comes to Óðin R Elsuson, the logic of this world somehow does not apply. He is a living legend, a man who few know, many talk about and everyone fears without really knowing why, and this is why Óðin R Elsuson is more like menace incarnate than a mortal man.

'Well, at least they didn't leave without us, eh?' says Rúnar when he catches sight of Sæli standing there, beating his arms to keep warm.

Jón Karl doesn't know what he should do; his mouth is dry and his insides all numb. He's not man enough for any conflict at the moment – that much is clear.

'Your brother-in-law said I could leave the Jeep just anywhere,' says Rúnar as he stops the car and kills the engine right by the old quay.

My brother-in-law?

Jón Karl glances at the petrol gauge, which has a red arrow pointing to the bottom of a red line. He can't continue his escape in this car.

Fuck it!

'Let's go!' says Rúnar, getting out of the vehicle. Jón Karl does the same. What else can he do? Rúnar locks the car and leads the way to the ship, which pitches by the quay, by turns pulling on its moorings or rubbing against the tyres on the quay, with accompanying screeches. It blows black smoke heavenwards and thrusts up seawater that foams across the concrete pier.

'Hello there – I'm Sæli!' Sæli offers Jón Karl his sturdy hand.

'Hello.' Jón Karl shakes his hand loosely, watching with an anxious expression as the black van drives through the gates at the top of the harbour area.

'Whatever happened to you?' asks Sæli, grinning at Jón Karl.

'I, well …' Jón Karl hesitates, the salt wind bringing tears to his eyes.

'Not now!' shouts Rúnar, who has already jumped on board and is holding his left hand out to Jón Karl and hanging on to the railing with his right.

The black van gets closer and Jón Karl can see the shape of Óðin's head behind the dirty windscreen. Jón Karl's thoughts turn to the gun and he flexes the fingers of his right hand, but they are as stiff as frozen lobster tails.

It's now or …

Jón Karl turns around, tosses his duffel bag behind Rúnar, places his left foot on the gunwale and grabs the outstretched hand of the bosun, who pulls him aboard through a gate in the railing.

'Fucking windy!' Rúnar shouts through the chilling howl.

What might their destination be? Isafjörður? Or Amsterdam? Doesn't make much difference. Jón Karl will be leaving the ship at the next port, and if it turns out to be a foreign port he'll phone Lilja and get her to wire him money for the airfare home.

'Come on, I'll take you to your cabin,' Rúnar calls out, walking ahead of him up an iron staircase and behind the bridge on the starboard side to enter B-deck, where the kitchen, fuse room and a toilet are, along with two dining or mess halls – one for the officers, one for the seamen.

'Everybody's on board,' says Sæli into the intercom and then waits for an answer.

'Cast off the bowline,' the captain, Guðmundur, calls back through the static.

'Cast off the bowline,' Sæli repeats as he carries out the order. He stoops under the ever-increasing wind, half closes his eyes against the salt spray, loosens the forward hawser from the bollard and throws the heavy loop in the water to be heaved on board.

'Bowline ready!'

Óðin steps out of the black van and watches Sæli cast off astern and then jump aboard the ship, which drifts slowly away and then sails west out onto the turbulent waters of Hvalfjörður.

The sea churns behind the giant ship and the heavy beat of the main engine echoes like a toneless drum over the deep fjord.

The last thing Óðin R Elsuson sees before the freighter disappears into the dark of the stormy night is the name that is painted on the black stern: *Per se*.

'May you sail straight down to hell!'

He spits out a cold cigar end and scratches his nose absentmindedly before getting back in the van, which is purring in neutral and rocking back and forth like a boat on the quay.

VII

Fresh or high-gale winds are expected in the waters of Breiðafjörður and Faxaflói Bay …

Guðmundur Berndsen, captain of the freighter *Per se*, sits alone at the kitchen table in his home, drinking black coffee and looking out the window as he turns the envelope on the table and listens to the weather report on a small radio. But his mind is wandering and the soothing voice of the meteorologist goes in one ear and out the other.

It's not as if the weather matters for him: his ship is so big you can sail it in any weather – if the captain is capable and bold, that is. And after thirty years at the helm, Guðmundur Berndsen is an old hand. It's his habit, however, to check the weather before leaving harbour, if only to prepare himself mentally for the long separation from his wife and family, and to make the connection between his mind and the open sea that is waiting for him, enveloped in silence and mystery, both seductive and dangerous, a massive great heart that rises and falls in a cold breast, luring him like a lonely mistress.

And, just like a mistress, the open sea has come between Guðmundur and his wife, Hrafnhildur. The separation – which used to be like fuel to the fire of love and longing – has become a desert where nothing can live; little by little passionate goodbyes have changed into embarrassed silences, and excitement at meeting again has become bitter foreboding that coils itself around their hearts like a snake, poisons their blood with doubt and gnaws at the foundations of their marriage, which is on the verge of collapse.

It isn't, however, the sea that separates them but death; the death of their daughter, in fact. The sea is just a symbol of the dark wasteland that death has left behind in their lives in exchange for the lost girl child. The dark wasteland that has, since that day, kept them apart, whether they sleep in the same bed or on different continents.

They already have a son, who was born when Hrafnhildur was nineteen and Guðmundur twenty-two. He left home around the age of twenty, to learn to tame and train horses in Vienna, half a year before his sister came stillborn into the world. His interest in Vienna had come from his mother, who loved opera and had always intended to go there herself to study singing. That never came about, but her son made his dream come true; since then thirteen years have gone by. He now lives in Austria, with his wife and son, but Guðmundur and Hrafnhildur live alone in a two-storey detached house and share the silence, the sorrow and the dark wasteland.

Hrafnhildur studied singing in Iceland and sang in a great many opera productions, besides giving solo concerts and singing duets on various occasions. She delighted in singing and music generally, so neither the uncertain revenue nor the irregular working hours diminished the pleasure it gave her to entertain people. After losing the baby she stopped singing altogether for several years, until a pastor and a psychologist supported her husband's exhortations to take up singing again so she could renew her contacts with other people and the pleasure that singing had always given her.

So Hrafnhildur did start singing again, but on her own terms. Grief had her in its grip, and from the first day she allowed her beautiful soprano voice to be heard again, she sang only at funerals. Clothed in her long black dress, she was surrounded by such a holy aura that the loveliest churches paled beside her and the hardest men broke down and cried like babies. There, in the presence of death and sorrowful mourners, Hrafnhildur found a new role in life. In the middle of the dark wasteland life awoke in her like the smile on the lips of a dying man, like a blossom that opens for the last time.

Guðmundur was happy to see his wife leave the sanctuary of their home to sing for people again, but soon regretted having pushed her to do so. Instead of helping her deal with her sorrow, singing allowed her to wallow in it even more. She was as sad as before; sadder, if anything. When Guðmundur came back from a long sea trip the house would be dark, the windows shut, the air stuffy and no sign of life. He would often arrive to stand, unmoving, and listen to the silence, his wife's name stuck in his throat like a potato. Then Hrafnhildur would float past him like a ghost, in that long black dress, made up like a corpse.

Guðmundur hates the black dress, that well-tailored death veil that hides his wife's body, sucks all the energy and light out of her, turns her into a zombie and makes her avoid him, and him avoid her. He believes that Hrafnhildur could stop singing in funerals and master her grief, but that she doesn't want to. Guðmundur reasons that she is addicted to grief, a slave to her own sorrow.

And Guðmundur is addicted to the sea, an old sailor who can't get in tune with life, himself and existence unless the world is rocking under his feet and infinity facing him in every direction. Distance is his eternal embrace, loss his most passionate love and intense homesickness the force that maintains a balance in his life. But Hrafnhildur finds this difficult to understand.

Probably they both would just like to make peace with their own fates and each other, but they have remained silent for too long, and nothing is as heavy as long silence.

They long to talk; the words are in the air but they can't open their mouths – or, at any rate, their hearts.

It's been like this for nine years.

Nine years.

Guðmundur sighs and lightly taps the envelope on the table with his finger. Then he takes a sip of his long-cold coffee and looks out the window, distracted.

He isn't looking out the window, though – rather, at his reflection in the dark glass. He is face to face with a bearded, half-bald old man in his sixties, but looking as if he retired years ago.

Guðmundur smiles weakly, turning his eyes into narrow slits that sink into the wrinkled, leathery skin.

There was a time when he seriously considered leaving Hrafnhildur, bringing to an end the long season of cold, dark and silence that was their marriage. Breaking the ice, the silence and the vows he had made in the presence of God and men. Demanding a divorce, moving out of the house and starting again.

That was two years ago. At that time he had come to hate Hrafnhildur. But the hate gradually changed to pity, pity to shame and shame to self-contempt.

Starting again?

He was an ugly old sea-dog, doomed to die alone and abandoned in some basement bedsit where his body would rot for weeks before the neighbours came to investigate the smell.

But it wasn't his fear of lovelessness, loneliness and death that made Guðmundur abandon all ideas of divorce; he wasn't that selfish and petty. No, it was love that defeated his doubt, the tediousness, the hatred and the shame. Love for the woman he had married and vowed to love and honour, in sickness and in health. Love for the woman who had accepted him, a self-important young ship's mate who had nothing to offer her but those very vows.

He loves Hrafnhildur and longs to express his love, renew the vows and the wedding night. He longs to begin anew, with her. He longs to embrace her, kiss her passionately and never let her go. But life isn't that simple.

Guðmundur catches sight of his watch – the gold watch

that the shipping company gave him when he turned fifty. It's twenty-five past eleven, only fifteen minutes until some landlubber from the owner's office comes to fetch him.

The bloody idiots! They're going to give up their lease on the ship and fire the crew. They offered him a job on another ship but he refused it. This coming tour is going to be his last.

Guðmundur Berndsen stands up from the kitchen table and walks with heavy steps into the master bedroom; he blows air out through his nostrils like a whale and turns the envelope in fingers as broad as a Polish sausage, hairy up to the last joint and rough as driftwood.

At the end of the bed stands his suitcase. His uniform cap lies on the bed, protected by a plastic bag, as is his captain's uniform, though its plastic is from the cleaners, while his spit-and-polished shoes are in their own bag by the suitcase. Hrafnhildur has done his packing all these years. She packed for his first tour as captain of a freighter and now she's packed for his final tour. But she doesn't know that this is the final tour. He hasn't the courage to tell her; he's too superstitious for that. He has never promised that he would come home. A sailor can't make such promises. A sailor says his final goodbyes to his nearest and dearest every time he sails. After that he trusts God and luck, and celebrates each homecoming as though it were the final homecoming.

Sailing is dancing with death. And whoever dances with death makes himself no promises about another dance. You simply do not defy death or tempt fate.

Guðmundur puts the heavy bag down by the front door, lays the plastic-packed uniform over the suitcase, the shoes on the uniform and the cap on top of it all. Now there is nothing left but to say goodbye to his wife, who is lying under a blanket on the living-room couch, watching television.

'Hrafnhildur, love.'

She stiffens and gasps when he addresses her, as if his voice were locking itself around her throat like an icy hand.

'Yes,' she says without taking her eyes off the television, where desperate actresses are playing desperate housewives.

He places his right hand very carefully on her shoulder. She softens and breathes more calmly, because his hand is alive and warm. Guðmundur Berndsen's hands are always warm. They are big paws that swallow the hands of women and children like the epitome of security.

Hrafnhildur looks briefly into her husband's eyes and a feeling awakens in him that he has not experienced for a long time. Suddenly he wants to make love to his wife, merge his flesh and hers, fall with her into love's hot ecstasy.

And he knows she wants it too. He can feel it. All he need do is bend down and kiss her on the mouth, hold her hand, whisper words of love in her ear and lead her into the bedroom.

It's been such a long time, though. An ocean of oblivion separates them, a deep void of silence, chill and inertia.

A void that could be dispelled with one word, one touch, one kiss.

If not now, then when?

A car honks in the driveway in front of the house. Guðmundur hesitates and Hrafnhildur turns her eyes back to the television.

Is he here? Damn him, Guðmundur thinks and looks at his watch. He could ask him to come back in an hour. It wouldn't be the end of the world. What could they do? Fire him?

'I could ask him to ...' Guðmundur starts, but he's not able to complete the sentence.

'Shouldn't you just get going?' says Hrafnhildur, clearing her throat. She's troubled by these goodbyes. Not that he enjoys them himself.

'I, umm ...' mumbles Guðmundur, turning the envelope in his beefy fingers. 'I'm going to leave this ... with you.'

Hrafnhildur sits up and looks at the envelope in Guðmundur's hand with intense fear. What is it? Divorce papers? A diagnosis of illness? A will?

'This is a plane ticket,' says Guðmundur, staring at the carpet.

'Plane ticket?' Hrafnhildur's voice is low.

'I want you to meet me in a fortnight,' says Guðmundur, then he takes a deep breath. 'Someone's coming to relieve me. The company has agreed to it. You can fly down south together, you and Captain Trausti. If you'd like. He's going to sail home. You remember Trausti?'

'And …?'

'Just think about it, Hrafnhildur, love,' says Guðmundur, handing her the envelope. 'We could do something together – go somewhere – anything. You and me. If you want. It's just …'

The car honks again.

'You'll phone me, won't you?' asks Hrafnhildur. She lies back down, turning her attention to the television.

'I'll phone.' Guðmundur stands stock still for a few seconds, then he bends down and gives his wife a clumsy kiss on the cheek.

'Have a good trip,' Hrafnhildur says without looking up. She widens her eyes and stares at the screen, which turns into a hot mist and fills with salt water, which is the great ocean – the void that draws Guðmundur to it and separates the two of them.

The emptiness grows larger with each unspoken word, with each touch that isn't touched, each kiss that isn't kissed.

The darkness is like a wall, the car heater blows hot and raindrops slam cold against the windscreen.

Guðmundur sits in the back seat and watches out the side window as lights and shadows race past. The lights become fewer and fewer, the shadows become longer and eventually there's unbroken dark.

'It's getting a bit windy,' says the driver when they come up out of the tunnel under Hvalfjörður. The headlights shine on the rain that pelts the car; the drops burst in time to the neurotic sound of the wipers.

'Yes,' says Guðmundur. He can't wait to be aboard the ship, to cast off and sail away from the house, the lovelessness and the silent pain. But where the pain ends, anxiety takes over.

Will she come and join him or not?

Doesn't matter, maybe, when it comes down to it. This marriage can hardly be saved any more. It would take a miracle to breathe life into something that has been in a coma for so long. Resolve, at the very least. The resolve of both of them to step outside the vicious circle and begin anew.

But she hadn't even been able to say goodbye properly. She pretended not to hear him, see him or be aware of him at all. It was almost as if she had already disappeared from his life.

Left him.

'Have a good trip,' says the driver cheerfully as he hands Guðmundur a folder containing the cargo papers, work orders, inspection certificates and other documents for the tour.

'Yeah,' says Guðmundur. He gets out of the car, a black Mercedes-Benz, takes a deep breath of the cool sea air and partially closes his eyes against the cold rain.

He watches the Mercedes creep away along the wet quay, looking no bigger than a rat alongside the freighter that rises and falls by the quay.

Lamps light up the front of the wheelhouse, the gangway and the weather deck; the generators are going full blast down in the engine room and grey-blue diesel smoke snakes up from the funnel.

'Hi there, Ási!' Guðmundur calls through to the galley, where the cook, Ási, is listening to the radio as he fills a big plate with cakes and doughnuts. 'Could you ask John to knock on my door in about an hour?'

'Yes, sir!' answers Ási, without removing the inevitable match from between his teeth. He clicks his heels, puts two fingers to his forehead and winks at the captain, who shakes his rain-drenched head and sets off up the steep staircase with his suitcase and folder in one hand, his uniform, shoes and cap in the other.

Behind the captain trots the ship's dog, a medium-sized black animal of uncertain parentage that answers to the name of Skuggi. Skuggi usually stays near the captain, but nobody knows where he spends the nights, because nobody has ever thought about it.

The captain's cabin is to starboard on F-deck, called the captain's deck. On the port side is the cabin of the chief engineer, the second in command. F-deck is on the fifth floor of the wheelhouse, counting B-deck as the ground, or first, floor. At the very top is the bridge or G-deck, where the view is like that from a high-rise balcony, while the A-deck – the so-called main deck – is actually below deck.

The captain's cabin isn't locked. Guðmundur enters and turns on the overhead light by pushing his left elbow against the switch by the door, which closes itself behind him. He puts the suitcase down beside a two-seater sofa, puts the folder on the coffee table, his cap straight onto a wardrobe shelf, the uniform on the rod under the shelf and the shoes on the wardrobe floor. Guðmundur doesn't wear his uniform unless he has official business ashore in a foreign port.

He takes off his shoes, socks and jacket and goes into the bathroom, splashes his face with warm water, checks that there's plenty of soap and paper in the shelves behind the mirror above the sink, sits on the toilet and pees while reminding himself to remember to fetch towels, a facecloth and bedding in the laundry room before he goes to bed.

The usual thing is for the captain to stand on the bridge, notify the harbour authorities of their departure and set the course, but Guðmundur isn't actually on duty until eight o'clock tomorrow, when he relieves Jónas B Jónasson. By then he'll have had at most three to four hours' sleep. On a long tour, though, there's more than enough time to make up for losing a bit of sleep.

Guðmundur opens the drawer beneath his bed, which is built into the wall, and pulls out a doona and two pillows. Then he lies down with the folder, turns on the reading lamp above the bed, puts on his reading glasses, opens the folder and leafs absently through the papers. The ship pulls at its moorings and soon rocks him gently to sleep with the steady beat of the generators, the hum of the air-conditioning and the mournful song of the wind outside the salt-encrusted window.

Around one-thirty there's a knock on the door of the captain's cabin and Guðmundur starts awake.

'Gummi?' says Big John through the closed door.

'Just coming, mate!' Guðmundur answers. He swings himself out of bed, puts aside his papers and glasses, stomps across the carpeted floor and opens the door.

'You wanted to see me about something?' Big John crosses his arms across the front of his red-checked shirt that smells of soot, sweat and oil, and which is unbuttoned halfway down his chest, the sleeves rolled up to his elbows.

'Yeah, I just wanted to check that everything was in order,' says Guðmundur, rubbing his tired eyes. 'Are all the tanks full?'

'Everything's in order,' says John a bit brusquely.

'You'll start the engines when the time comes, won't you?'

'I'll start the engines,' John says with a nod and a scowl.

'Good,' says Guðmundur, looking sheepish. 'I'd rather it wasn't – you know …'

'Don't look at me!' says John sharply. 'It wasn't me who hired the fucker.'

'Yeah – no,' mutters Guðmundur with a faint smile. 'But you know how it is – they call the shots, the landlubbers.'

'There's a lot of shots they call, the landlubbers,' John says, looking the captain in the eye. Guðmundur looks away, ashamed.

The hull of the ship creaks as it scrapes against the quay in its long battle with the wind, the sea and the mooring lines.

'It's getting bloody windy out there.' Guðmundur tips his head as if listening.

'Was there something you wanted to tell me?' John asks,

letting his arms fall and sticking his huge hands in the pockets of his dark blue trousers.

'I'll phone down around two-thirty.'

'Right,' says Big John. He turns his broad back to the captain, who watches him clamber down the stairs before he closes his door.

Something I want to tell him? What did he mean? He doesn't know about the lay-offs, does he? What then?

Guðmundur opens the drawer beneath the bed again, bends down, stretches his right arm and pulls out the shotgun that the company provides for these tours. It's a five-shot Mossberg pump-action gun, twelve-gauge, coal black with a sight, interchangeable chokes and a shorter version of barrel. Up on the shelf in the wardrobe are two boxes of twenty heavy-shot magnum shells.

Guðmundur loads the gun – five shells in the receiver and one in the chamber – puts on the safety catch and loads five more shells in a special clip on the left side of the gun. Then he places the weapon in the right corner of the wardrobe, vertically, with the barrel up, and arranges his uniform in front of it before closing the door.

From a drawer in the table Guðmundur Berndsen takes a worn Bible, which he presses against his chest with his left hand as he crosses himself with his right. He bows his head, closes his eyes, closes his hands around the holy book and prays silently.

Our Father …

★ ★ ★

At 2:35 a.m. the phone rings in the control booth of the ship's engine room.

'Yes?' says Big John, sitting on his worn chair in front of the engine controls.

'Start the engine,' says the captain on the phone. 'Half an hour to departure.'

'Start the engine,' John repeats and hangs up. He stands up, puts on his earmuffs and opens the door to the engine room. The air in there is stale and smells of cleaning fluids and the noise from the two 700 horsepower generators is as maddening as an alarm clock in a metal bucket.

John climbs backwards down the ladder to the ship's main engine, a nine-cylinder four-stroke MAN B&W engine, a copper-coloured giant that turns over serenely, pulling the ship with a giant's power. It is over two metres high and the chief engineer steps up onto a platform that reaches round the middle of it like scaffolding. He walks from piston to piston, forcing cooling water from the valves with an air gun and closing the lids of the pressure gauges that measure the combustion pressure and the heat of the exhaust.

The ship has numerous tanks, including four huge fuel-oil tanks for the main engine, which burns eighteen tonnes a day; two gas tanks for the generators, which burn around one tonne a day; two forty-tonne water tanks; lubricant tanks, storage tanks and cisterns.

Everything relating to engines and fuel is the responsibility of the chief engineer, as is the electricity and daily operation of the heat and steam equipment, as well as general maintenance and repair.

★ ★ ★

On D-deck, the lower living quarters, Methúsalem opens a starboard cabin and gestures to Jón Karl to enter before him. Methúsalem opens the door wide and shoves a stopper on the door into a clamp on the wall.

'There's bedding under your bed,' says Methúsalem, turning on the cabin light. 'You can get linen and towels down in the laundry room, as well as toilet paper, soap and stuff.'

'Yeah,' says Jón Karl, dropping his bag on the floor before sitting on the bed.

'There are seasickness pills in the bathroom cabinet,' Methúsalem says with a smirk.

'Yeah,' says Jón Karl again, nodding.

'You can pop down and have coffee and cakes and such,' says Methúsalem as he pulls the door off the clamp.

'Yeah.' Jón Karl nods once.

'You start work tomorrow at nine. Deckhands work from nine to five. Bridge duty for the bosun and the two deckhands is in three three-hour watches, from twenty-one-hundred to midnight, midnight to three and from three to six, moving forward by one watch every twenty-four hours. Rúnar will tell you more about it. Any questions?'

'No.' Jón Karl rolls his eyes like a naughty schoolboy.

'Okay then.' Methúsalem closes the door behind him.

★ ★ ★

Ási turns off the radio, throws the used coffee filter in the garbage and turns off the light. Then he picks up two plastic pails of newly made offal puddings in sour whey – one full of blood puddings, the other of liver sausage – and carries them down to the cold larder, to starboard on the upper deck.

The cold larder is on the right in a short corridor lined with stainless steel. Opposite the cold larder is the dry-goods storeroom, and at the end of the corridor is a walk-in freezer.

Ási puts down the pails, opens the cold larder by pulling on a long handle and walks in. On the shelves are 200 litre-cartons of milk, a hundred of buttermilk, ten litres of cream and 200 cartons of yoghurt; a case of butter and two of margarine; a hundred kilograms of eggs; ten litres of cod liver oil; twenty kilos of cheese spread; ten litres of mayonnaise; ten loaves of bread and twenty cakes; a shelf-metre of coffee and a case of tea; 100 litres of fruit juice and an equal amount of fizzy drinks; two cases of biscuits; sacks of potatoes, swedes, carrots, onions and other vegetables, and cases of fruit, as well as ten kinds of cold meats, dried fish, salt fish, a number of boiled meats and a barrel of salted lamb.

The dry-goods storeroom contains flour, sugar, sacks of meal; milk and egg powder in ten-litre pails; several cases of cereal and dried fruits; many shelf-metres of tinned foods in huge tins; cooking oil by the litre, spices in jars, dried vegetables in sacks, soup stock, and vitamins. In the walk-in freezer there are over 300 kilograms of lamb, beef and pork; thirty chickens; two ox tongues and 400 kilos of fish; fifty loaves of bread, fifty cakes, various sausages in large packages and twenty kilos of ice-cream in four flavours.

Ási closes the cold larder and taps all the heat, frost and humidity gauges, which show him that everything is as it should be in these important rooms. When he turns around he finds himself facing Stoker – Óli Johnsen, the second engineer, who is on his way up after fetching his bedding and towels from the laundry room, which is to starboard on the upper deck.

Stoker is around fifty, short and dark. He has something approaching a hump on his back, his hands are reminiscent of a bird's claws and there is a lot of dirt under his long, ugly nails. He nose is hooked and his teeth either yellow, brown or not there; his mouth has long been frozen in a sarcastic grimace; his beard is black, long and untrimmed, and over the years his staring eyes have turned into hellish lumps of coal.

'Is it true what they say?' asks Stoker, leering at Ási. 'Is your old lady there in the freezer, chopped up and packed in burlap?'

'You bet, pal!' Ási answers, laughing. 'And one of her thighs is what we're having for Sunday dinner.'

'Ha-ha, yep, I thought so, Ási, you bloody sadist,' says Stoker merrily, trying to look straight into the eyes of Ási, who swiftly avoids those black holes. 'I wouldn't put it past you! This I know: you are destined for a seat at the head table down below.'

'I'll lend you some shampoo, mate, when you take a bath,' says Ási in his light tenor voice, trotting light-footed up the steps ahead of the Stoker.

Not all the crew are so slick at avoiding the traps set by the Stoker, this evil-smelling scoundrel who is never happier than when people get angry at him and who tries to get rid of evil through evil temper.

★ ★ ★

Up in the bridge it's dark except for the soft lights from the gauges in the instrument panel and the red light on the coffee pot on the starboard side.

Guðmundur pours fresh coffee into a mug and strolls out to the starboard bridge wing, from where he has a view of the dimly lit quay.

'Everyone's on board!' calls Sæli through the intercom.

'Cast off the bowline,' says the captain into the microphone attached to the lapel of his parka.

'Cast off the bowline!' echoes Sæli.

Down in the engine room John has started the main engine that's idling heavily, heating up.

'Bowline ready!'

'Cast off astern,' says the captain into the microphone as he steers the ship's bow away from the quay with the electrically powered bow engine.

'Cast off astern!' echoes Sæli.

Guðmundur picks up the phone in the bridge and dials the engine room.

'Stern ready!'

'Slow ahead,' says the captain on the phone.

'Slow ahead,' echoes the chief engineer.

The propeller starts turning at the back of the ship and the captain steers its heavy bulk out into the fjord. Once he has the ship straightened out, he phones the engine room again.

'Full steam ahead!'

'Full steam ahead!' the chief engineer repeats and then carries out the order.

When the engine has reached its top revolutions and the ship is travelling at full speed, over thirteen knots, the captain reports their departure and destination to the harbour authorities.

'Echo, Lima, Whiskey, Quebec, 2, calling coastal station.' Guðmundur carefully enunciates the call sign for the *Per se*.

'Echo, Lima, Whiskey, Quebec, 2,' comes the reply. 'Coastal station here, over.'

'Leaving Grundartangi for Suriname,' says Guðmundur. 'Over.'

'Leaving Grundartangi for Suriname,' the coastal station repeats. 'Over and out.'

Guðmundur sits down in the captain's chair and takes a sip of the black coffee. He has a faraway expression as he stares through the window, where the pitch-black of the ocean welcomes him with open arms.

The ship makes its way out of the fjord, rises slowly on a heavy wave and then drops down at the front. The blow pulses back along the ship and all the way up to the bridge; the wave breaks and white foam splashes over the weather deck and pours out of the chutes on the sides.

The ship rises and falls, the wave breaks and the blow pulses back along the ship.

Boom, boom, boom …

Again and again, and forever again.

VIII

The *Per se* sails at full steam towards the south, with the dark blue of the Atlantic Ocean rough and unending in every direction, and black clouds, thunder and lightning in attendance. As the ship meets the heavy waves of the open sea it rises slowly then drops slowly but purposefully down at the front. The blow pulses back along the ship and all the way up to the bridge; the wave breaks and white foam splashes over the weather deck and pours in frothing rivulets out of the chutes on the sides.

The ship rises and falls, the wave breaks and the blow pulses back along the ship.

Boom, boom, boom …

Again and again, and forever again.

★ ★ ★

In through a square ship's window comes a flash of white, throwing a cold light on the fittings of a cabin on the starboard side of D-deck. Then everything goes black once again and thunder rumbles in the distance. The rain beats against the window, which is not completely closed and lets in the water through a narrow chink. Outside the howling wind competes with the so-called blowers on the boat deck – air intakes that suck oxygen into the engine room. Inside the cabin the air-conditioning system hums, pumping warm, oily-smelling air into the ship's living spaces.

Another flash of lightning and everything turns white. A staring, ghostly face floats in the air; there is dark and muttering thunder; the ship rises and falls, the wave breaks and the blow pulses back along the ship and through the bones of men. It echoes in the head of Jón Karl, who is tossing in his bed, writhing in pain and moving his swollen tongue around his parched mouth.

He has a fever and he doesn't know where he is. The only thing he knows is that his bed is floating somewhere out to sea. Sometimes it changes into a small boat or a bathtub. There is movement under his doona, but it is hard to discern the creature's outline. Jón Karl lifts up the doona but the creature darts into a black hole. He is dizzy and his head, heavy as lead, falls onto the sweaty pillow as the doona slides off the bed and sinks down in the dark.

There is no wind, the sky is clear and blue, and there is nothing to be heard except the gurgle of the sea. Jón Karl closes his eyes; he smells salt, wet wood and sunshine. Nothing happens until the ship bumps into a small buoy.

He opens his eyes.

The buoy rocks back and forth and the bed rotates gently. He can hear the squeak and rattle of rusty chains. The buoy is a goddess of destiny in the form of a handless skeleton with a black scarf over its head.

'Five dead men …' she says without opening her mouth. 'Four of them on a ship.'

Then she changes back to an ordinary buoy that gets smaller and smaller until it disappears, because Jón Karl's ship is sailing further and further out on the endless sea.

The waves grow higher and the boat grows smaller; he hears voices but doesn't understand what they say. Then a fog arrives like a grey facecloth, the sun disappears and it gets cold, so cold. The bathtub overturns and Jón Karl falls backwards into the sea and sinks down into the dark blue silence. Someone grabs his feet, someone else grabs his hands and a third pushes as hard as he can on his chest. Hands of sand, men of stone, and the buoy watches. He can't move, he can't breathe, he is pushed down on something hard and dry. His mouth and eyes fill with dust, the pressure is so great that the flesh is torn from his bones, and his bones break and crumble like biscuits; gears turn at terrific speed and sparks fly in every direction like daggers of light.

Jón Karl screams with all his might, kicks out, tears himself away from these deadly clutches and slams his right fist into the wall above his bed.

He comes round, gasping, sits up in the sweat-soaked, bloody bed and stares at his trembling hand. The pain is nearly unbearable. The skin is torn off his knuckles and blood trickles down between his broken fingers. Or are they only cracked? He shuffles, naked, from his bed and staggers like a drunk man across the cabin and into the bathroom. He has a high fever, aching bones and a savage headache.

Jón Karl runs water over his deathly white hand, rinsing away the black blood and flexing his stiff fingers under the cold stream until the pain is bearable. Then he tries to pee standing up but loses his balance and is knocked out when his head hits the bulkhead behind him.

The ship rises and falls, the wave breaks and the blow pulses back along the ship.

Boom, boom, boom …

Again and again, and forever again.

★ ★ ★

Jón Karl sits naked on the couch in his cabin, staring at the cigarette he holds in his right hand. He is pale and bleary-eyed, his hair a sweaty clump, his muscles twitching and his shrunken stomach a cavity.

Through the window come a greyish glimmer of light, the noise of the blowers on the boat deck and a cool breeze tasting of salt.

Jón Karl has laid out the contents of his duffel bag on the coffee table: three pairs of socks, three pairs of underpants, two T-shirts, a hunting knife in its sheath, ten shells, useless passports, share certificates, bank books and ten packs of Prince cigarettes. He has 200 cigarettes but not a single match.

The clothes he was wearing are in a pile on the floor. He steps with his bare feet onto the pile and feels the shape of the holstered handgun under one foot. Everything in its place.

The only thing he's lacking is a light. And maybe something to eat. The water in the sink in the bathroom is drinkable, but Jón Karl hasn't had anything to eat for … a long time.

His stomach contracts into a tight knot, sweat breaks out on his chest and back, and his heart pumps nutrient-low blood up into his dizzy head.

How long might he have been asleep? A day and a night? Longer? And what kind of doomsday trip is he on?

People had come into his cabin because he could hardly have added that extra safety rail himself. Maybe it was the guy who gave him a lift and brought him aboard the ship. Or the guy who brought him to this cabin. But they weren't looking for anything – the gun and everything else are in their place. Which means that either they trust him or they are afraid of him, or they have no idea who he is. None of them has had any objection to him being aboard this ship. In fact, it was as if the ship and the crew had been waiting all evening and half the night for him to arrive. As if this whole shipping company outfit was all about Jón Karl, nothing and nobody else; about getting him on board and sailing with him to somewhere … somewhere.

What should he do? Just act normal? Just go along with things and hope for the best? Or should he ask what the hell is going on? What he's doing here, whether they know who he is and where this fucking ship is going?

No, it's probably best to feel around a bit before …

A light!

'I need a light!' Jón Karl says to himself hoarsely and stares with red-rimmed eyes at the cigarette which is quivering like the needle on a seismograph between the swollen fingers of his right hand.

No sooner has he spoken than there is a knock on the door.

The ship rises and falls, the wave breaks and the blow pulses back along the ship.

Boom, boom, boom ...

Another knock.

Jón Karl blinks, straightens his back and tries to think clearly.

Slowly his features harden; his eyes become focused and reclaim their usual, ice-cold expression; the cigarette stops quivering in his right hand and his left hand stealthily slips the hunting knife out from under the duffel bag before he invites the guest into the dimly lit room.

'Come in!'

IX

Thursday, 13 September 2001

In the seamen's mess Rúnar, Sæli and Stoker sit at a square table with a high brim, covered with a green foam-plastic net, drinking coffee from white mugs labelled 'Polar Ships'. In an old tape recorder is the same Doors cassette that has been circling there, round and round, since the oldest crew member can recall. It has long been a tradition that the seamen forget to bring replacement cassettes after shore time; ages ago they came to a silent agreement to forget that they were sick of it, and just let it go on turning for as long as it continued to do so. Not that they have stopped being sick of these songs they've heard again and again, tour after tour – rather, these fine songwriters have become an unconscious part of their surroundings, just like the beating of the main engine; the rattle of the generators; the keening of the air-conditioning; the rolling, the rocking and the blows that come from the heavy kiss of the waves and pulse back along the ship like ripples.

'Could you check whether Jónas is on the other side?' says Rúnar, stirring sugar into his black coffee as Jim Morrison keeps singing about being strange. 'I need to speak with him.'

'Okay,' Sæli replies. He stands up with his mug in his hand and strolls out to the corridor, past the infirmary, the computer room and the kitchen, over to the mess on the starboard side, where Jónas sits alone, seemingly deep in thought.

'Why don't you just come and join us, lonesome cowboy?' asks Sæli, leaning against the doorframe. 'Rúnar wants to talk to you.'

Jónas slowly raises his head, looks at Sæli then nods and follows him over.

The Doors' song 'Horse Latitudes' starts.

'Jónas!'

'What?' says Jónas, jerking out of a buzzing daydream in which sand mites the size of trout squirm about in the wet, black sand that fills his head and runs like syrup out of his eyes and down into the pitch-black coffee.

'Hand me the bread, man,' says Rúnar, who is not known for being cheerful or sweet-tempered in the mornings.

'Sorry,' says Jónas, handing him the tray of sandwiches.

'Are you sick or something?' Sæli says, smacking his lips on rye bread with meat roll. 'You're kind of pale and wan and somehow without that broomstick shoved as far up your arse as usual.'

'No, I … don't know.' Jónas sighs and takes a sip of his coffee, which has grown cold in the mug. The remark about the broomstick is so old and meaningless that Jónas doesn't hear it any more.

'The winter darkness is getting to him,' says Stoker, grinning evilly. 'Darkness, depression … madness! The dark power overcomes even —'

'No,' says Rúnar, giving Stoker an extra-dirty look while he puts a slice of bread and liverwurst on his plate. 'It's probably some problem that's affecting the family.'

'The family … problem?' Jónas repeats, blinking bloodshot eyes that are rolling like marbles in their sockets between his purple eyelids and the dark blue circles under them.

'Yeah,' says Sæli, shrugging. 'Your brother-in-law still hasn't shown his face.'

'Ha … really? I'd forgotten …'

'Haven't you gone to check on him?' says Rúnar.

'No … I …' murmurs Jónas, who seems totally confused, as if he understands neither heaven nor earth at the same time as he's lost somewhere between these two worlds.

'I thought you'd keep an eye on the guy!' says Rúnar with a shake of his head.

'You're the bosun,' says Jónas, slumping down in his seat as if paralysed.

'He's *your* brother-in-law,' says Rúnar.

'He was all busted up, man,' says Sæli, taking a doughnut.

'Busted up?' Jónas says, blinking hard.

'Yeah, he was rear-ended,' says Rúnar, pouring himself and Sæli more coffee. 'His car was off the road and half in a ditch.'

'But Kalli doesn't have a car.' Jónas straightens his back.

'No, not any more,' Rúnar says with a grin.

'We have to check on the guy,' says Sæli, looking at Jónas and then at Rúnar, who nods.

'I don't know what car he can have been driving,' says Jónas, getting more confused with every passing minute. 'But he doesn't own a car … not himself … I think.'

'Well, of course he owns a car!' Rúnar laughs coldly into the ghostly face of the second mate. 'Otherwise you'd have had to take him with you in your goddamn Jeep, no?'

'He didn't ask me for a lift,' mutters Jónas, staring down into his coffee mug and turning it round with trembling fingers.

'Goddamn Jeep … goddamn Jeep!' says Stoker, grinning. 'Like in the movie *Christine* … The car was possessed, but in the book it was driven by a ghost. The ghost of a former owner who —'

'Shut up!' Rúnar barks at Stoker, waving his fist.

'Take it easy,' whines Stoker, wiping the devilish smile off his face and shrinking in his seat. Usually he keeps in the background in the presence of the bosun, who doesn't hesitate to beat him like a cur.

'Shall we go check the guy out?' asks Sæli, clapping the bosun on the back.

'Yeah,' says Rúnar, swallowing the rest of his coffee. Then

he points an accusing finger at Jónas. 'And you're coming with us!'

'Yes, but ... I ...' Jónas seems to have no idea what they're talking about, or what he's saying himself, for that matter.

'No buts!' say Rúnar forcefully.

The old tape recorder gives a click as the cassette comes to an end, stops, and starts turning counterclockwise. More 'Strange Days'.

Up on D-deck Rúnar opens the door onto the landing behind the wheelhouse. Wind and rain slam into the three men. They look out on dark clouds, iron-grey waves the size of mountains and a churning wake that stretches into the turbulent darkness like a river of boiling milk.

'Christ, but it's black!' Rúnar screams into the wind as he tries to control the heavy door.

'*Shut the door, man!*' shouts Jónas, who seems to have come back to life and shields his eyes from the pounding rain.

'We won't be working outside much today!' Sæli says loudly, poking his head out the doorway.

'*Nope!*' Rúnar answers with a laugh and shuts out the wind and rain again. 'And me with plans to scrape away rust and spot-paint the railings on the way south.'

'It's not worth the trouble, fixing this godless tub,' Jónas says, shuddering from the cold rain that's running down his bony face and under the collar of his shirt. 'It's nothing but a tin can with a wheel and an engine that's tossed around by wind and weather.'

'What do you mean?' Rúnar says with steel in his voice. He walks right up to Jónas, who avoids the bosun's sharp gaze and retreats until his back hits the fire extinguisher on the wall.

'You're talking just like that fucking Stoker!' says Sæli, throwing his hands up. 'What sane sailor would talk such crap?'

'Good question,' says Rúnar, waving his fist in the second mate's face.

'What's your problem?' asks Jónas, who takes to rubbing his

hands together like an old man. 'I was just saying. Didn't mean anything by it. I take it back, okay?'

'Do you know something I'm not supposed to know?' Rúnar says, poking Jónas in the chest.

'No,' replies Jónas, his eyes desperate as he faces the bosun. 'Such as what? Nobody tells me anything!'

'Maybe,' mutters Rúnar, taking two steps back.

'Do you know something?' Jónas asks in confusion.

'About what?' Rúnar asks him back.

'I don't know,' Jónas says with a shrug. 'About the ship, I suppose. Or the company. Maybe they'll cancel the contract?'

'You're not as dumb as you look,' says Rúnar darkly. 'But if they give up the ship, then we're let go too. Right?'

'I don't know.' Jónas sighs.

'No, you don't know anything in your born-again head!' says Rúnar, shaking his own head. 'Have you lost both your mind and your faith?'

'So, shall I knock?' asks Sæli, clearing his throat loudly to break up the argument. He hesitates in front of the cabin door of the deckhand, holding up his fist as if to knock.

'Yeah, knock,' Rúnar replies, snuffling rainwater up his nose and turning his back on the second mate.

'Heathen,' murmurs Jónas and brushes imaginary dust off his shirtsleeves.

Sæli knocks but nobody comes to the door.

'Try the doorknob,' the bosun orders.

'It's open.' Sæli pushes it into the darkened cabin that exhales hot, smelly air into the faces of the three men. 'Hello! Is anyone in there?'

'Come on – get in there, lad!' Rúnar pushes Sæli, who stumbles ahead of him into the cabin. The bosun turns on the light and stands blinking while they get used to it.

'What the hell!' he says when he sees what condition the deckhand is in.

Jón Karl is lying naked on the floor by the bed, pale, cut,

scratched and covered with palm-sized bruises. He is gaping like a fish and the whites of his eyes stare up at the ceiling.

'Is he dead?' whispers Sæli.

'I certainly hope not,' says Rúnar with a deep sigh. 'Come on, let's get him into the bed.'

Rúnar lifts Jón Karl's shoulders and Sæli grabs his legs. Then they take hold of his body with all their strength but only just manage to lift him off the floor.

'*Jónas!*'

Little by little they lose their grip on the naked body; the damp flesh slips from their hands and Jón Karl's head slams against the floor. Cuts open and blood runs out.

'*Jónas!* For Christ's fucking sake!'

Rúnar, crimson with fury, clenches his sinewy fists as he screams at the second mate, who is standing by the bathroom door as if turned to stone and staring at the man lying naked on the floor of the cabin.

'Are you going to give a hand here?'

This isn't his brother-in-law. Where's Kalli? What's going on? Has Jónas gone mad or …?

'*Have you finally gone mad or what?*'

But Jónas does know who it is. He knows who's lying there on the floor of Kalli's cabin. He recognises the face from pictures of crooks in the gossip magazines. He remembers that Gothic 'S' tattooed on the muscular chest. He doesn't know the lowlife's name but he can well remember what name he's known by in the underworld. The name is particularly disagreeable, but extremely descriptive of the man's character.

'Hello?'

But what is this human devil doing aboard the *Per se*?

'*Jónas!*'

And where is Kalli. What's going on?

'What's going on with you, man?' Rúnar screams as he steps over Jón Karl, strides up to Jónas and slaps him hard on the left cheek.

'Huh ... What?' Jónas straightens up, with a shaking hand on his reddening cheek, his lower lip trembling and unmistakable panic in his eyes.

'Help us, you motherfucker!' Rúnar yells in the mate's ear and grabs his shoulder.

'Yes, I ...' mutters Jónas and follows the bosun to the bed.

'One, two and ...' says Rúnar once they all have a good grip on Jón Karl, who is coughing with one leg twitching. '*Now!* And give it all you've got, lads!'

They manage to lift Jón Karl halfway onto the bed frame and then roll him like a barrel onto the mattress, where he ends up on his back with his left shoulder squeezed against the bulkhead under the window.

'Christ, what a hulk,' says Rúnar as he catches his breath.

'Definitely more than a hundred kilos,' says Sæli, wiping sweat off his forehead.

'Yeah,' says Jónas, who really has no idea what to say, think or do. Should he let them know about this stranger on board? Should he phone ashore and ask about Kalli? Or should he just act as if he knows nothing and hope for the best?

What if Kalli suspects his sister is lost or dead? What if Kalli goes to the police?

'Is he a weightlifter or what?'

Are Kalli's absence and this stranger's presence just a whim of fate, pure coincidence or the intervention of a higher power?

Whims of fate are an invention of the superstitious and coincidence is nothing but denial of the relationship between cause and effect in the nihilism of the Western world, which means that the hand of God has ...

'Jónas?'

'The Lord is my shepherd ...' says Jónas mechanically, blinking in the bosun's face.

'The Lord shepherd what-the-fuck?' says Rúnar, snapping his fingers in Jónas's face.

'Ha ... what?' says Jónas, gasping as if he's just been

pulled out of water.

'Goddamn but you lose contact a lot, man!' says Rúnar. 'You're worse than a mobile phone outside the service area.'

'Am I?' Jónas says, coughing a little.

'Yeah!' says Sæli, grinning. 'I think there's something seriously wrong with your head.'

'I just need to rest a bit,' says Jónas, sitting on the bed by Jón Karl, who is still staring out at the world with only the whites of his eyes.

Jónas contemplates this muscular replacement for his brother-in-law, sighs and silently rejoices that he won't have to look his wife's brother in the eye on top of everything else that's weighing on his mind, keeping him from sleeping and hollowing out his heart as a worm hollows an apple.

'You just rest, friend,' says Jónas, laying a paternal but trembling hand on the deckhand's boiling-hot forehead. 'We'll talk when you ...'

Jónas is silenced when Jón Karl suddenly sits up in bed and, without any warning, head-butts him in the face.

'Rúnar!' calls Sæli. He grabs Jón Karl's right arm, which throws him like a wet cloth onto the couch.

'Fucking hell!' says the bosun, and he jumps on Jón Karl, grabs his shoulders and forces him back down onto the bed.

All three of them jump on Jón Karl and manage to hold him down, until he gives in and stops struggling. Blood is pouring from the nose of the second mate, who sits snivelling on his attacker's legs.

'Okay,' says Rúnar. 'Let's try letting go of the bugger!' He releases the deckhand's neck.

'Is your nose broken?' asks Sæli after they've let go of Jón Karl and moved a safe distance away from his bed. Rúnar takes the safety rail from under the bed and puts it in place, so the seaman won't fall out of bed again.

'I think it is,' whines Jónas as he feels his swollen nose and snuffles up blood.

'Come on, we'll have a look at it down in the infirmary,' says Rúnar, putting his arm around Jónas's shoulder. 'This brother-in-law of yours can stay here and rot, as far as I'm concerned.'

'I'll check on him later today,' says Jónas. He looks over his shoulder at the stranger before they close the cabin door. 'I'd better be the one to look after him.'

'Up to you,' says Rúnar, slamming the door behind them.

Boom, boom, boom …

★ ★ ★

The slam echoes deep inside Jón Karl's head. He jerks around as if an electric current were running through his nerves, lets out a rattling cry and slams his right fist into the wall above his bed with all his might.

X

Jónas is empty inside. Cold and empty. Like a ghost ship that drifts, powerless, into a night that will never again turn to day.

Five years ago he had been head over heels in love with María, lost in her eyes, hypnotised by her laughter. Just seven months after he first saw her she was standing beside him at the altar, dressed in white and vowing to be his, before God, his parents and their friends. A year later their first child was born, a weepy son who adored his mother. Two years later came their daughter, the apple of her father's eye.

Then, without understanding when life in heaven ended and hell took over, he was suddenly rushing through the ice-cold night with María's dead body in the boot of his car. The dead body of his wife. The dead body of his children's mother. The woman Jónas loved was dead. Murdered by the man who had pledged her lifelong loyalty, in sickness and in health. Until death did them part. And now death had parted them.

In actual fact, though, it hadn't been death that parted them. Death is some inescapable phenomenon that works behind the scenes according to rules and regulations that no-one understands. When death takes a life it usually seems that there's no connection between whose life is chosen and the causes and effects of our existence. But María's death was due not to some imagined coincidence but to the single-minded will of Jónas, who – in a maelstrom of desperation, envy and jealousy – lost all control of his thoughts, words and deeds.

In the dark night of his mind he forgot all the good and the beauty that had united him and María, had been totally blinded by the single evil that had taken root in their relationship. The evil that he had, at first, loved to flirt with and watch, like a little boy playing with fire. The evil that later consumed him like an evil spirit. The evil that María did, again and again. The evil he could no longer stand. The evil María didn't want to stop. Or couldn't stop, if you took her word for it. But it didn't matter any more. She was dead, and the evil died with her. She could never do that evil again. *Never.*

It had begun with some innocent flirting at a crazy party. Men were attracted to María and that excited Jónas. As for him, well, he couldn't bear the idea of having sex with only one woman for the rest of his life. María wasn't very keen on the idea of an open relationship to begin with. She enjoyed flirting but didn't consider that flirting was necessarily the start of something more. But Jónas knew what he wanted and María didn't want to disappoint her husband.

Once María had ended up in bed with strange men two weekends in a row without being bothered by it; however, doubt began to gnaw at Jónas. He was, of course, not as attractive to women as María was to men. And his disquiet over María's adventures meant that he couldn't concentrate on his own urges which were, little by little, repressed; this made him irritated and frustrated.

When he came home from a tour María always welcomed him, but behind the warm smile and sparkling eyes was the shattered self-image of a woman who had become addicted to the attention and lust of men who fucked her once or twice and then disappeared forever. She had become a sex addict who used the internet and personal columns to find men who would meet her at lunchtime or in the evening, in a car on the edge of town, in a clean public toilet or a cheap hotel room. These countless assignations were hot and exciting, but essentially all the same. Afterwards there would be a period of regret and depression, a time of darkness of the soul that María would get herself through with the help of tranquilisers and alcohol.

He and María had tried to make love earlier that evening, before Jónas went to sea again. His mother had taken the kids – as she so often did – so they could say goodbye in peace. María had tried to calm him down, had massaged and caressed him, whispered words of love and sucked his member slowly and sweetly. But all for nothing. He couldn't get it up. He was too tense, too confused, too worried by the situation. He had pushed María away, gone out to the living room and turned on the television. When he had come back to the bedroom two hours later she was lying in bed, naked. She had washed down who knows how many pills with vodka. She was so fast asleep that there was no way Jónas could wake her up. Then he had gone to the garage and fetched the hammer. He hadn't quite known why. It was just something he'd felt he had to do. One blow and she was dead. One blow and his life was over.

Jónas breathes and his heart beats, but he is as lifeless as poor María, who lies in a frigid tomb. He is cold and empty, an abandoned house of flesh and bone, possessed by some kind of ghost, kept going by the shreds of the human being who once existed within him.

The ship rises and falls, the wave breaks and the blow pulses back along the ship.

Jónas sits on the side of the bed in his cabin on E-deck, staring at nothing while he rocks automatically in time with the slow, almost graceful movement of the ship; heavy, rhythmic movements that he knows as if the ship were an old dancing partner.

In his right hand he holds a rosary with a crucifix, and he squeezes the black beads until his nails dig into his palms and his knuckles whiten, while the cross hangs between his legs and swings like a pendulum, silently counting the seconds.

His swollen, broken nose is covered with gauze and brown tape. His nostrils are filled with clots of blood; the pain in his head rises and falls in time to his heartbeat; his stomach churns with nausea, and his mouth is dry and sour because he's been breathing through it all day.

On the table in his cabin are three gas lighters, two boxes of matches and an out-of-fuel Zippo, but he hasn't been able to find even one cigarette anywhere. To hell with a change of clothes, toiletries and reading material – how in the world is he supposed to survive the trip without tobacco?

'Shit!'

He's been awake for over seventy hours and hardly knows any more whether he's thinking or dreaming, awake or asleep, dead or alive.

When he sits or lies down his mind chases around in circles through the lands of dark horror, bloody fury and fast-forwarded nightmares; but if he tries to walk around and rid himself of hellish thoughts, it's as if his legs turn into an invisible mustang that gallops uncontrollably beneath him, while he floats giddily as if outside his own body, holding desperately onto the reins of common sense and mental health so he won't fall off.

'The Lord is my shepherd.'

God has sent a stranger aboard the ship. Whether the stranger is meant to show him the way back to the light, or Jónas is supposed to instruct the stranger and be rewarded with forgiveness in the arms of the Creator, isn't clear to him. But God will show him the way.

He is the light that will show the way.

'He is the light.'

However, why he should send that particular individual, of all men, is a mystery to Jónas. God certainly moves in mysterious ways.

'The ways of the Lord.'

According to the laws of society, Jónas is guilty of a crime. It's a crime that God has condemned, as the story of Moses and the tablets eternally witnesses.

Thou shalt not kill.

'Not kill.'

How far he has gone astray! Is there a sheep in the Creator's fold who is more lost than that sheep who has taken the life of his wife, the mother of his children?

'I am a lost sheep.'

Jónas is guilty and the guilt is about to destroy him. Jónas is sinful and the sin is drawing him into the deep as if it's a black stone tied round his neck.

He has, though, neither confessed nor given himself in. Rather, he has fled from the crime scene and attempted to hide the trail of evil.

He is following in the footsteps of Cain, the archetype of all who murder in a passion. He has shown criminal intent; he has destroyed evidence and perverted the course of justice; he has dishonoured the corpse of the dead.

But God forgave Cain! God was reconciled with him! God put a mark on Cain to protect him!

In the book of Genesis it says:

> *And the Lord said unto him, Therefore whosoever slayeth Cain, vengeance shall be taken on him sevenfold. And the Lord set a mark upon Cain, lest any finding him should kill him.*

Jónas is Cain and God loves Cain!

And what does that mean? Is Jónas going to take responsibility for his actions, step up and admit his guilt, lay down this heavy burden?

'The Lord is my shepherd!'

No! How would it change anything if he gave himself in and admitted his guilt? María would be just as dead as ever. The only thing Jónas would get out of that would be an arrest and custody, endless interrogations whose only purpose would be to cast a light on a crime that the murderer himself can't understand and, finally, a long trial and heavy prison sentence.

What for? So he wouldn't commit the crime again? As a warning to others? To salve the conscience of society? To provide dramatic entertainment for the citizens?

María is definitely dead. But she is also free. Free from the yoke of sin. Now she will rest until she rises up from the dead, washed white from sin, on the last day.

'On the last day!'

Then they will meet again; then they will be joined again before God.

Jónas has no reason to go to the prison of men. He is a lost sheep in the flock of God almighty, maker of heaven and earth. A sheep who wants to return home and commit his soul to Him who first placed it in transient flesh in a transient world.

God alone can decide whether this wretched flame will get a lamp to live in and burn forever or whether it will be blown out and the ultimate darkness made to swallow its foul smoke.

'God alone!'

The God who put him on board this ship and far out to sea, the God who sent him a stranger to accompany him, the God that wants him to …

'*Quiet!*'

Jónas puts his hands over his ears and walks around in circles in his cabin, so bewildered, confused and disoriented that he borders on total insanity.

He has to talk to that man before someone else does. Before that man talks to someone in the crew.

He has to know what that man is doing on board the ship.

First he has to figure out the will of God, who sent him that angel from hell.

Is the man in hiding? Or is he going to give the captain some kind of report or an explanation for his presence on board?

He mustn't come forward! That would threaten … everything. Like a stone falling into a quiet pool, his crewmates' sudden knowledge of who the deckhand really was would send ripples in all directions and call for unnecessary attention and questions and reactions and …

'I have to talk to him,' Jónas says to himself, beating his thigh with clenched fists as he walks in circles, counterclockwise, in the darkened cabin. 'He mustn't come forward.'

Jónas means to get all the way to South America without the crew finding out about the crime he committed just hours before he boarded the ship.

There he means to disappear. Once there he will look for signs and wait patiently for the guidance of higher powers. There he will walk in the way of God, penniless and humble, until he either dies or finds the light anew.

He means to end his days there or be reborn for the second time to eternal life in the merciful arms of God almighty, God the son and God the Holy Ghost. Amen.

'Amen.'

Jónas stops walking and takes a deep breath. Then he opens the cabin door and walks, straight backed and looking confident, down to D-deck, where he knocks on the cabin door of the deckhand.

'The Lord is my shepherd, my strength, my light,' Jónas says softly, standing in front of the door.

No answer.

He knocks again:

Knock, knock, knock …

Jónas lets his arms fall and clasps his hands around the rosary. He bows his head, closes his eyes and intones the simple prayer again and again while he waits for an answer to his knock, waits for the door to be opened.

The Lord is my shepherd, my strength, my …

'Come in!'

XI

Jónas puts his hand on the doorknob, opens the door and, putting on a look of authority, enters the cabin of the deckhand, who sits naked on the sofa behind the coffee table, studying his visitor with the cold eyes of a man who trusts nobody and is ready for anything.

'How do you do, deckhand,' says Jónas clearing his throat. 'My name is Jónas Bjarni Jónasson and I am chief mate on this ship. As your senior officer I bid you welcome aboard.'

Your senior officer?

'You got a light?' asks the deckhand calmly as he waggles a cigarette between the fingers of his right hand, taking the measure of the second mate, who stands shifting his feet, his tired eyes flitting about the cabin.

'Yes ... of course!' says Jónas, patting his pockets and finding a matchbook in his left hip pocket.

'Thanks,' says Jón Karl, taking the matches.

'May I?' asks Jónas, pointing to an open pack of Princes on the table.

'Sure,' says Jón Karl. He lights his cigarette, leans back on the couch, closes his eyes and pulls smoke into his lungs till the ember crackles.

'I forgot to bring smokes,' Jónas says, the cigarette hanging between his lips. He tears a match from the book, strikes it on the sulphur strip, shields the flame in the palm of his left hand and lifts it very carefully to the end of the cigarette, his rosary rattling between his trembling fingers.

What Jón Karl sees is an undernourished, insomniac, nerve-wracked, broken-nosed man with a three-day beard, smelling of sour sweat and clutching a Catholic rosary as if his life depended on it.

Fucking loser!

'Whaddaya want?' demands the deckhand.

'What do I want?' Jónas repeats in surprise, coughing as he shakes the match until the flame dies.

'How many mates are there on a ship like this?' asks Jón Karl, blowing smoke through his nostrils and lifting his arm to lay it carefully along the back of the couch.

'How many? There are two,' replies Jónas, taking a drag and shrugging. 'Why?'

'Who's the second mate?' asks Jón Karl, who knows that the same rules apply in conversations as in fights: the one who gives the first blow gets the advantage and is in control of the conflict from then on.

'Second mate?' Jónas coughs nervously. 'Nobody. Or … Technically I'm second mate, but since the next highest ranking in the bridge is called chief mate, then …'

'Take a seat!' says Jón Karl, pointing to the still-unmade bed, which is covered with large and small bloodstains.

'Yeah … thanks,' mutters Jónas. He removes the extra safety rail before sitting cautiously on the edge of the blue-striped mattress. 'But, look,' he tries again, 'as one of the officers from the bridge I've come to —'

'Try to shut up for a moment, man!' says Jón Karl, tapping his ash onto the floor without losing eye contact with Jónas, who goes bright red and blinks rapidly like a parrot.

'Shut …'

'One more word, my friend,' Jón Karl snarls, snapping his fingers in front of the mate's broken nose, 'and I'll twist your head so far that you'll have to walk backwards all the way to hell dragging that stupid rosary behind you like a tail.'

'I have never ...' Jónas stops in the middle of his sentence when he sees evil awake like a blind dragon in the eyes of the man who the underworld's gang leaders and messenger boys fear more than death itself.

'First,' says Jón Karl, holding the middle finger of his left hand up from his tight fist, 'what am I doing on this ship?'

'They think you're my brother-in-law,' Jónas says, drawing on the cigarette. 'But it's not as if you ... I mean, nobody asked you to ...'

'Second!' Jón Karl inhales deeply from his cigarette. 'How long have I been here?'

'Three days,' replies Jónas. 'Or, rather, it'll be three whole days tonight at –'

'*Fuck!* And third ...' says Jón Karl, the smoke coming out of his nostrils as he lights a new cigarette from the old one, 'where are we headed?'

'To Suriname.' Jónas allows himself a tentative, crooked smile as he sees the stranger's face become one big question mark.

'Suri-what?' Jón Karl stubs out his old cigarette on the edge of the table.

'We sail to South America every month to bring back eight thousand tonnes of bauxite. Suriname is bordered by Brazil, Guyana and French Guiana. It has the largest bauxite mines in the world, I think.'

'Bauxite?'

'Yeah, or aluminium oxide,' says Jónas, inhaling smoke. And, when he sees that the deckhand is still at a loss: 'It's just a kind of white sand that the aluminium plant at Grundartangi melts down with electrodes to make pure aluminium.'

'How long do we have to sail to get to ... there?' asks Jón Karl with a sigh.

'Two weeks each way, including port time,' says Jónas, shrugging. 'When everything goes well, that is. We sail inland up a river and it depends on —'

'No fucking way!' Jón Karl blows out smoke through his nose. 'I've got to get ashore. Can't I get someone to fetch me or something? Couldn't we order a speedboat or a helicopter? Or stop at the next port?'

'In the first place, we've already travelled almost 2000 kilometres, so we're in international waters,' says Jónas, inwardly smirking. 'In the second place, we neither ask for help nor sail to the nearest port except in an emergency: engine failure, illness and suchlike. And in the third place, you are the deckhand and have duties to carry out.'

'You're not putting *my* back against a wall!' Jón Karl barks, pointing at Jónas with his lit cigarette. 'If I say I have to get ashore, then I get ashore, whether you like it or not. Understood?'

'And might I ask who you are?' Jónas asks, feeling a bit more confident but still fearful in the presence of this naked madman.

'Jón Karl Esrason,' replies Jón Karl dramatically.

'Better known as … Satan,' says Jónas, unwillingly cringing a bit, as if expecting an attack.

'That's right,' says Jón Karl, smiling mirthlessly and raising his eyebrows.

'I saw a picture of you in —'

'Is there anyone else on board that knows who I am?' Jón Karl asks as he leans back in the couch.

'No, and I —'

And you don't want them to know,' says Jón Karl with a careless sniff.

'It would be awkward for me, since I'm the one who found the new crew member.' Jónas briefly looks in the eyes of the dark prince of the Icelandic underworld. 'But it would be even worse for you if the crew found out the truth.'

'Oh?' Jón Karl smirks.

'It's bad enough being stuck with a guy who hasn't been legally registered as a crew member,' says Jónas, putting out his cigarette by stubbing it up under the table. 'A lot worse if that same guy is a renowned criminal.'

'It's not as if I've been accused of anything, or wanted by the police,' says Jón Karl, blowing smoke in Jónas's face.

'You'd get your wish,' says Jónas, straightening up. 'They would phone for help or sail to the nearest port, which would probably be Newfoundland. For your sake, I hope you are ready with a good reason for being aboard this ship, along with a credit card or some dollars, proof of identity and a passport.'

'Are you wanted by the police?' asks Jón Karl with a cold smile.

'Me ... Why would ...?'

'You board the ship without cigarettes for a two-week voyage,' says Jón Karl, also putting his cigarette out on the table. 'And judging by the way you look, you didn't bring clothes or toiletries either. You must have been in quite a hurry. And where is this blessed brother-in-law of yours? Did you get into some drunken argument? Did you kill him, maybe? Oh, no! What have I done? And now you want me to pretend to be him so nobody will suspect anything.'

'Whatever you say,' Jónas says as he stands up. 'But that doesn't alter your situation. You are deckhand aboard this ship and I suggest you take that role seriously.'

'Nobody tells me what to do.'

'There's eight of us against one of you, an injured man,' says Jónas, pocketing his matchbook. 'And the captain is armed with a shotgun.'

'Good for him.' Jón Karl leans forward onto the table, which makes him grimace with pain. 'Do you mind if I keep the matches?'

'If I get a pack of smokes,' replies Jónas, digging the matches back out of his hip pocket.

'Okay,' says Jón Karl, throwing him the open pack.

'I want a fresh pack.'

'No way,' says Jón Karl, holding out a trembling hand for the matches.

'We're on watch together tonight, up in the bridge,' says Jónas as he passes the matchbook to Jón Karl. 'You turn up at three to relieve Rúnar and you're on watch with Methúsalem till four. Then I relieve Methúsalem.'

'Is there a phone in the bridge?' asks Jón Karl, opening a fresh pack of cigarettes.

'Yeah.'

'Where do I get something to eat?' Jón Karl knocks a few cigarettes from the pack.

'Down in the kitchen,' says Jónas and sticks his pack in his shirt pocket. 'Dinner is at six. You eat in the seamen's mess on the starboard side.'

'Eight to one is nothing. Send sixteen seamen against me and then maybe I'll take the trouble to tie my shoes.'

'Don't be an idiot,' says Jónas as he walks to the door. 'Think carefully before you do something you'll regret. You're not on your home turf here.'

'I'll be your brother-in-law for five million,' says Jón Karl, sticking a cigarette in his mouth. 'That's about how much I'll lose during this month.'

'We can talk tonight.' Jónas opens the door.

'Precisely.' Jón Karl grins as he lights his cigarette with the third-last match in the creased matchbook, then he winces, muffles a cry and drops the flaming match onto the rug when his broken collarbone sends waves of crippling pain across his chest, down his arm and up and down his back.

'I wouldn't bother,' says Jónas with a furtive grin.

'Bother with what?' asks Jón Karl in a hoarse voice, stamping out the match with his bare foot.

'Tying your shoes.' Jónas gives a dry and humourless laugh. 'There's only eight of us against you alone.'

XII

Friday, 14 September 2001

'Come in!'

Rúnar turns the handle, opens the door and walks into the cabin of the chief mate, who gives him an imperious nod and gestures to him to close the door.

'And put on the catch,' says Methúsalem softly. The catch is a hinged metal plate screwed onto the door, which can be hooked onto a peg in the doorframe, so the door can't open more than a few centimetres if an unwelcome guest wants to come in.

'Is all well up in the bridge?' says Methúsalem.

'Yeah,' Rúnar replies, looking at his watch. He sees that it's twenty past midnight. 'We've got just under fifteen minutes until the dead man's bell goes off.'

Methúsalem Sigurðsson and Rúnar Hallgrímsson have the same watch in the bridge, which is unattended while this secret meeting is taking place. The dead man's bell is an automatic system that lets the captain know with a warning light and bell if the men on watch don't clock in every fifteen minutes. People have fainted and died in ships' engine rooms due to poison gases; dead man's bells were first used to prevent such accidents and were named for the danger that is ever present for engineers on big ships.

Both Methúsalem and Rúnar started their watch at

midnight, but Rúnar will get off an hour earlier, at three o'clock, when the deckhand relieves him. The first and second mates have regular night shifts: Methúsalem from midnight to four and Jónas from four to eight. Big John Pétursson, chief engineer, who has just got off his regular six-to-midnight evening shift, is already in the chief mate's cabin, chomping on an unlit cigar.

The chief mate's cabin is a reflection of its occupant. Everything is clean and tidy; there is no mess of any kind; everything in its carefully organised place, whether clothes, books or toiletries. There is nothing missing and nothing that isn't needed. On the table are his diary and a ballpoint pen – nothing else. And the bathroom looks as if it has never been used.

Methúsalem is just under two metres tall, fair haired and slim, yet also big boned and sturdy. He is considered to be an honest fellow and a loyal friend to the few friends he has, but neither entertaining nor exactly boring. The worst you can say about him is that he's a fascist, but the tradition at sea is to disregard another's extreme opinions or, at most, make fun of them to cheer things up a bit; after all, people who are forced to be in each other's company aren't much interested in experiencing the unpleasantness that comes with seriously and hotly arguing about beliefs and sexual orientation.

A ship is essentially a closed world, a kind of microcosm in some part reflecting the wider world; but because it is small, specialised and thinly populated, it is free of serious environmental problems, political landscapes, wars and international disputes.

Methúsalem is one of those individuals who are one person in their private lives and a totally different one at work. At sea Methúsalem is quiet and remote, and takes his role as chief mate very seriously; he neither looks down on the hoi polloi nor kowtows to the 'king'. He simply has his mind on his job, day and night, for the whole tour; he doesn't allow himself to relax or lighten up while the ship is sailing; he is burdened with responsibilities and worries. But once ashore Methúsalem Sigurðsson becomes totally reckless and doesn't leave his crew mates in peace – he tries to get them to come drink with him at any time of the day or night, any time of year.

Drinking with Methúsalem always ends up the same way, and it's a way men can't be bothered to repeat more than once or twice. First he tells endless gay, black or Jewish jokes, then moans about 'bloody women', adding a few gross blonde jokes before he changes his tactics and starts praising Iceland and the Nordic race, and conservative Icelandic politicians. After the jingoism comes a long lecture on navigation, the running of a ship and the responsibilities of officers, which always ends with his rancorous complaints that the bosses of Polar Ships have still not promoted him and made him a captain.

Going by the book, the experienced and reliable Methúsalem Sigurðsson should long ago have been given his own command, but the years have passed and most, if not all, of his old mates have been promoted – all except Methúsalem, and this uncomfortable fact is becoming pretty embarrassing, both for Methúsalem and those who sail with him. But there is simply something wrong with Methúsalem Sigurðsson – something people can feel but maybe can't put their finger on – and it's this something that prevents him from being trusted to take on the demanding job of a captain. He's been divorced twice; he is either on his way to treatment for alcoholism or freshly out of it; he is bankrupt; he's a bloody fascist, and then there's something odd about him. Nobody who knows Methúsalem would maintain that he's crazy exactly, yet his fellow crew members all agree that there's something crazy about Methúsalem.

'Well, lads, now it's the real thing,' says Methúsalem, gesturing to Big John and Rúnar to follow him over to the bed. From underneath he pulls out his suitcase and lays it flat on the neatly made bed. From the suitcase he takes a heavy oblong bundle, something wound in canvas and tied round with twine. Methúsalem closes the suitcase and puts it back under the bed, then he places the bundle lengthways on the bed, loosens the twine and carefully unwinds the canvas. They can hear the soft clinks of metal touching metal, metal touching wood and wood touching wood.

'So how do you like that?' the chief mate asks, taking a step backwards. Big John and Rúnar take a step forward, the chief engineer on Methúsalem's right and the bosun on his left.

All of them stare in awe at the darkish artefacts lying side by side on the canvas, smelling of soot and oil. Three dismantled guns: one .22 calibre bolt-action Savage rifle and two double-barrelled shotguns, one an old Remington side-by-side with one trigger, the other a double-triggered over/under Ruger.

'These are my children,' Methúsalem announces.

'I'm not so sure this is a good idea,' sighs Big John.

'No revolution without weapons, my dear Che,' says Methúsalem, clapping the chief engineer on his broad back.

'It kind of gives you the creeps, I won't deny it,' says Rúnar.

'The Old Man is armed, don't forget that!' Methúsalem says, picking up the barrel of the rifle and carefully blowing off some invisible thing.

'Well, that's just a condition of the insurance company,' says Big John. 'Some international requirement because of piracy.'

'Besides, the gun belongs to the ship, not to the captain personally,' says Rúnar, then shrugs. 'Some shotgun provided by the company.'

On board the ship the freight company Polar Ships is never called anything but 'the company'.

'Exactly! A shotgun provided by the company!' says Methúsalem with a chilly laugh. 'A gun that is nothing but a tool for separating the few who are in control from the many who control nothing. A tool that only one man has access to, and that's the captain, of course, who – nota bene – is, in fact, the only representative of the company on board. Think about it! The rest of us are his subordinates, and the captain is the only one that bows to the will of the bosses.'

'You've started talking like a noxious leftie,' John says, smiling crookedly. 'Like a nationalistic left-winger – that is to say, a national socialist.'

'That's right, though.' Rúnar sighs. 'What he's saying about the company.'

'Of course it's right!' says Methúsalem, putting the rifle barrel back on the canvas. 'It's not as if I only started thinking about this yesterday.'

'There's one thing I totally agree with,' says Big John, chomping on his cigar. 'Guns are tools. And, as with all tools, everything depends on who's using them. What matters isn't whether you're armed or not, but what you do with the weapon you may be holding. D'you understand?'

'Of course,' mutters Methúsalem indifferently.

'The way I understood this, the idea was that if men knew we had weapons, then they wouldn't use their own,' says Rúnar, getting out cigarettes and a lighter. 'That one weapon would cancel out another, so that it wouldn't really come to weapons. A sort of ceasefire. Wasn't that it?'

'Why are you saying "men" and "they" when we're only talking about one man?' Methúsalem says as he takes hold of the bosun's right arm. 'There is one gun in the hands of the enemy, and that enemy is our captain. Don't smoke in here.'

'Let's not be talking about enemies,' says John, scratching his beard. 'And I agree with Rúnar. The idea behind these weapons was to strengthen our position and even up the odds. In an even game, neither adversary can oppress the other. That way we should solve this dispute quickly and effectively.'

'The captain isn't alone,' Rúnar says, putting away his smokes and lighter. 'People have a tendency to back up the person in power.'

'Now you're talking sense!' Methúsalem claps the bosun on the back. 'And these guns ensure our control over those who consider themselves above the three of us and everyone else.'

'But we keep the guns out of it for as long as we possibly can,' says Big John decisively. 'Showing these weapons is a last resort and nothing else. I remind you that the mere presence of these murderous tools aboard the ship can have serious consequences. Not to mention if men start threatening with them.'

'Yeah, I think we ought to keep the guns hidden,' Rúnar adds. 'Just knowing they're here will make us feel more confident, which is useful in itself.'

'These guns,' says Methúsalem calmly, looking over the dismantled guns like a pastor over his flock, 'these guns are meant to ensure that our forthcoming revolt will not just peter out and blacken our honour and reputations forever. These guns will distinguish between the victors and the defeated. They may not be the lamp that lights our way, but they will show the way and get rid of all obstructions.'

'Amen,' Rúnar says, giving the short, nervous laugh of a man who wants to win but fears the victory will be sour rather than sweet.

'Just remember, lads, that this kind of dust-up can end badly,' says John, looking at his companions.

'We could end up in jail, for fuck's sake,' says Rúnar, scratching his head.

'I don't know about you, comrades,' Methúsalem says, crossing his arms, 'but I'm not about to go on the dole.'

'No, nobody's about to do that,' mutters Big John.

'Let's finish this, comrades,' says Rúnar with a deep breath. 'I've gotta have a smoke, for Chrissake!'

'That makes two of us,' says Big John, spitting out wet tobacco. 'Who's taking which piece?'

'I'd better have the rifle, because there's an art to assembling it,' Methúsalem says as he waves his hands over the pieces of guns. 'Shotguns you can just slide together.'

'I'll take this one.' Rúnar grasps the over/under shotgun.

'Here's its back end.' Methúsalem hands Rúnar a magazine attached to a lacquered wooden stock.

'Then I'll take this one,' says Big John, picking up the other shotgun, which is both older and more worn.

'Meeting closed,' says Methúsalem, winding the canvas sheet around the rifle. 'Now go hide the guns in your cabins, either under the beds or in the cupboard. I'll go straight up to the bridge.'

'What about shells?' ask Rúnar.

'I'll get them to you when I have a chance,' says Methúsalem, gesturing them to leave. 'It's not a good idea to be wandering about with both hands full of guns and shells.'

'No, probably not,' Rúnar agrees with a shrug.

'I'm going to regret this,' Big John says quietly, undoing the catch before he opens the door and shows Rúnar out ahead of him down the narrow corridor.

'Thanks,' Rúnar says, stalking out with the shotgun parts upright in his right hand.

He walks straight into Jón Karl, who is on his way up to the bridge.

'Fuck!' says Big John when he sees the deckhand, and hastily closes the door.

'What? ... Who?' says Rúnar, backing against the closed door. He stiffens and stares in confusion at Jón Karl, who shows no change in expression and seems not to have noticed the gun.

'Evening,' says Jón Karl, nodding to the bosun, who hesitates in front of him, twists his body and sneaks the gun behind his back.

'Yeah ... evening ... I, uh,' Rúnar stumbles, but Jón Karl strolls on past him and up the stairs without looking back.

XIII

Like tumbling down a huge river in a closed barrel ...

Jón Karl stands spread-legged in the shower stall, steadies himself against the slippery walls, squeezes his eyes shut, breathes fast and shallow, and lets the ice-cold water splash over his head and trickle down over his back and chest. He grits his teeth and silently counts to a hundred.

And burning up in a cold flame ...

He had slept after the second mate's visit, but has no idea for how long. It's pitch black outside, but there is also a thunderstorm, so it's not easy to figure out what time it is. His watch and mobile phone had been left at home in Staðahverfi.

Cold, dark and eternal night ...

Without scientific instruments or a visible sun, time is just a relative experience, subjective evaluation or, simply, a dream.

And the dreams are madness ...

Sleeping on board a ship is really weird. Rolling back and forth as if in a swing, only more slowly, but with unpleasant sideways movements as well, and always the strange feeling that the roll down is both longer and deeper than the roll up, as if the ship is plunging over some kind of brink, shown in slow-motion like a replay on television, again and again. It's kind of relaxing in some hypnotic way, but first and foremost it's a state of endless lethargy that gets more and more unreal the longer you float about in this oppressive void that smells of oil and is as large or small as your mind, as deep as the echo of the slow drumbeat of the engines:

Boom, boom, boom …

The heartbeat of nightmare.

In a small first aid kit in the bathroom cabinet, Jón Karl found a bottle of painkillers – paracetamol with codeine – ten bitter white pills that he washed down with tap water. Maybe not the breakfast that the Public Health Centre would recommend, but the narcotic effects of the drug were now a welcome change from the screaming headache, bubbling nausea and steady messages of pain sent by his frayed nerve endings.

A hundred seconds in a shower provides a local anaesthetic …

Jón Karl turns off the cold water, opens his eyes and then stands still, staring at the clear whirlpool disappearing down the drain while his teeth chatter, muscles twitch and joints tremble. His skin is bright red and numb, fingers and toes virtually frostbitten, and each and every muscle so stiff with cold that he can hardly step out of the shower and walk from the bathroom to his bed.

The night of the living dead …

But he does it in the end. Cold and wet, he crawls under the sweaty doona, curls up in the foetal position and waits for the shivering, the biting cold in his nails and the muscle twitching to pass, and the extra-strong painkillers to kick in. The cold is a comfort but it only reduces the hellish pain to a certain point.

'Come on, then.'

His tongue swells, his lips go dry and a woolly drug fog fills his head …

He had felt tolerable after that long sleep or unconsciousness or whatever, at least while he sat and did nothing, but the second mate's visit had tired him more than three hours of heavy lifting would. While flesh, bones and sinews are healing there's no energy left over. You can't do anything but rest, gather strength and wait for the green light from your body's Department of Restoration.

Breathe and wait.

A million, trillion seconds in an itchy woollen cloud …

★ ★ ★

Lightning tears through the dark like a crackling electric sword cleaving the inner heavens of the skull.

Silence.

And the thunder rattles flesh and bones, growls and kicks the steel like a ragamuffin who spots a tin can in the gutter.

Another silence.

The ship hovers in the air, just for a moment … before it crashes down on the heavy wave.

Boom, boom, boom …

Jón Karl jumps, opens his eyes and sees nothing.

'STOP!'

He sits up in bed, clenches his fists and stares into the darkness while his heart pounds in his chest and his lungs pump foul air in and out of his flaring nostrils.

'Stop,' he mutters hoarsely, exhales like a dying man and falls back down on the sweat-soaked pillow.

Down into a pitch-black woolly cloud …

★ ★ ★

The lights are on, the window half open and Jón Karl has dressed in trousers, socks and a T-shirt. He sits on the couch with a lit cigarette clamped between his lips, the revolver in his hands and a glint in his eye.

He double-checks all the gun's movable parts, then pushes the cylinder to the side and empties it. Two empty shells and three whole ones fall onto the tabletop. He rubs soot away with his fingers, blows powder grains out of the barrel and reloads the gun, leaving eight whole shells.

'Speak softly and carry a big gun,' Jón Karl says to himself as he slides the gun into its holster.

The eight shells he drops into a sock which he then rolls

up and slides into the left pocket of his trousers.

He places the ruined passports, the bank books and the stock and share certificates in the bottom of his duffel bag and arranges his clothes on top of them.

He laces up his army boots, straps the handgun to the upper part of the right boot, sticks his sheathed hunting knife into the left boot and hides the weapons with his trouser legs. Óðin had slit the left leg but Jón Karl found a needle and thread in the first aid kit and sewed it back together. He stands up, tosses his cigarette out of the window and throws the bag into the wardrobe. The open pack of cigarettes goes in his right trouser pocket, along with the matchbook containing one unused match, then he puts the eight unopened packs in the bathroom cabinet.

He closes the cabinet door and looks himself in the eye in its mirror.

'Rock 'n' roll,' says Jón Karl, forcing a smile as he runs his fingers through his greasy tangles, then he winks at himself before turning off the bathroom light.

He takes one turn round, intently scanning the cabin, catches sight of the empty shells and tosses them, like the cigarette butt, out the window. Then he closes the window and turns off all the lights before opening the door and, for the first time, leaves this simple room that is neither a prison cell nor a hotel room, and least of all a home of any kind, yet some combination of all three.

A cabin.

On his way to the bridge he runs across that Rúnar who picked him up in the Jeep and brought him aboard the ship. Rúnar is coming out of one of the E-deck cabins, holding a dismantled shotgun. He's nervous and jumpy when he sees Jón Karl, who is experienced enough to know when to act as if you haven't noticed something someone else clearly doesn't want you to see.

'What? ... Who?' says Rúnar, backing against the closed

cabin door and trying to hide the gun behind his back.

'Evening,' says Jón Karl expressionlessly and then carries on climbing the steep stairs.

Just as well to be armed and ready for anything on this bloody ship, where men sneak around with dismantled guns when they think no-one's looking.

Jón Karl doesn't spend much thought on the bosun's skulking, though. He expects others not to concern themselves with him and what he's up to – whether under the cover of darkness or not – so he doesn't concern himself with others, as long as they keep themselves to themselves and don't mess with him.

At the top of the stairwell, up on G-deck, there are three doors. Directly ahead is a door with a window, leading to the landing of the iron steps on the outside of the wheelhouse; at the back, on the right, is the toilet and on the left is the door to the bridge.

Before opening the door to the bridge, Jón Karl steps out onto the landing behind the wheelhouse. Wide eyed, he looks over the edge of a swaying cliff and lets the wind and rain refresh him. The sea is deeply dark and rough, boiling and churning behind the stern, and in the distance lightning illuminates the black-clouded darkness, oppressive in its immensity. Jón Karl's legs shift under him, so he teeters and grabs an ice-cold iron rod to keep from falling, and then backs through the door and shuts the howl of the wind outside.

In the bridge there's not a soul to be seen. He hears nothing but the low clicks in some instruments and the creaking of the fittings. If it weren't for the yellow-and-green lights in the navigation instruments, he may just as well have been on a ghost ship.

'Hello?' calls Jón Karl, walking past the map room on the starboard side and in to the centre of the bridge, where an empty captain's chair on a high swivel foot moves slightly back and forth with the rolling of the ship.

No answer.

'Jónas?'

'Jónas doesn't come on till three o'clock,' says a voice behind Jón Karl; the door closes with a soft click. 'And you're not supposed to come until four.'

Jón Karl turns to look searchingly at the chief mate, who returns the stare with suspicion.

'What time is it now?'

'Twenty-five to one,' says Methúsalem, looking at his watch. He walks quickly past Jón Karl and clocks in on the dead man's bell, a simple device about the size of a garage door opener.

Not good having no watch …

'Yeah, okay … I'll just go and …' says Jón Karl, but he stops talking when his legs start to give way under him. His eyes roll up and he reaches out to grasp something to keep his body from falling.

'What the hell!' Methúsalem charges across and grabs Jón Karl in his arms before he falls flat on his face. Jón Karl clutches the chief mate's arm, then he lays his head and shoulders against the chief mate's chest, draws a deep breath and manages to regain his feet.

'Are you …?' asks Methúsalem, loosening his hold a little.

'I'm … fine,' says Jón Karl and calmly stands up without, however, immediately letting go of the chief mate's arm. 'I can't think what …'

'I expect you'll recover,' says Methúsalem dryly, loosening his arm from the seaman's grip. 'Just go lie down until your watch.'

'Yeah, I'll do that.' Jón Karl takes a deep breath. 'It's just seasickness or something.'

'No sea legs,' mutters the chief mate, opening the door for Jón Karl and waiting for him to leave the bridge. 'You'll get used to it,' he says more loudly. 'Good night.'

'Yeah, sure.' Jón Karl smiles weakly.

Methúsalem shakes his head as he closes the door behind

the seaman, who is still unsteady on his feet and grasps the railing with both hands as he walks backwards down the steep staircase.

'Fool!' says Jón Karl down on F-deck, laughing quietly. He pulls the chief mate's gold watch out of his waistband, slaps the strap around his left wrist and examines the diamond-studded white-gold dial before he continues on his way.

Rolex. Not bad. But he prefers Breitling himself.

On D-deck he stops and deliberates about what to do: carry on all the way down to the kitchen on B-deck and see whether he finds anything edible, or return to his cabin and sleep until his watch comes up.

But before Jón Karl can choose one of these options, an unexpected third turns up. Through the doorway of a cabin on the starboard side wafts a faint aroma that makes Jón Karl forget both hunger and fatigue. It's the sweet, heavy spicy smell of first-class oil of hashish that somebody is mixing with tobacco.

The third option is this: should he knock on the cabin door and refuse to leave until the occupant shares some of this, the strongest product from cannabis sativa, the one and only hashish plant?

Yes!

Jón Karl knocks on the door – three soft blows with a bent forefinger.

No answer.

So he knocks again – three determined blows with two bent fingers.

Then three with a clenched fist.

Then finally there's an answer.

The door opens a tiny crack and half the face of the first engineer appears in it.

'What?'

'Let me in,' says Jón Karl with the voice and attitude of a man who knows what he wants and isn't about to listen to any objections. 'I'm going to join you in a pipe.'

XIV

'Nobody ever comes in here,' says Stoker as he lets Jón Karl in to the dimly lit room, which is a mirror image of the cabin on the port side.

'Right,' Jón Karl says curtly, taking a good look at this wretched shipmate of his who is dark, skinny and hairy, with a lump on his back and a bald spot on the back of his head, and all shiny with grease – his own and the ship's. He stinks like a dog, is quick and antsy in his movements, and seems to be wearing nothing but a brown bathrobe. In his earlobes are holes but no rings, and through his smelly beard Jón Karl can just see an irritating skeleton grin and, above that, nervous raven eyes.

'You're like some homeless halfwit!' says Jón Karl, wrinkling his nose. 'What do you think you gain by looking and smelling like a beggar?'

'I've got other things to think about,' growls Stoker, looking sideways at Jón Karl like an abused dog at a new master. 'You'd be the new guy.'

'Or something.'

Jón Karl looks around the cabin. On the table he sees dozens of books – some open, all with notes or clippings sticking out of them every which way. There are various small objects in amongst the books, including a hashish pipe, but the most remarkable thing is a black tin canister full of black candles and candle ends. Its lid is in the middle of the table with five black candles burning on it, stuck on with blobs of melted black wax.

These flickering candle flames are the only source of light in Stoker's cabin.

On the unmade bed is an old, worn leather case full of books, magazines and odd bits of paper, and above the bed hangs a picture which provides the only decoration in the cabin. It's an elaborate pencil drawing that has an old-fashioned look about it, framed with thick matting and a carved wooden frame. The drawing is a portrait of some kind of monster or being that is also a man. It is dressed in the clothes of an upper-class Victorian but the head is like an octopus: bald, with neither nose nor mouth but wearing a long beard that resembles soft tentacles. The small black eyes look without doubt or fear into the eyes of the viewer, who can't help but admire the arrogant demeanour of this aberration that crosses its arms in the manner of a dictator and isn't the least ashamed either of its ridiculous head or the misshapen hands like long seal's flippers that hang out of its sleeves.

'Kutulu, king of the underworld,' says Stoker, rubbing his hands. 'He who doesn't live, yet dreams.'

'Who?' asks Jón Karl, tearing his eyes from the picture.

'Bought it on the internet,' says Stoker with a secretive expression, pointing towards the picture. 'A priceless treasure which the civilised world doesn't actually appreciate.'

'No. Quite,' murmurs Jón Karl and sits on the couch.

A priceless treasure? Did he mean the picture or the degenerate subject of it? Is it meant to be some famous elephant man? If there's one thing Jón Karl can't stand, it's innuendo. If people have something to say, they should say it or keep quiet.

'The only true mercy of creation, to my mind, is the inability of the human mind to see and understand the big picture,' says Stoker, waxing profound in the presence of this stranger. 'We live on the peaceful island of ignorance in the middle of the ocean of the darkness of eternity, and we were never meant to leave our birthplace. The sciences, fumbling about in different corners, have not yet caused us harm, but one day some shreds, some fractions of knowledge, seen as a disparate collection until that moment, will come together in a new and unexpected way, revealing a horrifying reality that will either madden us or drive us from the true light and into a period of rejection, stupidity and stagnation that could be called the new Dark Ages.'

'I came in here to smoke a pipe,' says Jón Karl, irritated. 'Not to listen to a lecture on the vastness of your granny's underpants.'

'So you smoke,' Stoker says with a foolish grin.

'Wouldn't be here otherwise,' says Jón Karl with a bored yawn. 'It's not as if I want to get to know a crackpot like you, understand?'

'I don't have any need for friends.' Stoker takes off his ragged bathrobe and tosses it on the bed. Underneath he is wearing grey cotton trousers cut off just above the knee to form sloppy-looking shorts. 'In fact, I make a point of keeping human company away from me and my personal space.'

'I see,' says Jón Karl, staring at the hairy, bony excuse for a body he's faced with in the dim light of the candles.

The stomach is sunken and distorted by a Y-shaped scar that pulls it together into an awful knot; Stoker's chest is virtually fleshless and his thin arms are covered with homemade tattoos – mostly upside-down crosses, five-pointed stars and letters or calculations – and in amongst the tattoos are raised scars from cuts or some kind of branding.

'I do that with a red-hot wire,' says Stoker with a victorious grin when he notices his guest's interest in this hellish body art. He stretches out his left arm to show Jón Karl a brand reaching from his left chest down to his wrist. It's a sentence that appears to have been burned again and again into the meagre flesh.

That which sleeps forever is not dead.
The letters, some of which are backwards or upside down, are highly ridged, some pink, some fiery red.

'Do you do that in front of a mirror?' Jón Karl asks, smiling crookedly.

'Yeah,' says Stoker as he sits down at the table, lifts an open book from a paper of hash oil, a pocketknife and tobacco in burned foil. 'Face to face with …'

He goes silent, clears his throat and looks at Jón Karl with his skull-like grin frozen on his face like a grimace.

'You're welcome to dance naked with the devil every night as far as I'm concerned,' says Jón Karl, taking a deep breath as he pulls over a black gas lighter and sneaks it into his left pocket. 'I couldn't care less.'

'They call me Stoker,' says Stoker. He scrapes a bit of the thick hash oil from the wax paper it's stuck to. 'They say I shovel coal for Satan and no one else.'

'Some would say that shovelling is a waste of time,' says Jón Karl with a low laugh. 'At any rate, I reckon that old guy doesn't pay well – if he exists, that is.'

'Satan exists, both as a shadow or inversion of the godly in the world view of Christians, but above all as a spiritual archetype in the society of men,' says Stoker as he ignites a gas lighter under the knife and melts the oil from its tip onto the tobacco. 'Satan is a dependable companion and a fun guy, but he is neither the beginning nor the end of the diabolical chaos at work behind the weak stage set that humankind is dancing on.'

'You're no different from any other Bible-basher!' says Jón Karl, laughing in Stoker's face. 'You've just turned everything upside down, that's all. The same self-righteousness, the same dogma, the same empty expression, the same arrogant tone, the same idiotic conviction of your own safety and everyone else's certain death.'

'What you don't understand —' Stoker begins, putting down the lighter and knife.

'What I know and understand is that life has no real purpose and there is nothing once it ends,' Jón Karl says forcefully. 'Good and evil are just ideas, God and the devil don't exist – the stage set is all there is. There's nothing behind it … nothing! Not even darkness or death.'

'Good, good,' says Stoker, smiling like a teacher who purposely challenges his pupil in order to get him to express himself. 'But can nothingness flourish without existence? Is it technically possible for some nothing to take over from some *thing* that is without at the same time gaining existence – that is, becoming something?'

'I can't be bothered to argue with people who …' Jón Karl trails off, pushing aside some books in English, German and French whose hard covers have been torn off. 'With people who have nothing better to do than read fucking books!' he finishes.

'Nothing, or that which is not, can only flourish as the shadow of something that is,' says Stoker as he starts to heat up the tobacco over one of the flames. 'If something which *is* disappears, that doesn't mean that something that is *not* takes over, but that the nothing disappears at the same time. Nothingness only exists as a phenomenon without independence on the surface of, or in the shadow of, existence.'

'Speak Icelandic, man!' says Jón Karl, whose mouth is beginning to water as the hash oil warms up on the foil.

'The nothing gets its existence on loan from the existence itself,' says Stoker, stirring the aromatic tobacco with dirty fingers.

'You've given this a lot of thought,' mutters Jón Karl.

'Yep!' Stoker grins again.

'But if the nothing is dependent on the existence,' says Jón Karl after a moment's thought, 'couldn't you just as well say that the existence is dependent on the nothing? I mean, otherwise it wouldn't be existence. It's the nothing that distinguishes existence from being, you know … not being, right?'

'Well …' Stoker shrugs his bare shoulder.

'I mean …' says Jón Karl, sitting up straight, 'the only thing that makes existence *is* is that it's not nothing!'

'Yeeaah … maybe …'

'So the nothing *does* exist.' Jón Karl smiles widely. 'In fact, it's the basis of everything that is. When something that *is* disappears, the nothing disappears as well. You said it yourself! And that which can disappear, that can also be. I mean, otherwise it couldn't disappear. So if the stage set that we sense, live in and call "the world" is the one and only existence, then the nothing must flourish in its shadow – it *is* its shadow and reigns beyond it, beside it, all around it. Where the stage set ends, the nothing takes over. So there you have it!'

'Yes, but ...' Stoker coughs a little. 'That doesn't alter the fact that when the stage set disappears, so does the nothing.'

'And then what's left? Nothing?'

'Which is logically impossible,' says Stoker calmly. 'Which tells us that the stage set won't disappear. It can't, from a philosophical point of view. But – nota bene – it's going to change! As day becomes night, so will —'

'But while the stage set is, then the nothing is as well.' Jón Karl leans back on the couch with a triumphant smile. 'Like two sides of the same coin. End of story!'

'Very well,' says Stoker with a careless sniff. 'But since you're granting a specific world view – that is, existence on the one hand and nothing on the other – you must grant some kind of purpose that —'

'Life is without purpose,' says Jón Karl, silencing his host with a piercing glance and domineering gesture. 'There is nothing in nature that could be called a higher purpose. Purpose is simply an empty word that humanity uses to excuse various actions. *Basta!*'

'A bit of a simplification, maybe. Your point of view is narrow, your attitude unyielding and your mental world black and white ... but, even so, you're not so dumb.' Stoker returns to his customary leer. 'I saw right away that there was some glint in your eye. Something that —'

'Take it easy, mate!' Jón Karl stands up from the couch and snaps his fingers in Stoker's face. 'Snap out of it. None of this "me and you" bullshit, huh?'

'Take it easy yourself,' says Stoker, wiping the leer off his face. Then he turns to concentrate on mixing the warm tobacco and the melted hash oil.

'Um, tell me ...' says Jón Karl. 'When did you get interested in all this ... this mumbo jumbo?'

'When?' Stoker turning his suspicious raven eyes towards his guest.

'Yeah.' Jón Karl yawns.

'"Lo, let that night be solitary, let no joyful voice come therein",' intones Stoker dramatically, his voice trembling. '"Let them curse it that curse the day, who are ready to raise up their mourning".'

'I see,' says Jón Karl, drumming his fingers on the edge of the table.

'So says Job in the Old Testament,' says Stoker and he stuffs a short, black, wooden pipe with the oily tobacco. 'The Leviathan he mentions in his Lament, where he curses the night he was born, is the Hebrew name for Tiamat, the snake or dragon of disorder that's coiled in the abyss and has been worshipped and raised up by the followers of Kutulu for hundreds and thousands of years.'

'Indeed,' says Jón Karl with a nod.

'Since I was born into this world I have been one of the few who fight against the many.' Stoker presses his thumb into the bowl of the pipe. '"Let that day be darkness" – to quote Job again – "for they will know nothing but misery and woe who know the truth and see through history's web of lies".'

'Aren't you going to light that, man?' asks Jón Karl, rocking back and forth.

'You asked,' says Stoker. He presses his thumb even harder into the bowl of the pipe and looks calmly at his guest, who is losing patience. 'And I'm going to tell you about the primordial powers that were worshipped and called to meetings with humanity long before the days of Kabbalahs and the early Christians. I'm going to tell you about The Ancients from the religious writings of the Sumerians, who are the oldest culture in the world and reigned in Sumeria where Iraq is now, and Mesopotamia was before. For some reason this great nation disappeared from the face of the earth, in the blink of an eye, but their language is still whispering in the Shadow beyond Time, and in the dark corners of the Western world you can find age-old manuscripts that tell of the ungodly and terrifying powers that wait beyond the Gate, ready to break through and usurp the power anew!'

'Yeah, great,' says Jón Karl, snapping his fingers. 'Just get that fucking pipe lit!'

'All good things to those who wait,' says Stoker with a cheeky grin. 'Hannibal Lecter, this time, not Job!'

'I'm warning you.' Jón Karl points a threatening finger at his host.

'If you don't start calming down, I'm going to spit in the pipe instead of lighting it,' says Stoker, his voice shaking. He takes a deep breath and straightens his back.

'Then I'll tear your head off and throw it all the way to hell!' Jón Karl thumps the table so hard with his clenched fist that the books bounce and the flames flicker.

'And there's a hearty fire in hell.' Stoker lights a match. 'Because I've worked so hard shovelling coal for the Master!'

'Just light the pipe. After that you can shovel coal in hell till the fire reaches God's arsehole.'

'Ha ha! Bloody good!' says Stoker, putting a match to the pipe and the pipe to his lips, then drawing the fire into the tobacco and the smoke into his lungs, between bursts of chilling laughter. 'God's arsehole! Ha ha! The fire reaches to heaven! Ha ha!'

'Yeah, yeah,' says Jón Karl, irritated, and reaches out his right hand. 'Come on, let me have the pipe.'

'Ha ha! The clerics may have managed to turn things upside down and got the masses to believe that the devil is inferior to God, that he's down there and really just a shadow of the Godhead, whose only purpose is to tempt man and punish him but the truth is something else entirely.' Stoker speaks while inhaling then hands the pipe to Jón Karl. 'The Sumerian creation myth recognises the personification of evil as the oldest of all ancient gods. Christianity teaches us that Lucifer was a rebel in heaven who fell into disgrace with God, who is supposed to have sent him to earth to be punished, taught and humiliated.'

'Yeah, right,' says Jón Karl, preoccupied with drawing the heavy, thick smoke into his lungs which then send it throughout his body like a burning-hot cloud.

'But, in truth, the future creator of the world and godfather of mankind rebelled against the gods of old, killed the eldest of the ancient gods and made the universe from his body, which was the body of an enormous snake,' says Stoker, blowing smoke through his nose. 'Our Icelandic Eddas confirms this. They tell how the sons of Bor killed the giant Ýmir and moved Ýmir's body to the centre of Ginnungagap and made the earth from it, the ocean and lakes from his blood, and the mountains from his bones … and woman, all humankind.'

'This is good …' Jón Karl closes his eyes and lets the smoke slide like a headless snake out of his open mouth.

'Therefore mankind's position in creation is eternally between a rock and a hard place,' says Stoker with a leer. 'In our veins runs the blood of the enemy, the vindictive and fearsome ancient gods who do not live but dream all the same, while our spirit is a gift of the gods of old, creators of the universe, mentors and protectors of mankind, this childish offspring of evil and the Holy Ghost.'

'Here,' says Jón Karl, handing back the pipe.

'But the snake that doesn't live but dreams all the same, it hides in that endless outer space and pitch-black abyss which they call man's subconscious,' says Stoker, taking the pipe and drawing in the smoke. 'That dragon of disorder coils and twists like a spring … like the galaxies of the universe … like the snake that twists in each of us and biologists call the code of life ... DNA.'

'Yeah, yeah, my fucking friend. You can go on talking as long as that pipe is lit.' Jón Karl takes the pipe again. The smoke coils and twists in his lungs like a spring and turns into snakes, dragons of disorder and endless galaxies ... that coil above the flame, merge with Stoker's incoherent stories, change their shapes and dance with their own shadows in the air of the cabin ...

'... Which is a story that starts in the darkness of the human soul, winds through valleys of shadow and ends in the continent of eternal winter, where death has reigned for more than forty million years and the awesome mountains are like abandoned castles in the ghostly light of dawn ...'

'Don't talk any more ...' Jón Karl says, putting the pipe down on the edge of the table. His head is full of hot darkness and his limp body melts into the couch. The smoke runs like glowing syrup into his blood, which is heavy as lead and brown as melted chocolate ... and nightmarish, chaotic images of his wife and daughter plague his mind like mosquitoes in the feverish heat of the East ... rotten flesh and putrid blood and infected eyes that weep metal splinters ...

'... But their day will come. That will be the day when the gates open and the dreadful truth will become clear to condemned mankind. The short-sighted man will wake to the nightmare that the ship they thought they were sailing towards progress and a bright future has been going in circles for thousands of years. It is a ship of fools, steered by fools who look to the stars and ignore the currents in the sea of eternity ... And not until then will they fetch new helmsmen in the insane asylums and in the dungeons of the big cities, but by then it will be too late!'

'Ha ... What ship?' Jón Karl half opens his eyes.

'They are there, always ... forever,' whispers Stoker, giggling through his beard. 'And Kutulu calls!'

'I hate this ship,' mutters Jón Karl, closing his eyes again.

'There is a curse on this ship!' declares Stoker, his voice rising. 'Originally it was named *Noon* and under that name it was infamous after a police investigation of two murders and three suicides that were committed on board over a two-year period.'

Silence.

'Originally it belonged to Jews, but now it belongs to Muslims.'

Silence.

'The fourteenth letter of the Hebrew alphabet is N or Nun, pronounced "Noon". Nun is the thirteenth tarot trump card, because the first trump is a zero. In the Kabbalah teachings "Nun" means the single fish that swims in the great sea and has all creatures in its stomach, and trump number thirteen is death.'

'I've got to go,' says Jón Karl, sitting up. 'Got to lie down. Nauseous … Haven't eaten for …'

'The ship itself may not be evil, per se,' says Stoker with a grin. 'But it is pregnant with evil!'

'Christ, you're boring company.' Jón Karl checks his watch. He sees that it's three minutes to two. Then he slides out to the end of the couch and stands up.

But he has to grab the edge of the table to keep from falling as the ship pitches violently.

Boom, boom, boom …

'Listening to you talk makes me want a cold shower,' says Jón Karl and he steadies himself like a drunken man against the table and walls as he lurches towards the door.

'Hey, pal!' says Stoker, catching hold of the pipe as it slides off the table. 'I still haven't asked you your name.'

'You've said my name three times this evening,' says Jón Karl after a moment's thought. 'So you must be able to work it out for yourself.'

'Eh? What?' says Stoker, scratching his tousled head. 'What name?'

His only answer is the click of the cabin door closing behind Jón Karl.

XV

04:10

Second mate Jónas's face is pale, almost blue, and he looks around with eyes that have stayed open so long they've stopped moving in their sockets.

'What is the meaning of this?' Jónas asks hoarsely when Jón Karl finally makes his appearance up in the bridge. 'It's ten past four! You were supposed to be here for your watch at precisely three o'clock. Methúsalem was furious! He talked about cutting your pay.'

'Relax, man,' says Jón Karl, feeling his way in the dim light, red eyed and unsteady on his feet. 'I just took a little nap. Did we hit an iceberg in the meantime?'

'It's no joke! Around here men are expected —'

'Is there anything to eat here?' asks Jón Karl, grabbing hold of the handles on one of the instruments in the middle of the bridge.

'You stink of hash, man,' says Jónas, throwing up his hands. 'Have you been with Stoker?'

'I don't know,' says Jón Karl with a crooked smile. 'Or in hell. I'm not sure.'

'Which means he's pretty fried down in the engine room.' Jónas sighs.

'Are we allowed to smoke hash here?' Jón Karl says, surprised.

'This ship belongs to Arabs. They allow hash but alcohol is completely forbidden.' Jónas shrugs to show he can't fathom the Arabs' attitude. 'But that doesn't mean men can be stoned on their watch.'

'Go, Muslims!' says Jón Karl with a low laugh.

'There's coffee and biscuits over there,' Jónas says, nodding towards the dim alcove near the back of the bridge. 'See if you can't shape up a bit.'

'Can't we turn on the lights in here?' says Jón Karl and steadies himself on the wall as he heads for the bridge's port wing, which is about the size of a studio apartment.

'No,' says Jónas as he takes a seat in the captain's chair. 'Then we couldn't see out.'

There's a red light shining on the coffee maker, which is attached to the wall beside a small sink, and the glass jug is full of hot coffee.

'Great,' says Jón Karl under his breath. He half fills a clean mug with steaming coffee, which he sweetens with ten sugar cubes and fills up with milk from the little fridge under the table. Then he takes out a whole packet of digestive biscuits from the cupboard above the sink.

On a long counter opposite the coffee corner there are two dimmed screens, two keyboards, two printers, three powerful transceivers, a long-wave radio and a sort of telephone which, like the screens and transceivers, is built into a specially designed console of varnished wood.

'Is that a regular phone?' Jón Karl nods towards the black receiver as he holds his balance with the coffee mug in one hand and the packet of biscuits in the other.

'Satellite phone and telex,' says Jónas, blinking dry eyes. 'We've also got an NMT-phone, but it doesn't always work.'

'Remind me to phone home later on.' Jón Karl puts the mug and biscuits down on the portside windowsill, which has a view over the lit-up weather deck and the bow, which sinks down, breaks the waves and tosses the foam high in the air.

Boom, boom, boom ...

And the salt-filled spray rains over the ship, from bow to stern.

'Listen,' says Jónas slowly, stepping out of the chair and pulling a chequebook out of his shirt pocket. 'I wrote you a cheque.'

'A cheque?' says Jón Karl as he sits down in a chair by the window.

On the windowsill there's a little dashboard Jesus on a glued-down spring. It wobbles back and forth with outspread arms, palms forward, and stares through the glass with its black-painted plastic eyes.

'Yes,' says Jónas, tearing out the cheque. 'It's for those five million you wanted. Or were you just joking?'

'No,' says Jón Karl, accepting the cheque, looking at it and folding it once before sliding it into his right-hand trouser pocket. 'But cheques aren't all that dependable a currency. You understand?'

'It's not as if I could get to a bank!'

'You could phone,' says Jón Karl, opening the biscuits. 'You could get them to transfer the money.'

'First I'm going to have to sell my house. You can't cash that cheque until we get back to Iceland.'

'For your sake,' says Jón Karl, breaking a biscuit before dunking one half in his sweet, milky coffee, '... it'd better not bounce!'

'That's my problem,' mutters Jónas, his eyes going dark.

'Did you kill him?'

'Who?' asks Jónas, stiffening.

'That brother-in-law of yours,' says Jón Karl, smacking his lips on the biscuit.

'No ... I ...' Jónas goes white and then purple around his nose and mouth, as if he's about to suffocate.

'Relax, man. As if I give a shit!'

'I'm just a weak man,' says Jónas, drawing a deep breath like a sheep with lung disease. 'But you are a devil in human form.'

'Whatever. At least I don't have to sell the roof over my head in order to silence people who don't even know what they're being silent about, do I?'

'You …' Jónas gives up.

'Did you say we're on our way to Sumeria?' asks Jón Karl, breaking another biscuit in two.

'Suriname.' Jónas rubs his swollen eyelids with the palms of his hands.

'Right,' says Jón Karl and looks distractedly out the window at the darkness outside. 'But it doesn't look as if we're going anywhere at all, for fuck's sake.'

'Listen. I'm going to the toilet. You just take it easy meanwhile.'

'Real easy,' says Jón Karl, noisily chewing the coffee-soaked biscuit.

'Just remember to clock in on the dead man's bell,' says Jónas, who is putting on an old parka marked Polar Ships back and front. 'That's all you have to do.'

'Right.'

'It's this instrument here.' Jónas points to the dead man's bell. 'When the lights flash and you hear a peep, you have to push the button within fifteen seconds. Otherwise you'll wake the captain.'

'Right,' says Jón Karl, standing up to refill his coffee mug.

'This instrument here,' says Jónas, still pointing at the little grey transceiver.

'Are you going outside for that crap, man?' asks Jón Karl, finally looking at the mate.

'Ha?'

'The parka.'

'Yeah. Might check on the weather while I'm at it.'

'So why don't you just go?' Jón Karl again takes his seat by the window. 'A guy could go grey listening to your bleating. You're worse than the engineer with the hash.'

'Just remember the dead man's bell.' Jónas zips up his parka. 'It'll peep in ten minutes.'

'Right.'

'I'll be off, then,' says Jónas. There's a click as he closes the bridge door behind him, then it rattles as he opens the door to the platform behind the wheelhouse, letting the wind into the stairwell.

Jón Karl sits at the window of the bridge, drinks coffee, eats biscuits, looks out and watches the ship rise and fall on its journey through the turbulent blackness that never changes yet is never the same.

The darkness of night, the ocean and the blowing clouds, the whole hellish spectacle, run together into a dark, seething whole which looks, from the bridge, like a vertical whirlpool turning counterclockwise, round and round, growing neither larger nor smaller, shallower nor deeper.

It's somehow relaxing, this movement of the ship, the interplay of natural forces, the roar of the engine and the many thousands of tonnes of steel. There's something hypnotic about the heavy, measured rhythm that keeps the slow dance going forever, with ever-new variations on this classic theme.

The blows that pulse back along the ship when the bow kisses the waves no longer echo in his head but, rather, pump salty blood in time to the lifeless heart of the engine.

Boom, boom, boom …

And before the voyage ends they will probably disappear from the surface of consciousness and merge with the low ticks of the clock of life itself.

Jón Karl sits completely still and silent, staring out the window like an eagle on a high mountain or, simply, the mountain itself. It must be at least twenty years since he has sat so still and let his mind wander. He's the man who can't sit still to watch a movie without making a few calls, fixing a meal, going to the toilet, eating, drinking and fast forwarding over all conversations.

There's something quite magical about sitting there in the dimly lit bridge and looking down on this gigantic ship as it sails into the night, as if one were an explorer, an astronaut or God almighty travelling through a spiritual sea of oblivion beyond space and time.

Jón Karl allows the ship to rock him in the exhilaration of the moment; it's almost as if his soul awakens and floats higher and higher while his sleepy body sinks deeper and deeper. This sleeping while waking and waking while dreaming is utter bliss, and Jón Karl feels as if he could sit there all night, all his life, forever and ever.

But after four minutes he starts to get bored.

★ ★ ★

Captain Guðmundur lies sleepless under the doona in his cabin, blowing like a whale and turning over at regular intervals.

He keeps the light on in the bathroom and the door open, to thin out the darkness that would otherwise engulf him and fill his head with heavy thoughts. Besides, he has to pee every half-hour whether he sleeps or not, so he may as well simply keep the light on.

04:27

The digital clock stares at him with its red numbers that look like broken letters and which will remain meaningless until 06:59 becomes 07:00. Then Guðmundur will get out of bed, take a hot shower and shave, whether he has had a wink of sleep or not.

04:28

Every time Guðmundur closes his eyes he sees the face of his wife, Hrafnhildur. She looks at him as if she were waiting for him to say something. Say what? Or is she implying that he forgot something? Forgot what?

Did he kiss her goodbye? He can't remember. It had all been so strange and awkward. But did he leave the envelope?

Yes, he left the envelope.

Did she say anything? She said nothing. Or did she?

Would she come? Probably not. Would she be at home when he returned from this tour? Or would she have left him? Would the house be lit up or dark? He hopes it will be lit up. But he fears it will be dark.

04:29

The silence is unbearable. It's more than unbearable – it's driving him crazy.

What he wouldn't give to have her here with him. What he wouldn't give to be able to kiss her now. Or just touch her hand. Feel her breathing. Her heat.

If only he could hear her voice. Even if she were just scolding him. Oh, how wonderful it would be if she could just scold him now.

'I must phone home tomorrow,' Guðmundur says to himself with a sigh as he turns to his other side.

First thing in the morning!

04:30

A red light blinks by his cabin door, then a loud bell starts ringing at three-second intervals, which means there is no-one on watch in the bridge. If they forget what they're doing in the engine room, or lose consciousness there, or if the main engine stops, then the bell rings at one second intervals. But if a fire starts, all the bells on the ship ring without stopping.

'What the hell!' says Guðmundur. He sits up in bed and looks searchingly at the expressionless face of the digital clock.

04:30

'What's Jónas up to?' Guðmundur throws off his doona and leaps out of bed in his pants and undershirt. He still hasn't felt up to unpacking his bags, but has at least arranged his toiletries and bathrobe in the bathroom.

'Goddamn the man!' mutters Guðmundur as he puts on his robe, but he can't find his slippers anywhere, so he runs barefoot up to the bridge.

'Hello!' he calls as he storms into the bridge, but there is no answer. He walks straight to the dead man's bell and pushes the button, at which the light stops flashing and the bell goes silent.

'What in the fucking fires of hell!' Guðmundur roars, so furious that his face has gone red, his hands are shaking and his tongue is dry in his mouth.

He looks over the instruments to check the ship's speed and direction. They're on the right course, the main engines are turning over at full speed, there are no warning lights on – but what's this?

The radar screen is as black as the night outside.

'What the …!' Guðmundur breathes hard through his nose. He taps the screen, pushes all the buttons and turns the brightness knob as far as it will go clockwise, but all for nothing. Instead of a ray of light going circle after circle around the image of the ship with a green blur in its wake, he can see only dark glass with grains of dust and fingerprints on it.

'I am completely …' Guðmundur stops and smoothes his damp palm over his head, then he tears his staring eyes off the darkened radar screen and turns them to the GPS navigation device, which is about the size of an alarm clock and displays the exact position of the ship in red letters on a black screen:

55°N 32°W

'Well, at least we've got …' Guðmundur falls silent as the red letters disappear from the black screen of the GPS device.

His heart skips a beat. He taps the instrument, turns the knobs to left and right, pulls the cord, flicks his nail at the screen, but the letters don't return.

'JÓNAS!' screams Guðmundur and beats the instrument

panel with his clenched fist, but there is no answer.

Guðmundur takes a deep breath and tries to calm himself; he rolls his head back and forth and silently counts up to fifty. He steps across to port and pours inky coffee into his mug, splashes some milk in it and sits down in the captain's chair. He rocks back and forth, drumming his fingers on the chair's arm while he sips the thickened coffee.

'Goddammit! I'll have to call somebody out to relieve me,' he says to himself after a while. He gets out of the chair, then stops to listen as a door opens and someone enters the bridge. Someone who stops to catch his breath by the map room, sneezes like a dog and then snorts something out of his nose.

'Who's there?' the captain asks frostily as he takes two steps forward, a murderous glint in his staring eyes.

XVI

04:17

Jónas opens the door to the platform behind the wheelhouse, but screws up his eyes and steps back when the wind and rain hit him. He grabs the doorframe with his left hand, holds the doorknob tightly with his right, steps over the threshold, out onto the platform and, on the third try, manages to slam the door behind him.

It's a little better standing on the iron platform outside than in the draught that's formed in the doorway, but it's still quite hard for Jónas to keep his feet. He's forced to let go of the cold, wet railing so he can tighten his parka hood. Then he loses his balance, falls flat on his back, slamming the back of his head against the wheelhouse.

'Holy Mary, mother of …' Jónas moans, rolling over onto his hands and knees. Through the X-pattern of the iron platform he can see the iron stairs winding all the way down to B-deck, and from the corner of his eye he sees the stern, poised like a lid above the cauldron-like sea.

Jónas scrambles to his feet holding fast to the railing and climbs up the top stair, which leads onto the roof of the bridge. It's a completely level green-painted iron roof, surrounded by the same kind of railing as the platform behind the wheelhouse.

At the back of the roof, directly above the stairs, is a twelve-metre-high radar and lighting mast with two radar scanners and three aerials for cellular and radio telephones, as well as the mandatory lights. Further up the mast, which is triangular and narrows towards the top, are two railed platforms; the lower one is quite roomy but the upper one is only half the size. Jónas makes his slow and cautious way up a vertical iron ladder on the mast, doing his best not to look down. This far above sea level, the ship's movements are fully exaggerated – Jónas is swinging back and forth so fast that his stomach lurches and heat streams into his head. The sideways movements pull so hard that he almost loses his grip on the rain-slick iron and when the ship pitches into troughs between the waves it feels as if his flesh is pulling on his bones and all his blood is flowing into his legs.

Jónas climbs all the way up to the lower platform but decides not to try to climb onto it. The rain smacks against him like a wet cloth and the wind tosses him back and forth, tears at his soaking parka, thrusts water into his nose and eyes. His trousers stick to his thighs, his shoes are full of water, his hands are red and his fingers stiff as thick rubber hoses.

In front of him are two horizontal iron tubes; from their ends insulated wires wind upwards and connect to such things as the foghorn, the little blinking red lights on the mast, the radar scanners turning circle after circle in the wind, and the aerials, long needles reaching into the black heavens. Jónas locks his left arm around the mast's frame and pulls big, yellow-handled wire-cutters out of his right parka pocket.

He wants to clip apart only the aerials, but doesn't know which wires lead to them, so he has to clip all the wires to be sure, although the ship can't really do without its radar. The wires are both rigid and wet; the wire-cutters are stiff and slippery in his cold hand. Jónas screws up his eyes in concentration. He mustn't drop the cutters, and he mustn't lose his hold on the mast. One by one the wires slip apart; the fingers of his left hand slip on the wet iron; he's blinded by the rain but finally all the wires have been cut. They dangle there like licorice straws with a copper filling.

Jónas slides the cutters back into his parka pocket and climbs down the steep ladder. When his shoe soles touch the roof of the bridge a foolish feeling of happiness washes over him. But he's not finished yet: he still has to cut the wire that leads down from the satellite receiver at the front end of the roof on the port side, a white dome standing on a narrow pole. It's about the size of the body section of a large snowman. Jónas stands still, holding onto the mast while he recovers from his climb. To his right is the ship's funnel, a square chimney out of which protrude four curved exhaust pipes. The black smoke merges with the darkness and disappears into the night, but off and on it blows in Jónas's face, causing him to lose his breath and cough in the sour and irritating fuel oil soot.

There are a few protrusions on the roof of the bridge, besides the satellite receiver. There's a searchlight on its stand, towards the front on the starboard side, and in the middle a magnetic compass on a six-foot platform, wrapped in green canvas. But the roof is mostly bare – just the green-painted metal, covered with slimy salt, soot, oil spills and running water.

The ship is lifted slowly onto the crest of a wave, listing a bit to port; in front of it clouds drift to the east and suddenly Jónas catches a glimpse of something that shines like gold in the sky.

It's a new moon that looks like a cradle, resting on top of the churning clouds.

Jónas gazes at the moon, heedless for just a moment. He lets go of the mast to shield his eyes from the wind and then the ship dips and rights itself. The wind hits Jónas in the back; he loses his balance, is thrown forward and slides at full speed across the roof on his belly until he comes to a stop up against the railings at the front of the bridge.

His right cheek hits a sharp piece of metal, his right shoulder takes a blow, pain flares up in his breastbone and there is a low hiss as his left hand closes round the boiling-hot searchlight on the front edge of the roof.

Jónas cries out and writhes in pain and fear, but his cries drown in the wind and the railing saves him from a lethal fall off the roof.

'Good God!' he cries, holding tight to the railing. He doesn't dare let go and needs a few minutes to build up the courage to stand up and carry on. The night is again dark as a coalmine, no gleam of light in the sky.

Step by step Jónas edges over to the satellite receiver on the port side. At times the wheelhouse tilts back, and he hangs from the wet railing and gazes, terrified, up into emptiness, and sometimes it tilts forward so the metal digs right into his bones and he stares with horror all the way down to the weather deck, which looks like farmland seen from an aeroplane coming in to land. But every once in a while the wheelhouse seems to be pretty horizontal, and then Jónas grabs his chance and dashes across the roof.

Once he has locked his left arm around the pole holding the satellite receiver, he gets the wire-cutters out of his right-hand pocket, then locks the cutters around the thick wire that sways out from under the dome before it disappears into the white-painted metal pipe surrounding the base. He squeezes the handles with all his might, using both hands.

Jónas's knuckles go white, the blades of the cutter sink slowly into the insulated wire, Jónas grimaces and whimpers with effort, the ship falls forward and the bow kisses the heavy wave.

Boom, boom, boom …

The wire snaps and Jónas loses his hold on the cutters, which slip from his stiff hands, bounce once on the roof and then disappear over the edge on the port side.

'*Shit!*' says Jónas and listens intently. But he doesn't hear the cutters land on anything – no blow, no clatter, nothing. They probably fell straight into the sea, which is the best place for them.

Jónas grabs the railing with both hands and catches his breath. He smiles crookedly and snuffles rainwater up his nose with a quiet laugh.

He did it!

The ship is free from the burden and fuss of telecommunication. No-one can contact the ship and the ship can contact no-one. It is out of reach. It sails away in peace and quiet, as ships are meant to do.

Now Jónas is sailing undisturbed to his rendezvous with God and uncertainty, free from worry about official interference and the attention of the media, confused relatives and mourning loved ones.

Actually, from the psychological point of view, it's not so good to have lost both the radar and the GPS, but it doesn't really make any difference. They still take their course from the magnetic compass and in good weather they can work out their position with a sextant, night or day. If people could do it in olden times, they can do it today. The radar keeps track of nearby shipping, but since other ships will still see this ship in their radar, there's almost no danger of a collision, especially not in daylight.

Jónas goes backwards down the stairs that lead to the platform behind the wheelhouse, then he grips the handrail, hurries to the door and grabs the doorknob.

'Jesus Christ!' he exclaims as the wind hits the door and blows it open, yanking him like a ragdoll over the high threshold. He loses his balance but doesn't let go of the door. He manages to resist the wind and push against the door with all his weight, so he closes out the whining wind and pounding rain.

Silence. The freezing rain is running down his neck onto his back and chest, his hands are trembling and his teeth chatter.

Jónas unzips his parka and pulls his soaking hood off before opening the door into the bridge. He closes the door, stops to catch his breath by the map room, sneezes like a dog and then snorts out a blend of snot and ice-cold rainwater.

Has the underworld guy fallen asleep?

'Who's there?' somebody asks frostily and takes two steps forward in the gloom. Jónas sees a murderous glint in staring eyes that he knows he should recognise.

'Eh? What?' asks Jónas, then stiffens as he realises that it's the captain himself who's receiving him in the unattended bridge.

'Where's the ... seaman?' says Jónas, just to say something, but of course Jón Karl's absence astonishes and angers him, while the captain's presence scares him to death.

'It's not up to me to answer that!' says Guðmundur, who is so angry he can hardly speak clearly. '*You* are the officer on watch.'

'He said he was just going to the toilet,' says Jónas, trying to think of some plausible story.

'The radar is out,' says Guðmundur, tying his bathrobe more tightly. 'And the GPS went out just now.'

'Huh? Yes, I was going to check that out, see. But it's madness to try to get up there now. The weather's insane and —'

'Did you abandon the bridge?' growls Guðmundur, taking a deep breath and blowing it out through flaring nostrils.

'Yes, the radar went out and —'

'You said the seaman had gone to the toilet!' says Guðmundur, throwing up his hands. 'And then you go exploring without letting anyone know. *In this weather.*'

'Well, I, look —'

'*Have you gone out of your mind?*' Guðmundur barks, spraying a blend of coffee and saliva over the soaking-wet second mate.

'Yes – no – look ...' mutters Jónas, scratching his wet head, but he has no idea what he should say, or what he shouldn't say.

'Jónas?' Guðmundur walks right up to the officer, who is about to collapse from exhaustion, sleeplessness and general distress. 'Is there something you ...'

Guðmundur stops in the middle of his question when somebody opens the door and enters the bridge.

'Evening,' says Jón Karl, slamming the door behind him. 'What's going on here?'

Jónas says nothing but Guðmundur looks searchingly at the deckhand, who is both red and wet in the face, as if he has just come in from the storm.

XVII

04:22

Jón Karl leaves the bridge and knocks on the door of the G-deck toilet, where he assumes Jónas is sitting on the throne.

'I'm going down below for a moment!'

Then he saunters down to F-deck, then E-deck, on down to D, then C and all the way down to the kitchen on B-deck. The stairs are steep and the treads are hard. Jón Karl is breathless and the pains in his stiff body come to life and send their silent distress signals to his head.

In the kitchen a light is shining under a shelf and below that shelf is a plate of sandwiches that Ási has covered with plastic wrap. Jón Karl strips the wrap off the plate and eats three slices of brown bread with meat paste, washing them down with cold milk which he drinks straight from the carton. Then he returns the empty carton to the fridge and locks the fridge door. At sea all cupboards are locked to ensure they don't open in high seas.

'Hello there,' says Jón Karl when he sees Skuggi's black head peering from the officers' mess. The look each other in the eye for a moment, then the dog turns and disappears into the darkened mess.

In the corridor between the kitchen and the seamen's mess is the ship's medicine cabinet and beyond it a room with a hospital bed and a closed air-conditioning system in case someone needs to be quarantined. Jón Karl walks into the medicine cupboard, turns on the light and closes the door behind him. He finds some strong painkillers and swallows a fair number, then his attention is drawn to a special locker where they keep ampoules of morphine, syringes and needles. Jón Karl takes one ampoule, a syringe and a few needles, wraps them together in a bandage and closes up the whole thing with adhesive tape. Then he fishes a pack of cigarettes out of his right trouser pocket and dumps the four cigarettes left in the pack into a steel tray, sticks the taped parcel into the empty pack and shoves it back in his pocket.

Jón Karl sticks two cigarettes behind his left ear, one between his lips and the last one behind his right ear. Then he turns off the light in the medicine cupboard and goes back out in the corridor. There he lights his cigarette, lets it dangle between his thick lips, blows the smoke out through his nose and thinks for a few moments before strolling down to A-deck to find himself clean bedclothes.

It's dark down there and confined; the air is stagnant and smells of soap and grease; the mats on the floor are slippery, and at the end of the corridor, to port, a faint lightbulb is blinking, as if it's about to go out. Jón Karl steadies himself against the greasy wall and walks across to starboard, where the soap smell's coming from. At the end of this corridor there's a closed iron door marked ELECTRIC WORKSHOP, to the right of which is the entrance to the laundry room, where there's a light on over the ironing machine.

In the laundry room there are piles of clean bedding on long shelves above a pair of washing machines and another pair of dryers. Jón Karl selects some hardly used sheets, four snow-white towels – two large and two small – a number of facecloths, an extra sheet and another two towels to use as bath mats. Jón Karl leaves with his pile of linen under his left arm and goes back along the dim corridor, across to the stairs leading to B-deck. But there's another staircase there too, which leads down to the engine room where the ship's heart is beating, sending out its shuddering shockwaves and boiling breath.

Jón Karl stops and looks down the stairs to the doorway of the engine room – a door with black handprints all over it and greasy smudges round the handle. A moment later he turns the handle and opens the door. The heat beats against him like a stifling breeze and there, in the depths of the ship, there is the usual stink of oil mixed with volatile cleaners, ammonia and galling poisonous fumes.

And the noise is fearsome, almost demonic.

First Jón Karl walks through a kind of storeroom where overalls, helmets and ear protectors hang on hooks, and bottles of detergent, buckets, scrubbing brushes and three pairs of well-worn wooden shoes rest on thick rubber mats. Two steps lead down from the storeroom into the engine room itself, an open space divided into two storeys by a metal-grid floor round the sides. In the open middle lies the gigantic main engine, like a stranded sperm whale that huffs and puffs and flaps its heavy flukes in the sand. Jón Karl walks out onto the metal floor, grips the railing with his right hand and looks down on the nine-cylinder engine with its 270 revolutions per minute, that consumes over seventeen tonnes of fuel a day and provides a constant 5300 horsepower day after day, week after week, tirelessly. Behind the engine is the dynamo, which produces electricity for their daily use, and then at the back of the ship is a huge propeller that drives it forward.

The engine-room control booth is furthest in to starboard – a white, windowless box the size of a garage. Jón Karl inhales cigarette smoke, screws up his face against the noise from the dynamo and walks fast over to the control booth, opens the door, pops in and closes the door behind him.

Silence! What a relief. Actually, it's far from silent in there but the walls are insulated enough to put the noise that does come through in the category of heavenly peace compared to the apocalyptic symphony outside them.

Jón Karl takes his cigarette out of his mouth, knocks the ash off and runs his eye over the contents of the control booth. It is oblong with a door at each end, and the long walls are covered from floor to ceiling with instruments. To his right the wall is hidden by some kind of fuse box where needles quiver in endless voltage meters, counters click and reels turn round and round while the left wall carries the actual operator control panel, which is no small affair. On its vertical face are dozens of meters, switches, warning lights, little screens and a device that keeps a record of all information as it comes from the sensors on the main engine. The horizontal part leans just a little forward, and on it there are open logs, a telephone, a microphone, more lights and switches, a dead man's alarm and, finally, the controls for the engine. There are long shelves of binders held in by the rod on the surface of the console; under it are drawers and cupboards, and in a chair in front of it sits Stoker, snoring, his feet and arms crossed and his head drooping towards his left shoulder.

'Fucking pothead!' says Jón Karl with a low laugh, then drops his cigarette on the floor and steps on it. He puts the bedding down on the console and takes a look at a newspaper cutting that someone has stuck between two meters. The picture shows a few members of the Iceland–Palestine Association demonstrating outside Parliament House. Most are holding placards with hand-painted slogans; all of them are the epitome of earnest tediousness, and some have Arab scarves round their necks. Jón Karl looks over the stupid-looking faces and finally recognises one: it's Big John, the guy who closed the cabin door up on E-deck when the bosun with the shotgun tried to back in through the door.

'Fucking Commies!' mutters Jón Karl and spits on the cutting before tearing it down, crumpling it up and throwing it on the floor.

At the same moment the red light starts flashing on the dead man's bell, so Stoker stops snoring, lifts his head and half opens his eyes. Then he turns his chair halfway round, pushes the button on the alarm with his right forefinger and goes back to sleep.

'Hey! You!' says Jón Karl, snapping his fingers in front of Stoker's nose, but Stoker settles down in his chair and goes back to snoring.

'I've never known … How'd he do that?'

Jón Karl shakes his head and picks up his bedding, turns around and is about to go into the engine room, but hesitates when he sees the picture on his side of the door.

It's a centrefold from a Danish porn magazine, Miss September 2001. The girl's name is Eva and she sits, open legged, on a chair by a window, her expression dreamy and sensuous. She wears white net stockings and a white lace bodysuit, see-through on the sides and with holes in front where her firm breasts push out. Her left hand rests on the left side of her groin, while the fingers of her right hand fool with a long string of white beads. Eva's lips are painted red and there is a gleam of white teeth between them; her fair hair ripples over her shoulders; her blue-painted eyelids have a whorish look, and the crotch of her bodysuit is hitched up between her well-trimmed labia.

'You're coming with me, sweetheart,' says Jón Karl, pulling down the picture, folding it and putting it in his right trouser pocket. Then he picks up his bedding once more, opens the door to the engine room and hurries past the dynamo, over the metal grid floor and into the storeroom at the back. But instead of turning right in the closet and going up the same staircase he came down, Jón Karl walks straight ahead through the oil-saturated gloom, through the storeroom and into the boiler room, where two diesel burners take turns maintaining the correct heat and pressure in a large boiler, whose job is to keep the ship's living quarters warm and ensure that there's always plenty of hot water. The heat in the boiler room is even greater than out in the engine room, The sweat pours off Jón Karl, who breathes quickly through his nose and turns in circles, looking for the exit. Innermost in the boiler room there's a green light and that's where Jón Karl finds a steep metal staircase leading in a half circle up out of this airless incinerator.

At the top of the staircase is a narrow corridor full of darkness, but Jón Karl knows he's reached the upper deck and he knows he's on the starboard side of the ship, so all he has to do is feel his way across to the port side, where there must be some door to the light.

And, sure enough ...

Jón Karl hasn't been feeling his way for long when he sees a dim light above a sturdy door with three hasps. As this doorway is on his right in the corridor, it opens out, towards the bow of the ship, which doesn't seem particularly logical to Jón Karl as he is sure he is very far forward on the deck. The door should be on the left and open onto the deck; for instance, into the corridor where the pantry is to port and the laundry room to starboard. And this is the only door in the corridor that ends there, which continues neither up nor down, forward nor back.

'Fucking ridiculous!' Jón Karl says, clamping his bedding under his left arm while he undoes the hasps with his right. The glass on the light above the door is both scratched and dirty, and the bulb under it is yellowish and pale, but in spite of the weak light Jón Karl manages to read what is painted in white on the red door: HOLD.

'Hold what? Hold it?' murmurs Jón Karl, making a final effort that tears open the third hasp. Going by the streaks of rust, the squeaking and the stiffness of the hasps, this door hasn't been opened for a long time, and when Jón Karl finally manages to pull the heavy door into the corridor he is faced with a darkened emptiness, full of foul-smelling cold, and just as he lets go of the door the ship pitches, smashing into a heavy wave.

Boom, boom, boom ...

Jón Karl loses his balance, stubs his toe on the high threshold and falls forwards through the doorway in a kind of somersault. His left hand gropes and finds something hard and cold, while the bedding, towels and facecloths soar like ghosts through the dark and disappear into the damp depths.

'Yeah, right,' he mutters. Jón Karl is hanging by one hand to some sort of railing and rubbing against a cold iron wall, surrounded by a dark and a terrifying void. He twists round and gets a grip on the metal with his right hand, then feels around with his feet and finds a notch or sill to step on. After feeling around some more and adjusting both his hands and his feet, he realises that he's standing on a vertical ladder that curves from the bottom of the doorway, down along the wall and deep into the ship's hold – a vast space as long, broad and deep as the ship itself, a rectangular tank full of cold and dark.

Jón Karl climbs up the ladder, turns around and sits in the doorway with his feet on the top rung. He feel around his ears and finds one cigarette behind each, which means that only one was lost in those acrobatics.

'Not bad,' he says and lights the cigarette from behind his left ear. He blows out smoke, holds onto the doorframe with his left hand and silently stares into the empty hold. He can't see them in the dark, but there are four hatches the size of football fields over the hold – he saw them from up on the bridge and if he didn't know better he might think he was staring into genuine night, not enclosed darkness.

Jón Karl sits there for a while, smoking serenely and looking neutrally at this rectangular eternity, this bottomless void, which is of course neither eternal nor bottomless, but it seems like that from where he's sitting, and while it seems so it *is* so – it's as simple as that.

Deep under the darkness the engine counts its eternal beats and the ship rises and falls, rocks and rolls, on the expansive dance floor of the ocean, and the ship breathes, the ship moves and the ship generates long, drawn-out screeching and creaking, and in the empty hold the sounds turn to the voices of the condemned, who writhe about in perpetual torment, wail like the newly born, roar like distant monsters and produce soulless sobs that echo between the iron walls and turn into pathetic whimpers in the head of the man who sits stock still and listens to the threads of his own mental health snap like guitar strings being pulled apart by faceless fiends.

The dark is simply dark, which is a black hole and a lifeless abyss, but suddenly there is a flash of brightness that blinds Jón Karl for just a moment. It lights up the pale face of his daughter, who makes an inhuman noise and looks helplessly into her father's eyes, then disappears in an instant, like a spark, into the leaden blackness inside his head.

'I hate this fucking ship,' he says, shooting his lit cigarette into the void. Then he stands up, steps over the threshold, closes the heavy door and slams the hasps into place so violently that rust rains into the corridor.

Jón Karl curses and walks back along the corridor, all the way to the ladder that leads down to the boiler room. But when he turns around to back down the ladder he finds himself staring into the gloom at the front end of the corridor, right by the bulkhead to starboard.

There's an open doorway right above the stairwell. He hadn't noticed it before because it's pitch black inside. Jón Karl decides to walk through the doorway and feels his way in the dark until he finds a light switch on the right-hand wall.

He turns on the light and is faced with a little workroom with a table, chair and long shelves, with countless little plastic drawers full of small items and electrical bits. Jón Karl walks through the room and opens a door in the wall kitty-cornered from the other doorway, and this brings him back to the corridor on the upper deck. To his left is the laundry room and, at the end of the corridor to starboard, the stairs leading up to B-deck, where a light is blinking as if about to go out.

Jón Karl closes the door behind him and reads what's painted on the door in white letters: ELECTRIC WORKSHOP. He fetches some more clean linen in the laundry room and makes his way up to D-deck and into his cabin, where he throws the bedding on the unmade bed and hangs the towels in the bathroom. The air in the cabin is stale and cloying; Jón Karl decides to open the window wide. To do this he has to loosen four big nuts and move an equal number of bolts out of the iron grip of the window, which opens into the cabin and lets in cool night air and cold raindrops, as well as the noise of the blowers.

Jón Karl stands, stooped over, on his bed, sticks his head out the window and lets the wind and rain refresh him. A faint light comes from somewhere and he can vaguely see the propeller and bottom of a big, orange plastic lifeboat that sits in white davits right in front of the window, on a forty-five-degree incline back along the ship, bow down and stern up.

'Amazing,' he says and sniffs rainwater up his nose, then he pulls his head in and steps down off the bed, turns off the cabin light and strolls up to the bridge.

Just before he turns the doorknob into the bridge, he hears a loud voice through the closed door.

'*Have you gone out of your mind?*'

Jón Karl smiles crookedly and lays his ear against the door, but the voices inside are both low and unclear, as if the men have suddenly regained their tempers.

What's going on in there?

Jón Karl is too curious to eavesdrop like this if he can't hear what's being said.

'Evening,' he says, slamming the door behind him. 'What's going on here?'

There are two men standing before him: Jónas and a middle-aged guy wearing a bathrobe.

The light is dim in the bridge but the air is so charged it almost illuminates the entire area.

The mate says nothing but the guy in the bathrobe looks searchingly at Jón Karl, who is both red and wet in the face, as if he has just come in from the storm – which, of course, he has, in a way.

'Where have you been?' asks the guy in the bathrobe, his

voice low and frosty.

'This is the captain,' says Jónas, looking at Jón Karl with eyes that beg for cooperation, restraint and mercy. 'I told him you —'

'Jónas!' says the captain, shutting Jónas up. 'Let me speak to the man.'

'Yes, I …'

'Not another word!' says the captain, turning to Jón Karl. 'You were where?'

'I was just getting my bedclothes,' says Jón Karl with a smirk as he takes the cigarette from behind his ear and sticks it in his mouth. 'But I knocked on the door of the toilet on my way down and told him to stop hanging about.'

'Who was in the toilet?'

'He was,' says Jón Karl, lighting the cigarette which is almost too damp to burn and smells awful. 'He'd been in the toilet for fifteen minutes or so.'

'Didn't you tell me *he'd* been in the toilet?' asks the captain, looking at Jónas, who turns bright red and gapes like a fish.

'Yeah – no. No. Definitely not.' Jónas falters and points at Jón Karl. 'He was the one who left the bridge, you heard what he —'

'Blah, blah,' taunts Jón Karl, drawing on his cigarette until the sputtering ember conquers the wet tobacco.

'It's your responsibility,' says Guðmundur, breathing into Jónas's face.

'Yes, I'm fully aware —'

'Not another word!' Guðmundur cuts the gloom with a sudden movement of his hand as he strides towards the door. 'We'll settle this in the morning.'

Guðmundur slams the door behind him and at the same moment the ship pitches deeply until it finally collides with a rising wave.

Boom, boom, boom …

XVIII

11:19

When Jón Karl wakes up it's nineteen minutes after eleven o'clock in the morning. He lies, fully dressed, on top of the still-folded bed linen and the wrinkled doona and stares at the ceiling, at the curtains that swing to and fro in the cold breeze, letting blue-white light into the dim cabin.

He's stiff and still tired, despite five hours' sleep. If you can call it sleep. 'Conscious unconsciousness' is more like it.

Christ but he's sick of being on this ship! Sick of the ship itself. And the guys on board. Sick of this fucking mess. What's he doing here? What was he thinking, to get on board this million-tonne washbowl?

And what's the matter with all these mates, engineers and whatever they're all called? First they drag him onto the ship and dump him in this cabin, as if it was the most natural thing in the world. Then this second mate comes and tells him everyone on board thinks he's his brother-in-law and he'd better act as if that's the case, since he's on board in the first place. And this same mate pays him five million crowns to play that stupid role.

Some guys creep around under cover of night carrying dismantled shotguns while others are smoking themselves silly and going on about ancient gods and the fate of humanity. The captain comes to the bridge wearing a bathrobe, just to find out who went to the toilet when, while the second mate confuses him and tries to blame Jón Karl for something he can't even understand. As if he should care about the nursery-school rules in this floating sandbox! But when the fucking satellite phone doesn't work – just when he finally remembers to phone home – then he *does* care. And it's not just the phone that's dead but also some bloody navigation stuff, and the ship's radio. All because of some aerials that have been damaged because of something nobody can identify. And so forth!

It's bad enough for Jón Karl to be fucking stranded on board this ship with some guys he doesn't know at all without these same guys being philosophically delusional, suspicious about the state of their own souls and those of everyone else on board, and sneaking about in the night and accusing each other of treachery, deceit and carelessness. Some of them have one of these faults, others all of them, and these are the guys who steer this ship, look after the engines and all that. And to make matters worse the ship doesn't even work the way it's supposed to – it's out of touch with the rest of the world and off the radar, or the radar's off of *it*, or something. All because of something that maybe happened while someone was in the toilet. Or was it when someone was *not* in the toilet? Doesn't really matter.

Or does it?

Jón Karl is stuck with deranged men on board a ship that seems just as deranged as the men who are supposed to sail it.

Could the second mate have been fucking with the communications equipment when he pretended to be in the toilet? So someone couldn't ... phone ashore? Hardly. Or so someone couldn't phone the ship? Who? His wife? His brother-in-law? The police? He doesn't want the police to be able to reach the ship because ... he killed that brother-in-law of his!

'I'll kill that fucking Jónas!' Jón Karl says darkly, sitting up in bed, but he stiffens and grimaces when the searing pain comes to life in the back of his head, his chest, his swollen hand and cracked collarbone. His acrobatics in the hold didn't exactly speed his recovery.

'*Fuck!*'

Yeah, sure, he's going to kill that Jónas – but maybe not today. Tomorrow. He'll just kill him tomorrow.

Or the next day.

The day after tomorrow he's going to kill Jónas and every single person on board and let this ship sail on its merry way. It's bound to hit some fucking land sooner or later, and as soon as Jón Karl sees that fucking land he'll just dive in and swim the final kilometre or so. The ship will run aground and he'll be out of this prison. *Basta*.

Why not?

Anything's better than spending a whole month with some salty sea-dogs who can keep neither the ship nor themselves in touch with the real world.

Jón Karl stands up, sighing as he looks at the bed. He couldn't be bothered to put a sheet on the mattress and clean linen on the doona and pillow before he went to sleep, and he can't be bothered now, either.

After having a piss and splashing his face with cold water, he grabs an unopened pack of cigarettes and wanders along the D-deck corridor and out onto the platform behind the wheelhouse. It's still pretty cloudy and the wind hasn't quite died down, but it's stopped raining and it isn't as cold as it has been. The deep blue of the sea churns behind the ship, which crests a high wave and, little by little, makes its way south, to where day and night are equally long and the mountainsides are covered with coca bushes.

Jón Karl rocks to the heavy rhythm of the waves, opens his pack of cigarettes, flicks his finger against the bottom of it and then lights the cigarette that pops up. He blows smoke through his nose and stares at the sea, which is grey in the distance and black at the horizon, rising and falling like a mountain range in the head of some dreaming creator. A lonely albatross hovers in the sky above the ship and Jón Karl follows it with his eyes until it flies so high that it disappears into the dark grey of the clouds.

'Lucky bugger,' he says, glancing to the right, where he catches sight of part of a lifeboat. It's pretty big and probably has room for all the crew. Underneath it there's a propeller in a tube; near the top there's a window for whoever's steering. A boat like that is probably unsinkable, as long as it doesn't break. Jón Karl walks under the boat, knocks on the bottom and tries to see how to free it from its davits, make it fall on its nose into the sea behind the ship. The boat seems to be fastened to an iron hook that locks into a cylindrical steel joist in the bottom, behind the propeller. All you'd need to do is jack the boat up until the joist came free of the hook, and you can probably only do that from inside the boat itself.

Jón Karl walks to the back of the platform, leans over the railing and looks down along the lifeboat that's hanging there, nearly vertical, thirty or forty metres above sea level. No small drop, and there must be quite a blow when the boat slams onto the surface of the water. Suddenly he sees a man's face down on B-deck. He's leaning over the rail like Jón Karl, twisting round and staring up along the back of the wheelhouse. The man's head is out over the rough sea and when he catches sight of Jón Karl he seems astonished.

'WHAT CAN I DO FOR YOU?' Jón Karl shouts down to the man, who is beardless, round cheeked, curly haired and cute in some weird way; he looks very pleasant, even from a distance and at such a strange angle.

'COME GET YOURSELF SOME FISH ON A DISH, FRIEND!' the man calls back, smiling over the whole of his childlike face before disappearing into B-deck.

Jón Karl grins, throws his cigarette overboard and opens the door to the D-deck corridor. He's hungry – so hungry his stomach is grumbling – but he also needs to take a shit. He goes into his cabin, turns on the light in the bathroom, pulls down his trousers and sits on the toilet. He's always thought shitting in an aeroplane was bloody good, and shitting on board a ship is even better. The heavy up-and-down movements help the bowels to do their work and add interest to this otherwise monotonous activity. As if it were the ship itself that is shitting, not him.

The ship takes a deep breath, climbs up to the crest of a wave and tenses its abdominal muscles, then it lets itself go down the side – one, two and …

Boom, boom, boom …

Jón Karl's backside is pressed down onto the toilet seat; his anus opens and manages to rid itself of a hard turd the size of a bratwurst.

'Way to go!' Jón Karl says with a sigh. He pats his pockets and mentally reviews their contents. In the left is the sock with the shells, morphine and syringe while in the right is a pack of cigarettes, a five-million-crown cheque and the picture of Miss September.

Jón Karl pats his trouser legs by his ankles, feeling for his gun and knife, and then considers that maybe he should leave the weapons in his cabin. But it's probably safer to carry them. His next idea is to try out the morphine. No, that can wait for a while. Eat first. He wipes his bottom and flushes, washes his hands and looks himself in the eye in the mirror above the sink.

He isn't tired any more. Or not dead tired, at least. Now he's got a healthy-looking gleam in his eye, blood in his hard muscles and self-confidence in his savage grin. *Looking a lot better, champ.* Got a bit of Satan in him, a kind of diabolical aura you can almost touch that pulses like an electric current, fascinating and frightening at the same time.

'Who's the king?' Jón Karl says, winking at his own reflection. Then they both laugh at their own joke.

The laugh bursts through flesh and bone, deforming the face in the mirror, like lightning that tears the rain clouds apart and lets the thunder through.

Silence.

Jón Karl stops his satanic smile, turns off the bathroom light and leaves the cabin.

The stairwell is newly scrubbed and smells of soft soap and ammonia. Jón Karl leans on the railing and swings himself down the last few steps at each landing.

The smell of fried fish and onion-butter wafts through the stairwell and makes his mouth water.

XIX

08:27

Guðmundur sits in his chair in the bridge, staring fiercely out of the salt-caked windows. The weather has improved slightly – it's stopped raining and calmed noticeably – but there are thick cloud banks ahead, heavy waves and strong ocean currents, none of which bodes well. Sailing in bad weather is both time consuming and dangerous, besides which it uses extra fuel to the tune of several tonnes a day.

At the captain's feet lies Skuggi, looking pensively up at his master.

But Guðmundur is thinking neither of the weather nor the cost of extra fuel. He is more worried about being held up. Most of all, he resents not being able to phone home to Hrafnhildur.

What's she going to think if she doesn't hear from him?

The fact is that the ship is totally disconnected from the world and that is almost driving the captain round the bend. Never before in his long career as a seaman has Guðmundur Berndsen had the misfortune to lose all three at once: radar, satellite phone and radio. Anything can happen at sea – that's true enough – but there's something dubious about this particular malfunction. It's simply too widespread to have come about without somebody noticing something. If lightning had struck the ship, for instance, everyone would have noticed.

A blow, a flash, fire and then the electricity would have been out for a while – the engine could even have died. It would have been the same if something had hit the ship: a small plane, a big bird, flying debris. A collision like that would either have come to their attention or had limited impact. No – there are little warning bells ringing in the head of this experienced captain. Not only is the malfunction extensive, it could just as well be called specialised, since it only affects the ship's ability to communicate. Coincidence? Imaginings?

No, by Christ! Something is not as it should be.

Guðmundur picks up the console phone and calls down to the engine room.

'Hello, John here,' Big John drawls.

'This is the captain. We've got a bit of a problem and I'm going to have a little meeting up here at eleven.'

Silence.

'What's the problem?'

'We've lost the GPS, radar and radio phone. Can you come up at eleven, and bring Methúsalem with you?'

'Yes,' says Big John, raising his voice. 'Who else will be there?'

'I'm going to get Rúnar to have a look up on the roof later on. Then he'll come to the meeting and report to us.'

'Okay. See you at eleven, then.'

Guðmundur puts down the phone and leans back in the chair. The sea has gone blue-black out at the horizon, the wind is picking up little by little and coal-black banks of cloud are drifting closer. If he's going to send Rúnar up on the roof, he'd better do it sooner rather than later. He looks at his watch and sees it's just past twenty to nine. The deckhands' watch starts at nine and Rúnar usually stops by the bridge soon after to check the weather and have a cup of coffee. Guðmundur gets out of the chair and walks slowly to the port side.

Better make fresh coffee before the bosun comes.

★ ★ ★

08:45

Big John pushes the dead man's alarm before he leaves the engine room and stomps up to E-deck, where he knocks on the chief mate's door.

'Who's there?' asks Methúsalem, opening the door as far as the metal catch will allow.

'It's me,' says Big John. Methúsalem closes the door so he can loosen the catch.

'Come in,' says Methúsalem, letting the chief engineer into the cabin.

'I thought you were asleep,' says John, fishing a chewed cigar out of a packet in his shirt pocket and then putting it back when he remembers the mate's ban on smoking.

'What do you want?' Methúsalem is not only awake but newly bathed, freshly shaven, smelling of aftershave and hair cream, dressed in well-pressed trousers and an ironed shirt, with his hair carefully combed.

'The Old Man just called. He says the GPS is out, and also the radar and radio.'

'What in the world?' says Methúsalem, his mouth falling open in wonder. 'And what?'

'He wants to meet us up in the bridge at eleven,' says John with a shrug. 'By that time Rúnar will have gone up on the roof and can presumably give us more information.'

'Do you mean the ship is entirely out of touch?'

'I expect so, yeah.'

'There's something suspicious about this!' says Methúsalem, his eyes going cold. 'Two days before we mean to stop the engines we lose all contact. Which means the Old Man can't phone the company when the time comes to get them to abandon their plans to lay us all off.'

'What do you mean?' asks John anxiously.

'They've discovered our plan,' Methúsalem declares, taking a deep breath through distended nostrils. 'This is their way of disarming us, the fuckers!'

'Are you saying the Old Man is lying about this? You can't be saying he had those instruments disconnected. That's just impossible!'

'All's fair in love and war,' says Methúsalem, rolling up his sleeves. 'Someone leaked our plan to the Old Man or the company and they've decided to play by our rules. But they're not going to get away with it!'

'Who could have talked?' asks John doubtfully. 'And besides, the Old Man's sending Rúnar up to check it out. He's one of us!'

'What Rúnar will find up on the roof is cut wires,' says Methúsalem calmly.

'How can you be so sure?' asks John, knitting his brows. 'You aren't responsible for this, are you?'

'Are you crazy?' Methúsalem scowls. 'What would I gain by having no communications? Nothing! But there are those who gain by it, and we both know who they are. Right? The only thing I'm not sure of is exactly who it was who cut the wires up on the roof. But they've been cut, believe me.'

'Yeah, maybe, I don't know,' mutters John. 'Ummm, tell me, what time is it?'

'The time, yeah ...' Methúsalem automatically looks at his left wrist, where there is no watch. 'I've lost my fucking watch. I've looked everywhere! Can't think what the hell I've done with it.'

'I thought you never lost anything,' says John, smiling inwardly.

'I know, I just ...' Methúsalem sighs as he rubs his left wrist with his fingers.

'I've got to get back down,' says John, walking towards the door. 'See you up there at eleven.'

'Listen!' Methúsalem stops rubbing his wrist. 'We're not going to let this put us off. We keep to our plan!'

'And kill the engine?' asks John, turning around with his

left hand on the doorknob.

'Yep,' says Methúsalem, nodding. 'And the sooner the better.'

'But –'

'No buts!' says Methúsalem, lifting his chin and hooking his arms together behind his back. 'We create a document clearly stating our demands and the Old Man can sign it on behalf of the company. A document like that must be valid in the maritime court, if it comes to that.'

'We'll see.' John squeezes the doorknob. 'But I'm not killing the engine unless the weather's reasonable. It's not a good idea to set a ship this big adrift in bad weather.'

'I can't see it makes any difference whether this pile of scrap iron sails lengthways or drifts sideways!' snarls Methúsalem. 'If you're giving in to these fuckers you'd better admit it right now – and I mean *this instant*.'

'I'm not giving in,' says John, going red around his eyes. 'But if seawater gets in the engine room I can't be sure of starting the engine again. You must see that!'

'I'm not going on the dole,' says Methúsalem, as calm as can be, staring into space as if he's alone in the cabin. 'Just so that's clear.'

'See you at eleven,' Big John says then tears open the door and disappears into the corridor.

★ ★ ★

09:17

'So, what's the outlook?' asks Rúnar as he comes into the bridge.

'Good morning to you, too,' says Guðmundur, turning round in his leather chair. 'Can I offer you some fresh coffee?'

'Yes, please,' says Rúnar, walking over to the coffee machine. 'I was hoping we'd be able to work outdoors today.'

'Looks to me like we're heading straight for another storm,' says Guðmundur and he turns his chair back towards the front.

'I guess we'll scrub the stairs, then, to start with,' says Rúnar as he pours steaming coffee into a clean mug. 'And when I say "we", I mean me and Sæli. The new guy hasn't shown his face.'

'Forget him,' mutters Guðmundur. 'Forget him for the time being.'

'Either we've got three deckhands aboard or we haven't,' says Rúnar. He shakes loose a cigarette and puts it in his mouth. 'If Sæli and I do all the work it seems obvious we get to divide the third man's pay between us. Right?'

'I've got a little job for you,' says Guðmundur softly, drumming on the chair's arms with the flat of his hand.

'Oh?' says Rúnar then lights his cigarette.

'Yeah,' says Guðmundur, looking out the window at the swirling cloud banks that seem to be eating up the daylight about ninety kilometres away. 'I want to ask you to have a look up on the roof before we sail into that storm.'

'On the roof? What for?'

'This is just between you and me … for the time being.' Guðmundur glances at Rúnar. 'Is that understood?'

'Yeah, no problem,' says Rúnar, nodding, with the cigarette stuck fast in the corner of his mouth. 'You can trust me.'

★ ★ ★

10:11

Guðmundur sits alone in the bridge, his arms resting on the arms of the chair while he watches, as though hypnotised, out the window.

Maybe the crew knows about the pending dismissals. They suspect something, at least. But it hasn't been decided. The CEO had spoken of it as a possibility – a last resort to help the business recover.

Goddammit! As if he doesn't have other things to think about! As if he doesn't have enough worries already!

There's anger in the crew, some bloody unrest, some upheaval that may break out into a genuine revolt if it is allowed to fester under the surface long enough. What can he do? Tell them the truth? Threaten them with serious consequences? Make them some promise he won't be able to keep?

Or just pretend there's nothing going on?

What if the ship's been sabotaged, though? Then what will he do? What *could* he do? Search out some culprit to appease the others? Who? The new guy?

Or maybe that's exactly what they're waiting for him to do? Are they expecting him to make a wrong move – string up the wrong guy – just so they can denounce him as a dictator? Is that meant to be the final straw?

The key now is to remain calm and not let difficulties, bad luck or challenges upset him.

To begin with, it's best to do nothing at all. Just take his time. Watch how the crew reacts to things.

The captain has been cornered. He's been outmanoeuvred in an unexpected way. Okay. If people want to play blindfold chess he's not afraid. But there's one thing they should know: he's going to think for as long as he wants before he reacts to the threats of this invisible opponent.

★ ★ ★

10:13

'Don't you want me to come with you?' asks Sæli, putting down his bucket of soapy water. He leans on a long-handled scrubbing brush and wipes the sweat from his forehead. He has already scrubbed the bridge and the stairs down to F-deck, and is beginning to wet the floor there.

'No, and not another word about it!' says Rúnar, zipping his fur-lined overalls up to his chin. 'The Old Man asked me to not let it go any further.'

'What do you think happened?' asks Sæli half to himself, letting the wet floor cloth slap onto the grey-speckled linoleum. 'What do you think you'll find up there?'

'I don't know,' says Rúnar, putting on a dark-blue woollen cap. 'You just be careful not to mention it to a single soul.'

'Yeah, I know,' says Sæli, scrubbing away. 'But what'll we do if it's sabotage or something?'

'I don't know.' Rúnar lights a cigarette. 'But if it is, then I think I actually don't want to know who it is on board who has such an evil nature. I mean, we'd throw a shit like that headfirst into the sea without a thought, understand?'

'Yeah, I understand.' Sæli pushes the wet cloth around with the scrubbing brush. 'But then we'd be the ones being grilled in a maritime court, not the guilty party.'

'That's exactly what I'm afraid of,' says Rúnar, putting on thick leather gloves. 'But not another word. I'm going up.'

'Listen!' says Sæli when Rúnar is halfway up to the bridge deck.

'Yeah?' says Rúnar, turning round, his cigarette smoking in his mouth and one eye half closed.

'Be careful up there.'

'Yeah,' says Rúnar, trudging up the stairs again. 'You just keep scrubbing.'

★ ★ ★

10:33

Rúnar stands at the forward edge of the bridge roof, holding onto the wet railing with both hands. The ship plunges down off one giant wave simply to climb up the next one; the inky-black cloud banks tower over the ocean to the south, roaring like a bull and shooting lightning in all directions; wind pounds the ship, buffets the waves and brings salty tears to the eyes of the bosun, who clenches his fists round the icy metal and stares out.

'Why didn't I become a joiner?' he asks himself, but the wind takes his words and whips them away. 'WHY?'

It's exhilarating to shout where no one can hear you. Rúnar stands at the top of the visible world and laughs in the face of the furious gale, which is speeding across the surface of the ocean and will be hitting the ship within the hour.

However, Rúnar laughs neither loud nor long. He doesn't feel much like laughing. He just needs to laugh. It is the only thing he can think of to do. Either that or lose his mind to the bewildering thoughts that are building up like those clouds, in his head, accumulating negative energy. Laughter releases tension and prevents the nervous system from burnout.

He has found what he was most afraid of: cut wires.

Someone sabotaged the radar mast and the satellite receiver.

There is a louse on board. A lowlife. A terrorist.

But who could it be?

Rúnar curses under his breath and holds on as tightly as he can while the ship attacks a wave the size of a mountain. The wind dies down for a moment then slams into the bosun's chest as the ship reaches the crest. He looks down across the ship and notices the rust seeping around railings, joints, bolts and the hatches of the hold. It's been a long time since they've had the right weather for working outside, and the forces of nature are quick to take control if maintenance is postponed. If this ship isn't to look like a Russian ghost-hulk it needs some time in the dockyard pretty soon.

Rúnar takes his right hand off the railing and looks at the palm of his leather glove. It's red with rust. In just a few more weeks the whole ship is going to be pretty much the colour of a dead leaf.

Painting will have to wait, though. There's a storm on the way and the crew has other, more serious matters to think about.

There is a traitor on board. A rotten apple in a rusty barrel.

XX

11:09

'Is someone in the engine room?' asks Guðmundur, breaking the silence that settled over them after Rúnar made his report on the situation on the roof of the wheelhouse.

'I sent Stoker down there,' Big John says, staring distractedly into his coffee.

'What the fuck does it matter whether somebody sits on his arse down there or not?' says Methúsalem, clenching his fists. 'There's a terrorist aboard the ship! A terrorist, I say!'

'What are we going to do?' asks Rúnar in a hushed voice. He leans forward against the windowsill and stares into the darkness.

Guðmundur sits, scowling, in the leather chair, rolling his empty mug in his sweaty palms; Big John is standing with his feet apart to starboard, sighing repeatedly, and Methúsalem can't keep still and either dithers near the captain or strides from one side of the bridge to the other.

'First and foremost, we must show restraint,' says Guðmundur with a quick look at Methúsalem. 'Though the wires have snapped, it doesn't mean someone on board damaged them.'

'What?' says Methúsalem. 'What did you say?'

'Someone could have damaged them while the ship was in dock with a view to their coming apart while we were under sail,' says Guðmundur slowly. 'If this was done on purpose.

Sabotage, I mean. As things stand, we can't rule out other possibilities.'

'And what possibilities are they?' Methúsalem says, raising his eyebrows. 'That insects gnawed the wires in two or something like that? Maybe seagulls flew into all of them?'

'Methúsalem,' says Big John, signalling to the chief mate to take it easy.

'They were cut,' says Rúnar, looking over his shoulder. 'I saw it with my own …'

Rúnar stops talking when something slams against the window in front of him. The pane cracks in all directions; Rúnar recoils and they all fall silent.

'What was that?' asks Guðmundur, staring in disbelief at the fourth windowpane from the port side, which is still hanging together but is shattered and looks like a badly made spider web.

Outside, the growing wind whistles, the ship rises on a huge wave and there is a rumble of thunder.

'It's a conch!' says Rúnar, pushing his face against the cracked glass and staring at the broken shell and greyish mess sliding down the outside of the pane. 'A conch hit the windowpane. I've never heard of that!'

The ship lists to starboard and falls, as if in midair, down off the wave; the sea gets rougher in the pounding wind, and the weather deck disappears in a dark grey haze that looks like a horizontal waterfall. The men in the bridge hold tightly to whatever is nearest and can hardly believe their eyes when the windows of the bridge all disappear at once in sandy ocean spray that hits the ship like black hail.

'It's raining sand, seaweed and shellfish,' murmurs Big John when the ship is more or less back on an even keel.

'It's a sudden storm,' Guðmundur says, switching off the autopilot and turning the small wheel counterclockwise a number of times. 'Hold on, lads! I'm going to turn the ship hard astern and see if we can't get to the east of the worst of it.'

'Sudden or not, it doesn't matter,' says Methúsalem, who's

holding onto the railing on the wall behind the captain. 'There is still a felon on board the ship, whether you're prepared to face that fact or not. Someone cut our connection to the outside world, and when I say "someone" I don't mean a seagull or a conch.'

'While this storm is raging, the safety of this ship and everyone aboard her is top priority,' says Guðmundur as he steers the ship to the east along a long, deep trough in the cliff-like waves on either side.

'So long as the captain refuses to face the real danger threatening the ship, the safety of everyone on board hangs by a thread,' says Methúsalem, icily composed. 'While this felon is loose, the danger of more terrorist attacks looms over us like a black shadow.'

'If you had your way, Methúsalem, the witch hunt would already have begun,' says Guðmundur as he steers the ship out of the trough and sails angled on to the wind. 'But it's the captain's role to look after the interests of every person on board and to ensure that they don't split into factions that are for or against individuals on board. If there is a felon amongst us, I will find that person – but I will do it using my own methods.'

'And what methods might they be, if I may ask?' asks Methúsalem.

'I will begin by speaking to those on watch,' says Guðmundur. He sets the autopilot, since the ship is free from the claws of the storm – for the time being, at least. 'That is to say, those that were on watch when we lost our communications.'

'He hadn't arrived yet, that new guy, when I left the bridge,' says Rúnar, pouring himself more coffee.

'And there wasn't a soul here when I came up at four-thirty,' says Guðmundur with a scowl.

'What in the world?' says Big John to the captain.

'What were you doing here last night?' asks Methúsalem.

'Dead man's bell woke me up,' says Guðmundur distractedly, looking through the sand-covered window at the storm that is, little by little, drawing near again.

'Then what?' asks Big John.

'Where were the men?' says Rúnar.

'And when did they come back?' asks Methúsalem.

'The radar was out by the time I got up here,' replies Guðmundur. 'Then I watched the GPS go out —'

'The bastard must have been up on the roof!' says Methúsalem, pounding his right fist into his left palm.

'A little later Jónas came in, soaking wet,' says Guðmundur, clearing his throat. 'Said he'd gone to check out the radar.'

'And left the bridge unattended, did he?' Big John says.

'Where was this brother-in-law of his?' asks Rúnar.

'Yes, where was he?' Methúsalem's voice is cold.

'I still have to get these facts sorted out,' says Guðmundur with a sigh. 'They didn't quite agree as to who had left the bridge unattended. But this brother-in-law of Jónas's was wet, too, though not as soaking as Jónas. But I don't know — why should any man damage the ship he's sailing in himself?'

'When had you been thinking of speaking to those two?' Methúsalem demands. 'After they've had time to get their story straight, or after they've muddled it even further?'

'I can't believe Jónas is involved in this,' mutters Big John.

'That leaves the other one,' says Rúnar, looking at Methúsalem, who nods in agreement.

'I will speak to Jónas when he comes on watch at four this afternoon,' says Guðmundur, turning off the autopilot and steering the ship even further east. 'After that I've got the evening watch with his brother-in-law. Then I can hear his side of the matter. But —'

'Don't you want to just put it off till we get to Suriname?' says Methúsalem, interrupting the captain. 'Or maybe till we get back home to —'

'But!' Guðmundur repeats, looking angrily at the chief mate before he speaks again. 'But I wish to make it quite clear that nobody — absolutely *nobody* — is under suspicion. Is that understood?'

'Yeah, sure,' says Big John, shrugging his broad shoulders.

'Yes, of course,' murmurs Rúnar with a sniff.

'Methúsalem?' asks Guðmundur without taking his eyes off the dark sea outside the window.

'If you like. But it's pretty obvious, if you ask me.'

'I'm not asking you or anyone,' says Guðmundur firmly. 'I alone am responsible for safety and working atmosphere aboard this ship. I will not have any conjectures, any backbiting or any witch-hunts! Shipmates must be able to trust one another, not least when there's danger. I trust you and must insist that you trust me. If there is a breach of trust between a captain and his crew, it's nothing but the first step towards mutiny.'

'I understand,' says Methúsalem, nodding. 'And now, in the light of this declaration of trust, I'm asking the captain whether or not he has any knowledge of the reputed plans of the shipping company to dismiss the present crew and hire a new one to replace it?'

Silence.

'Can we trust that the captain will inform us of the facts of this matter?' Methúsalem says, stepping nearer to Guðmundur. 'Or don't you trust us to know these facts?'

'I'm not discussing company matters in the middle of a tour,' answers Guðmundur. 'The company hires the men for the ship. My job is to sail the ship and ensure the safety of the crew, whoever they may be in each instance.'

'So the answer is no?'

'The answer is no,' says Guðmundur without looking anyone in the eye. 'If I did have knowledge of impending lay-offs I would not be free to speak about that knowledge. I would be betraying the trust of my superiors.'

'So they are going to lay us off?' asks Big John.

'I don't believe this!' says Rúnar, hands in the air.

'I *never* said you were going to be laid off!' says Guðmundur, putting the ship on autopilot once again. 'I just said that I couldn't talk about it *if* I knew such a thing. Is that understood?'

'Oh, perfectly – it doesn't need saying,' says Methúsalem with a sneer.

'Methúsalem!' says Guðmundur and he turns around in his chair. 'I need hardly remind you that you are chief mate on board, I think?'

'We could of course just phone the CEO and ask him,' says Methúsalem, staring coldly into the bloodshot eyes of the captain. 'No, that's right – we can't! Someone cut the wires.'

'Methúsalem!' says Big John, laying his great paw on the chief mate's right shoulder. 'Don't be stupid.'

'The meeting is adjourned,' says Guðmundur, giving the chief mate a dirty look before turning his chair forwards again. 'Return to work.'

Then he adds, in a softer voice, 'And God be with you.'

Guðmundur's subordinates leave the bridge but the captain remains in his chair, scowling out the window. The storm is still on its way, though his battle with it has been postponed.

★ ★ ★

11:50

In the kitchen on B-deck Ási, the ship's cook, is dipping the last of the haddock fillets in egg and then golden breadcrumbs before placing them in a frying pan that's wedged in a metal frame on an impressive gas cooker. The fillets swim around in a bubbling mixture of margarine and cooking oil; in a pot beside the frying pan peeled potatoes are boiling, and in a saucepan on the back burner five chopped onions are browning in a butter-and-oil bath.

Ási rinses the utensils he's been using and places them in the dishwasher, wipes the egg off his fingers on his apron, ties a knot on the bag of garbage and walks out to where four big garbage bins are fastened together with a long chain and padlock. He opens the first bin and throws in the bag, then lights himself a cigarette and checks on the weather. But just as he places his hand on the portside railing his right foot hits something. It's a large set of wire-cutters with yellow handles.

'What are you doing here?' murmurs Ási, who knows that all tools are kept down in the engine room. He takes his cigarette out of his mouth with his left hand, bends down and picks up the cold, wet cutters in his right.

He studies the tool and shrugs, but then it occurs to him to stick his head out and look up, in case he might see someone who could have dropped the cutters.

And what do you know – there's another head looking down from D- or E-deck, but it's neither of the engineers. It's someone Ási doesn't recognise. That would be the new guy, Jónas's brother-in-law.

'WHAT CAN I DO FOR YOU?' shouts the new guy, who seems to be hanging around the large lifeboat, which means he's up on D-deck.

'COME GET YOURSELF SOME FISH ON A DISH, FRIEND!' Ási shouts back, smiling at the newcomer before disappearing.

'What a weirdo,' mutters Ási, taking a last drag before he puts out his cigarette, sticks the clippers in his apron pocket and makes his way back to the kitchen.

Ási turns the fillets over in the pan, then scrapes freshly made remoulade from the mixer bowl into two smaller ones. He takes the saucepan off the fire and pours the water off the potatoes. Then he turns off the gas, opens the oven and takes out an oven tray full of fried fish that he's been keeping hot while he fries the last fillets on the pan, because he has to fry four full pans of fish to feed the crew.

'Right, lads!' Ási says when the first faces appear in the doorway. The clock strikes twelve and everything's ready: the fish, the potatoes, the onion-butter and the remoulade. The crew line up and each serves himself while Ási runs cold water into jugs and gets out two cartons of milk.

'Smells good, Ási,' says Big John, who is first in line. He takes four fillets, a few potatoes, a good spoonful of onion-butter and then drowns the whole lot in tepid remoulade.

Next is Sæli, then Rúnar, Captain Guðmundur is behind him and last in line is Methúsalem. Stoker is down in the engine room and will stay there until John relieves him for half an hour, and Jónas is sitting up in the bridge, because he offered to take the wheel while the chief mate had his lunch. Jón Karl has still not come down.

'There's plenty here, lads,' says Ási, sticking a toothpick in his mouth.

Sæli and Rúnar sit opposite each other in the seamen's mess, where the Doors tape is circling in the old tape recorder, while Big John, Guðmundur and Methúsalem sit in the officers' mess, John and Methúsalem side by side with their backs to the south, the captain at the end with his back to the door.

'Wouldn't he say anything?' Sæli murmurs as he takes a drink of water.

'No,' says Rúnar, mashing his fish, potatoes, onions and remoulade together. 'He said he couldn't tell us whether they were going to lay us off or not. Said he wasn't allowed to say.'

'Shit, man,' says Sæli, pushing a piece of fish around with his fork. 'But what about the sabotage?'

'The Old Man is kind of in denial,' says Rúnar as he divides his mash into even-sized bites. 'But Methúsalem suspects the new guy.'

'Jónas's brother-in-law?' Sæli takes a small bit of fish and samples it like it's a foul medicine.

'Yeah, it's not nice to back the relative of a crew member into a corner,' says Rúnar, shrugging. 'But he's the only one we don't know.'

'Do you think he's some kind of swindler or something?' Sæli chases his fish with cold water. 'Do you think Jónas knows something about him that we don't?'

'I don't know. I don't know what I should think. But the

man isn't exactly charming, if you know what I mean.'

'Wasn't it just some lunatic?' asks Sæli, putting down his knife and fork. His stomach is in a knot and he doesn't have much of an appetite.

'Yeah, probably.' Rúnar shrugs. He puts his knife aside and starts shovelling the mash into his mouth.

'And the Old Man won't say anything,' sighs Sæli. 'Which means we will be laid off, doesn't it?'

'S'pose so,' murmurs Rúnar, pulling a face with his mouth full of food.

'But what about stopping the engines? Is that still on?'

'Prob'ly not.'

'I wish I could phone home.'

'That makes two of us.'

'I can't stand this!' Sæli hides his face in his hands.

'Could you pass me the salt please, Methúsalem?' says Guðmundur as he feeds a potato to Skuggi, who is sitting under the table.

'Of course,' says Methúsalem, handing him the salt.

'What's the situation with that storm?' asks Big John, smacking his lips.

'I don't see how we can avoid it,' says Guðmundur.

'Well, we can't keep retreating to the east, can we?'

'I'd suggest we try to avoid the storm. It's better to take a small detour than to go through sudden gusts, undercurrents and breakers.'

'This is no storm,' mutters Methúsalem. 'Just a shower.'

'There's no need to take chances,' says John, putting a whole potato in his mouth.

'Prudence is the mother of all virtues,' says Guðmundur and starts eating.

'This is fucking ridiculous!' says Methúsalem with a sneer. 'Here we sit discussing the weather instead of talking about what we're really thinking about, all three of us. The crew is going to be laid off and there's a felon loose in this ship.'

'Right,' says Big John, then he shovels more food down his gullet, using his left hand to wipe remoulade from the corners of his mouth.

'A storm in a teacup has never sunk a ship,' says Guðmundur with a cough. 'And I'm referring to these supposed lay-offs. But sabotage will not, of course, be tolerated – that goes without saying.'

'*Denial and equivocation*,' says Methúsalem, white with fury. 'Jónas and I had a short talk just now and it seemed to me he was afraid of this brother-in-law of his. Doesn't want to talk about him and is evasive if you ask about him! I suggest we visit this guy and ask him the questions we need answered.'

'There's a time and a place for everything,' says Guðmundur, taking a deep breath.

'Rubbish!' says Methúsalem, spluttering fish over the table. 'I'm convinced he's a spy for the company, and that you know it.'

'What are you implying?' asks Guðmundur, giving his chief mate an angry look.

'You know something we don't.' Methúsalem no longer holds the captain's eyes. 'That much I'm sure of.'

'I think we should go back to discussing the weather,' says Guðmundur, clenching his fists round his knife and fork as he continues eating.

'This storm will die down like any other storm,' says Big John, still shovelling his food.

'If it was up to me this hooligan …' says Methúsalem and he is about to slam his fist on the table when Jón Karl appears in the mess, in one hand a dished piled high with food, in the other a glass of water.

'What hooligan?' says Jón Karl, sitting down opposite the first engineer, while Methúsalem is so astonished at this sudden presence of the deckhand that he's unable to speak.

The same could be said for Guðmundur and John, who look at each other and then at Jón Karl, who pretends not to notice.

'Were you maybe talking about me?' Jón Karl says, grinning

like a hyena in the face of the chief mate. Methúsalem blinks his watery blue eyes and is about to look away when he suddenly notices his gold watch right in front of his eyes, on the muscular wrist of the seaman.

'My watch!' Methúsalem attempts to grab Jón Karl, who moves a good deal more quickly, leaving Methúsalem empty handed.

'What are you talking about, man?' says Jón Karl, calmly salting his food. 'If you owned a watch you'd be wearing it, wouldn't you? This is my watch, obviously, 'cause I'm wearing it, see?'

'*That is my watch!*' says Methúsalem and he looks at Guðmundur as if he expects the captain to take his side.

'It's no good looking at him,' says Jón Karl, smiling at the captain. 'Is he maybe your daddy? Should Daddy take the watch off the bad boy and give it to you?'

'What's the matter with you?' asks Methúsalem, pounding his fist on the table. 'You must have found that watch somewhere. *That is my watch and I want it back this instant!*'

'Methúsalem,' says Guðmundur, giving the chief mate a paternal glance. 'Try to keep calm.'

'Aren't you lost?' says Big John, licking his chops. 'This is the officers' mess.'

'Are you tired of life?' asks Jón Karl, grinning at the chief engineer. 'The scar after your heart operation has hardly healed, man, and you're wolfing down remoulade as if it were yoghurt or something.'

'I don't see that's any of your …' John stops and coughs.

'Give me the watch!' Methúsalem tries again, giving the deckhand an icy look. Jón Karl just smiles back at him and eats his fish.

'Is that a freemason's ring?' asks Jón Karl without looking at the heavy, loose-fitting ring on the chief mate's ring finger. 'Are you a freemason?'

'None of your business!' says Methúsalem.

'You're no freemason. That ring doesn't even fit you,' says Jón Karl, continuing to eat. 'You've just found it somewhere and are pretending to be a freemason so people will think you're more important than you actually are. You'd have had the ring tightened if you weren't afraid of being discovered. The goldsmith might be a freemason, see? Or the ring might be on record as having been stolen. Highly unlikely, of course, but a guilty man's imagination can overpower his reason.'

'You're crazy,' mutters Methúsalem, attempting a sneer, but his mouth just goes crooked and his eyes blink rapidly.

'You do know this is the officers' mess, don't you?' says Guðmundur, completely calm.

'I couldn't care less,' says Jón Karl, shrugging. 'But I can't say I'm enjoying the company, so maybe I'll try eating with the plebs next time. They just all looked so gloomy, the guys next door.'

'On board a ship the men can't choose where to sit,' says Big John, clenching his right paw round his glass of water. 'You aren't welcome here, so you should move to the starboard side.'

'Tell me, captain,' says Jón Karl, taking a big bite of fish and visibly savouring it while he continues speaking. 'Is it true you're armed with a shotgun?'

'Yes, that's true,' says Guðmundur. 'But it would be truer to say there's a weapon on board, though it is in my keeping. It's one of the conditions set by international insurers —'

'And is that the only gun on board?' Jón Karl glances quickly at Methúsalem and John, who go pale and stiff in their seats.

'Yes. Why do you ask?' Guðmundur says, pushing his plate away.

'Just asking. I thought I saw some guys carrying guns last night, but it could easily just have been a dream, you know?'

'Carrying arms is forbidden on a ship,' says Guðmundur with a frown. 'If you know of any weapons other than the gun I am in charge of, I order you to make that knowledge public.'

'As I said,' says Jón Karl, sipping his water, 'it was just a dream or something, I think.'

'Young man,' says Guðmundur, leaning forward onto his elbows, 'I don't know what Jónas was thinking when he recommended you as a deckhand on this ship, but I do know that if you don't stop this insubordination and disorderly behaviour then I will make certain that —'

'Ask him about the sabotage!' Methúsalem breaks in, giving the table a smack. 'Ask him where he was when —'

'Methúsalem!' barks Guðmundur, black eyed with fury. He points at the chief mate with a trembling finger and is about to speak again when the deckhand interrupts him by striking his empty glass three times and standing up.

Kling, kling, kling!

Jón Karl wins complete silence and the undivided attention of the three men.

'We'd better get a few things straight here, gentlemen,' he says, leaning his fingertips against the table edge. 'This Jónas is not my brother-in-law. I have never seen him before. I am neither a deckhand nor a saboteur. I'm a criminal, just so you know. I hurt people for pay, I deal in drugs and I stab anyone in the back who is stupid enough to turn it towards me. My name is Jón Karl Esrason, also known as Satan.'

★ ★ ★

12.29

Satan leaves the officers' mess and ambles up to D-deck with a full mug of hot coffee in one hand and a smoking cigarette in the other, a hidden revolver by his right ankle and a hidden hunting knife by his left.

XXI

The engine room.
    They stand together in a tight little group up on the shuddering metal floor above and behind the ship's main engine: Big John, Rúnar, Sæli and Methúsalem, shouting to be heard in the unholy din and hot, oil-filled air. Ási has still not arrived for this secret emergency meeting of the 'gang of five', the first one since they met in the bar the night before they sailed.
    Rúnar: 'What are you saying? He's not Jónas's brother-in-law?'
    John: 'No!'
    Rúnar: 'Who is he, then?'
    Methúsalem: 'He said he's known as Satan.'
    Rúnar: 'Did you say "Satan"?'
    John: 'He said "Satan"!'
    Sæli: 'Satan! Are you sure? Satan?'
    Methúsalem: 'Yes!'
    Sæli: 'I can't believe it! He's followed me here. What does he want from me, anyway?'
    John: 'What do you mean?'
    Methúsalem: 'Do you know this guy?'
    Sæli: 'Yes! No! I don't know! Surely not. I'm just talking rubbish. I don't know …'
    Methúsalem: 'He's a spy from the shipping company, that's all I know.'
    Rúnar: 'ARE YOU SURE?'

Methúsalem: 'Of course I'm sure. The man walks around as if he owned the ship and needn't work. As if he has nothing to fear! Because he *doesn't* have anything to fear. They sent him on board, those fucking despots!'

Rúnar: 'To do what?'

Methúsalem: 'To cut our communications. To ruin things for us. To back up the captain if needed. To bear witness against us if it comes to a fight.'

Sæli: 'Shit, man!'

Rúnar: 'What are we going to do?'

Methúsalem: 'I'll tell you exactly what we're going to do!'

They close in even tighter to hear what Methúsalem has to say. Behind the main engine Stoker is rambling around with ear protectors on his head, a dirty rag in one hand and a grease gun in the other. He's greasing the dynamo but at the same time wondering what the four of them are discussing on the floor above him.

Methúsalem: 'John and I are going to relieve Stoker and Jónas and send them for their dinner. Stoker goes back on watch but Ási keeps Jónas chatting in the officers' mess. Where is Ási?'

Rúnar: 'He's on his way.'

Methúsalem: 'Rúnar, you fetch John's shotgun up on deck and take it down to your cabin on D-deck. then you fetch my rifle up on E-deck and take it to your cabin as well.'

Rúnar: 'Methúsalem, are you sure we —'

Methúsalem: 'We don't have a choice any more.'

Sæli: 'What guns are you talking about?'

Rúnar: 'I'll tell you later. Let Methúsalem finish!'

Methúsalem: 'Sæli, you'll be up on D-deck keeping an eye on Satan's cabin. We don't want to lose sight of him.'

Stoker sticks his nose in and takes off his ear protectors.

Stoker: 'Who's Satan?'

John: 'Go to hell, you nuisance! Can't you see we're talking here?'

Stoker: 'I'll just go to dinner, then.'
John: 'Yeah, just go!'
Methúsalem: 'When Stoker comes back down, you come up to me on the bridge, John. Then we'll go down to D-deck together and Sæli can go up to the bridge and be on duty till I come back.'
Rúnar: 'And then what?'
Methúsalem: 'The three of us'll be armed and we'll arrest that guy Satan and lock him in the forecastle.'
Rúnar: 'Christ!'
Sæli: 'What about the captain?'
Methúsalem: 'He said he was going to take a nap.'
Sæli: 'I mean, what do you think he'll –'
Methúsalem: 'He's a bastard turncoat! We really ought to lock him in the forecastle too.'
John: 'I don't know about this. We should have some better evidence. Something tangible.'

Ási comes down and joins the group. He takes the wire-cutters out of his apron pocket and hands them to John.

Ási: 'Don't these belong here?'
Methúsalem: 'The cutters!'
John: 'Where did you find these?'
Ási: 'Out by the rubbish bins. As if they had fallen from the sky! And when I looked up, there was the new guy. He was messing around with the lifeboat.'
Rúnar: 'Satan!'
Sæli: 'What was he doing to the lifeboat?'
Methúsalem: 'Do we still need more evidence? Something tangible?'
Everyone: '*No!*'
Methúsalem: 'Ási, we need to use the lock and chain you use to fasten the rubbish bins.'
Ási: 'What for? What are you guys talking about?'

Stoker stands inside the open door to the storeroom and peers into the engine room. The gang of five stands close together talking just three metres away, their voices as loud as a male philharmonic choir, but their words drowned in the noise of the dynamo. Stoker sees their lips moving but can't hear what they're saying.

'Satan,' murmurs Stoker as he hangs up his greasy ear protectors. 'That's the name. His name is Satan! Of course – he *is* Satan!'

Stoker smiles so widely that he shows his brown wisdom teeth.

XXII

D-deck

Sæli leans against the doors leading out onto the platform behind the wheelhouse, lightly drumming his fingers against the door. He's out of sight here if anyone should come along the newly scrubbed stairwell, and the door to Satan's cabin is just two metres away. He assumes Satan is inside the cabin. Where else would a man be when he can't be bothered to work?

But what's this Satan doing aboard the ship anyway? He told Sæli to bring back some bloody package from some contact in Suriname, and more or less threatened to hurt his family if he didn't do as he was asked.

'You bring the package,' the bastard had said on the phone. 'I look after the family. That's it.'

All because of that fucking gambling debt! A loss of a million that became a loss of two million, then three, four and five, like a hole that keeps getting bigger as you try to fill it, and before Sæli had realised he was falling, not flying, and the loss had become a soulless monster whose stomach had room enough for a whole flat in the Old Town.

Why should the bugger be on board the ship, though, if Sæli's supposed to bring the package? And how is he going to 'look after' the family if he's nowhere near them?

Sæli can't find answers to these questions on his own, but if this Satan guy is on board, then his wife and son must be safe back in Iceland, right?

But Sæli has to be sure. He has to get answers to these questions. He can't just behave as if nothing's happened – as if he doesn't know who this man is. He's the fiend who's made his life a nightmare! A devil who has, up to now, remained in the shadows, been just a deep voice on the phone. But now he's here. The man on the other side of that cabin door is Satan, the arch-fiend in the flesh. The terror of the underworld is cornered in a ship's cabin, trapped inside a narrow room, like a mouse in a shoebox.

Sæli has nothing to fear. In just a couple of minutes three armed men will enter the cabin and overpower the scum. But before they put him in chains and lock him in the forecastle, he ought to speak with Satan, face to face. Get answers before it's too late to ask. Before he realises he's nothing but a mouse in a shoebox. After Methúsalem, John and Rúnar overpower the man he may just close up and refuse to say anything at all. Hard guys like that are not exactly known for breaking down and crying when things go against them.

It's now or never.

'To hell with it.' Sæli takes three steps forwards and breathes deeply before he knocks on the door with three short blows. *Knock, knock, knock ...*

Satan is sitting on the couch, drinking coffee and smoking a cigarette when someone knocks on the door. On the table in front of him is the ampoule of morphine sulphate solution, the syringe and the needle. He's dying to inject himself with this heavenly stuff and float into a sleep that is deeper, longer and darker than any other. But a man who is in the power of the sleeping death of a morphine rush is totally vulnerable, and considering the situation on board this ship, there's not much chance it's going to be some Prince Charming who brings him back to life with a tender kiss. And unlike the seven dwarfs – who laid Snow White to rest above ground in a cushy glass coffin – these blockheads are as likely as not to throw him in the sea headfirst if they find him unconscious in his cabin.

There is another knock on the door.

'Just a minute!' says Satan, laying his cigarette down on the edge of the table. Then he winds the bandage back around the ampoule, syringe and needle, shoves the whole lot into the empty cigarette pack and puts the pack in his right trouser pocket.

Satan has a sip of cold coffee, then picks up the cigarette and takes a drag, leaning forward on his elbows and watching the door. He knocks his heels lightly on the floor to get a feeling for the gun and knife, both of which bounce lightly on his ankles, sending nerve impulses up to his brain and from there to his fingertips.

He's ready for anything.

'Come in!'

Sæli slowly opens the door and enters the cabin warily.

'What do you want?' asks Satan, knocking cigarette ash onto the table.

'Me? I want to know what you're doing here,' says Sæli. 'I want to know why you can't leave me alone!'

Satan looks at Sæli as if he has no idea what he's talking about and couldn't care less anyway. And indeed, he does have no idea what Sæli is talking about and he couldn't care less.

'You're Satan, right? You said that downstairs, didn't you?' says Sæli, standing in the middle of the cabin shuffling his feet. 'I've only spoken to you on the phone up until now, and maybe you haven't seen me before – at least, not face to face. I'm Sæli, the guy who owes money. Ársæll Egilsson.'

Satan takes a smoke, leans back in the couch and examines Sæli from head to foot as he casually blows smoke out through his nose. But he says nothing.

'Why don't you say something, man?' asks Sæli, going red with rage. 'You threaten my family on the telephone, order me to fetch some package and I don't know what else! And then when I face you, you can't say a word. I just want to know what you're doing here. Are you following me? Don't you trust me to bring you this package? Maybe you were sent here to kill me? Eh? Am I to be killed for a measly eleven million? Or is it twelve, now? Who sent you? The owner of the gambling joint? What's his name again – Sverrir?'

When Sæli mentions the gambling joint Satan raises his eyebrows. He sits up, leans forwards on his elbows, takes the cigarette out of his mouth and narrows his eyes.

'Goddammit!' Sæli throws up his hands and sighs noisily. 'You don't want to say anything – fine. But tell me one thing: is my family safe? I'm the one who owes money, not them. Are they safe? Answer me that!'

'What gambling joint are you talking about?' asks Satan, waving his left hand in a circle counterclockwise, as if wanting to rewind Sæli's speech. 'You said you owed money to some casino?'

'Yes. In Dugguvogur,' says Sæli, glancing sideways at the door and wiping the sweat from his forehead. 'Stop acting as if you know nothing! You're a collector for those pigs. You're Satan!'

'Hold your horses, boy,' says Satan, putting his cigarette out on the tabletop. 'You owe money to a casino in Dugguvogur and some Satan wants to collect from you? Is that right?'

'You're this Satan guy, aren't you? I mean, if you weren't him you wouldn't be here.'

'Have you ever seen this guy, the one who's collecting?' asks Satan, standing up and walking towards Sæli, who retreats towards the door. 'Can you tell me anything more about him?'

'Don't mess with me, man!' says Sæli, pale with fear. 'There's no sense in messing with me. I won't stand for —'

Sæli never finishes the sentence because Satan hits him open handed on his left cheek with a blow so heavy that Sæli sees only black and blood starts flowing from both of his nostrils. He leans against the wall and tries to remain upright but the pain is so severe that he's forced to sink to his knees.

'Yes, I *am* Satan,' says Satan, spitting on the top of Sæli's head. 'And Satan doesn't bother with minnows like you. Simply having to hit such a kitten makes me choke with contempt and shame. I don't collect debts for anyone but myself and I don't threaten any fucking families with anything!'

'I don't understand …' mutters Sæli, trying to wipe the blood from his face, making it even worse by spreading it around.

'Who phoned you?' Satan squats down beside Sæli and grips his throat tightly with his right hand.

'He said his name was Satan,' says Sæli, sniffing blood up his nose. 'I never saw him, but I saw his car. It was a big BMW, maroon.'

'Fucking hell!' says Satan, letting go his hold and standing up. 'We're being fucked around, my boy.'

'What do you mean?' asks Sæli as he totters to his feet, coughing.

'I'm not the guy who phoned you, the guy who's collecting the debt,' says Satan, lighting a cigarette. 'That idiot is pretending to be me, or else he doesn't know who I am. Shit! You get old fast in this business. After ten years you're a dinosaur in the eyes of beginners. And then you're suddenly stuck on a ship that's sailing with you straight to hell.'

'I don't understand. If you're not the Satan who phoned me, then who is?'

'What package were you supposed to fetch?' Satan blows smoke from his nostrils as he shoves the half pack of cigarettes and the gas lighter into his left pocket, on top of the sock with the shells.

'I'm supposed to smuggle a package home from Suriname. Probably drugs. Something from Colombia. To pay part of my debt, you know?'

'I'll tell you what we'll do,' says Satan, fishing Jónas's cheque from his pocket. 'We'll just keep that package and also buy as much coke as we can. Haven't you got some currency or a credit card or something? Here, take this cheque as security. You get hold of a pile of pesetas or shillings or whatever they use down there and I'll sniff out the cocaine and buy it. You hide the stuff, I'll sell it in Iceland and we'll split the profits. We're talking tens of millions here! What do you say?'

'But …' Sæli murmurs as he takes the cheque. 'This package – it's not mine. And this Satan – the *other* Satan – he threatened my family and he's home in Iceland and –'

'There's only *one* Satan! Just so that's clear,' says Satan and he pats Sæli on the left cheek, which is still bright red and throbbing with pain. 'And your family is safe until the package is delivered to these guys, right?'

'Yeah, I guess,' says Sæli uncertainly, then he folds the cheque in two and sticks it in the pocket of his overalls.

'But as long as I'm your pal, your family is safe from cradle to grave,' says Satan with a cold grin. 'I'll see to this BMW prick the minute I set foot on our fucking island. He's as good as dead, you see? He's *dead* but he just doesn't know that he *is* dead!'

'Yeah, okay,' says Sæli. 'But there's just one thing I still don't understand. What are you doing on board this ship?'

'That's a good question,' says Satan, his grin disappearing. 'You could say I'm here because of that guy who phoned you and threatened your family. When he made so bold as to call himself Satan he probably set off a course of events we still can't see the end of. But to my mind it's first and foremost because I didn't fuck two little girls I wanted to fuck. I hesitated …'

Satan takes a drag, shrugs, then goes to the open window and flips his glowing cigarette out.

'Now I really don't understand,' Sæli says with an embarrassed half-grin which freezes on his lips, turning into a frightened grimace when someone rattles the doorknob forcefully behind him.

Satan whirls round to see the door open and three armed men force their way into the cabin.

In the lead is Methúsalem, who handles his rifle as if it has a bayonet on it, and behind him are John and Rúnar, who have no idea how to behave, so they are more like hunters lost in the woods than armed housebreakers.

Satan bends over to stretch his right hand quickly but coolly towards his revolver in its holster but Methúsalem aims the rifle at him, his finger tightening round the trigger, so Satan decides not to show his trump card. Instead he calmly straightens up and runs his fingers through his greasy hair almost casually.

He's been in worse situations. These guys are just amateurs carrying guns too ridiculous for conflict in such a small space.

'I'm sorry, I'm … they …' Sæli steps to the side and looks back and forth between Methúsalem and Satan, who don't take their eyes off each other.

'You!' says Methúsalem, aiming his rifle at Satan's breast. 'Don't move! Don't even scratch your nose!'

'Sæli!' says Rúnar, letting the barrel of his shotgun sink to the floor. 'Look at you, boy! Did he do that?'

'Yes, but look …' Sæli says, looking at Satan, who gives him a wink and a crooked smile.

'You fucker!' says Big John, tightening his hold on his shotgun, which he clutches to his chest and points at the ceiling.

'He won't be slapping anyone else during this voyage,' says Methúsalem, nostrils flaring. 'And he certainly won't be sabotaging this ship any further. Mark my words, you motherfucker! You're not going to see daylight again until we get to Suriname. We'll make sure of that!'

'Methúsalem!' says Sæli hoarsely. 'He isn't who I thought he was. He —'

'You're scared of him, Sæli,' says Methúsalem, without taking his eyes off Satan. 'And I can understand that. This is a dangerous man and he's just thumped you. But that's over now! He's coming with us and everything will return to normal. Understand?'

'Yes, but …' Sæli looks desperately at Satan, who returns

his gaze and shakes his head gently back and forth, as if to tell Sæli that it'll be all right, that he shouldn't get himself in trouble on Satan's account; that their agreement will remain their secret; that he's not afraid of these men nor what they've got planned for him, that …

'No buts!' says Methúsalem emphatically.

'Okay,' says Sæli, hanging his head.

'You just go up to the bridge,' says Methúsalem, glancing briefly at Sæli and nodding his head towards the door. This movement – the glance and the nod – lasts less than a second.

But that's all the time Satan needs, and more.

The moment Methúsalem takes his eyes off Satan he grabs Sæli and pulls him close, jumping behind him in the same movement. He hooks his left arm around the front of Sæli's neck, locking his left fist around his own upper arm and his right fist around the back of his neck, so Sæli is stuck in a deadly wrestling hold.

'STILL!' screams Methúsalem, who doesn't know where to aim his gun and ends up aiming it in the reddening face of Sæli, who stares at Methúsalem, desperation in his eyes.

'God almighty!' says John, looking at Rúnar, who shrugs and shuffles his feet to the right of the chief mate.

'Methúsalem, don't …' Sæli manages to say before Satan tightens his grip. His neck bones creak, his windpipe narrows and his oesophagus closes tight.

'Let that man go,' says Methúsalem, trying to squeeze out some saliva for his mouth, which is painfully dry from right down to his stomach.

'Just one question, before I snap this boy's spinal cord,' says Satan calmly as, little by little, he tightens his hold on Sæli, who is going blue and standing on his toes to try to avoid being hanged. 'What are your plans? What's going to happen if you capture me?'

Satan has pretty well defeated this three-man invading army. All he has to do – if they don't have the sense to throw down their weapons and give up – is to sink to his knees, with Sæli in front of him, let his right hand go and get the revolver from his right ankle. Before these fools would have time to drop their jaws in wonder, as they feebly try to deal with the overwhelming fact that they have about a third of a second left to live, he'd shoot all three of them.

However, before he goes so far as to end the lives of three people, he wants to know if there's a better solution. If blood is spilled and men die, there will be chaos on board the ship. Then the projected cocaine smuggling he and the second mate were planning would come to nothing, and down the drain would go a business opportunity that could easily earn him millions without any serious costs, danger or trouble. And Satan is not the kind of guy who'd risk losing such an opportunity if he could possibly avoid it.

'We're going to lock you up,' says Methúsalem, hesitating in front of Sæli and Satan and aiming his rifle now to the left, now to the right of Sæli, who watches the chief mate's asinine posturing with a terrified, oxygen-deprived expression. 'We're going to see to it that you don't cause any more damage than you've already … caused.'

'You're welcome to lock me up somewhere,' says Satan with a laugh. 'But if you're looking for some saboteur, then you're barking up the wrong tree, whether you believe it or not.'

'We don't believe you,' says Methúsalem, his voice shaking. 'Let the boy go and we'll show some mercy!'

'He can't breathe, man!' says Rúnar, watching Sæli turn blue and black around the eyes as he dangles in Satan's head-hold.

'I can't stand this!' says John, who's breathing like an adenoidal sheep and wiping sweat from his burning forehead.

'*Let go!*' yells Methúsalem, spraying saliva all over the cabin.

'Will I get food and drink?' asks Satan.

'Yes!'

'And I won't have to work and stand the watch or whatever it's called?'

'*Yes!*' screams Methúsalem, on the verge of breakdown.

'And I'll be left in peace?'

'YES, YES, YES!'

'All right,' says Satan, slightly loosening his grip on Sæli, who manages to get his feet on the floor and draw in a little oxygen.

'Let him go!' says Methúsalem, clutching even more tightly the rifle that's shaking in his hands.

'Breathe slowly,' Satan whispers to Sæli, who's convulsively sucking and wheezing as he tries to inhale. 'And you'll get me out before we reach land. Otherwise I won't get you out of debt. Understood?'

'What are you saying?' asks Methúsalem, lifting his rifle. 'Stop whispering! Let the boy go.'

'Let him go,' says Rúnar.

'Do you understand?' whispers Satan to Sæli, who manages to nod between gulps.

'LET HIM GO!' shouts Methúsalem, aiming his rifle straight at Sæli's blood-red face. 'Let him go or I'll shoot the both of you!'

'*Methúsalem!*' shouts Rúnar, about to grab the rifle barrel.

'Rúnar!' John says, grabbing Rúnar's hand before he can grab the rifle.

'Cool it in here!' Satan yells at the three men. '*Put down your guns and I'll let the boy go.*'

'Methúsalem?' asks Rúnar with a shrug.

'We do as he says,' mutters John and he lowers his shotgun.

'Okay,' says Methúsalem, aiming his rifle at the floor. 'But only until he lets go. And be ready, boys. And you – let go now!'

'I'm letting go,' says Satan. He takes his hands off Sæli, who takes two steps forward, vomits on the floor and then leans against the nearest wall.

'Easy!' says Methúsalem, pointing his rifle at Satan's chest.

'Turn round and put your hands above your head.'

'Yeah, yeah, cool it, man! You've been watching too many police movies,' Satan says, turning around and putting his hands behind his head. 'So where are you going to lock me up?'

'You'll see,' says Methúsalem, wiping the sweat from his forehead. Then he looks at Sæli, who's coughing and whimpering and blowing snot. 'Bear up, boy, and hurry up to the bridge before the bell brings the Old Man out.'

Methúsalem then moves his eyes back to Satan, who bends his knees as he turns around. Satan grabs the rifle barrel with his right hand and pushes it aside. The chief mate's index finger jerks on the trigger and the shot goes off.

BANG!

The report isn't particularly loud but so sudden, unexpected and disturbing that it sounds like a cannon to the ears of the sailors, who stiffen and go cold inside, their mouths filling with the bitter taste of blood, as if death has breathed down their necks.

A small hole appears in the wall above the head of the bed, the air smells of burnt gunpowder and the fine smoke gets in the men's noses and their startled eyes.

'But let me tell you something,' says Satan, still holding the rifle barrel and looking directly in turn at each of the gunmen, who have turned to stone in the face of this self-confident madman. 'If in the end you *can't* prove I'm this saboteur you're looking for, I'll kill the lot of you.'

None of them can utter a word, because none of them knows what to say.

'Let's go, then!' says Satan, dropping the rifle. Then he turns around, stands with his feet apart and conscientiously places his palms on the back of his neck.

'Yeah,' mutters Methúsalem, clearing his throat as he looks at Rúnar, who shrugs and looks across at the chief engineer. Big John raises his eyebrows with a sigh.

The three gunslingers are faced with a man who turns his

back on them with his hands behind his head, but they hardly dare open their mouths to give him orders – because they're no longer sure whether they have captured him or it's the other way around.

★ ★ ★

B-deck

'Can I offer you some dessert? Ice-cream or something?' asks Ási the cook, pouring more coffee in second officer Jónas's mug.

Ási had promised Methúsalem to keep Jónas busy chatting in the mess for ten or fifteen minutes, or until they had managed to sneak this Satan guy unnoticed down the stairs and into the forecastle, where they were going to keep him chained up for the rest of the voyage.

However, Ási, the sociable charmer who can talk about anything with anyone, can't make any contact with Jónas, who already has a reputation for being pretty distant in any company. But on this trip he's reached the point where they can't get a sensible word out of him, and when he does look his mates in the eye it's almost as if he doesn't recognise them, or as if he simply looks right through them into some other world.

'No thanks,' mutters Jónas, standing up without tasting his coffee.

'Up to you, pal,' says Ási, removing the last of the plates and cutlery from the table in the officers' mess. 'But there's lemon cheesecake in the fridge that's looking for hot coffee with a view to a lasting relationship.'

'Thanks for the meal,' says Jónas. He leaves the mess and sets off up the stairs with heavy steps, his back bent by worry and anxiety.

When he's about halfway up the steps from D-deck to E-deck he hears movement on the port side on the deck below him. He stops on the third step from the top, holds on to the railings either side and listens. He hears a number of men who walk in a row to the stair and then march like soldiers down to C-deck without laughing, swearing or talking to each other.

Jónas feels that something is not as it should be – seamen don't often walk around in silent groups. He creeps back down to D-deck and peers through the stairwell. There he sees Big John and Rúnar disappearing round a corner on C-deck, straight backed and with serious expressions, and clutching shotguns to their chests.

What's going on?

He jogs along behind them and manages to see the whole group before they disappear down to B-deck, which will take them outside. At the head is Satan with his hands in the air, and behind him Methúsalem, handling his rifle as if it were equipped with a bayonet.

Good God!

'Easy,' Jónas says to himself, drawing a deep breath and rubbing his cold hands together.

They've arrested Satan, which means they think he cut the wires – which is good. But what if this criminal talks? What if he tells them he isn't Jónas's brother-in-law? Then what will they think of Jónas, who's been keeping it secret that he isn't? Why should he keep such a thing secret? What if Satan tells them that Jónas paid him five million to keep quiet? What if he shows them the cheque?

What can Jónas say then? That Satan had threatened him? That he had paid Satan to keep silent? To save his life?

Jónas runs up to D-deck and straight into Satan's cabin. The air smells of burnt gunpowder, there's a bullet hole on the wall above the bed and a pool of vomit by the bathroom door.

Jónas searches everywhere for his cheque. If he can find it, lying his way out of all this will be easier. Then he'll just say that Satan threatened him – that he threatened to kill Jónas if he told the others about him.

Jónas finds the duffel bag in the closet and empties it.

He digs around in the clothes and finds the passports, the bankbooks and the share certificates – but not the cheque. He shoves the clothes back in the bag and pockets the papers.

There's nothing in the bathroom cupboard but cigarettes. Jónas steals one pack and continues the hunt for the cheque. He can't find it anywhere. It's not under the mattress, not on the couch, not under the bed; not behind, inside or under anything. It isn't in the cabin.

The bastard's got it on him, of course!

'Damn!' Jónas mutters, then sits on the couch and lights a cigarette.

He has to do something. He has to *think* of something. Something brilliant. Something dramatic. Something that will draw his shipmates' attention away from obvious facts and logical conclusions.

It's now or never.

Jónas puts out his cigarette, turns off the lights as he leaves the cabin and closes the door behind him. He listens for movement, hears nothing, and opens the door to the platform behind the wheelhouse. The storm has approached the ship again, dimming the daylight and raising the wind so the sea is grey and choppy. Jónas holds onto the railing with one hand and throws Satan's papers overboard with the other. The wind grabs the ruined passports, the bankbooks and the share certificates, stirs its catch round in midair, lifts it high above the ship and then scatters it over the churning sea.

The less there is available about Satan, the better. No ID, no family, no papers, nothing.

Who's going to believe the word of a man who can't prove his identity?

Jónas smiles crookedly, but not for long. He still has to carry out the most difficult part of his plan; he has undermined Satan's credibility but he still has to prove his merciless cruelty. Once the crew sees what this man did to Jónas when he threatened to expose him, they won't doubt the evil of his character. Then they won't doubt his guilt. Then the cheque won't make any difference, whether it's found or not.

Jónas clambers over the railing behind the wheelhouse and climbs down on the outside until his feet are hanging free. The ship is rising and plunging deeply by turns so Jónas is either slammed against the cold metal or swung out over the wake that roils behind the stern fifteen metres below him.

After only thirty seconds his hands ache. The metal is cold and wet, sticky with salt, and his stiff fingers are slowly losing their grip. Jónas is panting and trying to think straight as he appraises the movement of the ship. He must neither end up in the sea nor land on the railing on the deck below. It's a question of the right moment, letting go just as the ship begins to lift after breaking a heavy wave, but not too soon and absolutely not too late ...

Boom, boom, boom ...

Now!

Jónas lets go of the wet railing. For just a moment he seems to float in midair. Then C-deck shoots past his eyes, his stomach is filled with a cold emptiness, his heart flames in his chest and the taste of blood fills his nose, and the blood tastes of rusty iron ...

XXIII

F-deck

Guðmundur Berndsen is sitting on the couch in his starboard cabin playing patience. The cards slide on the table when the ship rolls or plunges but Guðmundur has been playing this same game of patience at sea for twenty years and his clever captain's fingers have up to now straightened the cards as he went along without his focused mind even noticing.

But no longer.

Guðmundur is finding it difficult to concentrate and when the cards slide about it gets on his nerves, his fingers are unsteady, the cards stick to them and gradually the game falls apart into a ludicrous mess.

'Damn it!' mutters the captain, mixing the cards around before shuffling them again.

He's thinking about Hrafnhildur, about the sabotage on the ship, about the morale on board; and he's thinking about that storm that Methúsalem should have manoeuvred them around long ago.

'The devil take this cursed ship,' murmurs Guðmundur and stands up to fetch a flask of cognac and a heavy shot glass.

The captain doesn't usually bring spirits on board but this is his final voyage, after all. Isn't he definitely going to quit after this trip? Yes, by Christ – he's quitting!

'Just one, for my stomach,' Guðmundur tells himself as

he breaks the seal on the bottle and fills the shot glass. Then he tosses it back and closes his eyes, smacking his lips on the smooth aftertaste.

That's better!

He shuffles the cards and lays the game yet again. The ship rolls back and forth, the wind from the west is rising and the daylight outside the window has turned to a weak glimmer.

What would Hrafnhildur be doing right now? Is she going to come to Suriname? Is he still a married man – or has Guðmundur Berndsen become a divorced old fogey?

'King on the ace, queen on the king,' he mutters as he moves the king and queen, then turns up the cards that lie upside down underneath them.

Guðmundur sighs deeply and licks his lips. He unscrews the top of the bottle, fills the shot glass and tosses it back. Then he refills the glass and screws the top back on.

For a long time he turned a deaf ear when men in their late fifties talked about how dull it must be not to have anyone to share your old age with. How sad it was to maybe die alone.

Whingeing old women, he used to think, and he would sneer if healthy men allowed themselves to express such sentimental rubbish.

But now he is getting anxious himself. What if Hrafnhildur leaves him? Then what'll he do? Rent a basement? Buy a flat in an apartment block? And then what? Play patience until he dies?

Is he going to be one of those old guys who take root in their recliners watching TV and get cardiac arrest when someone knocks at the door? *If* anyone knocks. Is he going to be one of those old men with bad breath who walk about in unwashed tatters and eat sour blood pudding for every meal? Who live in smelly flats that are as dim and lifeless as themselves?

Will he die alone and unloved, without any help, sympathy or soft hands to stroke?

The ship takes a deep dive, rolls over to port and slams into a rising wave. The wind howls and the ship shudders from end to end; the full shot glass jumps and overturns so cognac flows over the cards, off the table and onto the rug.

'Fuck it!' says the captain, jumping to his feet. He collects the wet cards, rights the shot glass, throws the flask on the couch and strides to the window.

Outside the dark is churning, circling in on itself, tearing up the sea, screeching like a banshee and shooting lightning in all directions. The storm is just about to slam into the ship, which is moving so slowly in relation to the wind and the waves that it seems to be bobbing in one place like a rubber duck in a bathtub.

'Holy Mary ...' Guðmundur crosses himself in the face of the indomitable power of nature.

The crests of the waves are everywhere, whipped into white foam that grows ever greyer as the light fades.

' ... Mother of God.' The captain takes a deep breath. Then he stiffens as something heavy and wet slams into the closed window.

Some brown and leathery creature with eight tentacles and a large head.

'Have mercy on us!' cries the captain as he watches the creature on the window with revulsion.

A large octopus is glued to the glass and staring at the captain with a dead eye.

★ ★ ★

The bridge

Sæli is standing at the starboard window, helplessly watching the chaotic storm as it comes careering out of the west, black as the smoke from burning oil. Sæli is not authorised to pilot a ship, and even though he thinks he probably could disconnect the autopilot and sail the ship out of the storm, he is not allowed to touch the controls.

What should he do?

The waves are getting higher and higher, the sea rougher and darker; heavy gusts of wind are slamming against the ship like invisible punches; wood and metal are grinding and grating; the daylight is fading, the ship is dancing with death and the view is distorted by the foaming sea as it buffets the windows.

'What is going on here?' asks Guðmundur, slamming the door behind him as he enters the bridge. Steadying himself against walls and tables, he makes his way past the map room and into the middle. 'Where's Methúsalem?'

'Methúsalem?' echoes Sæli, looking at the most senior officer with a mixture of fear and relief. He's afraid because he's part of a secret mutiny, but relieved at the same time because someone has come up to the bridge to take command of the ship.

'I told him to sail east! There's a gale coming up, even a hurricane, twelve on the scale.' Guðmundur sits in the captain's chair. 'Where is the man?'

'He … He …' Sæli clears his throat so hard he starts coughing.

'What's the matter with you, boy?' says Guðmundur, studying him carefully. Sæli is as pale as a ghost and clearly in some sort of state: his hands are shaking, his eyes are wide and shiny, and if the dark stain on the front of his trousers is anything to go by, he's wet himself.

What the hell is going on?

'*Where is Methúsalem Sigurðsson?*' asks Guðmundur loudly as he disconnects the autopilot and grabs the helm.

The captain doesn't have to wait for the seaman's answer, though, because as soon as he looks out the window the facts are evident.

Down on the port side of the weather deck, four men are walking forwards along the ship in single file. They are halfway along, fifty metres behind them, fifty metres to go. At the front is the new deckhand with Methúsalem behind him; next is Rúnar with Big John at the rear. And all of them are armed, except the man in front, who has his arms raised and his hands behind his head. Rúnar is carrying a long chain on his left shoulder and John has a five-litre water container in his right hand. They're stumbling as the ship twists but making their way forward, step by step, their knees and backs bent, their bodies beaten by wind, rain and spray.

'What is going on?' shouts Guðmundur, staring out the window as if he can't believe his eyes. 'What are the men up to? Are they armed?'

'They're going to shut him in the forecastle,' says Sæli.

Disobedience! Defiance! Mutiny!

'I don't believe this!' Guðmundur screams as he reconnects the autopilot. Then he jumps down from the chair and strides into the chart room, where he rolls up the charts that are on the table.

Just as well these mutineers didn't get hold of the charts!

'Where are you going?' asks Sæli, holding on with both hands as the ship takes a deep dive.

'You're staying here, boy, and doing nothing and touching nothing!' Guðmundur says forcefully as he opens the door to the corridor with his left hand, clutching the rolled-up charts to his chest with his right. 'DO YOU HEAR ME, YOU IDIOT?'

'But the storm ...' says Sæli with tears in his eyes.

Guðmundur, red faced, gives the young man a disdainful look but says nothing. Then he steps over the threshold and slams the door behind him.

★ ★ ★

Weather deck

The forecastle door is shut. It's a waterproof metal door with three hasps. It's painted red, as is all of the front of the forecastle, and painted on it in white letters is the English name for this space: FORECASTLE.

'You open it!' shouts Methúsalem, poking his rifle into the back of Jón Karl, who stands with his feet apart in front of the locked door.

The bow of a freighter is usually covered and that space is called the forecastle. The forecastle is a closed, separate space, but is considered the forward part of the A-deck or upper deck and is usually a storeroom of some kind. From there you can walk down to the bow thruster area. Down there you will also find boxes for the heavy anchor chains as well as the forepeak tank, which is a ballast tank.

The weather is now making it extremely dangerous to be above deck – sheer foolhardiness if not utter madness. The four men slide back and forth, lose their balance, get blown over and slam against whatever's near them, lean every which way and hold onto anything they can possibly hold onto. They are either being thrown to the cold, wet deck or swinging loose several centimetres above it, since the ship is either falling through a vacuum into the trough of a wave or shooting like a rocket into the sky.

Satan leans forward at forty-five degrees with his left hand against the forecastle wall and loosens the hasps on the door with his right hand. The door is the same kind as the one that opens into the darkness of the hold, but the locks aren't as stiff and Satan manages, with some effort, to open them one handed. As the third and last hasp comes loose the bow lifts right into the air, as if the ship is going to sail into the clouds. The forecastle door swings wide open and the heavy door throws Satan like a doll against Methúsalem; they both lose their footing and slam against the foremost hatch, which is high enough so they don't tumble all the way to the wheelhouse and get washed overboard.

Big John manages to hook the middle finger of his left hand in a metal loop on the front of the forecastle, while the fingers of his right hand lock themselves round Rúnar's left arm. Then they both dangle in thin air over the deck until the ship rights itself.

'Everyone inside!' calls Methúsalem the minute the ship reaches a pitch fairly near the horizontal.

Icy seawater floods across the deck from starboard to port. Satan and Methúsalem scramble to their feet and run inside the forecastle; Big John frees his middle finger from the metal loop and pulls Rúnar to his feet. Then they support each other to the forecastle door, climb over the high threshold and disappear into the gloom.

The hinges scream, the metal door swings back with great force and closes with a loud crash.

Boom!

Everything goes black inside the narrow forecastle, as if the dark were outer space.

Fear engulfs the companions in arms. They clutch their guns tightly and stare helplessly into the void. They're trapped in a triangular iron box that bounces and shakes like a tin can on the back of a truck driving along a pitted dirt road; with them is a dangerous man, an invisible poisonous scorpion, and they don't know where he is or what he's doing.

'Lights! Turn on the lights!'

'Where's the switch?'

'By the door, port side!'

'Methúsalem?'

'Yes!'

'Where's John?'

'I'm over here!'

'I can't find the fucking switch!'

'Who's closest to the door?'

'Not me!'

'Who's me?'

The ship slams into a heavy wave, the forecastle vibrates like a drum, men slide about, gasp and fall flat over one another, then the bow lifts and the door opens wide again, letting the grey daylight in.

'I've got it!' shouts Rúnar as he jumps up and hits the light switch. A weak bulb lights up behind its dirty plastic cover above the door.

Rúnar holds onto a roof beam and looks at John, who is lying on his back in the corner to port, looking at the Methúsalem, who in turn is sitting on his rear at the front of the forecastle, his gun pointing at the prisoner. Satan is standing to starboard with his arms spread, loosely holding onto the edge of a long metal shelf.

John is clutching his shotgun to his chest with both hands, but Rúnar's gun is sliding back and forth on the metal floor halfway between him and Satan, along with the chain and the water container.

'Don't even dream about it, mate!' says Methúsalem, loosening the safety catch on his rifle.

'Cool it, cowboy,' says Satan with a mirthless grin. 'You'd all be dead already, if I'd wanted that.'

He could, of course, just tell them who the saboteur was. Tell them that Jónas pretended to go to the toilet just as Satan came on the night watch, was away for a good half-hour and then did what he could to make Satan look suspicious in the eyes of the captain.

Even though it had been Jónas who was wet through, deathly pale and nervous as a chicken.

What are these men thinking? Can't they add two and two?

Jónas killed that brother-in-law and now he's trying to get to South America without the authorities making contact with the ship.

Isn't it obvious?

But Satan doesn't really care. All he wants, for the moment at least, is for this idiotic bunch of boy scouts to leave him in peace, even if that means an unjustified imprisonment in a cold iron box. When he gets tired of staying in the forecastle he'll tell them who the guilty party is – if they haven't discovered it for themselves by then.

Until then, he's going to relax.

'Here's the heater,' says Big John, pulling a little electric heater out of a wooden box tied to an iron column in the middle of the forecastle. He connects the fire to a plug in the column and sets it on low.

The ship pitches violently, the metal screeches, the hinges groan and the door shuts with its usual clang. Rúnar uses the opportunity to fasten one of the hasps from the inside.

'So,' says Methúsalem as he gets to his feet, 'let's get this over with before we all get trapped in here by the weather.'

Methúsalem aims his rifle at Satan while Rúnar tightens one end of the chain around his waist. He hooks the padlock through two links behind Satan's back, sticks the other end of the chain through a metal loop on the starboard wall, hooks that end also onto the padlock and closes the lock.

'Excellent!' says Methúsalem, taking the key and putting it into his shirt pocket. 'You just try to get comfortable, mate. We'll leave the light on, of course.'

'You make me laugh, you stupid seamen, for you know not what you do!' says the still-standing Satan, laughing, as the three of them leave, slamming the door and replacing the hasps.

These imbeciles wrongly imagine that they've captured the evil in their little world and locked it in some sort of Niflheim when, in fact, they've made a little heaven for the stranger who woke up in the incomprehensible misery they live and work in, and have thus freed him from duties, responsibilities and the yoke of everyday life.

★ ★ ★

B-deck

Captain Guðmundur stands out of the wind on the port side of the wheelhouse, waiting for the trio to come back and walk up the metal stairs that lead from the weather deck up to B-deck.

He's clad in a parka, has a cap on his head and holds the pump-action Mossberg upright against his chest as he leans against a recess in the white-painted wall.

After a few long minutes the crown of Methúsalem's head appears at the top of the stairs; next comes Rúnar and Big John brings up the rear. They're holding their guns in their left hands and the railing with their right, their backs are bent to reduce their resistance to the wind and their grimacing faces are turned away from the salty sea spray.

Anger flares in the captain as he watches his shipmates of many years sneak about fully armed, having not only disobeyed his orders but also taken power into their own hands.

They are lawbreakers, traitors and rebels.

Guðmundur hides in the recess and watches every step. Methúsalem has reached B-deck; he holds onto the top railing and edges his way along. Rúnar steps up onto the deck and follows Methúsalem, while John is halfway up the stairs.

The back part of B-deck doesn't have an actual railing around it but, rather, a solid gunwale of black-painted steel.

The west wind whines, stirs up the waves and batters the ship; lightning flashes in the clouds and thunder rumbles in the distance; the wheelhouse bobs like a buoy and the black hull of the ship regularly disappears in seawater and salt spray.

When the ship straightens after pitching deeply the captain steps out of his hiding place, lifts his shotgun and strikes the first officer on the side of the face with the stock, then slams his right elbow deep into the bosun's solar plexus.

Methúsalem drops his rifle and falls forwards on the deck while Rúnar drops to his knees without letting go of the top of the gunwale or his shotgun.

'Don't shoot!' shouts the chief engineer, who throws his gun overboard then lifts his left arm above his head where he stands, on the top step.

'*I ought to shoot the lot of you!*' the captain responds, pointing the shotgun at each in turn as he fights to keep his footing on the wet deck, which is rising and falling and leaning every which way.

'Easy, man!' shouts the bosun and slides his shotgun through the gutter at the bottom of the gunwale and overboard.

'What are you doing?' the first officer yells at his mates and stands up. At the same moment the ship pitches and he loses his footing and is lifted onto the gunwale.

'Methúsalem!' shouts the bosun, throwing himself towards his shipmate and managing to grab one of the officer's ankles before he tumbles overboard.

'*Everybody inside! Everybody inside!*' says Big John, stepping up onto the deck and feeling his way along the gunwale. 'Everybody inside before someone ends up overboard!'

Methúsalem crawls back along the ship on hands and knees, managing to grab the rifle before it slides back to the stern, while John helps Rúnar back to his feet and steadies him with his left hand on his back.

'*Let go of that gun!*' roars Guðmundur when Methúsalem stands up with the rifle in his left hand, but then he slips and hits the gunwale in front of Rúnar. Rúnar grabs the captain, who accidentally pulls the trigger of the shotgun, sending a shot up into the inky sky.

'Are you trying to kill me?' yells Methúsalem, waving his rifle like a battleaxe.

'*Everybody inside! Everybody inside!*' John tries again, but Rúnar can't go any further because Guðmundur doesn't move.

'Throw that gun in the sea,' Guðmundur snarls, aiming his shotgun at Methúsalem, who grinds his teeth in fury, eyes bulging and nostrils flaring.

'Get going,' Rúnar exclaims, pushing at Guðmundur, who doesn't move.

'*Nobody is going inside until that gun hits the water,*' the captain responds.

'Take it easy!' shouts Methúsalem, pressing his right elbow hard against the gunwale, then holding the rifle vertical with his left hand as he loosens the bolt from the magazine with the fingers of his right hand.

'What are you doing?' yells Guðmundur, whose mouth is dry and his throat sore from all the screaming.

'This gun is a museum piece,' Methúsalem replies forcefully as he lets the bolt fall onto the deck, then kicks it towards the stair and over the edge of the deck. 'Now it's undamaged but useless. It's not going overboard!'

'*Everybody inside!*' John pushes Rúnar, who slams into Guðmundur.

'All right! For fuck's sake,' roars Guðmundur, locking in the safety on the shotgun. 'Everybody inside!'

They creep along the gunwale, past the big winch to port and back to the stern. There Methúsalem seizes the opportunity to leap in three bounds over the watery deck to the wheelhouse and through the door to the B-deck corridor. He puts down his rifle and holds the door open for Guðmundur, who makes a run for it, falls on one knee when a wave slams the ship but makes it all the way in the end.

'Come on!' Methúsalem calls to Rúnar, who is watching the ship's motion to find the right moment to run.

Too much wind … Too much roll … Too much seawater …

'*Look!*' John shouts in Rúnar's ear just as he's about to let go of the gunwale and run for the door that Methúsalem is holding open.

'What?' Rúnar shouts, grabbing the gunwale with both hands as the stern presses down into the sea, like a whale diving for the depths.

'It's Jónas!' John cries, pointing with a trembling hand to the second mate, who's sliding around the deck on his back, between the big winch and the starboard gunwale.

'Is he dead?' yells Rúnar, motioning over to starboard.

'I don't know,' John says and gives the bosun a push. 'Come on! We've got to get him inside!'

* * *

The forecastle

Satan pulls on the chain to see how much he can move. He can touch the metal pillar in the middle and that's it. The door might as well be light-years away.

Down on the floor is an open plinth course reaching from the front of the forecastle on each side and ending at the stern. On the port side it contains buoys and net-bulbs but on the starboard side, by Satan, it's full of painting overalls, bottles of turpentine, paint pots, rollers and brushes. Above the plinth courses, at shoulder height for the average man, are shelves on which there are big bolts of burlap and canvas, dirty overalls and various other things, all kept in place with a green fishing net stretched over the shelves with little hooks.

It is almost ridiculously hard to stay on your feet up here in the forecastle, but by keeping the chain at the stretch, his feet well apart and at least one hand on the shelves, it isn't impossible.

Satan starts to pile up the painting things in the bow end of the course, then he loosens the net from the shelves and stretches it over them. Once that's done he makes himself a lair inside the plinth course by spreading canvas and burlap on the bottom.

Now the plinth course has become a deep bed.

Satan lies down on his back in the lair and hooks one link of the chain over a metal hook in the wall right above the course. This ensures that he won't fly up and out onto the floor in the worst of the turmoil.

The bulb over the door throws a dull yellow glow over the contents of the forecastle. The heater slides around on the floor as it blows out hot air.

'Could be worse,' mutters Satan as he digs a crumpled cigarette packet out of his right trouser pocket. Then he peels the bandage off the ampoule, the syringe and the needle.

He puts the needle on the syringe, pushes it through the rubber membrane on the ampoule and pulls the liquid morphine into the syringe. Then he waits calmly while the ship ascends another wave. As soon as it stops, still at the top of the ridge, he clenches his left fist, sticks the needle into a vein in the crook of his elbow and pumps in the stuff with his right thumb, firmly and calmly.

The ship pitches forwards off the wave, Satan gets butterflies in his stomach and drops into the dark abyss.

XXIV

Saturday, 15 September

Methúsalem is holding on with both hands as he makes his way along the portside gunwale towards the front of the ship, towards the stair that leads down to the weather deck. It's almost eighteen hours since they locked the supposed terrorist in the forecastle and the storm is still raging. Methúsalem is dressed in a dark-green raincoat and black rubber boots and is holding onto the iron railing with his bare hands as he backs down the steep staircase. He steps carefully onto the weather deck, which he can't even see in the foaming seawater and blinding spray.

The first officer is looking for the bolt from his rifle but isn't that optimistic about finding it after all this time.

But he couldn't get here any sooner.

Guðmundur sent him directly to the bridge watch after they had carried the unconscious Jónas to the infirmary, and he didn't get off the watch until ten in the evening. Then it was too dark to go looking for such a small object in such a large area, especially out on the weather deck in a storm.

As long as Jónas is unconscious, the captain and the first officer will have to take alternating watches on the bridge. This means that they take eight-hour shifts. The captain relieved the first officer at ten in the evening and was on watch until six in the morning. Then he should be free until two o'clock.

It's already six o'clock, actually, but Methúsalem isn't going up to relieve the old man until he's found the bolt from his rifle.

He has to find that fucking bolt!

Just as Methúsalem lets go of the railing the ship pitches and rolls to starboard. He loses his balance, falls on his belly and slams into the last hatch, then the ship rights itself, the deck is filled with seawater and Methúsalem is washed over to the port side, under the railing and overboard.

'NO!'

Everything goes black, the icy sea fills his senses and for a few moments he can neither see nor hear.

As if he were sinking, falling, turning in circles and disappearing into a dark emptiness …

What's he doing? Why did he go and search for the bolt from his rifle? Because the gun's a museum piece? No. Why did he bring the gun on board? To balance the power? To challenge? Was it because of his fear of losing his job? He will not go on the dole! What's wrong with being on the dole? Couldn't he get a job on another ship if he wanted to? A man with all his experience? Why is he so afraid of losing his job? Is it because he'd lose money? Is it pride that's getting him all mixed up?

Or is it the fear of finally losing control of his drinking? The fear of having all the time he needs to drink himself to death? *Why should he drink himself to death?*

Because he knows it'll happen and he can't stop it. But of course he can stop it. *Just phone the AA helpline.*

No. The thing is he won't phone. Or will he?

Did he take the gun onto the ship because he's afraid of death?

Or was it because he longs to die?

Life is nothing but a hopeless dance on a high wire and we all lose our balance sooner or later and fall into the empty abyss.

Everything goes black for a few seconds and …

The first officer slams against the black hull of the ship, his mouth gaping and his lungs sucking in air; the briny seawater runs out his nose and his salt-filled eyes open wide. The fingers of his right hand clutch the lowest bar of the railing and the flaming pain in his arm fills his head like a choir of angels.

He's hanging on by a thread of his own flesh.

What a pleasure it is to feel how the steel pulls his body, presses the skin and bones of his fingers, stretches his nerves, muscles, joints and sinews and conjures up suffering.

Methúsalem swings his body forwards and manages to get both hands on the railing. While the ship rolls to port he hangs there unsupported and half submerged, wriggling like a mouse that's trying to get out of a galvanised washtub. He grits his teeth and waits for the ship to right itself and roll to starboard. When that finally happens he climbs up to the gunwale, slides under the railing and onto the deck.

'Great God in heaven!' he cries, crawls on his hands and knees to the stairs and hugs the bottom steps.

In the infirmary Ási and Big John are standing by the bed of Jónas, who's blinking and appears to be regaining consciousness.

They gave him a shot of morphine before they checked him over and attended to his injuries on Friday. His left arm is broken at the wrist, his left ankle is cracked or broken, as is his left knee and probably his hip besides. He's badly bruised on his back and the back of his neck, but as for any smaller broken bones, or any internal bleeding, they can't tell.

The second officer is lying on his back with splints and bandages on his left limbs, a collar bracing his neck and a cold cloth on his forehead.

'Water!' he whispers, licking dry lips.

'Yes, we'll help you, mate,' says Ási removing the wet facecloth that has become warm after only a few minutes on Jónas's hot forehead.

John helps the second mate sit up a bit while Ási puts a glass to his lips and helps him sip the cold water.

'There, not too much,' says Ási and he puts the glass down before drying Jónas's lips with a clean cloth.

'Don't overdo it,' says Big John, letting Jónas sink slowly

back down on the bed. 'You're pretty seriously injured.'

'What happened?' asks Ási when Jónas opens his eyes properly and looks around the white-painted room.

'He pushed me,' says Jónas slowly. 'He pulled me out and threw me down onto D-deck.'

'Who?' asks Big John.

'Satan,' says Jónas with a grimace.

'You could have died, man!' says Ási, drying sweat off the officer's forehead.

'He meant to kill me!' says Jónas with a tearful look at his two mates.

'Why?' asks John.

'He was threatening me … I knew who he was,' says Jónas, closing his eyes. 'But I couldn't keep quiet any longer … Not after he cut the wires. I had to expose him! That's why he tried to kill me.'

'Take it easy,' says Ási, stroking Jónas's cheek. 'He's been locked up.'

'That's good,' says Jónas with a weak smile.

'When did he push you over?' asks John, scratching his beard. 'After lunch?'

'Yes, I …' Jónas clears his throat.

'It must have been,' says Ási, patting Jónas on the head like a little kid. 'He ate some fish with me and then went up at about twelve-thirty.'

'That doesn't fit,' says John with a shake of his head. 'The guy had told us who he was. So why should he silence Jónas?'

'He just attacked me,' says Jónas with a sigh.

'The man is obviously insane,' says Ási, wetting the cloth before again laying it on the second mate's forehead.

'Yes, but it still doesn't fit,' says John, shuffling his feet by the bed. 'When you went up after lunch we were just about to arrest the guy – if we hadn't done it already. When did he have time to push you off the deck?'

Jónas moves his lips as if he's about to speak, but he doesn't make a sound until he produces a long, drawn-out moan which at first is reminiscent of mental anguish, but then turns to the familiar sound of physical pain.

'Easy, pal! Easy,' says Ási, trying to calm the officer. 'You've got broken bones here and there. I'll give you another shot.'

'I'll look in on you around noon,' mutters Big John and starts to head for the door.

'Have you spoken to Methúsalem?' Ási says as he unpacks a fresh syringe.

'No. Why?' asks John, looking away.

'Haven't we dropped the plan of killing the engines?' asks Ási, fishing a fresh needle out of a tin box. 'I mean, what with the weather and —'

'Ási!' says John, stomping his foot and nodding his head towards Jónas, who's breathing fast and open mouthed and appears to be asleep.

'Oh, sorry!' says Ási quietly, putting the needle on the syringe. 'What I meant to say was something sort of general about engines and maintenance and things like that, not —'

'Ási?' says John, opening the door.

'What?' asks Ási, waving the empty syringe.

'I'm off.'

'Would you mind making me some coffee?' Ási says as he draws the morphine solution into the syringe.

'Yeah, no bother,' murmurs John and he hurries out before Ási sticks the needle in his patient.

Out in the corridor John runs across Methúsalem, who has just come in, soaking wet.

'Look at you, man!' says Big John, staring open mouthed at his shipmate. 'What've you been doing?'

'Just checking the weather,' Methúsalem says, snuffling rain and seawater up his nose. His face is red and his left cheek swollen after the captain's punch. His left eye is sinking into his head, the skin on his cheekbone is blue-black and the teeth in his upper gum ache.

'Shouldn't you be up in the bridge by now?'

'Yeah, I'm on my way up.' Methúsalem pulls the hood of his raincoat off his soaking head. 'I'm just going to hang up my wet-weather gear downstairs.'

'Do that,' says John and steps into the mess. Then he stops and calls to the first officer.

'Hey, Methúsalem!'

'Yes?' Methúsalem turns around on the staircase leading down to A-deck.

'This foolishness is all over, isn't it?' asks Big John with a scowl.

'What foolishness?' asks Methúsalem, his salt-reddened eyes wide.

'All that gun shit,' says John with a hefty cough. 'Now we change course and try to make friends with the Old Man – right?'

'I guess so,' mutters Methúsalem, avoiding the chief engineer's accusing look.

'I don't know what I was thinking,' says John, sighing. 'But from now on I'm not taking part in any fucking mess-ups! If we get laid off, then we protest it in the traditional and legal way and fight for our rights with the help of the union. Understood?'

'Yeah, understood,' says Methúsalem, his head hanging. He carries on down the stairs and Big John disappears into the mess.

After hanging up his gear down in the storeroom and turning his boots upside down on the boot stand, Methúsalem makes his way up the stairs, his feet soaking, his thighs, back and chest all wet.

He'll have to put on some dry clothes before he relieves the captain on the bridge.

Methúsalem Sigurðsson's steps are heavy and he looks nothing like his usual forceful self. He is, after all, weighed down by thoughts as dark as the storm that rages around the ship.

Only ten minutes ago he was hanging by one hand over the side of a ship in a raging sea, looking death in the eye; faced with his final hour, he realised something.

Without his job he would die.

During shore time he lies in bed in an alcoholic blackout, floating through the widths of oblivion and nightmares. When he comes to he reaches for the glass on the bedside table and knocks back its contents. Then he staggers out to the kitchen and makes another drink.

Vodka and Coke, half and half.

And knocks back its contents. Then all that's left is to make another drink and stagger back to the bedroom with it before he loses consciousness again.

When he wakes up he reaches for the glass and knocks back its contents.

Sometimes he has to piss. Sometimes he has to puke. But mostly he just wakes up, drinks and makes another drink.

And then he falls into oblivion once again:

Boom, boom, boom …

Until three days before the next tour. Then bells ring in his head. Then it's time to sober up.

And so he pukes and then he weeps. Then he enters a true hell that seems never-ending: shaking, cramps, hallucinations, chills and a temporary insanity whose roots keep reaching deeper.

But he doesn't give up. He will turn up for work. He's too proud to sink so low as to give in to Bacchus.

Until the next shore time, that is.

More than once he has been hospitalised with alcoholic poisoning and he has kept off the booze for the odd week, the odd month – twice, even, for more than a year. But he's never really *quit* drinking. He's *meant* to quit; he's *dreamt* of quitting; yet he's never taken that final step of seeking help for his alcohol problem. He has, in fact, never admitted to himself or anyone else that he has a problem.

He has never stood up, opened his mouth and rolled the

heavy words from the mouth of his heart's cave: 'My name is Methúsalem Sigurðsson and I am an alcoholic.'

Why not?

Maybe he's too proud to admit to the weakness. Too proud to seek help. But maybe he's afraid of what's hidden in the darkness of his heart, of what will reveal itself when the abyss opens wide. Maybe he's afraid of finding what he's been fleeing from all these years.

Emptiness.

On board the ship Methúsalem Sigurðsson has duties. He has a role to play. He knows what he has to do and how to do it. He is part of a united and organised whole. He is a man chosen to fill a particular space; he cancels out a particular emptiness.

He is Methúsalem, first officer.

Without this 4000-tonne iron monster, though, he's like a cog without a machine. A dead object: useless, of no consequence. Perhaps he, just like the ship he sails in, is a soulless iron monster that has no idea where it came from or where it's going. Ships have no independent will, and that which has neither will nor thought of any kind has no aim, unless it is directed by someone who thinks and understands, as an arrow is directed by an archer.

Methúsalem directs the ship he is in but he has no idea who it is who directs him. Is it someone who wants to save him from ruin? Or someone who wants to run him aground?

Is he the pawn of evil spirits? A favourite of the angels? Or just a ghost ship adrift on the sea of life?

He doesn't know.

And maybe he doesn't want to know.

The first mate stops outside his cabin on E-deck and looks at the fingers of his right hand, which, only a few minutes before, grasped the railing and saved him from certain death.

As if by accident.

He was face to face with death and survived. *That was no accident!*

Someone seems to be watching over him. Someone believes he should live.

Methúsalem Sigurðsson has been given another chance, and he's not going to let it slip away. There's too much at stake.

This is a question of life or death. Isn't it time he gave life a go?

'My name is Methúsalem Sigurðsson,' he says loudly, then clears his throat, 'and I'm an alcoholic!'

He smiles crookedly and turns the doorknob, but the door doesn't move and his right shoulder slams against it.

'What the hell!'

He puts his weight against the door and pushes hard. The door opens a crack and a moaning draught forces its way out into the corridor.

Did he leave a window open?

The wind is whirling around his cabin, blowing things all over. The curtains are torn, there is broken glass on the floor and everything is afloat in rain and seawater.

Methúsalem squeezes through the doorway and lets go of the door, which slams into its frame.

'What the ...' Methúsalem stares at the window, which gapes above the bed like the mouth of a creature with a bottomless stomach and teeth of triangular shards of glass.

And the creature hisses and spits wind, sea and rain in the face of the first officer, who half closes his eyes and walks across the wet rug.

Why is the glass in the window broken?

Methúsalem pulls the blanket off the wet bed, bunches it together and is about to shove it in the open window when one of the glass triangles comes loose from the window frame and shoots at a rate of knots straight towards him. He barely manages to close his eyes before it embeds itself in his right cheekbone.

Methúsalem stops still, then touches the splinter of glass that's sticking out of his face. He can feel blood running down his cheek, but the cold wind directs it to the side, into his right ear and his hair.

'Good God,' he murmurs, blinking. He bunches the blanket more tightly and shoves the bundle in the window, managing to shut out the wind and rain.

Silence.

The wind dies down; the temperature rises; the flying tatters of curtain come to rest; the blood runs under his collar and water drips from the table, shelves and cupboards.

Methúsalem goes into the bathroom and looks at himself in the mirror. The glass shard is stuck fast in his cheekbone, poking into the air like a tiny shark's fin.

He pulls the glass from the wound. Then he disinfects the wound before closing it with sticking plaster. Once that's done, he cleans off the dried blood with a warm washcloth.

'Well, I'll be blowed,' says Methúsalem as he undresses in the bathroom. Luckily, his dirty clothes from the day before are still on the hook on the back of the bathroom door. All his other clothes must be wet or damp, like everything else in the cabin.

The first officer dries himself with a clean towel, splashes himself with aftershave and dresses hurriedly. He runs a comb through his hair, brushes his teeth and, finally, slips into his shoes before stepping over the bathroom threshold onto the soaking rug.

Methúsalem looks sadly around his cabin, then sighs and shakes his head, turns round and puts his hand on the cold, wet doorknob.

The door looks terrible from the inside. It's soaking wet and covered with glass shards which stick out like spikes.

Methúsalem opens the door to the corridor, but comes to a halt just inside the threshold when his toes hit something on the floor.

He looks down and the minute he sees what's lying there on the wet rug, surrounded by broken glass, strips of seaweed, sand and pebbles, it feels as if his heart stops beating and his blood runs cold.

There it is. The bolt from the rifle.

'Good God.'

★ ★ ★

Guðmundur Berndsen is sitting in the captain's chair and staring through the salt-encrusted windows of the bridge. He's put the ship on autopilot and has been sitting there without moving for four hours, since he last stood up to make coffee.

That coffee has long since turned to overboiled tar without the captain having even tasted it.

Rúnar turned up for his bridge watch promptly at three in the morning but Guðmundur sent him back down half an hour later. He's not in the mood to converse or spend time with men who disobey orders, engage in intrigue and take power into their own hands when their superior officer turns his back.

Over the weather deck floats a yellow haze reminiscent of dry-ice fog. It's salt spray that takes on this ghostly aura in the beams of the searchlights. The ship rolls, hovers and pitches in turns, so the captain is alternately lifted off his chair, as if weightless, or is pressed into it with so much force he can hardly breathe.

He doesn't allow these extremes to disturb him, though, but steers the ship to the south without having any real idea where it is situated on the globe. While the GPS is dead he knows neither how fast they are sailing nor how far they are drifting off course. Heading south has limited significance in itself if their starting point is uncertain – which it most certainly is.

Once the storm calms the captain can work out the ship's position with a sextant, a watch and a calculator, but until then he must keep calm, trust his own judgement and hope for the best.

Sailing in a violent storm is like flying blind. Little by

little what you see baffles your senses until your imagination overpowers what you know.

His eyes tell the captain that he's going in circles but the compass says differently: the ship is clearly heading south. If the captain were to abandon reason he would stop believing the compass, insist it was broken and start going in circles himself.

Guðmundur's eyes also maintain that the ship is sailing backwards, not forwards. The GPS could correct that misunderstanding within minutes, but without the navigation device the captain has to trust the experience he has gained from earlier battles with the weather in the open sea.

His guess is that the ship is struggling forwards at about five to eight knots. As to sideways drift, it's hard to say, but he's hoping it isn't more than three knots.

However, it's possible that the sideways drift is greater than their forward movement. In that case the distance they have to sail grows by that difference every hour, instead of getting shorter. In that case it would be better to remain in place, tread water in the roaring sea, maintain a kind of deadlock with the storm while it's raging.

Guðmundur's eyes tell him the ship is getting nowhere, and maybe they're right, but going by the butterflies in his stomach and the dizziness in his head, the ship is flying along on the tops of the waves at three times its top speed.

The captain no longer knows what to think. He's come to the conclusion that it's best not to think at all. When rational thought fails, common sense tells you it's wisest to stop thinking. Irrational thoughts lead to delusions, mistakes and temporary insanity.

So long as Guðmundur does nothing, he'll do no harm either. He's sailing south and that's all there is to it. South is all he knows. It's not much, but it's so much more than nothing.

South.

Guðmundur stares out the salt-caked windows and thinks about only what he sees.

There's a yellow haze over the weather deck, a briny mist that swirls like dry ice on a rock band's stage, obscuring everything.

'This storm has been raised by magic,' murmurs Guðmundur Berndsen, blinking, his eyes bloodshot, dry and swollen after staring for so long.

'Good morning,' says Methúsalem as he enters the bridge. The captain looks at his watch for the first time in hours and sees that it's twenty-three minutes past six.

'You're late,' says Guðmundur, getting out of the chair. He then grabs one of the knobs on the instrument panel to keep from falling when the ship suddenly rolls to port, with the attendant creaks and shockwaves.

Methúsalem holds onto a side table by the chart room and makes his way over the carpeted floor of the bridge. As the ship rights itself the men both seize the opportunity to reach the middle of the bridge without bumping into or knocking each other over.

Guðmundur gets a grip by the chart room and Methúsalem climbs into the captain's chair.

'The autopilot's on,' says Guðmundur.

'So I see.'

The men don't look directly at each other, but each is well aware of the uncomfortable nearness of the other.

Guðmundur is angry that Methúsalem went behind his back and challenged him, and he's sorry to have hit him with the stock of his gun – really sorry.

Methúsalem is about to lose his mind with fear. He's afraid of the gun that's waiting for him in his cabin because he knows he'll use it.

The only thing he's not sure of is whether he'll use it against himself or someone else.

He has a vision of putting the barrel in his mouth, closing his eyes and pulling the trigger.

And that vision frightens him – frightens him terribly.

But he also has a vision of aiming the barrel at Guðmundur's head and then slowly and surely pulling the sensitive trigger and enjoying his ultimate power with hate in his eyes and a devilish smile on his lips.

And this vision is driving him crazy.

'I'm having a little meeting in my cabin at two o'clock,' says Guðmundur as he takes hold of the doorknob to go into the corridor. 'Me, you, Rúnar and John.'

'All right,' says Methúsalem, sinking into the leather chair as the ship lifts itself.

'We have to bury the hatchet,' says Guðmundur, opening the door. 'We can't go on like this.'

'I know,' says Methúsalem, looking over his shoulder. At the same moment the ship drops down and he lifts up from the chair.

For just a moment they look each other in the eye and for that instant they feel the companionship of shipmates, captain and first officer, comrades in seas calm and stormy.

It's going to be all right, thinks Guðmundur. *We'll talk, sort things out and shake hands.*

It's going to be all right, thinks Methúsalem. *I'll just throw the fucking gun in the sea. Won't I?*

Then the ship slams into a wave so hard that Methúsalem almost flies out of the chair, the door closes with a slam, Guðmundur loses hold of the knob and falls to his knees.

Boom, boom, boom …

The noise is such you'd think the ship was breaking in two, and it rolls so powerfully to port that it's hard not to believe that the movement will continue and the ship capsize within seconds.

The men in the bridge have seen and heard all these things before, though; they know their ship and don't doubt all will be well, which is why they don't even bother to give a sigh of relief when the gigantic hull quietly emerges from the breaker and slowly rights itself, like a whale surfacing.

'See you, then,' says Guðmundur before he gets up and again opens the door.

'Okay,' says Methúsalem, grabbing hold of the chair's arms as the ship pitches down off yet another wave, like a roller-coaster car starting down the steepest slope.

The captain leaves the bridge and closes the door; the first officer sits motionless in the captain's chair and stares out the salt-encrusted windows of the bridge.

Over the weather deck floats a yellow haze.

XXV

Christ, but he can't be bothered with this!

Methúsalem knocks twice on the door of the captain's cabin.

His face aches, he's tired, hungry and sleepy after his eight-hour stint in the bridge, and he can't be bothered to sit down and talk about something that was meant to replace meaningless yakking.

In the beginning was the word, but the words 'let's mutiny' are now past their use-by date.

They brought guns aboard so they wouldn't have to talk. They were aiming for action, not words.

Weren't they?

But their actions had turned to dust, more or less. They had gone too fast, too far, and maybe given up too easily when they met resistance. By placing a 'bad apple' on the ship the owners had managed to create an atmosphere of suspicion and confusion, weakening the solidarity of the crew.

All the energy of the mutineering faction had been spent on finding and then restraining that dangerous foreign body, which had also meant the plans of the gang of five had been revealed sooner than they'd wanted.

While that terrorist was on the loose the mutineering faction couldn't concentrate on the interests of the crew, and once the terrorist had been overpowered those interests were overshadowed by the fact that there were mutineers.

Their adversaries had manoeuvred them into the position of ending on fool's mate, whatever they did or didn't do. They're a piece of work, those fucking owners, that's for sure!

Secrecy had been their trump card and now it had been knocked out of their hands. Once they lost the mask of the anonymous rebel, men were embarrassed when faced with the authority they had meant to overthrow.

An awed respect for the captain runs in seamen's blood.

John refuses to kill the engines and Rúnar, Sæli and Ási have gone soft.

The mutiny was stillborn. The company has won. The lay-offs are coming.

Aren't they?

'Come in!'

Methúsalem opens the door, breathes in through flared nostrils and walks, with spine erect, into the cabin.

He intends to listen with an open mind to what the captain has to say but he is also determined not to be steamrollered.

It's one thing to lose, another to be humiliated in front of witnesses.

'Have a seat,' says the captain to the first mate, pointing to the couch, where John and Rúnar are sitting, near the wall.

'What's happened to your face, man?' says Rúnar when he sees the bloodstained bandage on Methúsalem's right cheek.

'It's nothing,' Methúsalem mutters, taking a seat on the couch closer to the door. 'I just cut myself.'

'That looks bad,' says John, who's sitting in the middle to Rúnar's right and Methúsalem's left.

'It'll mend before I marry.' Methúsalem offers the old saying as he touches the hardening bandage with his right fingertips. His swollen face twitches.

'Comrades,' says Guðmundur Berndsen with a slight cough. He stands, balancing, in front of the table, his hands locked together behind his back. Skuggi sits behind him, his head on one side.

The three men go silent and watch the captain, who lifts his chin and stares intently at the wall above their heads while he speaks, as if he's addressing a huge crowd – or no one at all.

'All I'm asking is that we work in peace until we get to Suriname,' he says and leans forward some thirty degrees to compensate for the ship's movement. 'The minute we dock I will phone home and speak to the company director. I will ask him about the alleged lay-offs and if they are, in fact, planned I will demand that he reconsider that decision.'

Guðmundur lowers his chin and looks at each of the three men in turn, as if emphasising his words by means of personal contact and authoritative silence.

Is he telling the truth? Yes. He *is* going to phone home and attempt to have the decision to lay off the whole crew reversed, or at least postponed.

Does he expect to succeed? No. He has himself already resigned from the company, so his word and opinion no longer have any influence.

At best they would listen to him for the sake of courtesy; at worst they would take revenge for his meddling by breaking his termination contract or putting off his pension payments for a few years.

He is simply buying himself peace – possibly at a high price.

'What if they refuse?' asks Methúsalem.

'Then I refuse to load the ship,' Guðmundur replies immediately.

'But what if they threaten to fire you too?' says Methúsalem, leaning back into the couch. He can feel something hard behind the cushion.

'Then I resign on the spot,' says Guðmundur firmly.

'And abandon the ship?' Methúsalem shoves his right hand behind the cushion to find out what's poking into his back.

'Yes,' says Guðmundur with a nod. He has now told so many lies that his face is red and his temples damp with sweat.

'And us at the same time, then?' asks Methúsalem, his face splitting into a grin because he has made the captain talk himself into a corner. But his humourless grin changes suddenly to a look of fear when his reaching fingers feel rounded glass behind the cushion.

'What?' says Guðmundur, blinking. Damn it! He'd been over this conversation in his head time after time, forwards and backwards, and practised answers to every conceivable and inconceivable question, yet he had allowed that fucker Methúsalem to trick him like that.

Silence.

Methúsalem can't think clearly. He feels the flask with his right hand and listens to the liquid gurgling inside the thick glass, or inside his head – he's not sure. He sees double, smells the alcohol and moves his swollen tongue around his dry mouth.

'Methúsalem?' says Big John, gently nudging the first mate.

'Yes?' Methúsalem presses his back even tighter against the cushions, jamming the flask and his hand against the back of the couch.

'You asked whether he would abandon us, the crew,' says John as he watches Methúsalem turn alternately red and pale.

Silence.

'It won't come to that,' says Guðmundur, clearing his throat.

'How can you be sure?' asks Rúnar.

Guðmundur says something; Methúsalem sees his lips moving, but he can't hear what he's saying.

The only thing he can hear is his own heartbeat, echoing like drum beats inside his empty head.

Boom, boom, boom ...

He pulls the flask out from under the cushion and slides it under his waistband at the back. Then he untucks his shirt and hides the flask with the shirt.

Is it vodka? Rum? Gin? Whiskey? Cognac?

Cognac. He's certain it's cognac.

'Methúsalem?'

Silence.

'I just want to say one thing before I leave this company,' says Methúsalem, standing up from the couch. 'I'm satisfied with what's been said here. Guðmundur is a good man and I trust his word absolutely. That's all I have to say.'

Methúsalem has hardly finished speaking when the ship is hit by a heavy breaker. Guðmundur loses his balance and ends up flat on the floor, and John and Rúnar are lifted from the couch, their thighs hitting the edge of the table, then they thump down hard on their bottoms to the floor between the couch and the table.

Methúsalem, on the other hand, doesn't move. He stands steady on both legs, his back to the door, and watches his crewmates get tossed around the cabin. He's wearing a foolish, puzzled expression, as if he can't understand why they're acting like that.

You'd think the first officer was suspended in some kind of vacuum beyond the natural laws of our world.

★ ★ ★

After the meeting in his cabin, Ási takes Guðmundur a message that Jónas wants to see him. The captain asks Rúnar to assume his watch in the bridge while he quickly goes down to see the second officer in the infirmary.

'How're you feeling?' asks Guðmundur, taking a seat on a stool by the bed of his second mate, who looks and acts totally miserable.

'Well, I'm in agony. The drugs have some effect on the pain, but —'

'You wanted to see me?'

'Yes,' says Jónas, closing his eyes and lying back on the sweaty pillow. 'I'm worried about the situation on board.'

'You're not the only one. But I just had a good meeting with the crew, and the way things stand now —'

'I want you to stake out the ship,' Jónas interrupts, opening his eyes again. 'I want you to put a man down to guard the engine room and another out here in the corridor. I'm afraid that —'

'But haven't they already captured the saboteur?' says the captain with a scowl.

'Yeah. Maybe. But you never know. I don't trust anyone, Guðmundur. Except you, of course. And I certainly don't trust Methúsalem Sigurðsson, to tell you the truth.'

'It's exactly these suspicions that I'm trying to get rid of.' Guðmundur takes a deep breath to calm the anger boiling inside him. 'We simply can't have all this friction, and men plotting behind closed doors.'

'Yes, but —'

'Who am I supposed to put on guard, if nobody's to be trusted?' asks the captain, raising his voice. 'And who's supposed to steer the ship if everyone's on guard all over the place?'

'I'm just afraid of more trouble, that's all,' Jónas says softly, his voice trembling. 'You could let Sæli and Rúnar off their normal duties and get them to guard the engine. Then we'd be sure that —'

'I'm not listening to this rubbish!' Guðmundur stands up. 'Why should I put a guard on the engine?'

'Methúsalem is capable of anything,' says Jónas, closing his eyes again. 'I know what he's like. He hasn't given up, believe me.'

'I'll take care of Methúsalem. You just look after yourself,' says the captain and he leaves the infirmary.

★ ★ ★

Why not?

On the table in Methúsalem's cabin stands a flask of cognac that glitters like gold, like spiritual honey; a shining vessel full of bodily warmth and dreamlike light! This flask is the only good thing in the whole fucking ship – in the whole world, if it comes to that. Methúsalem sits on a folded towel on the damp couch and stares at the flask. He squeezes out some saliva, sticks out a slimy tongue and tries to wet his parched lips.

There are towels on the windowsill, towels on the floor, soaking-wet towels *everywhere*, and *everything* is wet and damp and the cabin smells musty, and it's only a matter of time before this *dump* becomes uninhabitable due to mould, germs and other horrors.

From the broken window hangs the soaking-wet bedspread like dead flesh keeping the light *out* but letting the wind *in*. Everything is as miserable as can be and Methúsalem's face aches, he's shivering with cold, he's hungry, he's tired, and he feels *awful*.

In the face of all this horror stands the flask, like the Holy Grail, like a delicate candle flame in a world of darkness, cold and whirlwinds.

A guiding light? An hallucination?

Methúsalem Sigurðsson isn't certain what he *should* do, but he knows what he *has* to do. He has to have one swig of cognac, if only to get some warmth round his heart and dull his headache, reduce the pain a little. He already feels better just thinking about it, so there's nothing for it but to take a swig to make the thought a reality, not let it vanish like some fucking figment of his imagination.

Why should he lose out on feeling better when his only prospect is discomfort? Discomfort is an exception to the natural condition while comfort is the natural condition.

'I need a glass,' murmurs Methúsalem as he stands up from the couch.

'*I need a glass!*' What was the question?

He has neither decided to have a drink nor deny himself one, but he needs a glass because he knows that he *will* have a drink, without really being conscious of knowing it.

The first officer goes into the bathroom, where a glass in a copper stand on the wall by the sink holds a toothbrush and a tube of toothpaste.

He puts the toothbrush and tube in the sink and washes the glass with hot water, then rinses it with cold.

The glass is clear, middle sized, with a heavy bottom.

He dries the glass with a clean towel but stops rubbing the smooth glass with the white cotton when he suddenly remembers the psychiatric drugs he washes down twice a day with a sip of cold water from this same glass.

Damn it! Did he take a pill this morning? Or last night? When did he last take a pill? Was it yesterday morning? Or the day before yesterday? Or the day before that? Has he stopped taking the drugs? Is he so forgetful? Or is his short-term memory letting him down? Is he taking the drugs without remembering?

Methúsalem puts down the glass, opens the cupboard above the sink and takes out the package of pills.

Lithium citrate – a drug for bipolar disorder, 500 mg, take one twice a day, five aluminium sheets in a pack, twenty pills per sheet, a total of 100 pills.

Eight pills are gone from the first sheet but the other four are untouched.

Eight pills, four days. When did he begin on this package – two days before they left? Four?

Lithium citrate is a strong psychiatric drug which is meant to prevent extreme wave action in your head, a sort of chemical Jesus that calms the storm of thoughts, evens out the difference between hyperactivity and depression and, thus, creates a kind of calm in the oceans of the mind.

This spiritual calm takes its toll, however. Common side effects are nausea, diarrhoea, frequent urination, thirst and endless fucking tiredness, not to mention the humiliation of having to take psychiatric drugs like some nutcase or madman.

'Fucking poison!'

Methúsalem quickly washes the pills down the drain, one

after another, and then places the empty package back in the cupboard, as if to cover up his 'crime' or deceive someone.

Who?

The moment Methúsalem Sigurðsson closes the cupboard door his own face appears in the mirror, and he quickly averts his eyes – but not quickly enough.

He saw the gleam in his eyes and he saw the abyss beyond the flickering gleam.

But he pretends to have seen neither the dream nor the bottomless dark. He leaves the bathroom, glass in hand; he heads for the couch expressionless and he sits on the couch without so much as a glance towards the flask.

He acts as if he has no idea what he's about to do and even pretends to whistle a little tune to increase his self-deception.

So? Can't a man whistle?

He watches his hands do what they're doing, just as if he has no power over them and doesn't, in fact, have any idea what they're up to.

Hey, how about that! They're pouring cognac in a glass! For me!

He could just as well stand in front of a mirror and watch the rifle barrel disappear into the mouth of his reflection and the mirrored forefinger pull the trigger, as if he were at home in his living room, watching a thriller on the TV.

Then he laughs at such a childish comparison.

And that laugh is so mirthless as to be almost terrifying.

It *is* terrifying.

'Laughter lengthens life,' says Methúsalem Sigurðsson, lifting his glass as he laughs at his own joke. 'I'll drink to that!'

Cheers!

Who said cheers?

'Did you say cheers?' Methúsalem says, putting down his glass and licking his wet lips. 'Who are you? Eh?'

He rocks back and forth and stares at the glass, which is empty except for a copper-coloured drop that runs down the inside then spreads out and somehow disappears on the bottom.

What!

'Who drank from that glass?' asks Methúsalem, savouring the sweet aftertaste of the cognac. 'Did I drink the glass? Are you joking? Who's joking? Eh?'

What's going on? Is he going crazy? Or is he drunk from one sip?

'You're not going crazy at all,' Methúsalem says quietly and sniffs carelessly as he pours another glass.

Just the wrong man in the wrong place at the wrong time.

Wrong man — that is, not the right man, I mean! Nothing wrong with me! Maybe a bit of a fool sometimes, like stupid, but not a fool like crazy or anything, eh?

'Stupid? Me? I think not!'

Methúsalem coughs. Is he getting a sore throat? That won't do. Cognac kills germs, that's been proven over and over.

I'd better ...

'Hey!' says Methúsalem, leaning forward and examining the glass.

Empty! It's empty again! There's something eerie in this bloody cabin. Is somebody drinking my stuff here?

'Do you know what one rabbit said to the other rabbit?' Methúsalem says as he fills the glass a third time.

No. I don't know.

'You don't know?' says Methúsalem with a crooked smile.

Who doesn't know? The rabbit?

'Are you feeling as eerie as I am?' says Methúsalem. He tosses back the contents of the glass.

Then it's as if he catches on to the joke. The cognac stops halfway down and splutters out his nose.

'Ha, ha, ha!'

Feeling eerie! Like with big ears! Rabbit's ears, see! Ay, me!

'This is some bad party!' says Methúsalem, wiping snot and saliva off his face with the back of his hand.

And speaking of bad parties ... there's the bolt from his rifle!

'You're quite the mischief-maker,' Methúsalem says as he reaches for the bolt, which is folded in a clean handkerchief.

He unfolds the cloth and picks up the bolt, which is heavy and cold but still as good as new.

'You just need to be rubbed with a bit of oil,' Methúsalem coos as he turns the bolt every which way and rubs dried salt off it with the cloth.

Methúsalem puts down the bolt, stands up and walks on unsteady legs across to the wardrobe.

'Bloody waves.'

He steadies himself on the right side of the wardrobe as he opens the left.

He takes out the rifle, a box of shells and a little jar of gun oil, closes the wardrobe, then shuffles back across the damp towels and the soaking rug to sit on the couch again.

What do you know? Somebody's filled the glass!

He wets a corner of the handkerchief with oil and carefully rubs the part of the bolt that goes in the breech of the rifle. Then he slides the bolt into place, moves it back and forth and finally loads the rifle, shell by shell.

The first mate's movements are slow, methodical and focused. His fingers handle the shells with the gentle deftness of a magician; his pupils widen like the aperture of a camera and don't move even a fraction of a millimetre, his mouth half gapes open and the tip of his tongue lies still on his lower lip.

But the minute the final shell is in place, this bizarre look of concentration disappears from the face of Methúsalem Sigurðsson; it is a look that contains both the willpower of an evil-doer and the true simplicity of someone dim-witted.

There!

Methúsalem grins and handles the weapon like a proud soldier before he puts it down on the couch.

You need more than a single clown with a shotgun to disarm a real man.

I'll drink to that!

No! Hello! Knock it off!

'Am I maybe losing my mind?' Methúsalem says, picking up the glass in his right hand and the nearly empty bottle in his left.

He drinks a drop or two and then shakes the bottle.

What's going on? Two drinks? Three? Has he finished the bottle?

'Well, it wasn't full,' he mutters and pours half of what's left into his glass.

It was about half full, just a bit over. The Old Man's been hitting the bottle, all right! Smuggling liquor on board the ship. Finished half a flask in just a few days.

'Here's to the Old Man!' Methúsalem lifts his glass, exchanges looks with nothing and nods to his invisible drinking companion before he throws back the cognac.

Cheers to you!

Cheers!

No. Why should he be drinking to the fucking old bully? The Old Man? He's a dinosaur! A weakling! A boss-lover! Says he's going to resign in support of the crew. Yeah, sure!

'*I'll leave the ship.*' *Blah, blah, blah.*

You just go to hell, liar! Ha!

'Just a fucking liar,' Methúsalem says, pouring the rest of the cognac.

He leans back on the couch and breathes out as he sinks into the damp leather.

His eyes no longer glitter. And they stare at nothing, they're like empty sockets.

What?

'Nothing.'

Wouldn't it be the thing to sabotage the main engine and shake up the lot of them and create proper chaos, then shoot the captain in the head, throw his body overboard and take command of the leaderless ship?

'What?'

Nothing.

What's in the glass? There's nothing in the glass! Who drank from the glass?

Was it you?

'It was me.'

The flask lies open on the table. It's empty. It's full of nothing. Methúsalem lies on the couch. His eyes are open but he's not awake.

He sees black, he thinks black, he is black.

Blackout, man!

'EH?'

And he's grinning like a skull.

★ ★ ★

It's eleven minutes after six on a Saturday afternoon when Ási, Big John, Rúnar and Sæli meet in the mess to exchange information and go over the situation.

'I spoke to that Satan before you took him up to the forecastle,' says Sæli, holding onto the rack above the cooker. 'The shipping company didn't send him here, that's for sure. He has nothing to gain and that's why I don't think it's likely he did the damage to the ship. Why should he do that if he gains nothing from it?'

'Hard to say,' says Rúnar, who is standing in the doorway to make sure nobody eavesdrops. 'But quite apart from who this guy is or what he's doing here, there are at least two things I don't understand. *If* he isn't Jónas's brother-in-law, why did Jónas keep quiet about it? And if he *isn't* Jónas's brother-in-law, where *is* his brother-in-law?'

'Good point,' says Ási, leaning up against the fridge and moving his match from one corner of his mouth to the other. 'I think Jónas has something to hide. There's something strange about that accident. Something about his story that doesn't fit.'

'Jónas does have something to hide,' says John, grabbing

hold of the table as the ship pitches. 'But what it can be I can't imagine. If this Satan isn't the saboteur, then who cut the wires up on the roof? Jónas?'

'I can't quite see that,' says Rúnar.

'Somebody did it,' says Sæli. 'Anybody could have cut the wires, but why that person did it is another matter entirely.'

'Methúsalem maintains that the shipping company's behind it,' says Ási. 'He says the company's the only party that gains something from the ship being out of touch. While they can't hear from us, we can't be protesting.'

'Speaking of Methúsalem,' says Rúnar with a look at John, 'what was he thinking at that meeting earlier?'

'Dunno,' mutters John and shakes his head. 'I knocked on his door just now, but he didn't answer.'

'What did he do?' asks Sæli.

'He kind of went blank. It was as if he lost all connection to his surroundings.'

'Maybe somebody cut his wires,' says Ási with a grin.

'Then he just went,' says Rúnar. 'He just stood up, declared his full support for the captain and left!'

'There was something weird about it,' John says. 'That he should just suddenly stand up and declare his support for the Old Man, after everything that went before. I didn't find it convincing, to tell you the truth.'

'It was as if he was drunk,' Rúnar adds.

'Yeah, I know,' says John, looking at Rúnar. 'That's exactly what I was thinking – "Is the fucker drunk?"'

'Was he drunk?' asks Sæli.

'No,' says Rúnar. 'But, still, there was something not right about him.'

'Who can a guy trust?' says Sæli.

Silence.

'I suggest we put our trust in the Old Man,' says John with a cough. 'As things stand now I think that's the wisest thing for us to do.'

'But the lay-offs?' asks Sæli.

'As I said,' says John, 'I think we need to trust the Old Man. I don't want to take part in any more mutiny, that's for sure.'

'You and me both,' says Rúnar. 'I agree with John. We drop this foolishness and trust the Old Man.'

'All right,' says Sæli with a sniff.

'Ási?' says John, looking at the cook.

'I've always trusted Guðmundur,' says Ási, biting on his match. 'It's the shipping company I don't like.'

'Then that's decided,' says John with a nod. 'Now we stand by the Old Man and concentrate on getting this ship to harbour in one piece.'

The chief engineer's words get the agreement of a serious silence.

'I wish we were already in Suriname,' says Rúnar.

'We can agree with that, every one of us,' says John.

'I wish we'd never set off on this tour,' Sæli adds.

Silence.

'Don't you remember what he said?' says Sæli, looking sideways at his companions. 'The drunk guy in the bar?'

'The one who was scrounging change?' asks Ási.

'Yeah, that one,' says Sæli, nodding.

'He didn't say anything,' says Rúnar with a scowl. 'Nothing sensible, at least!'

'He looked at us and said, "Five dead men"!' says Sæli, wide eyed. '"Five dead men on a ship", that's what he said.'

'Did he?' says Ási.

'No,' says Rúnar with a shake of his head. 'He said nothing of the sort!'

'Yes, he did too say that!' says Sæli, looking at the bosun with tear-filled eyes. 'And then we saw him again … we drove past him in Mosfellsbær. We should've given him a lift or something. Maybe he put a curse on us? Maybe he was a gypsy or something? We should've —'

'Don't think like that, Sæli, lad,' says Ási. 'You never know how things'll turn out, eh? Broken mirrors and black cats don't alter the movements of the stars, my boy.'

'He was just some drunk,' says Rúnar, clapping Sæli on the back.

'Maybe.' Sæli gulps air as if to smother a sob. 'But if I never see my boy again, I …'

Silence.

From the seamen's mess comes the sound of the final song on *Strange Days*, playing low, Jim Morrison singing about the music being over and turning out the lights.

'Well!' says Ási, clapping his hands before opening the fridge and taking out ground beef, eggs, butter, milk, tomato puree and a few onions. 'Now I have to ask you to leave this battleground, because I have to mix up some meatloaf. Able seamen, officers, traitors, liars, saboteurs and stowaways – they all have to eat, my friends!'

★ ★ ★

Methúsalem is walking up the stairs that lead from E-deck to the bridge. He has black Ray-Ban sunglasses on his face, drops of cold sweat on his forehead and dried toothpaste in the corners of his mouth. His head is full of imaginary applesauce and the applesauce is full of a hot buzzing that overpowers all thought.

His ultra-sensitive fingertips touch the cold railing and his heavy feet step carefully from one step to the next. The first mate is empty and fragile, a floating glass bubble full of darkness, smoke and nausea. His half-open mouth pulls in air like the dirty-air intake of an old engine and his nose is as hot as an exhaust pipe, full of dust, soot and the smell of rust.

Smell of rust! What does rust smell like?

'Jesus …'

He is never going to drink again, never again.

Never!

Not cognac, at any rate,

'What a fuck-up,' Methúsalem tells himself, forcing an uneasy smile on his deathly pale face.

A smile that changes to a grimace as the nausea gushes up in his stomach, like milk on the verge of boiling over.

'Don't think about warm milk!'

Methúsalem stretches out a ghostly hand and opens the door to the bridge.

The lock clicks and that metallic click echoes like a shot inside the creaking shell of his head.

'I wish I was dead,' he murmurs and closes his eyes behind the lenses.

'What?'

'I just said good evening,' says Methúsalem, taking a deep breath as he straightens his back and walks slowly and confidently into the dim bridge.

'You're late,' says Guðmundur and glances at his watch as he turns around in his chair. 'You're *very* late! It's four minutes to eleven.'

'Isn't Sæli with you?'

'No. I let him off until three. Why?'

'Just … nothing.' Methúsalem gasps as the ship pitches so suddenly that it's as if the floor had been pulled out from under him.

'What's up with you, man?' Guðmundur says, getting down from the chair. 'Are you wearing sunglasses in the dark?'

'Yeah, I …' Methúsalem cautiously clearing his throat. 'I've got something in my eyes. An infection or something. They feel like they're full of sand.'

'So maybe you can't relieve me?.

'It's all right.' Methúsalem feels his way forwards in the bridge. 'The sunglasses help, and Rúnar is coming later on, isn't he?'

'He's on at midnight,' says Guðmundur, surreptitiously studying Methúsalem. 'Yeah, well, so, I'll just leave you then, eh?'

'Yeah, sure, I'm fine,' says Methúsalem, getting into the captain's chair. 'Don't worry about me.'

'Right, goodnight then,' says Guðmundur and opens the door.

'Goodnight.' Methúsalem leans back in the soft chair and closes his eyes behind the black lenses.

So get the hell going, Old Man!

The door closes, the ship hits a wave, and the blow pulses back along the hull of the ship.

Boom, boom, boom …

Coffee.

He should maybe have got himself some coffee.

Methúsalem Sigurðsson opens his eyes but sees only black. He takes off his sunglasses and looks out the window for a few minutes, motionless.

Over the weather deck floats a yellow haze.

His eyelids sink down, Methúsalem twitches and starts out of his catnap.

'Coffee,' he says with a sigh. He has to have some coffee if he doesn't want to fall asleep on watch.

He gets down from the chair and crosses to the port side, where some two-hour-old coffee is thickening in a glass pot standing on a warm hotplate.

'Fucking disgusting.'

Methúsalem pours coffee into a clean mug.

The smell is more than enough. He can't drink this! It's like diluted tar, this shit!

Methúsalem pours the coffee into the sink, then he has to breathe deeply and slowly to keep his nausea down.

Should he drink some water? No, water just gets warm in your stomach and increases the discomfort.

Coke.

He'd give everything he owns for a can of cold Coke.

'I'm not asking much,' says Methúsalem as he gets to his knees and opens the little fridge.

UHT-milk, UHT-milk, UHT-milk, an apple, an orange, UHT-milk, UHT-milk, more UHT-milk, and then something cold and hard at the back of the top shelf.

It's a can!

'Be Coke, be Coke!' Methúsalem whispers, tasting the sour slime in his dry mouth as he feels with his fingers and gets a hold on the ice-cold can.

There. It's coming, it's coming!

Coke, Coke, dear, dear Coke.'

Methúsalem pulls the can into the bluish light in the doorway of the fridge.

But the can isn't red – it is *not* red but green – fucking green! Is it Sprite? Don't be Sprite – no, it isn't Sprite and it isn't Fresca either ...

'Heineken,' murmurs Methúsalem, staring at the frosty can rolling back and forth in his trembling hand.

For fuck's sake!

Methúsalem Sigurðsson stands up, opens the can and takes a long, cold foamy sip.

★ ★ ★

Big John looks at the clock in the engine room and sees that it's ten to twelve.

He's off at midnight but he can't be bothered to hang around for even a minute longer.

'Fuck it,' he says as he turns off the dead man's alarm then gets out of his chair, puts on his earmuffs and walks out the door at the front of the control booth.

From there he walks directly to the stairs leading down to the floor in front of the main engine. He'll walk once around the engine before he goes up to bed, give it a pat, tap the meters and listen for unexpected noises.

As he walks past the engine on the port side he is aware of movement up on the metal platform on the starboard side of the space, in front of the generators.

It's the shadow of a man who's sneaking along the wall.

'Who's there?' John calls out, but his words are swallowed by the noise of the engines and the shadow disappears into the shadows behind the control booth.

That was a man, wasn't it?

'What the hell!' says John, striding behind the machine and up the stairs that lead up to the iron platform.

Nobody has any business in the engine room except the two engineers, and if that is Stoker, John wants to know what he's doing there outside his work time.

If it *isn't* Stoker then the chief engineer *really* wants to know what that person is doing wandering around there, and at this time of night.

'*Hello!*' John calls out when he reaches the place where the shadow disappeared just ten, fifteen seconds ago, but there's not a soul to be seen there on the platform between the storeroom and the control booth.

Had he been seeing things? Is the engine room haunted?

'If there's a ghost in here …' John shouts, shaking his fist at nothing in particular, 'then he'd better …'

John stops talking as he steps on something that crumbles under the coarse soles of his shoes. He takes a step back, bends down and sticks his right forefinger into white sand or powder that's drifting down through the metal grid and disappearing into the oily dark below.

What's this? Salt?

He smells the coarse, pale substance but it seems to have no smell. John decides to stick his tongue in it.

If it's some kind of poison he'll just spit it out and rinse his mouth.

'I'll be damned,' the chief engineer mutters after carefully tasting the coarse grains. 'Sugar!'

★ ★ ★

At two minutes before midnight Rúnar opens the door to his cabin on C-deck and steps into the corridor.

'Who's there?' asks Big John, who is halfway up the stairs from C-deck to B-deck.

'It's me, Rúnar,' he answers, closing the door behind him. 'Who are you looking for?'

'Did you see anyone going up?' asks John as he reaches C-deck. He's red faced, sweaty and out of breath.

'No. Like who?'

'Nobody,' says John and he stops to catch his breath. 'I thought I saw somebody down in the engine room. But I was probably just seeing things.'

'Have you started seeing ghosts?' asks Rúnar with a grin.

'I expect so. Don't we sailors all get more or less screwed up eventually?'

'Yeah, maybe.' Rúnar shakes a cigarette out of its pack. 'Are you on your way up?'

'Yes and no. I'm on my way to bed, but I need clean linen.'

'I'm on my way up to the bridge,' say Rúnar, lighting his cigarette. 'See you in the morning, then.'

'Yeah, okay.' John scratches his head. 'Is Methúsalem on the watch?'

'Yeah,' says Rúnar, blowing smoke through his nose.

'Yeah, right.' John shrugs. 'Just say hello from me, or something. Just keep an eye on him.'

'Will do,' says Rúnar, then he sets off up the stairs while John goes back down to A-deck to get clean bedding.

When Rúnar enters the bridge he sees no-one else up there – not Methúsalem nor anyone else.

'HELLO!' he calls.

Silence.

'What's all the noise?' asks Methúsalem as he turns around in the captain's chair with a huge grin on his face and his hands hanging limply from the arms of the chair.

He is so pale that his face is nearly incandescent in the dim light, and from a certain distance the Ray-Ban lenses look like black holes.

'Christ but you startled me, man!' says Rúnar with a snort. 'I thought you were a phantom!'

'A phantom?' says Methúsalem, his grin disappearing.

'What are you doing with those fucking glasses?' asks Rúnar, knocking ash off his cigarette. 'And what's that running down your face?'

'Eh? What?' asks Methúsalem, wiping a milky substance off his forehead. 'That's just sweat. I've got some virus or something. My eyes sting.'

'You weren't down in the engine room just now, were you?' asks Rúnar, hiding an impish grin by taking a drag on his smoke.

'Me? Down in the engine room? No! Why?' asks Methúsalem, his jaw hanging like that of a corpse before its ablution.

'Because,' says Rúnar, 'John thought he'd seen a dead man down there.'

XXVI

Sunday, 16 September

It is four minutes to 1 p.m. when Guðmundur opens the starboard bridge wing door and goes out into the storm, wearing a raincoat and a knitted cap. He squints through the salt spray, steadies himself with his left hand on the waist-high iron rail and feels his way along to the edge of the bridge wing with a half-century-old sextant under his right arm.

Guðmundur takes up a position farthest out on the bridge wing, spreads his legs to steady himself and leans against the iron railing while he aims the sextant. The sun's rays have penetrated the cloud cover off and on during the last hour, and if the captain isn't mistaken the sun is about to reach its zenith – which means noon, no matter what a man-made clock may say.

The ship dances crazily over the rough seas and Guðmundur finds it almost impossible to aim the sextant. He has to guess where the horizon divides itself from the threatening waves, and it's impossible to see the sun at the moment, but the minute its rays find a path through the darkness the captain will try to read the height of this fire-breathing mother of all life.

Stiff fingers handle the precise and finely adjusted instrument, and middle-aged eyes try to maintain focus and concentration. Guðmundur Berndsen has only calculated the height of the sun with a sextant on one sea voyage since he passed the exam on its use, in beautiful weather on the balcony of the College of Navigation more than three decades ago, and he's been trying to forget that voyage for thirty years.

Bloody hell, this simply isn't possible!

But he has to succeed. The longer the captain has no idea where the ship is, the sooner his underlings will lose faith in his ability to get the ship safely to Suriname.

The captain narrows his right eye and looks with his left through the little telescope on the back of the sextant. He peers through a slanting half-mirror and circular sight on the front of the instrument. The horizon divides the middle of the sight while the mirror at the top of the instrument reflects the rays of the sun, stars or moon through a coloured glass, down to the half-mirror and then to the eye of the user – that is, if the conditions are right. What the user has to do to find the height of the moon or sun is to keep the horizon steady in the sight and move the graduated arc at the bottom of the instrument, until the light is reflected from one mirror to the other and reaches his eye. Then all he has to do is secure the graduated arc and read from it the number that the pointer on the vertical part of the instrument indicates.

Technically this is a very easy thing to do, but at the same time it is complicated and difficult, especially at sea.

'Come on, then!'

At seven minutes after one o'clock, two and then three strong rays of the sun appear to the south. The captain tries to make up for the motion of the ship by stretching out his legs and bending them alternately. He holds his breath and manages to concentrate long enough to estimate with some accuracy the height of the sun over the horizon, before he loses his balance and rams into the iron wall and falls on his backside, grasping the sextant like a fragile work of art.

This sextant *is* a fragile work of art and, as things now stand, worth more than a thousand times its weight in gold. All the satellites of the world are little more than dusty electronic junk compared to this classical invention that has the lustre of scientific aesthetics, man's desire for truth and his unshakable faith in the reliability of God's creation.

A mere instrument on land; the breath of life at sea.

Guðmundur scrambles to his feet, with the sextant in his arms, and manages to get it into the bridge, where he places it on the desk in the chart room without disturbing the adjustment.

But the desk is empty. No charts.

'Of course,' Guðmundur says under his breath. For a moment he thinks someone has stolen all the charts, then remembers he removed them himself – rolled them up and hid them in the wardrobe in his cabin.

He had meant to make sure that no irresponsible person got hold of them and then sailed the ship somewhere other than was intended. When he became aware of the mutiny of the gang of five he didn't know what they were up to, and automatically thought the worst.

Guðmundur finds the walky-talky, turns it on and adjusts it to an open channel.

'Rúnar, can you hear me? It's the captain calling,' Guðmundur says into the transmitter. 'Rúnar, can you hear me?'

Skuggi lifts his head off the floor and looks at the captain. Crackling sounds are heard from the receiver.

'Rúnar here. Over.'

'Will you get Methúsalem to relieve me? I'm going to calculate the position of the ship. Over.'

'Give me two minutes. Over and out.'

★ ★ ★

Rúnar hangs up his overalls in the storeroom and saunters up to E-deck, a lit cigarette between his lips.

'Methúsalem?' he calls and knocks on the door of the first mate's cabin.

No answer.

'*Methúsalem!*'

The bosun grabs the doorknob and opens the door with his left hand as he knocks politely with his right.

'Methúsalem! Are you there?'

The first mate must be in the cabin, because the hasp prevents the door from opening more than a few centimetres.

'Methúsalem? You asleep?' Rúnar knocks again on the door, which rattles against the hasp.

No answer.

It is pitch black in the first mate's cabin and a strange smell floats into the corridor, a sort of mixture of mould, bad breath and strong body odour.

The bosun drags on his cigarette, grimaces, and then blows the smoke through his nose.

'*Methúsalem!*'

Still no answer.

'To hell with you then,' the bosun says and slams the door.

Rúnar draws on the cigarette until it's burned up to the filter before throwing the stub out the door behind the wheelhouse up on F-deck, then he shuts out the storm and saunters on up to G-deck.

'Where's Methúsalem?' Guðmundur asks when Rúnar enters the bridge.

'He didn't answer,' says Rúnar as makes his way to the port side and pours a mug of coffee.

'Wasn't he in his cabin?'

'Yeah, the hasp was in place. He's just fast asleep. Unless he's ill or something. There's a bloody stench in the cabin.'

'He wasn't feeling too good yesterday,' mumbles Guðmundur.

'Yeah, that's right. He's probably got some kind of bug.'

'Damn it!' Guðmundur shakes his head. 'It's hard enough to man the watch as it is.'

'I can relieve you for a while,' says Rúnar, grabbing a handle with his left hand as the ship rolls to starboard. 'What are you going to do?'

'I'm heading down to my cabin to calculate our position,' Guðmundur answers, picking up the sextant as if it were an infant. 'The charts and calculator are below. I won't be long.'

'Take your time,' says Rúnar as he gets into the captain's chair. 'I was thinking of taking him some food to the forecastle.'

'Doesn't the man have any food?'.

'No. But we left him some water.'

'That'll have to do for now. There's no way I'm letting men risk their lives outside when the weather like this.'

'I see,' Rúnar says into his coffee.

'We'll look into it this evening,' says the captain as he opens the door into the corridor. Skuggi stands up.

'Are you okay with that?'

'Yeah.'

'Good. I'll be back in a few minutes.'

The captain leaves the bridge with Skuggi at his heels.

★ ★ ★

Methúsalem?

Methúsalem!

Who is Methúsalem?

Is he the man who drove to a party and drank maybe one glass of white wine to be polite, and then another, and another, but still just one glass – the same glass – over and over again, and then drove home to prove to himself that he wasn't drunk, since he'd been sober for five weeks, four, three, two …?

No! Who'd want to talk to him?

Methúsalem is me.

Me? Yes! Who am I?

The first mate of death!

Death? What rubbish!

Knock, knock, knock …

Come in!

I mean …

Methúsalem Sigurdsson opens his mouth but no words come out.

Is it possible to be so hung over from one beer? The beer was just a pick-me-up. One beer. He was sober when he drank it, there's no doubt about that, see!

The beer must have gone off. How long had it been hidden in the refrigerator? A year? Two? Ten?

'Methúsalem!'

The first mate lies on his back in the hot dark and hears someone call from a vague distance.

A black skull speaks through a faint yellow light that sneaks in like fog through the doorway that opens beyond a dark room full of nothing.

Is he dreaming? Or is someone knocking on the door? On what door? The door to his head? Is there a door in his head?

Where is he? Outside his head? Is he knocking? Or has he got the DTs?

'To hell with you then.'

The door slams shut, the skull disappears and the furry darkness is filled with a feverish silence.

'Hello?' Methúsalem says, making a feeble effort to clear his throat. He is hoarse and tries to wet his parched lips with his swollen tongue.

No answer. Who should answer him? Is his head empty? Nobody home?

Shut up!

He means to open his eyes but nothing happens. He can't open his eyes.

They are glued shut.

'What the hell,' he says and feels his closed eyes with the fingers of his right hand. On his eyelashes he finds some kind of crust or something congealed that can be picked at and pulled off his slimy lashes and crumbled like bits of cake between his fingers.

His eyes are burning, he is nauseated and his nose is stuffed.

'Goddammit,' mutters Methúsalem and stops picking at the crust that glues his eyes closed.

He's come down with some fucking bug.

A virus.

There was no way he could have been so hung over!

Better sleep a bit longer. Restore his energy. Get better. It's hardly all that late.

What did he do yesterday? Who? Did he do anything yesterday? What?

The engine!

Did he go down to the engine room? Or didn't he?

Methúsalem puts the palm of his right hand on the bed frame. Through the wood and steel the tips of his fingers sense the slow beat of the engine.

So, had he not gone down to the engine room?

He sighs deeply and tries to fall asleep again, but he feels lousy and it's hard to relax when your thoughts wander across the border between dreaming and being awake, while your stomach is heaving like a bubbling mud pot.

His fingers meet a white cube …

Suddenly he remembers something. He makes his right hand crawl like a large spider into the pocket of his trousers, and when his trembling fingers finally find a hard cube his heart skips a beat, and then starts pounding in his chest like a rabbit fucking.

A lump of sugar!

The darkness buzzes like a huge bluebottle fly, the veins in his eyelids light up like the wires in a light bulb and the heat in the cabin seems to rise about twenty degrees.

'Shit!' Methúsalem tries to swallow, his mouth is bone dry.

★ ★ ★

This *can't* be right!

Guðmundur Berndsen sits at the table in his cabin and

stares in disbelief at the chart laid out in front of him, where two lines intersect like a cross far from their intended route:

33° W 7° N

He could accept thirty-three degrees west, which is the longitudinal coordinate. Guðmundur was hoping the ship was closer to thirty-seven degrees west, though drifting about four degrees east was of itself not impossible, though it is much more than all the models project.

But seven degrees north? That's simply not possible.

By normal standards the ship should be east-south-east of Newfoundland, somewhere nearer forty-four degrees north latitude. But according to his calculation the ship was positioned north-north-east of Brazil.

Seven degrees north of the equator.

South of the Tropic of Cancer.

The ship is right over the curved Atlantic Ridge, as if it had skimmed along it at three times its top speed.

'This can't be right,' Guðmundur mutters to himself.

But what if it *is* right? Can it be right? No, this simply can *not* be right!

Or can it?

If these coordinates are right he needs to change course and sail west to Suriname, which is only three days away *if* these figures are to be believed.

If the figures are sheer bullshit, though, and he accepts them and sails to the west, he could end up in New York after three days instead of continuing on to South America.

And then there is a third possibility: the co-ordinates are correct and he chooses not to believe his own calculations and continues to sail south, which means that he would not reach land until the ship ran into Antarctica ice after two weeks.

It would have been better not to use the sextant under these conditions. An hour ago he knew little, but now he knows absolutely nothing.

'Hell and damnation!'

Guðmundur rolls up the chart, pushes the sextant to the side and turns off the calculator.

What should he do?

The captain snaps the rubber band off his deck of cards and lays a solitaire to calm his nerves and ease his mind.

But it doesn't do the trick.

After losing track of the game, forgetting what he's doing and getting mixed up seven times in a row, the game is just an incoherent pattern of cards. So Guðmundur pulls the cards together into total chaos, shuffles them and puts the rubber band back in place.

Maybe he should unpack his suitcase?

Guðmundur Berndsen stands up, pulls out his suitcase and lays it flat on his made-up bed. The minute he opens the case and sees the ironed, folded clothes he thinks instinctively of Hrafnhildur.

What might she be doing now?

Is she still wondering whether she should fly to meet her husband? Has she maybe already started to pack? Started the flight in her thoughts?

Or has she thrown the ticket away in the garbage?

'If I just …' Guðmundur draws his fingertips over the stiff shirts and the soft flannel pants.

If he just *what*?

If only he'd pulled himself together and asked her straight out whether she really was interested in saving the marriage, instead of forcing her into a corner like that and leaving her there. If only he'd told her that he had resigned, and then maybe talked with her about her grief, the black dress and the singing at funerals. If he had just let her have the plane ticket a day sooner so she could sleep on it all, think it over and then give him an answer before he went to sea for the last time.

If he had just sat down with her sometime and asked her whether she was ready to turn her back on shadows of the past and walk with him into the light again, instead of remaining silent like a brute the whole time he was on shore and letting four precious weeks burn up to nothing.

What then?

Then there wouldn't be this damned uncertainty gnawing at the roots of his heart like a worm that eats the fruit from within.

Personal relations have never been one of Guðmundur Berndsen's strengths, though; he's always preferred being at the helm of a ship to being near sensitive souls. He's a ship's captain and what ship's captains do is find the most sensible path between two points; they sail around dangers, avoid collisions, and think only about getting the ship safely over the sea and into a safe port, together with its cargo and crew.

That's just how it is; that's how it's always been …

Guðmundur Berndsen heaves a sigh and continues to unpack the case.

He hangs the shirts and trousers on hangers in the clothes locker, arranges his underwear on one shelf and socks on another.

'Well …'

Guðmundur clears his throat loudly before continuing to unpack his case, sort his luggage and put it away.

He wipes away a tear from the corner of his right eye with the back of his rough, veined hand and then takes out several short-sleeved T-shirts, lays four silk ties on the bed and hangs up a light jacket and light-coloured trousers. There is nothing left in the case except something folded in brown wax paper that covers the bottom.

Hrafnhildur has never put wax paper around his clothes. Is this a gift? No, hardly. He'll be home long before Christmas and his birthday isn't until May.

This couldn't be …

Guðmundur feels a cold stab in his stomach and his neck stiffens as if he's about to suffocate.

For thirty years a dark brown velvet suit has hung in the clothes cupboard in their bedroom. This is the suit that Guðmundur Berndsen wore on their wedding day. It hasn't fit him for nearly twenty-five years but he is very fond of it, so Hrafnhildur has never been able to get him to throw it away despite pleading with him tearfully every single time she arranges the clothes in the crowded wardrobe.

For some reason she's never been able to stand that suit. Perhaps she can't stand it because it reminds her of the day she married Guðmundur Berndsen and now she is sending it with him to sea to tell him that the marriage is over and that he can go to hell, him and his crummy suit.

Or is she?

Guðmundur touches the package, this wax-paper wrapping that perhaps draws the line between love and unhappiness, the past and the present, marriage and loneliness.

'My love,' murmurs Guðmundur, lifting the soft package that crackles in his trembling hands.

My love?

He's never said that before. Has he never said that before? No! Why hasn't he ever said that before?

Because he's a brute.

A brute!

A heartless brute who doesn't deserve to have a wife and children!

Guðmundur Berndsen is angry with himself and his brutish nature and rips the wax paper off the clothes. He throws the paper on the floor, grips the suit with both hands and shakes out the folds. The material straightens and slides between his thick fingers, all the way to the floor. The captain blinks his eyes because the material is not brown but black, and it's not velvet. This is not his suit! He's holding a long dress with a low-cut back and short sleeves.

This is Hrafnhildur's black dress! Which means that …

'She's coming,' Guðmundur says softly, looking at the dress

that he has hated for so long. He's smiling from ear to ear. They had been thinking the same thing: when he had decided to stop going to sea, she had decided to stop singing for the dead.

But instead of expressing themselves in words they had each decided to send the other a symbolic message. She wrapped the black dress in brown wax paper in the bottom of his suitcase, and he bought a plane ticket and left it behind with her before he went off to sea.

As soon as he had handed her the ticket, Hrafnhildur knew she would use it but she chose to say nothing – because she didn't need to. She knew that when Guðmundur found the black dress he would realise that it stood for 'yes'. That was her answer. Taking off the black dress is her answer: *Yes, I want to save the marriage. Yes, I will come to meet you.*

Yes!

So they are linked after all. In harmony through thick and thin, until death do them part. Two people who are one whole.

A couple.

If only he'd told her he was through with the sea. But that can wait – he'll tell her that as soon as they meet in Suriname. How surprised she'll be! How happy she'll be!

'Thank you, Hrafnhildur! Thank you ... my love!' says Guðmundur in a voice as husky as the croak of a raven. He holds the shoulders of the dress and takes two steps back and one to the side. He wants to dance. He *is* dancing! He is dancing with an empty dress.

Brute! Who's a brute? He's the most romantic man in the entire world!

Guðmundur Berndsen feels he is floating on air, even though he's probably stomping around his cabin like a newly awakened troll. And it's almost as if the ship wants to dance too: it slows suddenly, as if bowing before an unseen dancing partner, then tilts to starboard, it tilts, and it tilts ...

The captain stumbles, falls on his back and hits his head on the edge of the table.

What's going on?

He blinks his eyes and looks dizzily up under the table. Blood runs from the scalp above his left ear and his right shoulder hurts.

'What the …? Is the ship …?' grumbles the captain and rolls out from under the table. Something's not right. The ship isn't managing to right itself and it almost seems to have turned so it's drifting side-on to the wind. As if it were …

Guðmundur Berndsen stares at his hands that are pushing against the rug on the floor but feeling neither vibrations nor thumps.

The engine has stopped. The ship is dead in the water.

'What the devil is going on?' says the captain, his voice shaking. He stands up, flings the dress into his open suitcase and then goes quickly to the door, uphill over the rug-covered floor that is tilting at a thirty-degree angle to starboard. But he hasn't opened the door into the corridor when the bell on the wall starts to ring.

Loud warning bells resound throughout the ship, as if the end of the world were near.

XXVII

14:45

When the captain enters the tilting bridge Rúnar is trying to phone down to the engine room.

'What's going on?' shouts the captain.

'I don't know!' Rúnar shouts back and replaces the phone. 'There's no answer from the engine room. Stoker isn't on watch!'

'Stay here! I'm going down to the engine room. The damn bell won't stop ringing until someone either cuts the power to the main engine or restarts it.'

The captain sets off down the stairs and the bosun grabs the wheel with both hands and looks out the window, terrified, at the starboard side of the bridge, which seems to be hanging in midair over a turbulent sea.

'What's going on?' asks Sæli, meeting the captain on the landing of C-deck.

'You know the regulations!' cries the captain, throwing up his hands. '*All crew to go to the boat deck.*'

'Is there a fire?' says Sæli, spreading his arms to keep his balance. 'Is the ship sinking?'

'I don't know yet. But the engine has stopped and …' Guðmundur stops talking when the warning bell stops, which means one of the engineers has arrived in the engine room.

The ship's hull creaks as monstrous waves bend and batter

the steel; the heavy beat of drums echoes in the hold and a long high-frequency tone resounds in the head of the crew. Then that slowly gives way to the symphonic whining of the wind.

'While the ship is dead in the water we have a state of emergency on board,' says the captain, gripping the handrail by the stairs. 'But since the bells have stopped we're hardly in immediate danger. Tell the men to stay put until I give the order to do anything else.'

'Right!' says Sæli, and he sits on the floor so as not to fall down.

★ ★ ★

14:51

Big John stands on the platform to port of the cooling main engine and opens the valve housings one after the other with a wrench, while below him stand the captain and Stoker on the floor of the engine room, waiting for a report from the chief engineer.

'FUCKING HELL!' screams Big John and he flings the wrench away, but because of the rattling of the generator the others can't hear the wrench landing or bouncing about in this oil-soaked iron cellar. 'Every single piston is broken. Repair is out of the question.'

'What's happened?' asks Guðmundur.

'I saw someone down here yesterday,' says Big John as he climbs down off the engine.

'Who?' asks the captain.

'Where?' says Stoker.

'Come with me!' calls John. He walks ahead of them up the stairs leading to the iron platform on the starboard side. He goes to where he stepped on the sugar cube the night before.

'Somebody was here.' Big John gestures as if to mark off the area behind the generator.

'Who?' says Guðmundur, wiping the sweat from his soot-covered face.

'Doing what?' asks Stoker.

'I don't know! He got away from me,' says the chief engineer as he looks around, examining the empty platform. 'But I found …'

He stops talking and looks thoughtful as his eyes rest on a ten-litre plastic container resting on an iron frame just inside of the ship's hull, behind the generator and this side of a large water pump. The container is half full of some kind of oil, and sticking up from a hole in the stopper are two black rubber hoses held together with plastic bands.

'Found what?' the captain enquires.

'I've got an idea,' says Big John as he climbs over the water pump and rips the hoses out of the container. 'Come with me!'

John lifts the container off the iron framework and walks off with it towards the storeroom.

'What's your idea?' asks Guðmundur as he follows the chief engineer over the iron platform. 'What's that container?'

'It's an additive for the fuel oil,' says Stoker, who has followed behind.

'What?' asks the captain.

'Óli! Find me a big pan,' says Big John, opening the storeroom.

'Aye, aye!' says Óli Johnsen and runs off. The chief engineer only uses Stoker's given name when there's a great deal at stake.

On the port side in the engine room are various containers that the engineers use for volatile liquids and strong soaps, for example, to scrub off spilled oil or clean parts after disassembling an engine. Stoker finds a big tin pan that's half filled with congealed grease. He cleans it and then hurries back over the iron floor. When he is a few steps from the storeroom he spots something on the floor. Something that reflects the light like a silver coin.

Stoker bends down and reaches his dirty fingers towards

the glittering piece of metal that resembles a coin but isn't.

It's a small key.

★ ★ ★

14:54

'What's that oil?' asks the captain when the chief engineer has closed the storeroom door.

'It's a fuel oil additive.' Big John unscrews the stopper. 'They're mixed together with the heated oil before it's pumped into the engine.'

'And you think that …'

The captain stops talking when Stoker opens the door, letting the rattling of the generator into the soundproofed storeroom.

'Here's a pan. I rinsed the shit out of it,' says Stoker, putting down a large tin pan that smells of pure gasoline.

'Good,' says the chief engineer as he starts pouring the contents of the container into the pan.

'But I don't understand what …' Guðmundur shrugs his shoulders.

'What did you find on the floor?' asks Stoker, looking at the oil and his superior by turns.

'Look!' says Big John, putting down the empty container.

'What?' says the captain as he leans over, the better to see what he's supposed to see. 'I don't see anything!'

'Salt?' asks Stoker, and he looks at John.

'No,' says John. 'Sugar.'

'Sugar? Where?' The captain looks from one engineer to the other.

'Look,' says Big John, pointing to very small drops that glitter like tiny stars in the dark oil. 'It's almost completely dissolved but it still glitters.'

'Sabotage,' murmurs Stoker and he sits on the floor.

'I think I see it but I don't understand ...' The captain shakes his head.

'I stepped on a lump of sugar here shortly before midnight last night,' says Big John, then he too sits on the floor.

'Has someone put sugar cubes in ...?' Guðmundur stops talking when Sæli comes running down to A-deck.

'What's up?' asks Sæli, standing in the doorway at the bottom of the stairs, bracing himself in the doorframe.

'Nothing!' answers Big John. 'What're you doing down here?'

'I was just –'

'I told you everyone should stay put!' says the captain with a scowl.

'Yes, but ...' says Sæli, reddening. 'Rúnar sent me down to get Methúsalem, but Methúsalem didn't answer me so –'

'The engine's stopped! It's kaput! It's an emergency!' says the captain hoarsely.

'What happened?' asks Sæli.

'It doesn't matter ... not for the moment,' says the captain. 'The ship's dead in the water.'

'What can we do?' says Sæli to the chief engineer.

'Nothing,' says John. He looks at his reflection in the oil. 'Nothing except send out an emergency signal.'

'I see,' says Sæli quietly.

'The radio is unusable,' says Guðmundur. 'How can we send out an emergency signal while the aerials aren't functioning?'

'There's an emergency transmitter behind the port bridge wing,' says Big John, looking at Stoker, who nods his head.

'The white box?' asks the captain.

'Yes,' says John, nodding to the captain. 'If the ship sinks, the pressure lock blows the box open and then the emergency transmitter floats up and start sending out an SOS along with the ship's call signal.'

'What do we have to do to activate the transmitter?' asks Guðmundur. 'Do we have to submerge the box?'

'No,' says the chief engineer, shaking his head. 'All we have to do is unscrew the box and turn it upside down. The transmitter is upside down in the box but in water it rights itself and then the transmitter turns on automatically.'

'That's it!' says the captain, clapping the chief engineer on the shoulder. 'Sæli, go up to the bridge, unfasten that box and turn it upside down on the floor.'

'Yeah, okay,' mumbles Sæli with a nod.

'Here's a screwdriver,' says Big John, fishing a medium-sized screwdriver from the toolbox and tossing it to Sæli, who catches it.

'Thanks.' Sæli sticks the screwdriver into his right trouser pocket.

'Be careful,' says the captain. He looks at his watch. 'We'll hold an emergency meeting in the mess at four o'clock. Let the others know.'

'Will do,' says Sæli, who then turns around and runs up the slanting staircase.

'You were talking about the sugar,' says the captain, looking at Big John and then at the pan, which tilts like the ship, disgorging thick oil over the edge and out onto the floor.

'Yeah,' says John, tossing dirty rags onto the sticky spilled oil. 'Sugar dissolves in the additive and then runs into the engine as a liquid. Once there it crystallises in the heat and the hard crystals damage the pistons, make them crack.'

'No deckhand would do that,' says Stoker, sneering nastily. 'If I didn't know better I'd say only a trained engineer would know enough to think of such a thing.'

'That's true,' says John, nodding.

'How about an officer?' asks Guðmundur Berndsen.

'Not out of the question,' says Stoker, leering at the captain. 'But, with all due respect, *you* didn't work it out, and you're a highly trained seaman.'

'You've got a point there,' says the captain, 'but if I had intended to damage the engine I would doubtless have remembered enough textbook learning to have thought of something similar.'

'That's right,' says the chief engineer. 'Every single graduate of the Navigation School knows enough to damage a ship in uncounted ways.'

'Yeah, maybe,' says Stoker with a shrug.

'But others wouldn't, you think?' asks the captain.

'If we don't count the three of us, the man in the forecastle and Jónas, that leaves only four,' says Big John. He puts a fresh cigar in his mouth. 'Of those, I trust two completely, if not three.'

'Which means that ...' Guðmundur looks questioningly at John, who lights a match and sucks life into his cigar.

'Which means there's only one left,' says Stoker.

'Ási is completely reliable, Sæli is an innocent ... and the devil take me if Rúnar is involved in this,' Big John says as he sucks on the cigar.

'Agreed,' says Stoker.

'That leaves Methúsalem,' groans the captain. He sighs. 'Is that possible?'

'You'll have to answer that,' says Big John, blowing a thick cloud of smoke out through his nose.

'Yes, you're right. It's up to me to answer it.' Guðmundur stands up. 'It's up to me to ask the questions and up to me to find the answers. It's my responsibility to decide who is trustworthy and who is not.'

'Yes, exactly, that was –'

'Thanks for your help!' the captain says, interrupting the chief engineer as he steps over the pan and walks to the stairs that lead up to A-deck. 'See you in the officers' mess at four o'clock.'

'Yes, of course ...' mumbles Big John, going red around the eyes.

'Don't forget one thing, John Pétursson,' says the captain as he turns at the bottom of the stairs. 'When we went to sea less than a week ago I trusted every member of the crew. *Each and every one.*'

★ ★ ★

15:21

What should he do? What should he *not* do?

Sæli holds onto the railing behind the wheelhouse with both hands, strains his eyes in the salt-laden wind and stares at a white plastic box the size of a cigarette carton which is screwed onto the iron wall farthest back on the port bridge wing.

If he turns the box upside down the ship will send out an emergency signal, which means that someone will hear the signal and tow the disabled ship to the nearest harbour.

Where is the nearest harbour? It could be St John's in Newfoundland, Halifax in Nova Scotia or Boston in Massachusetts. But that isn't so important. What's important is the package that Sæli has to pick up in Suriname and deliver to Iceland. If he does not pick up the package his family will suffer. If the ship is towed to North America it will be impossible for him to pick up some package in South America. Unless he flies to Suriname, gets the package and flies all the way home to Iceland. But he can't afford to fly anywhere; and besides, he could never smuggle this package between continents by air.

But what'll happen if the emergency signal does *not* get sent?

They're dead in the water in the middle of the Atlantic Ocean, without any contact with the rest of the world and surrounded by high seas and storms. Actually, the storm has abated somewhat, but even so ... Even if the ship drifts straight to Suriname – which, of course, would never happen – the drifting would take at least three to five weeks.

What should he do? Of two bad choices, the emergency signal seems better than drifting over the ocean out of control.

Or is it? If the ship is towed to the nearest harbour everybody will have to show their passport. Does Satan have a passport? Probably not. Which means he'll be arrested. The man who was going to help him deal with the 'debt collector' back in Iceland and at the same time save his family from his clutches would be handcuffed and locked in prison.

Then there'd be no hope left. If nobody comes to the rescue, though, Satan will be in the same hopeless position as everybody else on board. If it comes to the worst there's nothing ahead but misery, starvation and death.

What should he do? What should he *not* do?

The cold wind whips Sæli's hair, pulls at his clothes, bites at his face and fingers, dries his lips and draws salty tears from his eyes.

What will that bully do if he comes back to Iceland without the package? If he so much as touches one hair on the head of Lára and Egill …

'I'll kill you if you touch them, you fucker!' Sæli screams into the wind and tightens his grip on the ice-cold railing.

'What are you saying? Is everything okay?' shouts Rúnar from inside the wheelhouse.

'Yeah, sure – take it easy!' Sæli calls back and pulls the screwdriver out of his pants pocket.

Damn. Damn! He has to loosen the box and turn it upside down – it's their only fucking hope. If he doesn't it'll be the end of them. Damn it all!

Sæli bends down and tries to use the screwdriver under the box without losing hold of the railing. The box is screwed to two angle irons that are bolted fast to the back of the bridge wing, one screw for each angle iron. But the screws are swollen with old rust that runs in long streaks down from the angle irons. Sæli has trouble getting the screwdriver to stick in the head of the screw, and it's even more difficult to get the rust-brown screws to move at all. Every time the screwdriver slips out of the screw head the grooves are further damaged, and

Sæli bangs his hand hard on the angle iron, which doesn't help.

'This is impossible,' Saeli says and looks hopelessly at his hands, which are pale, shaking with cold and covered with scratches, sores and half-dry streaks of blood. 'Goddamn it all to hell. *Fucking, fucking hell!*'

In his fury Sæli pushes the screwdriver like a knife into the box lid. A crack appears on the lid and the screwdriver sits fast in it. He jerks the screwdriver slantwise up out of the box and then the lid splits apart from one end to the other. One half blows away but the other half is still there.

Not so bad!

Sæli sticks the screwdriver back in his pocket and makes his way along the bridge wing. He holds onto the edge of the wing wall and peers into the broken plastic box. There lies the transmitter, horizontal in a specially designed Styrofoam compartment. Sæli sticks the fingers of his left hand into the box but can't get the transmitter out. He needs to break the lid completely off. In the front of the box is the pressure lock that is supposed to blow up at a certain depth; Sæli is slightly frightened that it's delicately set and will explode straight in his face at any more disturbance. But that's a chance he'll have to take.

Big John was clearly wrong when he said the transmitter was upside down in the box. Which means that it would not have been enough to turn the box upside down in order to start up the transmitter, as then it would be as horizontal and just as inactive as before. To start the transmitter he'd have had to set up the box vertically, and take care that the transmitter was vertical inside it and not upside down.

'Come on,' murmurs Sæli, grasping the broken box lid with his right hand. He holds onto the wall with his left hand, turns his face away, pushes with his feet, then gives the lid an unhurried but determined jerk.

Nothing happens. Sæli grimaces and holds on fast to the sharp piece, which all at once splits apart so that he loses his hold on the metal wall and falls flat on the floor of the bridge wing. He lets go of the broken piece of plastic and watches the blood pour from a deep cut on his fingertips. On the floor beside him lies the circular pressure lock; up on the metal wall sits the bottom half of the box.

Sæli stands up. He wipes the blood from his fingers on his trousers then grasps the edge of the wall on either side of the plastic box. Inside the box lies the transmitter, shaped like a disposable gas canister with a stout aerial sticking up.

Now he holds on tight with his left hand and picks up the transmitter with his right. As soon as the transmitter is vertical a red light begins to blink on the top of the aerial.

One blink, two blinks, three blinks …

The transmitter works! He is calling for help! This little instrument is the most beautiful thing Sæli has ever seen – or nearly. Nothing is as beautiful as a newborn baby – a man's own child, that is – but this little blinking red light …

Boom!

The ship falls sideways off a huge wave and crashes with all its weight on the surface of the water, which explodes to all sides. Sæli loses his hold on the wall, flies backwards and lands on the forward wall of the bridge wing. The transmitter skids over the iron floor, spins in a circle in the middle and then rolls back behind the wheelhouse.

'No, *no!*' Sæli scrambles to his feet but he's only managed two steps before the transmitter rolls under the railing back of the bridge wing, off the platform and out into thin air.

NO!

Sæli runs across the floor, grabs the top of the railing and looks down on the blue-grey emptiness below the top deck of the ship.

But there is nothing to see, nothing there except salt-laden wind and rough seas as far as the eye can see. No blinking light; absolutely nothing. Did the transmitter land in the sea or did it land on the stern and break into a thousand pieces?

'I can't believe it.' Sæli hangs his head and clenches his stiff and bloody hands around the salt-encrusted metal.

★ ★ ★

16:03

Six of the nine-man crew have come together in the officers' mess. At the head of the table, furthest from the door, sits Guðmundur Berndsen, Big John and Stoker on his right, Rúnar and Sæli on his left. Ási stands in the doorway, gnawing on a toothpick.

'I'll keep it short,' says the captain, leaning forward with clenched hands. 'The ship is dead in the water. We have an emergency situation on board. You know this.'

The ship is dead in the water.

No matter how often Guðmundur Berndsen says it, he can't get used to it. To be adrift on the high seas is a captain's worst nightmare. Only a collision, a fire or icing up would worry him more.

And mutiny ...

'No hope of repair?' asks Rúnar after a short pause.

The chief engineer shakes his head.

'Stuff has got into the engine that doesn't belong there,' says the captain, who has to make an effort not to raise his voice. 'Every single piston is ruined. Repairs are out of the question.'

Silence reigns among those present, who glance at each other but don't feel up to saying what everyone was thinking.

Sabotage.

'Yes,' says the captain, nodding his head. 'The engine has been sabotaged.'

'But ...'

'The man in the forecastle?' says the captain. 'It wasn't me who locked him up. It looks like he is innocent. Unless he has an accomplice.'

Silence.

'We'll fetch him as soon as the storm subsides,' says Guðmundur, taking a deep breath through his nose. 'But until the crew is safe in harbour *no-one* will be suspected of anything, *no-one* will be punished for anything and *no-one* will be shut in anywhere. *Is that understood?*'

The captain bangs his fist on the table.

'Yes,' murmur his listeners, nodding.

'We are in a life-threatening situation, each and every one of us.' The captain clenches his fists again. 'We will all pitch in to help, and we will get through this difficult situation together. When we are back in a safe harbour there will be a maritime court inquiry, whether people like it or not. But until that time we are men in danger at sea and, given those conditions, we must set aside all our differences and stick together.'

His listeners nod again.

'Any questions?'

Silence.

'Where is Methúsalem?' asks Ási, who is leaning on the doorframe with his arms crossed.

'He appears to be sick,' says the captain. 'If he doesn't show tomorrow morning we'll have to break in to his cabin.'

Silence.

'Methúsalem is falling apart,' mumbles Sæli.

'How sad,' says Big John, grinning, as he picks up a box of artificial sweeteners. 'And he was so calm after we put Ritalin in his Canderel.'

Silence.

Methúsalem. It was Methúsalem who ruined the engine. It was Methúsalem who dropped that key on the floor of the engine room.

Stoker puts his palm flat against the right trouser pocket of his overalls and feels the key under the thin material.

What's it a key to? Maybe it fits something important? Should he mention it? Let them know he found it?

No. Not unless someone asks about it. Until then he intends to keep it, guard it well …

'Isn't the storm abating a bit?' asks Stoker.

'Yeah, looks like it,' says Guðmundur, tilting his head. 'Thank the lord. Such high seas could easily break the ship in two.'

'Has the emergency signal been sent out?' John asks, looking at Sæli and then at the captain.

'The transmitter fell overboard,' says the captain, sighing heavily. 'But of course it'll continue to transmit and with any luck it should drift in the same direction as the ship.'

'What happened?' says Big John and he looks at Sæli.

'It was just an accident,' Sæli says, barely audible, and he avoids looking the chief engineer in the eye. 'The box broke and …'

Sæli shrugs his shoulders and sighs.

'He did his best!' says the captain, decisively. 'Let's not despair. There is, of course, an emergency transmitter in the lifeboat but we'll wait to start it up until we get in the boat.'

'Why shouldn't we start it up at once?' asks Rúnar.

'We might be stuck in the lifeboat for several weeks,' says the captain. 'I don't want to risk having the battery in the transmitter give out before we find land or are saved.'

'When are we going to get in the boat?' asks Ási.

'When the weather has completely calmed,' the captain replies placidly.

'Why don't we get in the boat at once? Isn't it safer?' Rúnar demurs. 'The ship could break up at any time but the boat is really strong. The fuel should last us three weeks, which ought to be more than enough.'

'All of which is correct,' says Guðmundur. 'But before we get in the boat we need to know where we are. Otherwise we won't know which direction to sail in. When the weather calms I'll calculate our position exactly and then we can head for the nearest port.'

'I thought you calculated our position earlier today?' says Rúnar.

'We can't take that calculation seriously,' the captain says, almost to himself. 'There's no accurate reading to be had in such high seas.'

'So you don't know where we are?' Sæli asks hesitantly.

'No!' says the captain firmly, lifting his chin in the manner of stubborn children and dictators. 'I don't know except in a very limited way.'

Silence.

'Until we get in the boat I won't leave the ship's bridge,' says the captain firmly. 'Rúnar and Sæli will have eight-hour watches and take turns being with me up on the bridge – first Sæli for eight hours, then Rúnar for eight hours, and so on. As for me, I shall rest in the chart room every sixteen hours. *Nobody* besides us three has any reason to enter the bridge for the rest of this voyage. *Nobody!* If someone has to get in touch with me, he can phone the bridge or ask the seaman who is not on watch to get the message to me.'

Silence.

'When will you eat?' says Ási.

'Rúnar and Sæli can bring me food and something to drink.'

Silence.

'The engineers will keep their regular watches,' Guðmundur says. 'They need to look after the generator, the heating and so on. Ási will, obviously, see to the kitchen, in addition to looking after Jónas while he's stuck in bed. Outside of mealtimes and watches everyone is to stay in his own cabin, without exception. Is that understood?'

The men look questioningly at each other.

'Why?' asks Big John.

'If anything else threatens the ship I'll ring the warning bell,' says the captain. 'Then everybody is to meet on the boat deck, ready to abandon ship. If there's anyone who doesn't show up then the others have to know he's in his cabin so they can fetch him there. If he's not in his cabin, nothing more will be done to find him. Is that understood?'

'Yes,' comes the unanimous mumbled response.

'Any final questions?' The captain gives each of the men a serious look.

Silence.

'Then this meeting is over.' The captain stands up from the table. 'Sæli, you have the bridge watch until midnight.'

★ ★ ★

16:27

In the galley Ási, Big John and Rúnar have a quick discussion before the latter two leave for their cabins, as the captain instructed.

'The Old Man has never been like this before,' grumbles Rúnar, taking a sip of fresh coffee. 'I hardly dared open my mouth for fear of having my wages cut, or worse!'

'You get to go up to the bridge, though,' says Big John, spitting out a bit of tobacco. 'I'm the next to top officer on board and I'm forbidden access to the bridge!'

'He has his reasons,' says Ási softly as he puts out applecake and doughnuts. 'He's always been a flexible and just man, has Gummi. Maybe he's been too lenient with us through the years. I mean, he's always stood by us, listened to our bullshit and let us get away with various antics, and how have we repaid him?'

'Yeah, maybe.' Big John sighs. 'But *we* weren't the ones who cut the wires on the roof, and it wasn't *our* idea to destroy the engine. All we did was shut some idiot in the forecastle. That's all!'

'We were going to kill the engine,' says Rúnar and shrugs. 'That was a fucking stupid idea, now I think about it.'

'Yeah, but we had also decided not to,' Big John says,

lighting his half-smoked cigar.

'After the old man disarmed us!' says Rúnar with a soft laugh.

'You guys should never have smuggled those guns on board,' Ási says, shaking his head. 'I could have told you no good would come of it.'

'Yeah,' mutters Big John and he exhales sour cigar smoke. 'We should have asked your advice, Ási, lad, instead of listening to Methúsalem's nonsense!'

'Methúsalem,' Rúnar says and sips his coffee. 'There's something not quite right with Methúsalem.'

'Do you think he …?' Ási looks questioningly at his comrade.

'I don't know,' says John. 'But I can't understand how we —'
Boom!

The ship slams sideways into a rising wave. The blow is unexpected and heavy and the three men are thrown about in the galley and fall onto each other, as hot coffee, baked goods, milk, cigar ash, embers and sugar are strewn all over the floor.

★ ★ ★

16:30

Guðmundur Berndsen grabs the table in the chart room when the ship slams into the wave and holds on tight while the bridge shakes like a skyscraper in an earthquake. The weather deck fills with seawater and the windows on the starboard side are about to kiss the dark-grey sea, but then the ship's hull rights itself, about halfway.

'Sæli!' calls the captain when the worst is over. 'Are you okay?'

'I'm fine,' Sæli replies, sitting up on the floor and blinking his eyes. He had been spun around in the captain's chair, thrown out of it, flipped over on the floor and left with his head in the doorway to the starboard bridge wing.

'I think we'd better forget about sitting in chairs while the weather stays this bad,' says Guðmundur, releasing his grip on the chart table. 'It's actually insane to be up here at all, but we have no choice. Here we can keep track of other ships and send a signal light or shoot up a flare.'

'I know,' says Sæli. He positions himself on the port side of the bridge. He stands by the window with his legs spread wide, holding with both hands onto the copper rail that runs the length of the windowsill.

On the floor of the chart room lie the mattress from the captain's bunk, his doona and a pillow. Guðmundur had piled all this up and lugged it up to the bridge, where he tied the mattress to the cupboards in the chart room.

This is where he's going to sleep for the remainder of this voyage.

'If it's all the same to you, I'm going below to get a few more things,' says the captain. He still has to get his charts, sextant and calculator.

And the shotgun.

'Fine by me,' says Sæli without looking back over his shoulder.

★ ★ ★

20:39

Ási is in the galley, almost finished clearing away after supper. Conditions on board don't encourage much in the way of fancy cooking, so he just threw some pork chops in a pot, browned them in the oven and served them with thick mashed potatoes. No gravy, no caramelised potatoes, no peas, no red cabbage and no fuss.

Nobody complained, though – the men have other things to think about, and it's hard enough to eat simple meat at a forty-degree tilt without having to wrestle with caramelised potatoes, peas and thick, creamy gravy as well.

Even Jónas contented himself with flat-tasting tomato soup, despite the fact he'd hardly had anything to eat for two days. But while he's running a high fever and on morphine, liquids and a minimum of nourishment is all the second mate's getting. That's by order of the captain, who's responsible for the health and safety of each and every man on board as long as the ship is afloat.

'My good old lads!' says Ási with a sigh, chewing a toothpick as he turns on the dishwasher. While the main engine is out of commission and thus the dynamo also, the generator is working on full power to ensure there's no shortage of electricity for cooking, freezing and washing.

Ási wipes the work surface in the galley with a damp cloth, turns off the coffee machine and locks the fridge before he turns off the light and closes the door to the galley behind him.

'How are things with you, friend?' asks Ási as he enters the sick bay.

'Just ... the same,' mumbles Jónas and he tries to lick his dry lips. He is both sweaty and pale, and he lies absolutely still under a thin doona, a collar around his neck, his left foot in a pressure bandage raised on two pillows and his left arm in a sling across his stomach.

'Do you need anything for the night?' Ási moves the toothpick from the left side of his mouth to the right.

'I need to piss.'

'Of course,' says Ási and hands him the urine bottle. 'Can I help you with it?'

'No, no ... I can manage,' Jónas says, but he struggles a bit with the flask under the doona.

'Storm's dying down.'

'Yeah ...' says Jónas, grimacing.

'Shouldn't I pour you some water?' says Ási, pouring water from a pitcher into a glass on the bedside table.

'Yeah ... thanks.' Jónas sighs with relief when his urine starts to trickle into the flask.

'Good man,' says Ási. He stands on tiptoe. 'Should I give you a shot for the night?'

'No, I don't think so,' says Jónas, rolling his eyes. 'It gives me such a lot of nightmares. Just leave the pain pills by me.'

'Of course.' Ási fetches two sheets of paracetamol-codeine and puts them on the bedside table. 'Have you finished down below, pal?'

'Yeah ... I think so.' Jónas pushes slightly, then he moves something under the doona before he hands Ási the half-full flask. 'Here you go.'

'Thanks, pal,' says Ási. He examines the dark-yellow liquid before he pours it into the sink and rinses the flask.

'Thanks,' mumbles Jónas and closes his eyes.

'No sweat,' says Ási, turning off the light as he opens the door to the corridor. 'Goodnight, pal.'

'Ási!' says Jónas, opening his eyes and rising up on his right elbow.

'Yeah?' asks Ási, turning the light on again.

'Leave it on – it's better,' Jónas says and drops back down on the pillow.

'Okay,' says Ási with a shrug. 'Goodnight.'

'Goodnight.'

Ási saunters up to C-deck, where he, Sæli and Rúnar have their cabins. Ási's cabin is on the port side, Sæli's in the middle and Rúnar's to starboard. C-deck is the only deck in the ship that is completely manned, as the middle cabins on the other decks are empty.

'Rúnar, you there?' asks the cook as he knocks on the bosun's door.

After a few seconds the bosun opens the door.

'Something the matter?'

'No, no, I was just wondering if you would ask the captain something for me.' Ási takes the chewed toothpick out of his mouth. 'Don't you have night watch later?'

'Yes, I'm due up about midnight,' says Rúnar and yawns. 'What do you want to know?'

'I was just wondering how much I should take out of the freezer. If we're about to abandon ship I'm not going to defrost loads of food.'

'You might just as well shut off the freezer, Ási, lad. This ship is heading for hell.'

'Which means we abandon ship sooner or later, right?' Ási sticks the worn toothpick back in his mouth.

'Yeah,' says Rúnar and grins. 'Unless you want to stay on board?'

'And sail to hell?' says Ási, making a face. 'No-oo. Hardly. But I won't turn off the freezer for all that.'

'Up to you. Was there anything else, Ási?'

'Nope!' says Ási, and he clicks the heels of his wooden clogs together.

'Goodnight,' says Rúnar, nodding to the cook.

'And sleep well!' Ási bows to the bosun, who smiles and closes the door to his cabin.

★ ★ ★

23:47

Sæli is standing by the window to port in the bridge, staring out into the darkness. The storm is dying down little by little, the ship isn't tilting as much as before, and the weather deck has neither water nor briny mist on it. In the bow the forecastle is tilted and inside is a chained man who has no idea what's going on, although he must realise that the ship is drifting before the wind and waves, instead of cutting through the waves and heading in a definite direction.

Would his light be on?

'When can we fetch the man?' asks Sæli, who jumps hearing

his own voice break the hour-long silence.

'First thing in the morning,' mutters the captain, who is standing at the table in the chart room and writing a list on the lined paper of a notebook, lit by a low lamp.

It is a list of the things to take with them in the lifeboat. The boat holds eighteen people, so there's plenty of extra room for fuel, clothes and supplies.

'At dawn, that is,' says Guðmundur a little while later, as he adds 'reading material' to the list. If they are in the boat for a long time it is better if they have something to do besides stare at their hands in their laps.

'I see,' says Sæli softly. He continues to look out through the salt-encrusted windows; there is nothing to see except the ocean and eternal darkness around the lit-up weather deck, and sometimes the odd star in the far distance.

Stars that someone at some time had told him were maybe long dead, although the light they once gave out still travels through the universe.

But that's either a lie or some kind of astrophysics that Sæli doesn't understand.

His legs ache but, after having stood for almost eight hours, the pain has become a buzzing numbness that is almost closer to comfortable than uncomfortable. A fatigue that's unpleasant but which you get used to. What you don't get used to is the way the ship drifts off to the side this way, making you feel like a passenger in a car that skids sideways and is always just about to run off the road.

Is he getting seasick?

'I think I'm getting seasick,' says Sæli as he lets go of the copper pole and moves slowly across the slanting floor and over to starboard.

'Wait till Rúnar comes up,' says the captain. He closes the notebook and looks at his watch. 'It's only a couple of minutes.'

'Yeah, okay.' Sæli grasps a knob on the control panel. 'Should I take the dishes down?'

'No, no,' says Guðmundur, glancing down to the floor where a food tray containing the dirty dishes, cutlery, a coffee mug and a glass is jammed between the mattress and the filing cabinet. 'Rúnar can take it down in the morning.'

'All right,' mumbles Sæli. He takes a deep breath to counteract the nausea that washes over him.

'Are you going to be sick?' asks the captain, turning off the table lamp. As the light goes out they seem to see something blinking on the sea only about fifty metres off the starboard side of the ship.

'Yeah, I –'

'Hush!' says Guðmundur, putting a hand behind his ear as he stares out the window to starboard. 'Did you see that? Something's blinking out there!'

'Wasn't it just the lamp?' says Sæli, who sees nothing but darkness wherever he looks. 'The light was reflected in the glass and when you turned it off it was as if something blinked.'

'No! It was something else.'

The captain rushes to the control panel. He presses his finger on the switch that turns on the foghorn but there's no sound.

Of course not – all of the wires on the mast have been cut.

'Bloody hell!' says Guðmundur, running across the floor to open the door out onto the starboard bridge wing. 'There's a ship out there! I'm certain there is a ship out there!'

'Why ...' Sæli says, then inches across to the door to the wing, which tilts towards the black sea. 'Watch it!'

The captain reaches out and grasps the end of a searchlight that's shining at an angle down to the sea on the starboard side; he jerks at it until the cone of light moves up and over the sea, where the waves rise and fall.

'Come on!' says Guðmundur as he holds on to the light frame with one hand and stares out over the endless sea.

'There's no ship there!' shouts Sæli out the open door. 'What kind of ship do you think would sail without a light ...'

Sæli goes silent as the cone of light reveals sharp outlines on the sea north of the ship.

There is a ship there. A ship without lights.

'Did you see that?' shouts the captain, clenching his left fist. 'There *is* a ship there!'

'Gummi, come back in!' Sæli calls him back. 'I don't like the look of this!'

'Sæli! Go get the emergency flare! We'll shoot up a flare! Quick! The flare gun is in the drawer on the right of ...'

The captain stops speaking when the approaching ship turns on lights in front and behind and on both sides. These are no ordinary lights. They're green and, rather than lighting up their own ship, they're all directed away from their ship, which disappears in a sea of poisonous green light.

'Green lights?' asks Sæli. He stares open-mouthed at this oval sea of light that glows like a weird flying object in a cheap movie. 'Who uses green lights?'

'They can't be seen from a distance. *They can't be seen from a distance,*' mutters Guðmundur as he lets go of the searchlight frame and sneaks backwards through the door without taking his eyes off the green light that's following his ship, coming closer and closer. 'Christ almighty! And I thought things couldn't get any worse.'

'What is it?' asks Sæli, his heart in his mouth as he watches, bewildered, while the captain hits one switch after another, turning off all the lights on the outside of the *Per se*, which gradually becomes lost in the darkness.

Too little, too late. 'We don't have much time,' says Guðmundur as he looks at the dial of his watch, where the second hand is beginning to eat up the last minute before midnight. 'Go up on the roof and shoot off an emergency flare. If we're lucky there'll be other ships in the area.'

'Captain?' says Sæli, his voice trembling, and he grips Guðmundur Berndsen's left arm hard.

'*Up on the roof, now!*' screams the captain and he slaps Sæli across the face with the palm of his right hand. 'If nobody comes to help us we'll all be dead before tomorrow dawns.'

* * *

23:59

Big John is standing in front of the generator with an adjustable spanner in his right hand, a dirty rag in his left, grimy ear protectors on his head, and a dead cigar clamped in the right corner of his mouth.

The chief engineer listens carefully to the rhythmic rattling of these big diesel engines as he reduces the fuel injection in one of them. At night the use of electricity is at a low, so he's decided to run the generators one at a time at half speed, both to reduce fuel consumption and limit wear and tear and, thus, reduce the danger of a breakdown.

'*There!*' says Big John to himself as he gives the rattling engines a friendly pat. He puts the wrench back where it belongs, wipes the oil off his fingers with the rag and saunters over the iron floor and into the storeroom.

The evening watch is over and the chief engineer is on his way to bed. He takes off his ear protectors, steps out of his overalls and hangs them up, kicks off his work shoes and slips on his clogs.

Whatever happened to that picture of a girl he'd hung up inside the door of the control room?

John lights a match and sucks life into his cigar stub before he turns out the light in the cubbyhole and saunters up to A-deck.

In front of the food locker a light blinks, as if the bulb is about to give out. But it's been acting that way for the whole voyage.

'I'll change you tomorrow,' says the chief engineer as he grasps the stair rail leading up to B-deck, but he stops when a black shadow appears at the top of the stairwell.

'Who …' Big John Pétursson half closes his eyes under his hairy eyebrows and wrinkled forehead.

A light blinks in front of the shadow. A light like a candle that flames and dies at incredible speed.

And with this light comes a terrific noise. Rhythmic, thundering blows with a metallic undertone. Like a heavy iron chain running noisily over a sharp iron edge.

Ratatatata!

Then silence as empty as the night, which smells of bitter smoke and blood.

Warning bells start to sound throughout the ship and at the same time the chief engineer falls slowly but surely backwards, like the last tree in the forest.

The light blinks, the light dims, the light goes out.

His heart stops.

Stop.

And everything goes black.

XXVIII

00:00

Guðmundur is standing forwards on the starboard bridge wing, watching five black-clad men sail a hard-bottomed inflatable up to the ship's side, where they kill the outboard motor and throw a line with a three-pronged hook on the end onto the weather deck.

What should he do?

The captain runs into the bridge to get his shotgun. He flips off the safety catch, clutches it to his chest and, bent over, sneaks back out onto the bridge wing. When he looks out from the wing he sees that the men in black have tied the dinghy to the railing on the overhanging side of the ship; three of them are already up on the weather deck and the other two are about to leave the boat. They are dressed like terrorists, in black military boots with black berets on their heads and machine guns on short shoulder straps.

Skuggi coils up under the table in the chart room, whining like a puppy.

The captain shudders as he bends his knees, leans on the metal wall and aims the gun at the men, who are running single file along the weather deck. He aims at the leader of the group, his cold index finger trembles on the trigger, his eyes fill with salty liquid, his heart hammers, his blood rushes through his veins, and he breathes quickly through his open mouth.

He can't do it! But he must. He has to!

Guðmundur Berndsen pulls the trigger. The gun goes off and slams him hard in the shoulder. For one second he sees only black and it's as if time stands still, but then his eyes open, his lungs draw breath and the ship moves up and down. He lifts the gun and peers over the wall. Below on the weather deck run four black-clad men, stepping over their comrade, who lies curled up on the cold metal.

Is he dead? It doesn't matter.

Guðmundur pumps the shotgun and aims again. He has to hit at least one or two more before they get under the bridge wing and up to B-deck. Once they are on B-deck they're as good as into the wheelhouse.

But before the captain can pull the trigger a second time he hears the monotonous bark of a large machine gun, and heavy lead bullets crash into the bridge, making a fearsome commotion. Sparks fly in all directions and slivers of metal, shards of glass and chips of paint rain down. The captain throws himself face down on the floor and covers his ears while the pirates' mother ship pumps lead over the ship's wheelhouse.

Silence.

Guðmundur takes his hands away from his ears and opens his eyes. Beside him lies the shotgun, covered with pieces of glass and white chips of paint, like the captain himself.

The alarm bell! He has to ring the alarm bell! There are bloodthirsty gunmen on board the ship and the only thing to do is get the crew into the lifeboat and abandon ship before it is too late.

The captain clasps the shotgun close and crawls on all fours into the damaged bridge. Then he runs across to the red box in the middle of the bridge, opens it and pushes the fire alarm. Immediately, all the bells in the ship begin to ring.

Guðmundur looks at his watch.

00:02:30

The captain intends to wait for up to two minutes on the bridge, then go straight down to the boat deck and be the last to get on board the lifeboat. It doesn't matter what danger threatens the ship and crew: the captain does not abandon ship until the last minute and he is always the last to leave the ship, or loses his life if it comes to that.

Guðmundur takes a few steps over to the starboard side of the ship and peers out the door that opens onto the bridge wing. A sea of green light floats above the black water while a red globe flames up in the heavily clouded sky.

The noise from the bells makes it difficult to think clearly and every nerve in his body is incandescent as a lightbulb. Skuggi has crawled into hiding and is keeping quiet.

'NO SUDDEN MOVES!' shouts someone behind him.

The captain clenches his hands around the shotgun, looks to the right and slowly straightens up …

★ ★ ★

00:00

Sæli stands on the platform back of the wheelhouse on the bridge deck holding the flare gun in his right hand and the flare cartridge in his left. A flare gun is like an ordinary handgun except that the barrel is as wide as the exhaust pipe on a car. Sæli opens the gun with shaking fingers, puts the cartridge in place and shuts it again. Then he climbs up onto the roof of the ship, which is running wet and tilting uncomfortably to starboard.

Sæli is cold, his every muscle is twitching, his teeth are chattering and his stomach is clenching into a tight knot.

He has to manage this. *He has to!*

Sæli crawls out onto the roof and rolls onto his back in the middle. His legs point to the disconnected satellite receiver and at the back of his head the radar mast rises like an oversized scarecrow. Under the seaman 4000 tonnes of cold iron are rocking on the surface of an abyss; above him there is only darkness.

He holds the gun with both hands and points the barrel straight up to the night sky. But he doesn't pull the trigger. He can't pull the trigger. Why should he pull the trigger?

They are dead! Dead. All of them!

Hesitating up there on the roof, Sæli startles when the captain fires the shotgun down on the bridge wing.

What was that?

But when the shooter on the pirates' ship starts pumping lead into the ship's bridge, it's as if the seaman's blood freezes in his veins and his soul leaves his body. The machine gun barks thunderously and the ship shudders under the heavy hail of lead. At first the bullets pelt the bridge wings and the outside of the bridge, but then the shooter raises the barrel of his gun and aims his gunfire at the radar mast, which splinters like a henhouse in a hurricane.

Bits of plastic, screws and bent and broken metal rain over Sæli, who squeezes his eyes shut and cradles the flare gun to his chest like a child with a soft toy.

Silence.

Sæli opens his eyes and stares up into the sky, no longer feeling the cold or his body. The mast still stands but the two radar scanners are simply unsightly scraps and tangles of wire.

Time stands still and eternity smells of salt, smoke and broken plastic.

Sæli doesn't know what he's doing, what he should do or what's happening.

Maybe he should just fall asleep and never wake up?

Yes.

It's best to try to sleep.

All of a sudden the bells resound throughout the ship and the seaman blinks his eyes and blows shreds of something out of his nose. Then he lifts an arm, aims the gun at the heavens and pulls the trigger.

Pow!

There's a solid bang and the gun recoils so hard that Sæli almost drops it in his face, but the flare streaks vertically into the night sky. It leaves behind a white stripe as it flies higher and higher, until it stops climbing and pauses for a second, then comes a bright red light that glows like a jewel and changes the darkness into a rose-red dome that grows smaller as the flare sways calmly down, hanging from a white parachute.

* * *

Stoker, wearing nothing but a pair of cotton trousers, is sitting by the table in his cabin, mixing himself a pipe, when a green glow lights up the beige curtains.

A green glow?

'What the hell?' he mutters, putting down the pipe and the burnt aluminium foil with its hot blend of tobacco and cannabis oil. He stands up from the table and walks over the slanting floor, kneels on the bed and pulls the curtains to both sides.

Out in the sea north of the ship is a wash of green light that's gradually getting nearer.

'Pirates!' declares Stoker and he clutches the curtains in his fists. He has read several books about this perpetual threat on the high seas which, contrary to what many people think, has never in the history of sailing been as real as it is now.

* * *

'One, two, three, four,' murmurs Ási as he moves the red piece over an equal number of squares. He is sitting alone at the table in his cabin, playing ludo against himself. The blue piece has two sixes in a row, the green is close behind, the red has got started but the yellow one has hardly left the starting square.

'Come on!' says the cook as he shakes the die in his right

hand, releases it and rolls it over the table. Before it stops, some kind of hailstorm slams into the starboard side of the ship. It clangs against the steel, and sudden thumps pulse through the wheelhouse like someone knocking at the ship with a big hammer.

'What was that?' Ási says, stands up and walks over to the window, which is on the port side and faces at an angle up into the night sky.

Outside there is nothing to be seen but darkness.

'Where had we got to?' Ási sits back down at the table, where the red die lies motionless, showing two black pips. 'Wasn't it yellow? It was yellow. Yellow forward two. You'd better get a move on, my little yellow friend, eh?'

Ási moves the yellow piece two places and now all the pieces have started on one more go around the square board. The cook shakes out a cigarette from a fresh packet and lights up with a match.

'Whose turn is it?' asks Ási of no-one, shaking the match out before putting it back in the matchbox. Then he squints, sucks on the cigarette and blows smoke out his nose.

'Is it green?

The cook takes the cigarette out of his mouth and stubs it out in a tin can half full of sand and stubs.

'No, wasn't it blue?'

Yellow's turn has come round again when the alarm bells resound throughout the ship.

'What's all the fuss?' says Ási, absentmindedly throwing the die.

Four.

Outside of the window a red light starts glowing, but the cook doesn't notice. He stands up and walks slowly to the door, and opens it just as if the raging clatter of the bell was the doorbell and there was an impatient visitor waiting in the corridor.

Now what's up?

In the corridor stands a man dressed all in black, who turns suddenly when he becomes aware of the cook and stares at Ási with wild eyes.

'What can I do for you —' But before Ási can finish his question the pirate pulls the trigger of his machine gun.

Ratatatatata!

Ásmundur Sigjónsson from the Westman Islands blinks his eyes, moves his lips and tries weakly to hold onto the doorframe, but his fingers are as soft as butter and his body so terribly heavy. So heavy. So …

* * *

'I'd better let Satan out,' says Stoker, jumping down off his bed. He opens the door into the corridor and runs barefoot and bare-chested down the stairs and out the door at the back of the wheelhouse, to B-deck, where he turns right, runs past the wheelhouse and in three jumps down the stairs reaches the weather deck on the port side.

At the same time five black-clad men throw a line with a three-pronged hook on the end over the railing on the starboard side.

When Stoker is halfway across the icy-cold, wet deck the captain lets off a shot from his shotgun and then the second engineer throws himself on his face on the ribbed iron floor. Seconds later the shooter on the pirates' mother ship pulls the trigger of the big machine gun and rains lead over the bridge of the ship.

Stoker grimaces and crawls forwards along the deck like a soldier in a shallow trench. When the shooting lets up he has about a third of the way still to go. Then he stands up and runs the last bit, back bent, head stretched forward, and when he sees the red-painted front of the forecastle he throws himself on his abdomen in front of the forward hatch.

He lies there for a short while to catch his breath, then rolls over on his back. Just then the emergency flare swooshes into the black sky.

'FUCK!' screams Stoker, knowing that in a few seconds the flare will light up the night – and himself, where he stands defenceless in the bow of the ship, half naked and unarmed.

Why turn out the lights when idiots with a flare gun are loose on board?

Stoker jumps to his feet and runs over to the red door in the middle of the forecastle. He takes hold of the rusty hasps with his bare hands and tears them loose, and just before he manages to loosen the last hasp and open the door to the forecastle the flare ignites in the sky. It sways like a soap bubble at the highest point of the dome and casts a rose-red gleam over the ship and the surrounding sea.

★ ★ ★

Rúnar is half sitting in his bed reading *The Good Soldier Svejk*. It's dark in the cabin, except for the reading lamp that shines above the bosun's head. He's supposed to have reported to the bridge but he only has a page and a half of the thirteenth chapter to go and he might as well just finish it, rather than leave this little bit unread.

Always best to begin a new chapter each time a book is opened.

I think it must be wonderful to be run through with a polished bayonet, says Svejk in the book, and the bosun laughs aloud. He knows the story almost by heart, having read it on more or less every tour he's been on for the last three years, but the matchless nonsense spoken by that idiot Svejk never stops being funny.

And it's pretty decent to get a bullet in the stomach. But the most wonderful ...

The bosun stops reading when the page takes on a green tinge.

'What?' he says and looks up. Then he sees that this

mysterious light is coming from outside and filtering into the cabin through the light-brown curtains. He sits up in the bed, pushes the curtains to the side and looks out through the clouded glass of his window.

A sea of green light?

'Is that a ship?' the bosun mutters and shades his eyes in order to see out more clearly.

Yes, it must be a ship. But green lights! Who uses green lights?

'What the fuck!' says the bosun, eyes wide. Is he seeing things? No: there are men boarding the ship's weather deck from an inflatable. They're on board! Somebody heard the emergency signal after all!

We're safe!

'I knew it!' says Rúnar, his face pressed to the glass. 'I knew it all the ...' But he goes silent and stiffens when he hears shots fired in the distance and see the first of the five rescuers collapsing on the weather deck.

What?

The other four act as if nothing has happened. They run, stooped over, stepping over their comrade, heading for the stairs that lead up to B-deck on the starboard side. There's a glint of light out on the black sea and a split second later the noisy bark of the machine gun reaches the bosun's ears. He throws himself on the bed when lead bullets slam onto the bridge, ripping up iron, wood and glass.

Silence.

★ ★ ★

Why can't I open my eyes?

'Damn,' murmurs Methúsalem as he claws at the caked pus that's stuck to his eyelashes, gluing his eyes shut.

After about a minute he manages to open one eye and then the other. He is lying on his back in bed and looking up into the damp darkness.

What day is it? What time?
He hears a shot.
Silence.
And then a large machine gun barks in the distance and shots rain on the starboard side of the ship.

'What's going on?' wonders Methúsalem as he gets out of bed and tears the sodden blanket from the window.

A cold and refreshing wind hits the pale face of the chief mate, which takes on a green tinge from the strange light north of the ship.

Green light?

Methúsalem Sigurðsson sticks his head out the window and sees men in black with machine guns run, bent over, behind the wheelhouse and up to B-deck.

'Fuckers!'

Methúsalem jumps out of bed, naked. He steps on myriad glass shards that cut the soles of his feet and stick into flesh and bones, but he is too angry to feel pain.

He goes into the bathroom, splashes cold water on his face and looks at his eyes in the mirror. They are fiery red, swollen and sore, and full of yellow clots of pus.

Infection!

He had told the captain that he was getting an eye infection and now he's got an eye infection.

What's happening?

Methúsalem slathers soap on the mirror and spits at the distorted reflection in it, then he puts on some trousers and gets his rifle from the wardrobe.

'I'll kill those fuckers,' says the first mate as he releases the safety and wraps the shoulder strap loosely over his right arm. 'Kill the damn boss-men … Those treacherous vermin. That brute of a captain!'

Brute of a captain? Yes! Who else is behind it all? Who else was needing reinforcements?

The captain, that's who.

'That he should dare!' grumbles Methúsalem. Salt wind comes in the broken window, bringing up goose bumps on the corpse-white body of the first mate, who's breathing hard through flared nostrils and gnashing his teeth in fury.

Seawater is as salty as blood and …

Suddenly the alarm bells resound throughout the ship and a second later a red light flares outside the window.

That's the sign!

Sign? What sign?

'Doesn't matter!' Methúsalem mutters, opens the door and steps out of his cabin dressed only in beige trousers. Holding the rifle in both hands, he runs up the stairs, leaving bloody footprints on every second step.

He's going to capture the captain before these black-clad henchmen of the shipping company get control of the bridge.

No! He's not going to capture that fucking pig! He's going to shoot him in the head and watch him die!

Wow! It's come to that.

A cold current runs up the first mate's spine and he weaves up the last steps as if in a dream, stopping in front of the door leading to the bridge.

★ ★ ★

Rúnar is sitting on the side of his bed, rocking back and forth like an old man.

What's going on? Who are they? What should he do? Stay still? Go up to the bridge?

Suddenly the alarm bells clamour in every cabin, in every corridor, on every single deck at the same time.

The bosun stands up and clenches his fists. Is there a fire? Or is the captain warning the crew of danger? When the bells stop they're supposed to meet out on the boat deck. If the ship is in serious danger, the crew's supposed to abandon ship.

I've got to …

Rúnar walks towards the door but stops in the middle of the floor and looks at the closed door in bewilderment.

What if those men have boarded the ship? What if one of them is waiting on the other side of the closed door?

What if …

The bosun jumps and gasps as someone grabs the handle and opens the door of his cabin, then he takes two steps backwards as a black-clad man appears in the doorway.

'DON'T! DON'T! DON—' shouts Rúnar Hallgrímsson, covering his eyes with both hands as the stranger opens his own eyes wide and pulls the trigger of his machine gun.

Ratatatata!

The rapid-fire bullets tear asunder clothes, skin, flesh and blood vessels; they blow up entrails, cartilage and bones, before drilling their way through the bosun's back, slamming into the wall behind him and ricocheting, sticky with blood, along the rug.

★ ★ ★

Jónas is lying awake in the sick bay with a sweaty pillow under his head, staring at the closed door.

He can't stay any longer on this cursed ship that's floating dead in the water, en route to disaster. He just can't! But what can he do?

What?

He could sneak up to the boat deck, crawl on board the lifeboat and shoot it overboard. Then he could sail to land. If anybody asks, he can say that the ship sank and he survived. But with any luck he'd come ashore without anyone noticing.

He could do it. Or could he? Could he, physically? If he took enough painkillers he should be able to hop on one leg up the stairs, supporting himself with one hand on the railing.

Maybe not …

The pain is so hellish that he almost faints every time he coughs or gets a cramp.

And what about his shipmates? If he takes the lifeboat, their hopes of survival will be seriously reduced. But it wasn't Jónas who killed the engine! Why should he accept the conditions that others have put him in? Why should he think about the survival of men who haven't given a moment's thought to *his* survival? Why should he, seriously injured as he was, be worried about his fully fit shipmates?

Those idiots have dug themselves a grave that Jónas has no desire to lie in.

And how does he know they don't plan to leave him alone on the ship? How does he know they haven't already abandoned this drifting heap of iron? How does he know he isn't the only soul aboard this godless ghost ship?

No, that was too frightful to be true!

Or was it?

'Hello!' shouts Jónas, sitting up in the bed. 'Is anybody awake? Hello! HELLO!'

I don't believe this! Have they really …

Jónas gasps when the alarm bells start up.

What's going on? Is there a fire? Is the ship sinking? Is …

'Help! Help! ÁSI! SOMEBODY!' shouts Jónas, throwing the doona off. 'DON'T FORGET ME! DON'T FORGET …'

Jónas shouts himself hoarse and then it dawns on him. Nobody will come to help him, whether he yells or not.

Nobody.

'They're going to let me die here,' Jónas wails, wiping the sweat from his ruddy forehead as he moves his right leg carefully out of the bed.

He has to get up to the boat deck! He has to get in the boat with them!

He has to …

★ ★ ★

'No sudden moves!' shouts Methúsalem Sigurðsson as he opens the door and steps into the bridge.

The captain clenches his hands on the shotgun, looks to the right and slowly straightens up.

'*Stay still!*' commands Methúsalem, aiming at the captain from his waist. He steps into the bridge and checks that there are just the two of them.

'Methúsalem!' shouts the captain. 'Don't turn your back to the door! They're on their way up.' He beckons the first mate over to him, where he stands in the middle of the bridge, his back to the controls and the broken windows.

'They don't matter. *Now it's just you and me!*' yells Methúsalem, grinning with the pleasure of power.

'METHÚSALEM! BEHIND YOU!'

'No such tricks, old man,' Methúsalem growls, wiping the grin off his face as he grasps the rifle more firmly.

'METHÚSALEM!' shouts the captain again, as he lifts the shotgun and aims it in the direction of the first mate, who pulls the trigger of the rifle without hesitation.

Bam!

***

00:02:30

The bells are ringing throughout the ship. Guðmundur Berndsen glances at his watch as he sinks down, with his back to the wall and his shotgun in his arms, and sits on the floor in the middle of the mess, right under the red fire-alarm box.

'Easy now. You've got to keep calm,' the captain tells himself and takes a deep breath. Then he leans on the shotgun and stands up. He mustn't let down his guard. He has to be prepared for everything. These devils might appear in the bridge at any moment!

When great danger is imminent, life suddenly becomes so

very valuable but, at the same time, as delicate as a baby bird in a snowstorm. All you can do in such a situation is to blindly trust in the unlikely, while simultaneously closing your eyes to the obvious, and thus meet your fate armed only with absurdity.

Guðmundur takes a few steps across to the starboard side of the ship and looks out the door leading to the bridge wing. Green light shines over the black waters, while up in the darkly clouded sky, the red globe flares.

'No sudden moves!' shouts Methúsalem Sigurðsson as he steps into the bridge.

The captain clenches his hands around the shotgun, looks to the right and slowly straightens up. The bells are making so much noise that a herd of rhinos could have run into the bridge without his having been aware of it.

The door! Of course he should have watched the door. Goddammit! What if it had been the pirates and not …

'*Stay still!*' shouts Methúsalem and aims from his waist at the captain.

'Methúsalem! Don't turn your back to the door! They're on their way up!' shouts the captain, and he beckons the first mate to come over to him.

'They don't matter. *Now it's just you and me!*' Methúsalem grins coldly with an insane gleam in his infected eyes.

Is he joking?

'METHÚSALEM! BEHIND YOU!' shouts the captain as a black shadow appears in the doorway behind the first mate.

'No such tricks, old man!' Methúsalem Sigurðsson wipes the grin off his face and grasps the rifle more firmly.

'METHÚSALEM!' the captain cries again as he lifts up the shotgun and aims it in the direction of the first mate, who pulls the trigger of the rifle without hesitation.

Bam!

The shot streaks by the captain's left ear. Guðmundur blinks and hardly notices that blood is beginning to run down his neck. The only thing he sees is the look of astonishment on

Methúsalem's face as the pirate grapples him from behind and a sharp knife cuts his throat from below his left ear quickly down to his right collarbone.

Blood gushes in rhythmic pulses into the air and down to the first mate's chest. Methúsalem collapses helplessly onto his knees and then right on his face. The pirate sheathes his knife in an instant, waves the machine gun around, puts his index finger on the trigger and finishes off the few rounds of shot left in the vertical chamber.

Ratata–

Click, click, click.

The captain is faster. He takes one step to the side as he aims the shotgun, and as the bullets from the machine gun slam into the ship's controls. he takes a firm grip on the trigger and shoots the intruder straight in his staring face.

★ ★ ★

00:02:30

He's standing on a curved balcony looking over a brightly lit assembly room the size of a ship's hold. If this hall has a name it must be 'The Golden Gallery'. The walls are covered with golden squares from floor to ceiling. In front of the squares are smaller squares and, between them, lights that flicker on the smooth gold like fire in a dream. From the ceiling hang cylindrical chandeliers the size of ships' funnels, made up of crystal threads. The chandeliers are two-layered, the inner cylinders reaching below the outer ones. Inside them shines a light that refracts, creating thousands of lights that give the impression of stars in the sky or diamonds in water.

In the distance is the sound of old-fashioned jazz, though there is no band to be seen.

He walks down the broad, curved staircase to the assembly room. As he steps out on the polished wooden floor he sees a similar staircase on the port side. Above him is the balcony, but there's no-one there now.

He walks through the middle of the room. There are formally decked tables to each side. First he passes tables set for two and four but then he comes to long tables for eight, sixteen and thirty-two. There are white tablecloths and heavy silver cutlery, linen napkins in silver napkin rings, handpainted porcelain dishes and cut-crystal glasses arranged on them.

Very good, he thinks, as though he is responsible for it all, that things are exactly as he requested, that nothing in the assembly room disappoints the guests or upsets them.

Off and on the room seems to fill with the sound of chatter, light laughter and the clink of glasses, then he turns around and looks at first one table then another. But the moment he looks over his shoulder the voices are silenced and the clinking of glasses dies out between the echoing walls.

Or was it the screech of metal and rattling of chains?

At the front of the assembly room is a cognac lounge. Heavy leather chairs around uncovered circular tables of dark wood, a thick carpet on the floor and the aroma of cigar smoke, although no-one is smoking. He walks up a broad staircase leading to a doorway with heavy wooden double doors opening into the bright room.

Beyond the door is another room: a vast, stinking space – dark, cold and empty. At first he can see nothing – it's as if the bottomless dark absorbs the light – but little by little pictures appear in the darkness, like large fish that stick their colourless bodies up out of black water.

He sees eyes that are dark pits, gaping mouths and skin stretched like a rubber sheet over fleshless bones, and the people are singing a song as lifeless as the whining of wind in a half-open window. They stretch thin arms up in the air and all those emaciated arms turn into a leafless forest of arms in the bottom of the hold; the song changes into drawn-out lustful moans; these living pictures of the dead are fucking each other down in the deep, and their nightmarish faces – which had, at first, run together into one terrible mask of hunger – have now become fitful distortions of the face of his daughter, who thrashes about and fucks herself in a rotting stew of cold flesh that engenders flesh and –

He hears a heavy thud, turns and sees a man lying face down in the middle of the Golden Gallery. It's Stoker. He is dressed in evening clothes and beardless, his hair newly trimmed. His fingers twitch and he blinks his eyes. His head is open and a thick bloody soup oozes from the rug and into the opening that little by little closes again – *Daddy!*

He feels cold fingers pull at his clothes. He loses his balance and falls backwards, down into the darkness. He stretches out his arm and manages to grasp the brass doorknobs on the two doors with both hands but he isn't able to lift himself up; he can't keep his balance on the edge of the abyss. His arms grow longer and longer, he holds onto the brass knobs and closes the double door like a trapdoor behind him. The slit contracts, the light dims, he tumbles into the dark void.

He falls into the plinth course; he hears heavy metal pulled aside, hinges screeching, and a moment before he lands on the hard metal floor someone calls.

SATAN!

★ ★ ★

00:03:03

The noise of the bells is maddening …

With his right hand, Jónas takes hold of the railing on the right-hand side of the stairs that lead up to B-deck and then the boat deck. He takes a deep breath and tries to control his trembling muscles, then he bends his right leg a little before he hops up to the next step.

He is wearing nothing but a white nightshirt; he is

trembling with weakness and suffering torments of pain. Sweat pours off him and the bandages on his left ankle and left wrist are swelling from the rhythmic beating of his arteries; his left side itches all over and his broken limbs send a continuous message of distress. The fingers of his left hand hold the four aluminium sheets of paracetamol-codeine in a deathlike grip. One sheet falls onto the step below him and two steps above another sheet drops from his numb fingers. Only two sheets left, and one is beginning to slide …

One step, then another, and another …

He has to be able to do this!

When he finally makes it to the top of the boat deck stair he can hardly stand. The fingers of his left hand are holding weakly to the final aluminium sheet, snot and blood run from his nose, and his gums, skin and eyes all itch.

'*Further, further,*' Jónas cajoles himself, hops to the side and leans his left shoulder against the wall at the top of the stairs. Just rest a little, one second, only to …

Ási and Rúnar's cabins are wide open and they are lying inside on their backs in their own blood. Shot to pieces. Stone dead.

'What's going …' Jónas says and blinks. The paralysing din of the bells wreathes this horrific scene in an aura of unreality, but after staring at the corpses of his shipmates for a few second, the second mate realises that this is stark reality.

The men on the ship are being killed.

'Good God!' cries Jónas. He hops one short step forwards towards the bosun's cabin, but when he hears someone running up the stairs, he hops with all his strength over to the door leading out to the platform at the back of the wheelhouse, on the port side.

There he pushes his back against the door and holds his breath, while a man dressed all in black with a machine gun strapped over his shoulder studies the corpses of Jónas's shipmates for just an instant before running up to D-deck.

Who …? Is everyone dead?

Jónas takes hold of the doorknob with his right hand, opens the door and hops out under the open sky. He grabs the railing with his right hand and hops backwards along the iron floor.

Above him the emergency flare sways slowly down, like a dwarf sun setting.

When he reaches the lifeboat he has to hop up two more steps – first up to the raised platform back of the boat and then up to the boat's stern, which points forty-five degrees up into the rose-red night sky.

His sweat-soaked nightshirt is stuck to his clammy skin, a cold wind blows up his bare legs and his right leg has gone numb from the hard, cold steel.

When Jónas finally reaches the stern of the lifeboat he realises that the fingers of his left hand are not holding anything. The last sheet of painkillers is gone.

No!

He opens the door aft on the boat by turning two handles up, then he lifts up a heavy door with his other hand while he struggles to keep his balance on one foot. This is all so difficult that he mostly just wants to give up, to sit down and cry, but since he's got this far, he has to go the whole way. He has to!

The door falls to the side and the open boat lies before him. If Jónas should lose his balance and fall in through the door, he'd fall all the way to the bow, the boat slants at such an angle.

But Jónas makes it through the door, manages to close it after him and climb up to sit in the helmsman's seat, which is higher than all the other seats in the boat and is the only seat of the eighteen that faces forwards and not backwards. On top of the boat is a raised section with four windows, two facing forwards and one to each side. The first mate fastens the five-point safety belt, turns the current onto the controls and starts moving a long rod back and forth.

With every movement of the rod the boat lifts up a few

millimetres and slowly a short iron hook comes loose from a thick joist on the bottom of the boat. When the joist has risen above the hook the boat is free, and then it drops down off the davits and straight into the sea, which spurts dozens of metres in all directions.

The blow is so heavy that Jónas B Jónasson loses consciousness.

★ ★ ★

00:02:33

'SATAN!' shouts Stoker as soon as he manages to open the forecastle.

'Huh? What?' says Satan and his fumbling hands reach for nothing as he suddenly wakes from a deep nightmarish sleep. 'Who's …'

Where is he? Who's shouting? What …

Satan opens his eyes and sees the black shadow of a man lit by red light, framed by a doorway with rounded corners. He smells metal, tar and paint thinner; he is being lifted up and down, tossed about in a narrow and uncomfortable space; he hears the sea knocking against the steel, the wind moaning and the low squeal from the heater; his forearm stings from the needle prick and he can feel how the lock on the chain pushes into the small of his back …

The ship!

'Leave me alone, man,' says Satan. He leans his head back on the folded burlap. 'Don't wake me until we've got to Suriname. Is that clear?'

'GET UP, YOU!' Stoker screams, jumping over the sill. Then he lowers his hoarse voice to say, 'The ship is dead in the water and we've got pirates on board.'

'What!?' says Satan and opens his eyes lazily. 'What'd you say?'

'*The ship is dead!*'

'You said *pirates*, you idiot.' Satan snaps his fingers as he sits up in the plinth course.

'Yes, and they've come aboard!' says Stoker stepping from foot to foot like a little boy who needs to wee. 'Their ship is alongside and shoots a machine gun at the slightest provocation!'

'It's about time something happened on board this tub,' says Satan, climbing out of the plinth course. When he stands up the chain around his middle pulls taut. 'If there is one thing this boring crew needs, it is precisely entertainment from elsewhere. For some reason I didn't fit the bill, but pirates with machine guns are something everybody can enjoy. Right?'

'I'm not kidding, man!' Stoker points with a shaking finger out the open door, where the pirates' inflatable can just be seen in the water by the weather deck, halfway between the forecastle and the wheelhouse. 'I heard shots earlier on! They'll kill us all if —'

'I never said that I don't believe you,' says Satan, shutting Stoker up with the palm of his right hand. 'Did you bring the key?'

'The key?' asks Stoker as Satan removes his hand.

'Yeah, the key!'

'Oh shit, man!' Stoker stares at the chain. 'Who has the key?'

'The long, ugly one,' says Satan. He fishes a cigarette packet and lighter out of his left trouser pocket. 'White, dumb and badly dressed.'

'Methúsalem! Of course. Shit! Hold on.' Stoker grabs the pocket of his cotton trousers. 'I think –'

'What are you doing, man?' asks Satan and lights his cigarette.

'Here it is!' says Stoker, grinning broadly as he feels something hard in his right pocket, then he turns his pocket inside out and grabs the key before it falls to the floor.

'Clever boy!' Satan lifts up his arms and turns around,

holding a lit cigarette in one hand and the pack and lighter in the other.

'Okay, here we go!' Stoker sticks the key in the lock and turns it clockwise, so the lock pops open and the chain rattles onto the iron floor.

'Excellent!' says Satan and blows smoke out his nose as he sticks the cigarette packet and the lighter in his right trousers pocket.

'Now what?' asks Stoker, grabbing the iron column in the middle of the forecastle to keep from falling down.

'Do what I do.' Satan sticks the cigarette in his mouth, then tears the net off the paint cans at the front of the plinth course and screws the lids off a five-litre can of thinner. 'Find more of these thinner cans and hand them to me.'

'Okay,' murmurs Stoker and drops to his knees by the plinth course as Satan goes over to the door and tosses the cans in the direction of the pirates' inflatable.

He could, of course, shoot at the boat but it could be hellishly difficult to hit a moving target from so far away – besides which, there's not all that much ammunition.

The can lands in the sea in front of the boat. It washes back up on the weather deck on the next wave.

'Here!' Stoker hands Satan another can. 'There's just one more.'

'Quick!' says Satan with the cigarette hanging from his mouth. He takes the can and flings it with all his strength back along the ship. The can spins in the air and spits thinner in all directions, before landing on the weather deck behind the inflatable and at the feet of the black-clad man who's lying face down by the railing.

One down – way to go!

'This is the last one,' says Stoker as he passes Satan an open can only half full of thinner.

'*Watch this*,' hisses Satan out of one side of his mouth. He waits a moment while the ship rights itself and then he throws the can high up into the sky, watching as it swings in a long arc out over the weather deck and directly over the unmanned inflatable, which lifts on a wave as if to receive the can.

'Wow! That was really —' Stoker stops when a light begins to blink in the sea of green light and a shower of lead bullets slams into the starboard side of the forecastle, the outside of the door and the forward hatch.

The sound of the pirates' heavy machine guns carries to them shortly after the first bullets slam into the inch-thick steel, raising sparks.

Stoker grabs his head and throws himself to the side, while Satan jumps out of the door and disappears from sight.

'Wait! *Wait!* WAIT FOR ME!' cries Stoker, clambering over the sill and running barefoot over to the port side and from there back along the slanting weather deck. When Satan is halfway to the back of the ship he stops and sits down on the weather deck with his back to the hatch. He looks up to the sky, where the emergency flare is glowing, and curses the man who shot it up.

What halfwit lights up the field of battle when the enemy has come so close? The battlefield that, in this case, is the crew's home ground! These guys are so stupid! In close combat, darkness is the best comrade in arms, any sensible man knows that — if he's got any balls.

'Now what?' asks Stoker, red with cold, kneeling beside Satan.

'Wait a second,' says Satan and he sucks on his cigarette until it glows white, then stands up and throws the stub over the hatch cover.

'I get it. You're going to burn the dinghy so they can't get back if —'

'Take a look!' says Satan, nudging Stoker with his elbow.

'All right,' mutters Stoker as he stands up and looks across the hatch cover.

The machine gun retorts and bullets slam into the hatch

cover and fly with a loud whine into the night.

Stoker throws himself back on his knees and looks at Satan without saying anything. He doesn't need to say anything.

Disappointment shines from his eyes.

'Fire or no fire, doesn't matter,' says Satan under his breath. He gets to his feet without straightening his back. 'Come on, let's face these bandits!'

Stoker struggles to get up, then follows Satan over the weather deck.

'How many did you say there were?' Satan asks when they reach the stairs up to B-deck.

'I have no idea. But that inflatable couldn't carry more than six.'

'One's down already. So there are, at most, five left. Five men with machine guns. It's not going to be any fucking child's play getting bullets into all their guts.'

Satan runs over to the starboard side of the wheelhouse, sits on his haunches under the white-painted iron wall and pulls his hunting knife out of its holster on his left leg.

Inside the thick walls, the alarm bells are sounding.

'What are you going to —'

'*Shut up!*' hisses Satan and gestures to Stoker to sit behind him. 'Take this knife. If you unexpectedly find yourself in close combat, make eye contact with your enemy, get as close to him as you can and then push the knife into his stomach. It's best to surprise them if you can.'

'Yeah, I ...' Stoker takes the heavy knife. 'But where's it best to —'

'Stay here back of the wheelhouse,' says Satan. He gets the sock with the shells out of his left trouser pocket. 'If anyone comes out of the door or down the stairs, stab the guy in the gut.'

'Okay.' Stoker looks at his reflection in the broad knife blade.

'And don't think about death or anything like that,' says

Satan as he tips out the eight shells into the palm of his left hand and closes his fist over them. 'While we're alive we can kill others, and that's the only thing that matters. A dead man is of no use, and that's why it's no use thinking about death – got it?'

'Yeah, I guess so,' mutters Stoker, clenching his ice-cold right hand around the haft of the knife.

'May as well get on with it.' Satan draws the handgun from its holster by his right ankle. 'I'm going in!'

'But what do I do if …' Stoker begins, but he doesn't get to finish his question before Satan jumps up and disappears around the corner.

Stoker gets hesitantly to his feet, grits his teeth and peers around the same corner. Behind the wheelhouse there is nothing to be seen. Nothing that shouldn't be there. The stern is empty of people.

What should he do? Stand guard or …

Suddenly he hears a heavy blow and seawater splashes over the deck. Stoker cowers down, circles his head with his left arm and closes his eyes.

What was that? Has he been shot? Is he wounded? Is he …

He blinks, lets his left arm drop, turns around, sidles into the wheelhouse and braces his bare back up against the wall between the door to the wheelhouse and the stairs leading up the back of it.

The boat!

Behind the ship the lifeboat is rocking to and fro. It spins slowly counterclockwise as it drifts east away from the ship.

Who shot the boat overboard? And why doesn't whoever it is start the engine? Who is on board the boat? Everyone? No one? Are they going to leave him behind?

'HELP! HELP! HERE! TURN AROUND!' screams Stoker, running back to the stern and waving his hands like a madman. 'DON'T GO WITHOUT ME! TURN BACK! DON'T …'

The lifeboat drifts further and further from the ship until

it's lost in the darkness.

No, this can't be happening!

'Fucking traitors,' Stoker says and walks back to the wheelhouse, trembling with cold.

What should he do? He can't hang around out here – he'll freeze to death. But what else can he do? Where can he go? Where is he safe? Nowhere?

Down to the engine room! He can go down to the engine room. It's warm there, it's dark there, it's …

Stoker opens the door to the B-deck corridor and squeezes through.

The noise of the bells rages on.

He hurries over to the stairs that lead down to A-deck but then freezes in his tracks.

No!

On the floor at the bottom of the stairs lies the chief engineer in a pool of blood, already stiff with rigor mortis and blue around the mouth.

★ ★ ★

00:05:02

The bells peal through every deck and shut out all other sounds.

Satan runs up the stairs with the revolver gripped in his right hand and the eight shells in his left. He turns in a circle on each deck to be sure that no one will catch him unawares and points the gun alternately up and down the stairs.

If only those fucking bells would stop!

On C-deck he took a quick look at the corpses of the cook and the bosun before he carried on. It was neither the time nor the place for sentimentality. On D-deck there was nothing to be seen, nor on E-deck, but when he looks around on F-deck he hears for the first time something other than the bells.

He hears voices. Voices from above. Excited voices calling

to each other in a strange language. Two men, one up on the bridge deck and the other high on the stairs that lead up to it.

Satan presses his back against the wall beside the stairwell, then turns to the right, points his gun upwards and fires three shots towards the black-clad legs at the top of the stairs.

Bam, bam, bam!

The first two shots miss, but he thinks the third one might have hit the pirate in the back of his left calf.

Somebody screams up on the bridge deck.

Satan takes a short break after shooting the gun, moves one step to the left and silently counts to two, then jumps sideways, stretches his right arm up, aims at the chest of the pirate standing at the top of the stairs who's about to pull the trigger of his machine gun, and fires two more shots.

Bam, bam!

With that the gun is empty but another pirate has fallen, crumpling onto his knees and then tumbling forwards down the stairs, firing a few shots from the machine gun into in his own thigh as he falls.

Ratatata–

Satan steps to the side, opens his gun and empties out all the shells so they bounce, steaming, over the lino on F-deck. Then he loads the five compartments in the revolving cylinder of the gun with sweaty, shaking fingers: one shell, two, three …

The fourth shell slides on his palm, drops between his fingers and bounces along the floor.

Shit!

Four and five. He slides the cylinder into place, spins it and pulls back the hammer. The gun is loaded and there are two more shells resting in his palm. That makes a total of seven. That'll have to do.

Satan squats to the side of the stairwell and aims his gun up towards the bridge deck.

Nothing is happening there: no movement, no voices. He looks at the pirate who lies on his belly in the stairs above him.

Does he have a wound in one calf? Yes, he is wounded on his upper left calf, which means that his mate up in the bridge deck is unhurt.

'Fuck!' mutters Satan, now and then aiming the gun down the stairs leading to E-deck. As far as he knows, one or more of the pirates might be below him in the ship.

Fuck it! How long should he wait for someone to attack? He could make a rush up to the bridge deck, but it's not good tactics to attack up the way. And the fucker waiting up there knows it. He's going to wait until Satan gets tired of waiting and storms up there to his death.

Unless he's waiting for reinforcements from below ... *Fuck, fuck, fuck!* Satan can't wait here forever! Time is either running out or standing still – he can't be sure, because the fucking bells are driving him *mad*.

'*Come on out, fucker!*' screams Satan up to the bridge while directing his eyes and the barrel of his gun down to E-deck. 'COME OUT IF YOU DARE!'

No answer, no attack – nothing but the endless pealing of the bells.

DRRRHHHRrr...DRRRHHHRrr...DRHHRHHHRRRrr...

He's not waiting any longer. He can't wait any longer. He'll lose his mind if he ...

'Who's there?' someone shouts suddenly. Whoever's calling is yelling with all his might, but it's barely loud enough for the words to carry down to Satan.

Who's that? Someone on the bridge? The captain himself?

'Can you shut off the bells?' Satan calls up through the stairwell.

No answer.

Sweat runs down Satan's forehead and he blinks his eyes and aims the gun up and then down. His back and shoulders ache; he can't stand there much longer.

'CAN YOU HEAR ME?' he shouts so loudly it stings his throat. 'LET ME KNOW IF YOU —'

He stops shouting when the bells fall silent, all of them at once.

★ ★ ★

00:06:11

Guðmundur Berndsen is standing inside the bridge wing on the starboard side, hiding behind a tall cupboard and aiming his shotgun across the table in the chart room at the door leading to the corridor.

When one of the pirates had grabbed the doorknob and opened the door into the bridge, Guðmundur shot at the door and blew it in two lengthwise. Out in the corridor there are at least two pirates, waiting for the captain to give up or run out of ammunition.

He's not about to give up, but his supply of shells is certainly dwindling. The pirates are shooting their machine guns through the door at regular intervals and then Guðmundur responds with a shot or two.

Dear Christ! How long can he hold out in this hell? Ten more minutes? Five? One? To make matters worse the ship's dog is whining under the table in the chart room like an hysterical woman.

Where is the rest of the crew? Dead? Hiding? In the boat and …

The captain's thoughts are interrupted by a volley of shots in the corridor.

Who is shooting?

He pricks up his ears but hears nothing except the ringing of the bells. If only he could …

'*Come on out, fucker!*' screams someone in the distance. 'COME OUT IF YOU DARE!'

Who is shouting? Who is …

'Who's there?' the captain shouts in the direction of the doorless doorway that opens onto the corridor.

'Can you shut off the bells?' someone shouts back.

Shut off the bells? Of course! He can shut off the bells.

Hunched over, the captain creeps further into the bridge. He aims his shotgun at the open door and walks sideways across to the middle of the bridge, where the red fire-alarm box is.

On the floor between the chart room and the door lie the bodies of Methúsalem and his killer, the former in a black pool of blood with a gaping neck wound, the latter with no face and his brain spread on the outside of his shattered skull.

The air smells of blood, gunpowder and insanity, and the silent presence of the bodies of the men cries out for attention, but the captain doesn't let his gaze drop – he mustn't let his gaze drop – he has to watch the door, he mustn't look at the dead bodies, don't look at the dead bodies …

'Christ, have mercy on us,' mutters the captain and mentally crosses himself.

He hopes that the pirates are not watching him, because the minute he steps to the middle of the bridge he'll lose sight of the door, and if they see that he's out of sight they'll realise they can get to the bridge without his seeing them and then …

To hell with it! It's no good thinking like that!

Guðmundur takes three steps to the side; the door disappears from sight, he is facing a grey wall and the red box is right in front of him.

Just press the switch …

'CAN YOU HEAR ME?' cries someone from below. 'LET ME KNOW IF YOU —'

The captain presses the switch and releases it; there's a click and the bells stop ringing.

'Who's down there?' calls the captain and takes three steps to the left. He can see the door to the corridor, but he is utterly exposed if any enemy should come in. He has to get back under cover before someone shoots into the bridge.

'How many black coats up there?' comes the shouted response.

'Two, I think!' the captain calls back. Step by step he creeps back to the cupboard beside the door that leads out to the bridge wing. Two more steps, one, and he's covered again.

'I got one just now!' A shout from below.

'Then there's just one more out here! If there are any at all. Is that Rúnar who's – '

The captain jumps and stops talking when a black-clad man shoots past the doorway and opens the door to the landing back of the wheelhouse.

Is that …? Was he …?

Guðmundur Berndsen squeezes the trigger of the shotgun but hears only a click. The gun is empty and anyway, he was far too late pulling the trigger.

'*He got out! He ran out! He's gone!*' calls the captain, straightening up.

Someone is vaulting up the stairs to the bridge deck, and before Guðmundur can blink Satan appears in the doorway to the bridge, dressed in black like a pirate, a mad gleam in his eyes, beads of sweat on his forehead and a smoking revolver in his right hand.

Satan glances briefly and expressionlessly at the bodies on the floor, then looks up and spies the captain, who is still half behind the cupboard.

'You've done bloody well!' says Satan, nodding to the captain. 'I'm going to chase the one you missed and put a bullet in his neck, but you stay up here and guard the bridge.'

'You're the guy who was shut in the forecastle,' says Guðmundur as he steps out of his hiding place, but Satan doesn't hear a word he says. He's gone from the doorway, has kicked open the door to the platform aft of the wheelhouse and is leaping down the steep iron stairs with Skuggi at his heels.

★ ★ ★

00:07:06

Stoker paces round and round on the metal floor at the back of the engine room, thinking about the chief engineer lying dead on the floor up on A-deck.

Poor Johnny ...

The clatter of the generator manages to drown out the sound of the bells and that's good, because the hum of the generator is a normal part of the engineers' work environment, while the ringing of the bells is a noisy disturbance, a mechanical insanity, an ongoing warning, a herald of danger ...

Stoker stops walking when he is notices a movement up on the narrow platform at the front of the engine room. He sees the shadow of a man go out the front of the control room and over to the port side towards the machine shop.

Who's that?

'JOHNNY?' Stoker shouts and blinks his eyes, but when he sees that the shadow has both hands on a machine gun that's hanging from a shoulder strap, he shuts his mouth and backs, barefoot, over to the darkness at the back of the engine room, where containers and cleaning fluid are kept under a dirty sink.

A pirate in the engine room! What should he do? Hide? Run? Face the bastard?

Stoker gnashes what's left of his teeth, tightens his grip on the knife and creeps on dirty toes over to the open door behind the machine shop. There he stands still in the shadow behind a two-metre-tall gas canister and waits. And waits ...

Stoker's bony chest expands and contracts, his milk-white skin stretches over his ribs and his black chest hairs rise around his brown nipples. His staring eyes wait for a movement in the gloom; his nostrils flare, and dark yellow teeth and greyish gums gleam in the black beard.

This is the bastard who killed Johnny, the bastard who killed Johnny, the bastard ...

When the pirate finally appears behind the workshop,

Stoker relaxes slightly. His chest eases, his eyes become narrow slits and his chapped lips close over his crooked teeth.

Stoker takes two steps forwards and turns left. He is standing opposite the pirate, who opens his slanting eyes wide and stares in wonder, and some horror, at this ghost of a man who's staring back from a distance of just one metre.

Stoker takes care not to lose eye contact, and steps towards the man as he brings his right arm back, ready to stick the knife into the pirate's abdomen.

By the time the bewildered pirate has recovered sufficient wit to pull the trigger of his machine gun, Stoker has moved inside the line of fire.

Ratatata!

The bullets slam into the engine-room walls, the gun goes quiet and the pirate stiffens as the sharp steel tears into his stomach, cuts apart his entrails and finally penetrates to the pirate's spine. His mouth opens; life slowly drains from his eyes; his legs weaken and give way under the weight of his body.

'This is for John,' says Stoker, drawing the knife out of the wound and pushing the pirate onto his back on the floor. Then he kneels on top of the man's bloody body and sinks the knife into the flaccid flesh, again and again.

★ ★ ★

00:07:17

Satan throws himself down on his abdomen on the boat deck landing when the pirate turns around and fires his machine gun at him.

Ratatatata!

The bullets hit the metal all around Satan, who curls up, shielding his eyes from flying sparks. Behind him Skuggi circles and whines.

The machine gun goes silent and Satan opens his eyes, rolls

onto all fours, sticks the gun between the bars of the railing and sends three shots after the pirate, who runs to the stairs leading down to the weather deck on the starboard side.

Bam, bam, bam!

Shit! Missed!

Satan opens his left hand. No shells! He's lost them in all the commotion. Only two bullets left in the gun. *Two.*

Fuck. *Fuck.*

'FUCK!' he screams as he grips the rail with his left hand and jumps over it without thinking. He lands on both feet in the stern and steadies himself with his left hand on the floor before he straightens up and runs after the pirate, who seems to be aiming to get back to the inflatable.

Could he be the last? Hopefully he's the last.

When Satan reaches the metal stairs down to the weather deck the pirate is already on board the inflatable and has untied it from the railing.

Fuck!

Satan aims the shotgun at the boat but the ship rocks, and the boat is moving up and down. The pirate pulls the cord of the outboard motor and Satan tenses his muscles, holds his breath and pulls the trigger.

Bam!

He doesn't even see where the bullet lands.

'Fuck it!' Satan mutters. He aims again, the pirate pulls the cord, the outboard motor starts up, his index finger clenches gently round the sensitive trigger and the last shot rips off.

Bam!

Nothing happens. The bullet lands in the sea. The pirate turns the boat and heads for the green light that's covering the sea about 300 metres away.

Skuggi comes trotting up and lies down on the deck to the left of Satan.

'I don't believe this,' says Satan, letting his gun drop as he turns his face to the sky.

The emergency flare is about to burn up; it comes floating down out of the dark red dome and will land in the sea after just …

Unless.

Satan follows the flare with his eyes. It's floating at an angle over the ship, then the wind catches it and steers it directly into the inflatable, which is speeding north. Nothing happens at first, and then there is an explosion in the boat. It fills with fire that surges up in an instant and then leaps as a fireball up into the dark night

Everything goes black.

'YAAAHHHOOOO!' Satan screams over the ship's rail, and then Skuggi howls beside him. 'WHO'S THE KING? WHO'S THE KING? I SAID, WHO'S —'

The green light goes out as the big machine gun starts to spew fire. A burst slams into the ship, which trembles from end to end, and a second later comes the hollow bark of the gun.

Kra-ka-ka-ka-ka-ka-ka!

Satan throws himself on the iron floor – but not fast enough. Two bullets hit his head, like miniature cement trucks travelling at three times the speed of sound.

XXIX

Monday, 17 September

It is almost four in the afternoon but it seems the world can't be bothered to wake up today. The sky is grey as far as the eye can see; the ocean dark grey to the east and black to the west; the breeze smells of rotting ocean vegetation; it's neither hot nor cold, and a muggy salt mist surrounds the ship, which drifts south across the heavy waves that seem like nothing so much as undulating mountains.

The starboard side of the ship is covered with pockmarks, scratches and holes left from all the artillery salvos. The scratches have gone rusty; they collect damp that gradually condenses, forming reddish-brown drops that run down the cold steel.

Guðmundur and Sæli stand in the stern of the ship, over the bodies of two of the pirates who are lying side by side across the stern with pillowcases over their heads. One of the pillowcases is soaked with black blood but the other is still white and reveals the outlines of the dead pirate's face. Guðmundur and Sæli have been struggling with bodies all day long. These two are the last and they're going to throw them overboard.

First, though, they catch their breath.

It took them more than two hours to get these bodies all the way from the bridge down to B-deck. They are soaked with sweat, their lungs are burning and their shoulders, arms and backs ache. It's hard enough carrying heavy objects down the steep and narrow stairs even when those objects aren't cold, stiff corpses.

But it was a piece of cake manhandling these two compared to the emotional ordeal of carrying Ási, Rúnar and Methúsalem. The captain and the seaman had wrapped their comrades in white sheets from head to toe before they set off with them down the stairs. All the same, being in such close contact with their lifeless bodies was so overpowering that they were thrice rendered powerless on the way down from A-deck. Then they collapsed under the weight and burst into silent tears, each keeping to himself and not looking at the other.

Guðmundur has not yet told the survivors about Methúsalem, how Methúsalem had somehow lost his mind and tried to murder the captain. He isn't sure he should say anything about it. There was no reason to blacken the memory of a fine man, even though he had fallen apart at the very end.

It was difficult to keep quiet about such a huge secret, though, and his silence about the first mate's madness preyed on the captain and further increased the grief that filled his heart on that blue-grey Monday. Every time he closed his eyes he saw the distorted face of the chief mate …

'Smoke?' asks Sæli, offering the captain an open pack.

'Yeah, thanks,' says Guðmundur and sticks one in his mouth.

Sæli gives the captain a light, shielding the flame with the palm of his right hand, then lights up his own cigarette behind the lapel of his jacket.

They pull life into the cigarettes, exhale smoke and look out to sea, as if thinking of something else. Pals taking a smoke break.

'Did you see the game yesterday?' asks Sæli without the faintest change of expression. He doesn't know himself whether he is trying to be funny or just losing his mind.

They look at other, washed out and exhausted in body and soul.

'No,' says the captain. He smiles wryly as he claps Sæli

lightly on the back. 'How did it go?'

'I don't know,' says Sæli, shrugging his shoulders.

They stop smiling; it is no longer funny.

'Listen, are you sure it's right to throw them overboard, these two?' Sæli says after a short silence.

'No, I'm not,' says the captain without looking at the men. 'But I don't think I want to have them on board.'

'I see,' murmurs Sæli and throws his burning cigarette into the sea. 'Shall we?'

'Yeah.' Guðmundur takes a drag before he stubs out the cigarette and puts the stub in his pocket.

The captain takes the shoulders of one of the men while Sæli takes the legs. They swing the body twice back and forth before releasing it and flinging it into the sea.

The other pirate then goes the same way.

'May God have pity on your souls on the day of judgement,' says the captain, panting, and makes the sign of the cross with the fingers of his right hand, 'because until then they will suffer in the fires of hell.'

'Amen,' says Sæli and he spits after the bodies, which drift away from the ship, rock back and forth and then slowly sink under the surface. Stiff fingers grasp at nothing and drag it with them into the darkness.

'Come on, pal,' says the captain and puts his arm around the seaman's shoulders. 'The day's work is as good as finished. Let's get a cup of coffee.'

★ ★ ★

16:01

Satan is lying on his back in the bed, masturbating while looking at the picture of the Danish girl that he stole from the engine room.

Then he closes his eyes and tries to think of Lilja, but Lilja won't stay still in his head; she rushes around and changes, little by little, into the Danish girl in the picture.

'Shit,' mutters Satan. He opens his eyes and looks at the picture he is holding in his left hand. But then his eyes mist over and the Danish girl looks like his baby daughter.

★ ★ ★

17:21

Captain Guðmundur knocks lightly on the door before he opens it into the sick bay, where he expects to find Satan lying asleep or half conscious under a sweat-soaked doona. They had pulled him, blood soaked and unconscious, into the control room after the gunfire stopped, bandaged his wounds and pumped him full of morphine. The bullets had torn off his scalp above the left ear, leaving deep gashes and fractures in his skull.

'Hello?' says the captain and turns on the light. 'Are you awake?'

No answer.

There's no-one in the bed.

'What the hell!' mutters the captain, turns off the light and closes the door.

He looks into the mess and the galley, but finds no-one.

'Are you looking for someone?' asks Stoker on his way up the stairs from A-deck to B-deck. He is wearing clogs and filthy overalls, and wiping oil and soot off his fingers with a blackened rag.

'Yes and no,' says the captain, looking over Stoker's shoulder and down to the floor of A-deck, where the engineer has put down a thick layer of sawdust over the spot where Big John breathed his last. 'What's the situation down in the engine?'

'Okay – no change,' says Stoker, sniffing. 'I'm running the generators one at a time at full power and making sure there's enough hot and cold water and stuff. As long as nobody fools with anything down there, life on board will go on as usual, for what it's worth.'

'Yes, right.' The captain claps Stoker on the back. 'Nobody will fool with anything, you can count on that!'

'Nobody has any reason to go down there,' says Stoker, scratching his beard with oily fingers. 'Nobody but me.'

'No – yes – you're right,' the captain says, nodding to the engineer. 'I understand your point of view and trust you completely, Óli. Completely.'

'That's how it should be.' Stoker strolls into the galley while the captain starts up the stairs.

On C-deck the doors to Ási's and Rúnar's cabins are closed and locked. Behind the doors are bloody rugs, darkness and silence. Of these, the silence is the worst. You can clean the blood out of the rug; you can get rid of the darkness by opening the curtains or turning on the light, but no matter how much the survivors talk or how loudly they scream when no-one hears them, the silence their dead comrades leave behind will follow them for the rest of the voyage – even for the rest of their lives.

Silence like a hole in their existence.

The captain goes up to D-deck and opens the door of Satan's cabin. Nobody there.

Up on E-deck, Jónas and Methúsalem's cabin doors are closed. Methúsalem is dead and nobody knows where Jónas is. It's as if the earth has swallowed him – or the sea, more likely.

Guðmundur walks up to F-deck, the captain's deck. There his foot strikes something brass coloured that skitters like a pebble across the floor, bounces off the wall on the starboard side and spins in the middle of the corridor. Guðmundur leans over and picks up this small cylindrical object, and he thinks he knows who dropped it there. On the stairs up to the bridge deck is a white sheet covered with footprints; it hides the blood from the pirate Satan shot dead.

The doorway into the bridge has no door in it. Inside, the

floor is covered with white sheets from the threshold over to the controls. The sheets lie on top of each other but, even so, blood and brains have leaked through in a few places.

'So here you are,' says the captain as he enters the bridge, which still slants to starboard, as does the entire ship.

Satan is sitting in the captain's chair with a coffee mug in one hand and a burning cigarette in the other. He is dressed only in black jogging pants; he is barefoot and barechested. His head is wrapped in a bandage that covers his eyebrows and both ears, and which is bloody above the left ear. Dark hanks of hair hang from the top of his head and also, from under the bandage, down the back of his head and in front of his ears.

At his feet lies the ship's dog, which looks up and whines softly when the captain enters the bridge.

'Yep,' says Satan, without turning the chair or looking over this shoulder. He's looking out of the broken window, lost in thought, as if he were keeping track of everything without being interested in anything – worldly wise but pretty tired of life, like a helmsman or captain who has spent a lifetime sailing the seven seas.

The custom is for subordinates to get out of the captain's chair when the captain enters the bridge – if not out of common courtesy, then out of unconditional respect for the man who alone is responsible for the ship and everyone on board, dead or alive. But Satan doesn't show his superior even the minimum courtesy of looking in his direction, let alone greeting him like a civilised human being or offering him a seat in the chair that is intended for the highest-ranking man on board, or his stand-in on the bridge.

The captain's temper flares up, but dissipates so fast that his blood hardly has time to heat his face. This is perhaps neither the time nor the place to vent his rage on anyone – least of all on a landlubber who knows neither the written nor unwritten rules of the sea. And besides, this lad is a friend in need, to put it mildly.

Guðmundur goes to the controls, lays his palms on the edge of the control board and pretends to be looking out the windows, but then turns his head casually to the left and surreptitiously examines the interloper.

Savage is the first word that occurs to the captain. He remembers having seen, in an old travel book, a picture of the village chief in some small South Seas island, a fat and meaty native who sat on a bamboo throne and looked over his meagre domain with eyes revealing both naive simplicity and fathomless cruelty. An amoral savage who had many wives and diddled his children when he wasn't worshipping idols and eating his enemies.

For some reason, Satan reminds the captain of that native chieftain who, despite his foolish appearance, is so powerful and dangerous that no-one dares smile at him. Maybe that's because of the way Satan sits in the chair: completely at ease, without seeming careless or open to attack, like a lion that sleeps with one eye open. Perhaps it's the bare flesh: all that meat filling the chair, ready for love or attack. Or his eyes, those dim holes that –

'Coffee's hot,' says Satan, rolling his head to the right and looking the captain straight in the eye. Guðmundur glances away, like a young girl at her confirmation who's been caught staring at a virile boy.

'Yeah, thanks, I guess I'll …' The captain trails off and walks behind the chair, over to the port side of the bridge.

'Get me a refill while you're at it,' says Satan, holding out his empty coffee mug.

'Of course,' says the captain, his face turning red with anger, but he grits his teeth as he takes the mug.

Damn him!

'Two sugars and a dash of milk,' says Satan, leaning back more comfortably and pushing with his feet so the leather creaks.

Guðmundur Berndsen is speechless at the rude and demanding manners of this street kid. Isn't he meant to be a grown-up? The captain almost loses control of his temper, but with an effort he manages to swallow his rage and, with it, his pride. He sighs deeply, shakes his head and counts up to twenty in his head while he pours the coffee into the mugs.

Not today. He's not going to get angry today. Not the same day that four of his crew have been murdered and another one vanished. Not the same day that he murdered a man for the first time …

The memory of the killing pours over the captain like cold tar. He grabs the edge of the sink with both hands, takes a deep breath, holds it, and then exhales calmly. He hasn't slept a wink since he killed that man.

'Are you getting that coffee?'

Guðmundur opens his eyes and straightens his back. Spots dance before his eyes and hot winds whirl in his head.

Could it be that he understands this, this underworld man? Could he have taken a life before? Could he maybe tell him how …

'Coming,' says the captain and he picks up the coffee mugs, carries them across to the middle of the bridge and hands one to Satan. 'Here you go.'

'I asked for milk and sugar,' says Satan, looking into the black coffee and then at the captain, who takes a seat on the chair by the port side window.

'I have something that belongs to you,' says the captain as he pulls a white package from the side pocket of his jacket. It's the handgun, loosely wrapped in a handkerchief.

'It's empty,' says Satan, then blows some smoke rings.

'I know.' The captain puts the gun down on the window ledge.

'Otherwise you wouldn't have let me have it back, right?' asks Satan. Or, more precisely, declares.

Silence.

'Had you already, um, you know …' mutters the captain. He looks out the port windows – the only windows on the bridge that are intact.

'Killed a man?'

'Yes. Exactly. Killed a man.'

'Are you feeling blue about that thug you popped?' asks Satan with a grin as he taps ash from his cigarette onto the floor.

'Maybe.' The captain hesitates. 'It gets to you, I won't deny it.'

'It was either him or you, don't forget that.' Satan sticks his cigarette in his mouth and sucks smoke into his lungs.

'Yes, I know, but the thing …' The captain sighs. 'What I'm thinking is … isn't it better to die innocent than to live with …'

'Are you crazy, man? If you can't be grateful you're alive, you should have the guts to hang yourself instead of whimpering like a spoiled kid!'

'Yes, no … sorry!' fumbles the captain. 'I didn't mean to —'

'Sorry?' says Satan with a laugh, blowing smoke out his nose. 'Do I look like Jesus?'

'No, I just —'

'I know how you feel, man! That was quite a rush last night. A hell of a lot going on. You popped a guy and … you know, all blood and frenzy! Now it's just over, quiet and that … but in your head the frenzy is still at full steam, see? Anger, fear, hate, speed, everything that happened is still there inside and happens over and over … *boom, boom, boom!* And then all of a sudden that's over too, man … I'm telling you: life just goes on … as if nothing had happened.'

'Yes, maybe. If *you* say so.'

'I'm telling you, man!' Satan takes a drag on his cigarette before letting the stub fall into his coffee. 'After blood come the blues, but no-one wants to be blue forever … it's just too fucking boring!'

Silence.

'You didn't answer my question just then,' says the captain.

'You didn't give me any sugar and milk in my coffee,' Satan retorts.

Silence.

'I don't know whether you know this,' says Guðmundur, straightening his back and raising his voice, 'but the chair you are sitting on is the captain's chair, and the captain *is* the highest-ranking officer on board the ship.'

'Right,' says Satan with utter indifference, then he yawns like a lazy cat. 'Listen, I need some clean clothes. Do you think that big engineer could loan me something? He's the only one on board who wears grown-up sizes.'

★ ★ ★

18:45

When Satan enters the engine room there is no-one to be seen, but he knows that Stoker is in there somewhere.

It's pretty dusky down there: only the most vital lights are on. It's warm as a good summer's day and the rumble of the generator communes with its own echo in this greasy-smelling metal box.

After walking through the empty control booth, Satan strolls across the platform at the front of the room and into the machine shop to port, where the door is wide open. He sees Stoker standing barechested on a footstool, peering into a large pot that sits on a small electric hotplate up on the work surface. Stoker is holding the lid with his left hand while, with his right, he fishes for something in the pot with a piece of bent wire. Steam rises from the pot and the smell filling the workshop is disgusting, to say the least.

Satan stands in the doorway, holding his nose and breathing quickly through his half-closed mouth while he watches Stoker, who drags the wire out of the pot and knocks bits of hair and shreds of something off it before replacing the lid.

'I sure as hell hope that's not supper.'

Stoker is so startled that he falls backwards with the bent wire in his hand, and comes perilously close to hooking one handle of the pot and dragging it with him as he falls. He knocks the footstool out from under him and screams like a little kid when he lands flat on the hard metal floor. Cans, flasks and spare parts fall from the shelves under the counter, and the pot spits dirty water which runs onto the hotplate and turns into black smoke.

'*Johnny?*' cries Stoker and he blinks his eyes as he rolls over onto his belly.

No, this isn't Johnny. Of course it's not Johnny – but …

'*You're wearing Johnny's clothes!*' shouts Stoker, standing up and examining Satan.

'Yeah,' says Satan, closing the door so the noise from the generator drops by several decibels. He's wearing a blue-checked cotton shirt, dark blue trousers made of some synthetic material and tightly laced military boots.

'What are you doing down here?' says Stoker, pointing at Satan with the bent wire. 'Nobody has any business down here, nobody but —'

'Shut up, man!' says Satan, grimacing at the smell that issues from the pot. 'I just need something to cover the broken windows in the bridge – plywood or a sheet of aluminium or plastic or something. What is that god-awful stink, man? What the fuck are you boiling?'

'Nothing. Nothing at all,' mutters Stoker, backing towards the pot with arms outstretched as Satan steps forward. 'Just want to get some oil and junk off … off something.'

'Goddamn liar!' says Satan, trying to force a grin, but the smell is so disgusting that he's feeling seriously nauseated.

'There's some plywood out there, up on the shelf above the sink,' says Stoker, backing all the way to the counter. 'You can use it for the windows. And there's a saw on the hook beside it.'

Stoker knocks his left heel into a can of axle grease, which hits an empty turpentine container that falls over and rolls out on the floor, and then Satan sees brown fingers on the floor below the shelf under the counter.

Brown fingers?

'What are you up to here?' says Satan, leaning down and pulling at the brown fingers, which are stiff and cold and blue under the nails.

'DON'T!' screams Stoker. 'DON'T TAKE —' He grabs Satan's arm, but it's too late. On the floor in front of the work table lies an arm that belongs to neither Satan nor Stoker. It's the bare right arm of someone who was, hopefully, dead when the arm was chopped off at the elbow.

'What have you done?' says Satan with a sigh. He looks under the work table and, as far as he can see, there are other body parts hidden there. He sees a leg, another arm and, furthest in on the shelf, something large, maybe a torso.

'Who's that?' Satan says, straightening up.

'A pirate.' Stoker scratches his head.

'Did you kill him?'

'Yes.'

'You're quite the guy.' Satan spies his hunting knife and picks it up. The knife is covered with congealed blood, the edge is nicked and dull, and there are pieces of bone and flesh in the grooves.

'I wasn't going to …' Stoker rubs his dirty palms together. 'I just …'

'Listen,' says Satan, stabbing the tip of his knife into the surface of the work table, 'you are going to dump this carcass in the sea. And don't let anyone see you. Understood?'

'Yes, of course,' says Stoker, breathing more easily.

'If the others should see this!' says Satan and whistles softly.

'Thank you – *thank you!*' says Stoker, looking at Satan with tearful puppy eyes. 'You're the only one who has –'

'None of that!' says Satan, snapping his fingers in Stoker's face. 'Get rid of the carcass and then clean up my knife and sharpen it before you give it back. Understood?'

XXX

21:13

They sit silent at the table in the seamen's mess, the two seamen and the engineer, drinking coffee after a late supper of sandwiches, apple wedges and a few doughnuts. The eternal Doors cassette is now telling them about a moonlight drive.

Satan sits at the end, away from the door. Stoker sits on his right and Sæli on his left.

Sæli sniffs and looks at Stoker. He blinks and looks at Satan, who yawns, a cigarette in one hand and a lighter in the other. Skuggi, who is lying under the table, doesn't take his eyes off Satan.

'What happened to Jónas, anyway?' asks Sæli, just to say something and break the heavy silence.

'Didn't he take the lifeboat?' Satan says, lighting his cigarette and puffs it into life.

'That's one theory,' says Sæli and shrugs. 'But he was kind of handicapped.'

'Maybe nobody took the boat,' says Stoker, turning his coffee mug around on the table. 'Perhaps it just shot itself overboard. I saw the boat land in the water. There wasn't anybody in the window, nobody started the engine and the boat just drifted away.'

'And the fifth pirate?' says Sæli. 'Nobody knows what became of the fifth pirate. Maybe he took the boat?'

'Maybe he just fell in the sea,' says Satan, looking at Stoker as he exhales smoke.

'Yeah,' says Stoker and nods at Satan. 'It seems likely to me that he simply fell overboard when nobody was looking.'

'Yeah, maybe,' murmurs Sæli. 'I hope, at least, that he isn't just hiding somewhere. Have we definitely searched everywhere?'

'Yep,' says Satan. 'As far as we could. But it's probably safer to sleep behind locked doors.'

'Yeah.' Sæli sips his warm coffee. 'If we can sleep at all, that is.'

Silence.

There's a soft click from the tape recorder as side A of the eternal Doors cassette comes to an end, one motor stops and the other takes over, the wheels turn clockwise and the B side of the tape moves across the magnetic head.

'Well, boys,' says Guðmundur as he enters the mess with four shot glasses in his left hand and an ice-covered bottle of liquor in his right. 'I think it's about time we drank a nip or two in memory of our dear departed.'

He sits down at the door end of the table, puts the shot glasses on the foam-covered table and unscrews the top of the bottle.

'What have we there?' asks Stoker.

'I found it in the freezer,' answers the captain as he pours a thick clear liquid. 'I think it's Icelandic schnapps.'

He fills the glasses to the brim before passing them out to his shipmates.

'In memory of Methúsalem, John, Rúnar and Ásmundur, good lads who all died far too young,' says the captain, standing up with his glass in his hand. 'We bow our heads and show our respect with a minute of silence.'

The remaining crew stands up, bow their heads and remain silent for one minute.

'God rest their souls,' says the captain as he opens his eyes and lifts his glass.

'Amen.'

They all toss back their drinks and then sit back down. The captain collects the glasses and refills them.

'Enjoy,' he says and screws the top on the bottle.

The ice on the outside of the bottle has become clear; it is melting onto the table.

'Why did those men attack us?' Sæli says, sighing. 'I mean, what were they after?'

'There's a curse on this ship,' grumbles Stoker and gnashes his teeth. 'A curse that –'

'Óli! Not now!' says the captain, giving the engineer a severe look. Stoker looks away shamefaced, but Sæli straightens up, all eyes and ears, as if there's nothing he wants more at this moment than to learn from Stoker's lips about the alleged curse on the ship.

'They probably imagined that the hold was full of something valuable,' says Guðmundur, clapping Sæli's right shoulder.

'Couldn't you tell them the hold was empty?' asks Stoker, grinning impishly.

'Unless they were going to steal the ship itself,' the captain replies, looking askance at Stoker. 'We just don't know.'

'That reminds me of something … I read,' says Sæli and looks up at his shipmates, as if not sure whether or not they want him to continue.

'What was that?' asks Guðmundur.

'There's a tribe on the islands of Micronesia,' says Sæli, rocking back and forth and sniffing repeatedly, his face going red. 'They're primitive islanders who believe their ancestors will one day appear in a ship loaded with food.'

'Really?' says the captain with a crooked smile. 'And they just wait for it, year after year?'

'Yes. Something like that. This belief is called "cargo cult".'

'They wouldn't be very happy if we ran aground there!' says Stoker, giving a low laugh. 'A dead-in-the-water ship laden to the gunwales with darkness!'

'Yeah – no – probably not.' Sæli coughs. 'It would have been more fun if Rúnar had told us about this. He told stories so well, did Rúnar. Knew how to stretch it out and tie up the loose threads at the end.'

'Yeah, but it's not the storyteller who makes all the difference,' says the captain, smiling paternally at the seaman. 'Rather, it's the story that's told. And this was a pretty good story!'

'Yeah, maybe,' mumbles Sæli, blushing. 'But what difference does a fucking story make when your life's hanging by a thread?'

'We have to keep up hope, Sæli, lad!' says the captain, putting his hand on the seaman's shoulder. 'Without hope we are lost.'

'Nothing can be changed that's written in the stars,' says Stoker into his beard. 'Nobody can flee his day of judgement.'

'Óli Johnsen!' growls the captain, so that Stoker jumps and accidentally bites his lips.

'Whether you live life laughing or crying, it's still just life,' says Satan and tosses back the contents of his glass.

Silence.

'He who bears arms is not an educated man,' says the captain, looking directly at Satan. 'He who is educated does not bear arms.'

Sæli turns a questioning look on Stoker, who shrugs.

'God allows even those whose intentions are evil to have their way,' says Satan and smirks.

'Those who live by the sword die by the sword,' responds the captain calmly.

'The fact that men die means that men are doomed to death when they are born. And if a person is born dead he can't die,' answers Satan without blinking. 'Only those who believe they're alive fear death. I'm dead. I fear nothing!'

'I haven't heard that one before,' says the captain, opening his eyes wide. Then he smiles crookedly, picks up the bottle and passes it over the table to Satan.

'What was that about?' asks Sæli, smiling faintly.

'Thanks,' says Satan, taking the bottle from the captain.

'Dear friends,' says the captain once Satan has filled his glass. 'Now let's drink to those of us who are still alive. Here's to life! Cheers!'

'Cheers!'

They empty their glasses, grimace and lick their lips. In the distance they can hear the loud, mournful song of whales calling to each other, and the ship's hull creaks as it slips sideways down the side of a wave that had lifted it up towards the starry night sky.

'No, things don't look so good, dear friends,' says the captain and smiles at his men like a pastor attempting to hearten the mourners at a funeral. 'But whether you believe it or not, it's not the worst trouble I've been in.'

Silence.

'After I graduated from Navigation School I wandered around Europe and signed on to the odd tub, both to get experience and to have a look round on shore. Lisbon, Liverpool, Rotterdam, Hamburg. That was a great time, boys!' says Guðmundur with a faraway look in his eyes. 'Then, in communist Estonia, I was offered a job I was too young and foolish to turn down. The only thing I heard was the word "captain". They wanted to take me on as captain. A group of about sixty people had bought a sailboat named *Lootus* and needed someone to sail it over the Atlantic, first to Sweden and then to the US. The people were desperate. One mother looked at me pleadingly. She held an infant swaddled in tattered clothes, a dark-haired girl with a hare lip. How could I refuse these people?'

He pauses briefly to fill their glasses. He looks at each of his shipmates in turn, hands them back their glasses and licks his lips.

'The boat was a sorry sight. It was actually criminal to go to sea with all those people – men, women and children – in a rotten old bucket like that. It wasn't until things came to a head that I found out that hiring me had been the refugees' last hope. Nobody else had liked the look of the enterprise.'

Guðmundur half smiles, but the smile doesn't reach his eyes, which stare into the boundless distance.

'The deck leaked and there was always a line outside the head, which actually was just a crummy shed. The people lived on rotten potatoes that were stored in wooden crates on the deck, the water tanks were corroded and those poor children got dysentery, and they were covered with red rashes and sores. But I turned a blind eye to all of this because I had an irrational belief in the job I was doing. I was helping these people to free themselves from the chains of communism and begin a new life in a new world.'

Guðmundur drains his glass and refills it. Then he carries on with his story.

The navigation equipment available to him had consisted of an ordinary wristwatch, a sextant, a compass and a two-bit map. But he had succeeded in keeping on the right course for about 8300 kilometres – or until they hit a storm. According to the captain's calculations the ship was about 2000 kilometres south-east of Florida when threatening thunderclouds began to pile up on the horizon. The radio batteries had gone dead and there wasn't even a barometer on board, so the captain had no way of confirming his suspicions about an impending storm.

In the evening they were hit with hurricane-force winds that went on to rage for four days solid. The boat was about to fall apart and at least one man had fallen overboard.

Below decks the passengers crowded together in the airless damp. The stench from sweat, vomit and unwashed baby clothes was unbearable. Mothers and sick children lay together in the bunks but the others stood. Seawater rained down from the leaky deck and, little by little, the boat filled with water.

The merciless battering of the waves eventually loosened the planks of the old sailboat's hull, so that it began to leak below the waterline. People bailed furiously and the hand pump was in constant use, but the water level in the boat still rose steadily. In the engine room the sea slopped onto the already overheated engine, forming a cloud of steam so you couldn't see your hand in front of your face. They were also bailing furiously down there. Soot-covered men passed pails from one to the other, silent and exhausted after three days of continuous struggle. Women and men down in the cabins stuffed their ragged clothes into the cracks and lay on top of them to stop the leaking.

For three days they'd had no food other than hardtack, wet by the sea. The sick children had had nothing to eat. The drinking water was just a soup of rust and dirt.

During the night, a three-month-old girl breathed her last. It was the dark-haired child with the hare lip.

The storm died down and they were able to see blue-green waves around the boat. There was less spray, so they opened the hatches and everything else that could be opened. The men were bailing with buckets, the women with pots and pans, and they used blankets and overcoats to wipe the rest. After two hours the boat was virtually dry, and they started caulking the cracks with hemp and tar. The boat leaked steadily but the hand pump managed to keep up.

Hope – which had never died in the hearts of the refugees – quickened hour by hour.

Most of the crew lay, exhausted, and soaked up sunlight on the deck. The sick children had been dressed in dry clothes and were on the mend. One young man got out his accordion and started playing a mournful folk song.

The others joined in and sang …

Guðmundur stops talking, sniffs, gently clears his throat and empties his glass.

Silence.

'And then what?' asks Sæli in a low voice. 'Did the boat sink?'

'No, not while I was at the wheel. After sailing for five days we crawled into harbour in Jacksonville. The boat sank there just a few days later. After a few months in quarantine, the refugees were let loose. Fifty-four Estonians spread themselves over the US from one end to the other, and some went north to Canada, and I returned to Iceland, the wiser for the experience.'

'I didn't know about that,' says Sæli, looking at the captain with admiration. 'I've never heard this story, but everyone must have been talking about it.'

'No,' says the captain, shaking his head. 'I've never told anyone before – not a living soul.'

'Why not?' asks Sæli.

'Why not?' echoes the captain and takes a deep breath. 'Because I shouldn't have gone on that trip. If I had refused, the ship would never have sailed. Then all those people would still be alive today.'

'But you're a hero, man!' says Satan, smiling at the captain. 'It must be seen as a great achievement getting all those refugees safe and sound across the ocean on a tub like that, even though one or two died on the way.'

'Well, maybe you could say that.' The captain sighs as he fills his glass with a shaking hand. 'But I'll be damned, and so help me God, if I don't think it the lesser of two evils to drown in a storm every day for all eternity than to sail with the corpse of a child and a mourning mother for one single moment. That poor woman.'

Silence.

'But what of that – the boat was named the *Lootus*. That's Estonian for "hope",' says the captain, then lifts his glass and breathes in through flaring nostrils. 'Now let's drink a toast, my friends. Now we drink to hope! Cheers!'

'Cheers!'

They all knock back their drinks, grimace and lick their lips. The bottle is empty and the glasses are sticky inside and out.

Jim Morrison continues to sing about the music being over, about turning out the lights.

'I can't stand that song,' says Sæli with tears in his eyes. 'I just can't stand it!'

He stands up from the table and pushes some knobs on the tape deck, but the tape keeps turning and the song plays.

'For fuck's sake!' he mutters. He rips the electric cord from the socket but it makes no difference. The tape continues to turn and the song still plays.

'What the fuck is ...' Sæli shakes the tape deck. 'Sæli, lad, are you all right?' asks Guðmundur, but Sæli doesn't answer him. Instead, he stalks out of the mess with the tape deck in his hand and his eyes full of tears.

'Sæli?' The captain stands, his eyes following the seaman.

'Let him be!' says Satan, signalling the captain to sit back down.

'That was Rúnar's tape,' says Stoker, sniffing up into his coal-black nose. 'I think the poor guy misses the bosun.'

'Yeah, perhaps,' mumbles Guðmundur and sits back down. 'I'm just worried that he'll do something stupid.'

'Something more stupid than attacking a radio?' Stoker says with a smirk.

'Yes,' says the captain thoughtfully. 'But it is perhaps best to leave him in peace. People act weird after a shock.'

'That was quite the incident,' says Satan and he laughs softly. 'I mean, it isn't as if the song was "Killing me Softly", or something, is it?'

★ ★ ★

23:58

Sæli tears open the door in back of the wheelhouse, leaps over the threshold and runs back to the stern, where he flings the tape deck as far out to sea as his strength allows.

The tape deck flies in a long arc into the night, the music fades away little by little, and a soft splash is heard as it disappears into the silent deep.

'SO SHUT UP, THEN!' shouts Sæli over the railing. He holds the edge of the cold railing with both hands, clenches his jaw, widens his tear-filled eyes and tenses every muscle in his body as if he's about to kick off and jump over the iron wall.

All he can see is darkness as far as his mind can reach: thousands of kilometres of hopelessness, gloom and certain death, and somewhere beyond this all-encompassing void are Lára and Egill in a lit-up flat in the Old Town, like a distorted scene in a dewdrop light-years away.

Like a little star in the night sky, receding at the rate of several thousand kilometres an hour.

The mother and son are so far away that the thought of them at home is becoming ever more unreal. As if they're no more than a memory. She's happy and the boy is young, forever. A picture in his mind, nothing more. A picture that, with time, is becoming hazy, remote and confused.

Home. What's that?

Ársæll Egilsson is stuck on a ship that is the beginning and end of all there is. The ship *is*; everything else is only imagination. The ship is home and home is the ship.

Those who are not on board the ship may just as well be on another planet.

He wants to jump into the sea without really knowing why. Is it death that draws him, or the mother and son who are disappearing into the distance?

But he doesn't jump. Not because reason gains the upper hand, but simply because he can't.

XXXI

32°W 4°N

According to the captain's calculations, the ship is now located just north of the equator. So it has drifted one degree east and three degrees south from Sunday to Tuesday. That's about twice as much drift to the south as the average international model allows for, but there are very powerful ocean currents around here that doubtless distort all the conditions for the model. There's no point in comforting yourself with statistical wishful thinking and imprecise predictions when the facts speak for themselves.

The ship is drifting fast to the south, whether Guðmundur Berndsen likes it or not.

One and a half degrees of longitude a day. That's up to ninety kilometres a day – even more. Seven hundred to 740 kilometres a week.

'Am I going mad?' mutters the captain, punching numbers into his calculator as he sits, sweaty and exasperated, at the table in his cabin.

If no-one turns up to help them, the ship will drift all the way to Antarctica in only three months. Unlikely, yes, but statistically possible.

'For the love of …' The captain reaches for his sea chart. He puts his index finger on the point where the ship is situated at this moment and moves it slowly down along the thirty-second line of longitude west of the Greenwich line, which is marked zero.

Over the next three weeks they'll drift south along the coast of Brazil, where it juts out furthest to the east. After a week or so the ship should be situated about 110 kilometres east of the port of Recife. One hundred and ten kilometres! On the map, the distance looks so short that it should be no trouble for a fit man to swim it. But it is 100 kilometres, even more, which is almost three trips across the English Channel.

The dinghy! There's a rubber dinghy on the ship, an eight-foot Zodiac not unlike the one the pirates arrived on, but shorter. It's admittedly only meant for three, but Stoker's nothing but skin and bones. The outboard motor is five horsepower and there's more than enough petrol, and in good weather it is perfectly possible to sail a dinghy like that on the open sea, even if it is a bit overloaded.

'It's going to work out!' the captain tells himself with a sigh of relief. 'It's all going to work out.'

Guðmundur Berndsen turns off his calculator, closes the navigation log, rolls up the chart and drinks the last of his coffee, which has long since gone cold and bitter.

★ ★ ★

31°W 2°N

They're standing, lightly dressed, on the starboard side of the boat deck: the captain and the engineer, staring at the Zodiac dinghy that's drooping like a sail without a wind in the sling that holds it, because it's been shot to pieces and ripped wide open after the artillery barrage.

An easterly wind is blowing across the dark green ocean and the temperature is a good fifteen degrees Celsius and rising.

'Can it be repaired?' enquires the captain as he runs his hands over the deflated rubber.

'Everything is possible,' says Stoker and scratches his beard. 'I have plenty of line and glue. The only thing I need is rubber to make patches.'

'Isn't there anything on board you could use?'

'I could use rainwear. But it has fabric on the inside. The fabric doesn't glue to rubber as well as rubber to rubber.'

'Anything else?'

'No, probably not. I could try rasping the fabric out of the clothes.'

'Go on, then, do that,' says the captain, clapping Stoker on the back. 'You have five days to complete the job.'

'That should be enough,' says Stoker with a nod. 'When will the ship drift south across the equator?'

'Late tomorrow,' says the captain and he looks at sun, which will be reaching midday in three hours. 'Or early the day after.'

'And then the Brazil current will pull us into its endless flow to the south, is that it?'

'Yeah. It'll take the ship most of the way to Cape Horn.'

Cape Horn. Where cold ocean currents run riot like monsters from the deep in the west.

'But we'll have left the ship long before it reaches that chaos,' says the captain.

'It's just as well,' replies Stoker, wiping sweat from his forehead. 'No ship is safe east of Cape Horn, least of all a pile of dead-in-the-water scrap metal like this one.'

★ ★ ★

30°W 3°S

Satan puts on a parka that might have belonged to anyone before opening the walk-in freezer on A-deck, which is thirty degrees below zero. At first he can see nothing except the white steam that forms when the hot air from outside meets the frost in the freezer. The steam circles around as heat and cold fight it out, but after Satan closes the door the steam calms and gradually sinks to the floor where Big John, Methúsalem, Rúnar and Ásmundur lie side by side under a white sheet.

This is the why the captain begged Satan to do the cooking. The deceased's shipmates couldn't stand the thought of walking in to the freezer, which has, in fact, become an energy-intensive tomb.

Satan isn't disturbed by such things, however. To him a corpse is just a corpse: dead meat that does neither harm nor good and is, thus, irrelevant. Why be afraid in the presence of dead meat? They were fond of these men when they were alive but avoid them like the plague once they stop living!

Life is war and death is peace, not the other way around. Is that so difficult to understand? A living being fights for its existence until it dies. Then it sleeps forever and does no-one any harm.

Those who pray for peace on earth are actually asking for the end of the world. And, of course, they're exactly the people who are most afraid of death.

Fools!

The shelves in the freezer are split into compartments, each of which is closed with a door made up of a wooden frame covered with chicken wire. Satan steps over the bodies and takes a shoulder of pork from one compartment and four chickens from another. He's thought it all out. First, he's going to cook all the meat that needs to be cooked. If the generator fails there'll be no cold in the freezer and no current for the electric cooker and then it wouldn't be very clever to be left with pork and chicken. Beef can be eaten raw and lamb and fish can be salted, dried or pickled. When all the meat and fresh vegetables are finished there'll be porridge and tinned food for all meals. With this plan there'll be enough to eat for the coming weeks, even if they lose the electricity.

The captain says that if they are not rescued within the next few days they'll abandon ship and sail to Brazil in the dinghy, but Satan takes such pronouncements with a pinch of salt. At the very least, he is convinced that it always pays to keep something in reserve.

For the next few days meals will consist of pork and chicken morning, noon and night. He's the cook and he's in charge. End of story.

★ ★ ★

31°W 5°S

Guðmundur opens the door of his cabin, yawns and walks slowly into the dark. He doesn't turn on the lights because moonlight is filtering through the curtains. He takes off everything except his socks and underpants, walks to his bunk and …

It's as if an ice-cold fist has grasped the captain's heart. The pain is deep and excruciating, extending along his left arm. He gapes and stares and he can't breathe …

There's a dead child in the bed.

His mouth goes so dry that his throat and the insides of his cheeks sting, his veins fill with rust and acid and his stomach is on fire.

A dead child, so very long dead. The body is embalmed, wrapped in swaddling so old and brittle that it crumbles off the baby's brown body. Its eye sockets are empty and its nose gone, and its teeth project from shrunken lips.

A tickling sensation passes through the captain's genitals, the heat in his stomach reaches all the way to his head and urine begins to filter through his underpants and down his stiff legs.

What child is this?

He can hardly move but just manages to reach out a stiff arm that shakes like a leaf in the wind and takes on the colour of death in the cold light of the moon.

Is this his daughter? Or the girl with the hare lip?

His quivering index finger comes closer to the child's face – this fragile shell that may crumble at the slightest touch.

Should he …? What should he …?

The boat lists to starboard, the curtains move and a shaft of moonlight enters.

It's not a child! It's … The captain blinks and leans forward.

The sextant! It's been lying there on his raincoat since midday!

Guðmundur wants to laugh but he can't. He sits on the bed, hides his face in his hands and tries with little success to control his violent sobbing.

★ ★ ★

30°W 7°S

In the stern of the ship, Stoker is standing over the inflated Zodiac, which is so heavily patched that it looks like a homemade camouflaged punt. The engineer had moved the boat down to B-deck, where he worked day and night on stitching the torn rubber together. He glued large patches over the stitching with contact glue and then bonded the seams with a soldering iron. When this was done he inflated the boat, which still leaks in two places.

Stoker uses a marker pen to draw circles around the holes before he deflates the boat. Then he cuts patches from the rainwear that was sacrificed for this job. Next he spreads a thin layer of contact glue around the holes on one side of the patch and gets on with other tasks while the glue is drying. He lifts up the outboard motor and attaches it to the vertical plywood board that he has screwed securely to horizontal wooden blocks using angle brackets.

'How's it going?' asks Guðmundur, looking at his watch.

17:21

'Just fine,' murmurs Stoker and pulls the cord, starting the outboard motor. 'I EXPECT TO FINISH IT THIS EVENING!'

'That's good!' shouts the captain, frowning in the dark blue smoke. 'WE LEAVE FIRST THING TOMORROW MORNING!'

'YEAH, OKAY!' Stoker cuts off the one-cylinder, four-stroke engine by pressing a red button. 'Then all we still have to do is pour some petrol into smaller containers and cut out a canvas tarpaulin, in case it rains.'

'Yeah, that's a good idea,' says the captain, nodding his head. 'Is the engine okay?'

'Yep' says Stoker as he gets down on his knees, places the patches over the holes and applies pressure with the tips of his fingers. 'We just need to top up the oil and tune it a little.'

'I thought you'd finished patching the dinghy?'

'As good as finished,' mumbles Stoker, standing up to fetch the soldering iron and aluminium foil. 'I'll inflate it after I've bonded the patches with the rubber. If it's still hard tomorrow morning, then we're safe to go.'

★ ★ ★

31°W 7°S

Stoker ambles down to the engine room in his clogs to fetch the screwdriver that he's going to use to tune the outboard motor. He's wearing overalls but he's taken off the upper part and tied the sleeves round his waist. Even though the sun has set, it's still twenty degrees outside, a densely humid equatorial calm that smells of salt and sunbaked land in the distance.

He crosses the steel floor, turns on the lights in the machine shop, finds the screwdriver he is looking for and sticks it in his pocket. But he doesn't turn the light off straightaway, because there is something he wants to do before he goes back up to B-deck.

On a shelf under the working bench, a heater fan slowly revolves and in front of it there is something black and sticky, about the size of a tomato, sitting on a five-page-thick pile of newspaper, opened to a double-page spread. Stoker pulls the newspaper off the shelf and places it on the workbench. The black sticky thing glued to the newspaper is the heart of the fifth pirate. It's shrunk to half its size and become much darker, but it's still resilient to the touch and the newspaper is still absorbing blood, which colours it black and brown almost out to the edges.

Stoker grins to himself and slides the paper back onto the shelf in front of the heater. Once the heart is completely dry he's going to grind it into a fine powder and keep it in a locked copper casket. Powdered heart of pirate! How much for a gram of that on the black market in New Orleans or Casablanca? If it's even on offer!

But he's not going to sell this treasure. No, he's going to … Stoker is startled out of his daydreams when he hears a heavy thud.

Or was it?

He listens carefully but hears nothing but the tiresome rattle of the generator engine.

Boom, boom, boom …

There!

'What …' Stoker switches off the lights in the machine shop and walks out to the engine room. What's that banging? Who's hitting …?

Boom, boom, boom …

He walks over to starboard side and into the storeroom. Is the banging coming from above or …

Boom, boom, boom …

Stoker walks into the boiler room and from there up the steel ladder leading to the electrical workshop. That's where the banging is coming from, he could be pretty …

Boom, boom, boom …

Yes! He turns to the right and along a corridor, totally unlit apart from a faint green light from above the door leading to the empty hold. On the cold steel floor are pools of oily dampness, the walls are covered with old and new rust, and the clacking of his wooden clogs echoes along the corridor.

Clack, clack, clack …

'Is somebody there?' calls Stoker, who has figured out where the heavy blows are coming from. Someone has left the door to the hold open, and the heavy metal door swings with the movement of the ship, slamming every now and then into the doorframe, which shudders, and the metallic blow is magnified in these empty metal surroundings.

Who opened the door to the hold?

Stoker holds the door with his left hand and the doorjamb with his right. then sticks his head into the darkness and calls into the cool emptiness.

'IS SOMEBODY IN THERE?'

There is no answer. Of course there's nobody in there! Who could be there? Jónas? No. The door opened by itself. It's the only logical explanation.

'Bloody stupid,' mutters Stoker and straightens up. Just as he's about to step aside, the ship takes a heavy blow and he slips on the floor, losing his grip on the door, which swings …

XXXII

31°W 8°S

It's now or never! Well, maybe not *never*, but this is the *right time*, that's for sure. If they mess up this opportunity, there's little or no hope of another one.

Guðmundur stands out on the starboard bridge wing and checks the weather, then glances at his watch.

The sun is shining in a clear sky, the temperature is nearing thirty degrees and it's ten past eight in the morning. He goes back in the bridge and looks over the control board and the table. He has compass, charts, pocket calculator and sextant. He's recorded all the necessary information in the ship's log: everything about the ship, the crew and the events of the past few days, in both Icelandic and English. Everything's ready. If the foghorn were working he'd blow it as a sign that everyone should prepare to depart.

But since the foghorn is out of commission, the captain keeps shouting out to his shipmates as he makes his way down to B-deck.

'IS EVERYONE READY? WE ABANDON SHIP IN TWENTY MINUTES. ALL HANDS ON DECK!'

When he walks out onto B-deck Sæli and Satan are there already, so he could have saved himself the shouting. Stoker is doubtless down in the engine room, fetching something or making some final adjustments.

'Hello, lads!' says the captain, who is both excited and anxious about the pending boat trip. 'Ready to go?'

'Yeah,' says Sæli. 'I guess so.'

'Are you abandoning ship in this thing?' asks Satan. He gives the inflatable a kick so it turns in a half circle on the slippery deck.

'Yes,' says Guðmundur, putting on a lifejacket and then tossing one to Sæli and another to Satan. 'This boat is our only hope.'

'How far is it to land?' Sæli asks as he puts on his lifejacket.

'About 110 kilometres, maybe more,' says the captain with a shrug. 'We should get to shore before dark, if all goes well.'

'I'm not going anywhere,' says Satan, throwing his lifejacket to the deck. 'This thing's going to sink, that's for sure. I'm not leaving a million tonnes of steel to get in a bath toy. No way!'

'You have no choice!' says Captain Guðmundur, his eyes going red. 'This ship is on its way to hell! One hundred and ten kilometres is quite a way, I'll grant you that, but sunset tonight marks the end of any chance we have that this ship will ever be found! It could drift out beyond the earth's atmosphere, as far as that goes – there's just about the same degree of shipping traffic out there as in the godless depths this rustbucket is heading for. So there!'

'No need to get all worked up, man,' says Satan, squinting against the sun and lighting a cigarette. 'Can't we just drop anchor and hang out here until some losers find us?'

'We might as well hang Christmas lights on the ship as drop anchor,' says the captain with a grim laugh. 'At a guess the water here is a good five kilometres deep.'

'You must be joking!' says Satan, his eyes widening as he blows smoke through his nose.

A good five kilometres! That's about the length of the drive from the Höfðabakki Bridge all the way to Snorrabraut in the west of Reykjavík. Satan is dizzied by the thought of water so deep and dark that it may as well be bottomless. How long would it take a human body to sink a good 5000 metres? Six hours? Twelve? A full twenty-four? Or would the enormous pressure have turned it into pâté halfway down?

'If we don't go now,' says Sæli, slapping the side of the Zodiac, 'we'll never go.'

'All together now!' says the captain and grabs one of the Zodiac's handles. 'Let's get this dinghy afloat.'

'Fuck it!' says Satan and sticks his cigarette in his mouth before also grabbing a handle. 'I'll help you launch this junk but I'm staying on the ship, thank you very much. This wading pool is going to sink and I don't plan to sink with it. No fucking way am I going to bob around in the water for days on end just to be smelled out and eaten by a shark. No way!'

'Up to you,' says the captain with a sigh as they lift the boat and head for the steps leading down to the weather deck.

'There aren't any sharks around here,' says Sæli. 'Are there?'

★ ★ ★

31°W 8°S

Desert upon desert as far as his distorted consciousness can reach; a burning hot desert, yellow and deadly …

The sun is shining on Jónas's sickly face, salty sweat runs into his eyes, there's nothing to be seen but the flaming sand and dancing mirages in the distance …

He's walking and walking but can't feel his legs …

Maybe he's on horseback?

He doesn't know where he's going but he carries on, he has to carry on, he can't do anything but carry on, gliding as if in a dream …

Maybe he's dreaming?

Buzzing heat that paralyses his lungs, scratches his flesh and forces its way into his rotting body, which glows like the thread in a lightbulb …

When he's just about to give up …

Give up? He has no choice. He just is until he stops being.

… and die …

Dying's not so bad. Not when life is desert fire. Hopefully death is cold and crisp, endless depths of blue water.

… he catches sight of something that sticks up out of the soaring mirage fires …

Intersecting lines …

A house!

He remembers the house in Mosfellsbær.

There's a house up ahead, and it's slowly coming closer, and little by little becoming clearer …

Maybe it's a roadside café?

Water, water – he must have water …

The heat is overwhelming and the sun paralysing. It sucks away life like a fly sucking blood …

But there are people coming, people coming out of the mists! Two men coming to help him …

Somewhere a door opens, there are voices and …

'Water!'

His eyes are full of hot seawater and his legs drag along the hard sand. They hold him up and carry him towards the house, which throws a triangular shadow on the sand …

Shade!

He must have water! His head is full of red fire, the sun has bored a hole in his forehead and lights up the dark …

The house, the house …

The house isn't a house but an iron pyramid that lists to one side like …

A rusty pyramid that …

That isn't a pyramid but the bow of a freighter that's sticking up like …

'NO, NO, NO! NOT THE SHIP!'

He tries to resist but the men won't let him go. He looks closer and sees that they aren't men – not living men …

Two skeletons wearing beige suits drag him to the altar of the iron god that towers over them like a man-made mountain and stares out at the desert with empty, square eyes ...

★ ★ ★

31°W 8°S

The captain is on board the Zodiac, which is roped to the starboard side of the ship. Sæli and Satan are holding the outboard motor out to him over the railing.

'Don't drop it in the water, skipper,' says Satan as he lets go of the motor. Guðmundur crawls to the back of the boat holding the motor as if it were a baby, and attaches it to the platform in the stern. The others toss twenty-five Coke bottles on board: twenty containing petrol, five water.

'That is a ticking time bomb, lads,' says Satan, who's bare to the waist, tanned and shiny with sweat.

'Do you need help?' Sæli calls out to the captain.

'You're welcome to call it off and stay on the ship with me,' says Satan and he lights a cigarette.

'No, it's all right,' says the captain, wiping the sweat from his forehead. 'Why don't you just jump aboard?'

'What about the engineer?' asks Satan, scratching the bandage above his left ear as he blows out blue smoke. The bandage is dirty and soaked with sweat, which is dissolving the dried blood.

'I'd forgotten all about Stoker!' says Guðmundur as he tosses the bottles of petrol into the compartment at the bow of the Zodiac. 'What's he thinking of, the fool?'

'Guys!' says Satan, shading his eyes with his left hand. 'Do you see what I see?'

They all stare out to sea, where the waves glisten like mountains of silver in the strong sunlight.

'Is that ...?' mutters Sæli, squinting.

'For Christ's sake!' says the captain, standing up in the Zodiac.

About a hundred metres south of the ship is the big lifeboat, rocking to and fro as it approaches.

'Lads, jump aboard!' says Guðmundur as he tugs on the mooring line to pull the Zodiac up to the railing. 'We should head out before the lifeboat runs into the ship.'

'Are you crazy?' says Satan, tossing his cigarette overboard. 'You're not going anywhere in this inner tube when we can use that big one! I'll come with you in *that* one.'

'We have no idea what condition it's in!' says the captain, his voice sharp. We leave now – THAT'S AN ORDER!'

'How about the engineer?' says Satan, picking up a coil of rope from the deck. 'Are you going to leave him behind?'

'ALL ABOARD!' screams Guðmundur, clearly quite frantic. 'If we don't leave now we all die! *Can you understand that?* If you don't jump on board I'll go ashore alone!'

Skuggi is running back and forth on the weather deck, looking from the captain to Satan and whining constantly.

'Gummi? Gummi?' says Sæli, hesitantly. 'He's right, we should …'

The captain starts the engine and begins to loosen the mooring ropes.

'YOU GET ON BOARD, BOY! I DON'T CARE WHAT —'

'*You shut your bloody mouth, motherfucker!*' Satan screams at Guðmundur, who goes silent and stares at the seaman, a hysterical gleam in his eyes. 'You're not leaving anyone behind and nobody's going anywhere in that inner tube of yours!'

'*You* …' The captain clenches his pale fists and closes his mouth in mid sentence to control his trembling lips.

'I CAN'T SWIM, FOR FUCK'S SAKE!' shouts Satan, expanding his chest muscles like a wild animal preparing to attack.

'Look! It's Jónas!' says Sæli, pointing at the lifeboat, which is now only ten metres from the ship.

The ghostly face of the second mate can be seen through the window off and on. They can see no sign that he's conscious.

'Is he dead?' asks Satan, breathing deeply through his nose.

'I can't see,' says Sæli.

'He's going to hit the Zodiac! I knew it!' says the captain, escaping onto the weather deck and abandoning the boat. 'Don't let him hit the Zodiac!'

'You and your dinghy,' spits Satan. He climbs onto the railing with the coil of rope over his right shoulder and launches himself onto the bow of the lifeboat.

'NO! NO!' shouts the captain as the Zodiac gets jammed between the lifeboat and the ship.

The outboard motor mutters in neutral; the rubber groans when the heavy plastic lifeboat shoves against the Zodiac and twists it; two patches pop off, and several petrol bottles fall in the water.

'Here comes the rope!' says Satan, throwing the coil across to Sæli after tying the end of it to a hook on the bow of the lifeboat.

'*See what's happening?*' bellows Guðmundur, pointing at the Zodiac, which is losing its air as it is squeezed into a knot, until its motor dies and pulls the rubber boat down into the deep.

Sæli ties the lifeboat to the railing then leaps aboard, while the captain sits down on a hatch and wipes the sweat off his neck and forehead with a white handkerchief.

'Hello?' says Satan, knocking on the window of the lifeboat. Then the second mate blinks and licks his lips with a swollen tongue. 'He's alive!'

'We can get in at the back,' says Sæli, feeling his way along the enclosed lifeboat, which is rounded and difficult to negotiate.

'We sail at noon!' the captain shouts from his hatch. 'We load petrol and supplies and sail at noon!'

'What's the matter with you, man?' Sæli calls back. 'We

have to look after the second mate!'

'I'm going to take a nap,' says Guðmundur, sliding off the hatch and setting off for the stairs up to the starboard side of B-deck. 'We load petrol and supplies and sail at noon.'

Skuggi lies down on his belly on the hatch and watches as the captain leaves.

'I'll go in and get him loose if you help lift him out,' says Sæli as he opens the entrance at the back of the lifeboat.

'Christ, what a stink!' says Satan, holding his nose as foul air streams out of the lifeboat.

'Water!' says Jónas hoarsely as Sæli lifts him up.

'Take it easy!' says Sæli, dragging the second mate towards the door. 'You'll get water.'

'Got 'im!' says Satan as he gets a grip on Jónas's shoulders.

'He's dehydrated,' says Sæli, gripping the second mate's legs and pulling him, back bent, out the door of the lifeboat, which is lying parallel to the ship, its stern banging by turns against the railing and the side of the ship, depending on just how much the ship lists to starboard.

They choose their moment and manage to heave Jónas onto the weather deck, where they each take an arm and carry him between them into the shade of the wheelhouse.

'He's pissed and shit himself, for Christ's sake,' mutters Satan with a grimace.

'Yeah, I know,' says Sæli softly.

Just before they reach the staircase leading to B-deck, the second mate comes to, opens his swollen eyes and tries to resist.

'NO, NO, NO! NOT THE SHIP!' he screams, his voice breaking as he struggles with his shipmates.

'Stop it, man!' says Satan, taking a firmer hold on Jónas, who is staring at Satan with terror in his shiny eyes.

A slow, heavy wave tips the ship, then it straightens as it lifts up on the wave.

'Satan! *Look!*' calls Sæli, twisting around and looking along the weather deck.

'Oh, fuck. NO!' screams Satan, letting go of the second mate, who falls forward onto the deck.

As the ship lifts, the lifeboat is sucked under its gigantic hull. Its mooring line snaps under the pressure and the eighteen-man plastic boat disappears in front of their eyes as the ship settles all its weight onto it, thrusting it deep into the water.

'Oh my God!' says Sæli, on his knees. 'I don't believe …'

A muffled explosion can be heard when the plastic boat caves in underwater, then the sea foams violently as air, petrol and debris shoot up to the surface.

★ ★ ★

32°W 10°S

'Right, it's ready, finally,' says Satan as he places a casserole dish on the table in the seamen's mess. Then he takes off his oven gloves and sits at the end of the table nearest the door. Captain Guðmundur sits at the other end and Sæli in the middle, to the right of the captain.

'Have some before it gets cold,' says Satan, serving himself.

He has dismembered two chickens and thrown them in the pottery casserole along with cabbage, onions and potatoes, and seasoned the whole with salt and pepper before tossing it in the oven and cooking the whole show for three hours.

Silence.

'It's time you dropped this fucking gloom,' says Satan as he shakes the meat off a wing and a thigh. 'If you don't start showing some signs of life I'm going to lock you in the freezer with the other stiffs.'

Skuggi is under the table, waiting for Satan to sneak him a bone.

'Yeah.'

Sæli takes a sip of cold water and Guðmundur serves himself half a chicken breast.

Silence.

'If we don't want to go insane then we've got to carry on no matter what. Organise each day from A to Z and make sure everyone has plenty to do, that everyone has tasks to complete and so on. That's what life is like in prison – that's how men survive there, one day at a time, year after year,' says Satan, enthusiastically gulping down the bland food. 'We'll take shifts in the bridge. We've got to watch for ships and shoot up a flare if we see any ships. The engineer'll look after the engine room. Sæli'll see to keeping the ship tidy and I'll do the cooking. There are several things that need to be fixed, like, we could have a go at repairing the communications equipment. I mean, we hardly need a scientific genius to reconnect the aerial for the radio, do we?'

Silence.

Sæli looks at the captain, who is poking at the yellowish chicken breast with his fork.

'Do we?' Satan repeats, wiping his mouth.

'No,' says Sæli. 'It's worth a try.'

'Of course it's worth a try!' says Satan, taking a drink of water.

Silence.

'Is Jónas in the infirmary?' asks Guðmundur.

'Yeah,' says Satan, nodding. 'He's lying there, the bastard.'

'Unconscious?' asks the captain.

'He's not opening his eyes,' says Satan with a shrug. 'He's probably just ashamed of himself.'

'Why did he take the boat?' Sæli says. 'I just don't understand it!'

'But where's Óli?' says the captain, looking up. 'I haven't seen him since —'

'I checked in the engine room a while ago,' says Satan, serving himself more cabbage. 'He wasn't there.'

'Sæli, would you check whether he's in his cabin?' says the captain.

'No problem,' says Sæli, getting up.

Sæli has no appetite anyway, so he's sort of relieved to have an excuse to leave the table. The nauseating smell of the overcooked food accompanies him up to C-deck, and the climb doesn't help. Still, anything's better than sitting at the table in the mess looking at the colourless chicken floating in its own juices alongside the slimy cabbage.

Up on D-deck he knocks twice before opening the door to the engineer's cabin.

'Are you there, Óli?' asks Sæli, peering into the dark cabin where the close air smells of dirty socks, sweat and something that seems to be rotting. 'Are you asleep, or dead, or …'

Sæli holds his nose with his right hand and turns on the light switch with his left.

No!

He takes two steps back, eyes wide and glued to the horror that is displayed in the middle of the table, like some work of art. Then he retches and vomits all over the rug.

XXXIII

32°W 10°S

'Do you know who it is?' says Guðmundur, breathing through a handkerchief and looking at the *thing* in the engineer's cabin.

'Yeah,' says Satan absentmindedly as he looks round the squalid cabin. 'That's the fifth pirate. I asked him to throw the body in the sea but he must have kept *that* as a souvenir.'

Those empty eyes, that grotesque smile …

On the table sits the pirate's skull, still with hair on the back of its head and jaw muscles and flesh between its teeth, surrounded by half-burnt black candles.

'I don't understand,' says the captain, shaking his head.

'You don't need to understand anything. I'll throw this in the sea in a minute,' mutters Satan, walking over to the picture that hangs above the head of the bed. 'That's strange.'

'What's strange?' says Guðmundur, looking at Satan, who is staring at the picture and the frame around it.

'Nothing!' says Satan with a shake of his head. 'You just go on out. I'll clear up in here.'

'And are you going up to the bridge after?'

'Yeah, I'll go up to the bridge.' Satan takes the picture down off the wall. 'You guys let me know when you find the engineer. *If* you find him.'

'Yeah, we'll do that,' says the captain and he hurries out of the smelly cabin.

Strange!

Satan turns the framed picture every which way but there's no sign of its having been tampered with. All the joints are firm, the glass is in place and the back is covered with faded brown paper.

But, then, how can it be that the pencil drawing is gone from the frame? What used to be a drawing of an octopus man wearing a suit is now nothing at all. Nothing but a sheet of cream-coloured paper, framed in thick matting and a carved wooden frame.

★ ★ ★

31°W 11°S

'We can't find him anywhere,' says Guðmundur when he comes up to the bridge to relieve Satan.

'He has to be somewhere,' says Satan, getting down from the captain's chair.

'Yeah. Is there hot coffee?'

'There's some sort of poison simmering there, yeah. Goodnight, old man.'

Satan makes his way down the stairs and into his cabin on D-deck. He turns on the light in the bathroom, opens the cupboard above the sink and checks his supplies.

Four packs of cigarettes and thirty-two paracetamol tablets.

Fuck it!

There's nothing to do aboard this ship but drink coffee and smoke, and he's had the devil of a headache ever since he got hit by those bullets.

Satan turns on the cold water and washes down four paracetamol. Then he closes the cupboard door and examines his reflection in the mirror.

The bandage is disgustingly dirty; his eyes are red from exhaustion and lack of sleep; his skin is suntanned and salt-burned, and his beard is getting pretty impressive after being neglected for two weeks.

'Like a fucking pirate!' Satan says with a leer but then his face starts twitching because he itches dreadfully under the sweaty bandage.

This can't go on – he simply has to peel that horror off his head.

He takes off his shirt, finds scissors in a first aid kit and starts cutting the bandage away behind and in front of his left ear. Then he takes the whole bandage off his head, except for the bit that's stuck to the wounds. His hair is not only stringy and dirty, it's dark brown at the roots because the black dye is growing out. Satan cuts it all away, lock by lock and tangle by tangle, until there's nothing left but a centimetre of hair in his natural colour.

Before he pulls the last bit of bandage off the wounds, he wets it with warm water that softens the dried blood and loosens the hard cotton. He carefully pulls at the strips, which split off the half-healed wounds and bloody hair. His heartbeat rises, the veins in his head swell and sweat runs into his eyes. As soon as the final strip is free Satan holds a cold washcloth against the bleeding wounds. They are horizontal, one about two centimetres above the other. Once the bleeding has slowed he cuts the rest of the long hair away, cleans the cuts with disinfectant and ties a red bandanna around his head – he has to hide the wounds with something: they're open to the bone. He had found this fine bandanna in a drawer in the chief engineer's cabin.

A red bandanna and a silver earring: he definitely resembles a pirate. A pirate in a Hollywood picture, that is.

'Could be worse,' he tells himself and lights a cigarette with shaking hands. The pain is as hellish as ever, but at least he's rid of the itch.

Too bad not to have more cigarettes – the thought of maybe running out of tobacco is not a good one.

Those dead guys must have a few cartons hidden away, and Stoker must …

'Stoker,' mutters Satan, blowing out smoke through his

nose. He'd forgotten about him, that he was lost. How can you get lost like that aboard a ship? Unless he fell in the sea? No – no way.

The ship's big, no doubt about it, but somehow not big enough for men to just …

Suddenly he remembers one place nobody probably thought to look.

The hold!

He might have fallen into the hold. Far-fetched, yes, but he, himself, had fallen in through the door in the fucking corridor down there. Maybe such things didn't happen to experienced sailors, but it would be stupid not to check it out.

Satan puts his blue-check shirt back on without buttoning it. He lopes down to A-deck, where he crosses to starboard, through the electrical workshop and left along the corridor leading to the red doors with the white sign on them.

HOLD

The corridor is cold and dim; his heavy steps echo between the iron walls and Satan feels the hairs rising on the back of his neck. He's keeping his cigarette in his mouth and squinting to avoid the bitter smoke.

Ahead he can see the green light above the doors to the empty hold.

No.

The doors are locked, as he left them.

'I guess I knew that,' Satan says, grabbing the handle of one of the hasps – but it's so stiff he can't move it.

★ ★ ★

31°W 11°S

Guðmundur is sitting in the bridge staring out through one of the unbroken windowpanes.

It's night-time and the waning moon resembles a sickle,

hanging in the distance above the black sea.

The captain's hands grip the chair's arms, his eyes bulge and the lower part of his face – deathly pale and ghostly in the faint moonlight – twitches violently.

After drinking untold cups of black coffee, he has heartburn and a bitter taste in his nose and mouth. The captain calmly looks to the right, towards the doorway to the starboard bridge wing, where the shotgun no longer leans against the cupboard inside the door. He threw it in the sea, along with the pirates' machine guns, after he started tasting gunpowder on the tip of his tongue.

The ship drifts south, drawing away from mainland South America at the rate of four to five kilometres an hour.

Nothing awaits them except …

Nothing awaits them.

The idea of sticking the cold gun barrel in his mouth is getting less and less unpalatable. The imagined taste of gunpowder is actually not all that different from boiled coffee. The taste of the barrel itself is metallic and cold, with a trace of soot and oil. His teeth slide along the barrel, his eyes close, his fingers touch the cocked trigger and the end of the barrel pushes against his palate –

'What!'

The captain snaps out of a kind of waking dream, his fingers bury themselves in the leather of the chair's arms, his legs twitch involuntarily and drops of cold sweat break out on his temples.

★ ★ ★

32°W 51°S

'DYNAMOES ON FULL POWER! DYNAMOES ON FULL POWER!' roars the captain into the telephone, but nobody in the engine room answers.

There is nobody in the engine room.

Guðmundur Berndsen throws the telephone away and straps himself tightly to the leather chair.

Outside the sea has got rough and the only thing the captain can do is drive the ship into the waves by using the electrically driven bow thruster.

'Great God above!'

The captain battles heroically against the forces of nature, which in this part of the world are associated with Cape Horn, Drake's Passage and Antarctic winds. He is, of course, very fearful as to the fate of the ship and its crew, but while he struggles with these ancient enemies of all seafarers, his mind empties of all thought.

A hero's death is a good deal more acceptable than insanity, suicide or starvation.

The waves break over the ship, which shudders all along its length. He can see virtually nothing through the windows, the wind screams like a siren, the bow cleaves the waves and the weather deck is more or less underwater.

★ ★ ★

33°W 66°S

The ship …

The ship is still moving, damaged, rusty, weather-beaten yet afloat, though the hold is half full of water that has forced its way under the hatches. The only thing that has changed is that it no longer lists to starboard but has rolled over to port. The bow, in other words, no longer faces east but west. It's left leaning now, not right leaning, which changes nothing because the ship is still drifting south, athwart the waves.

Sæli is standing in the middle of the radar mast up on the roof of the wheelhouse, attempting to reconnect the aerials for the radio. He hooks his left arm around the frame of the mast and exposes the ends of the cut wires by cutting off their insulation with his pocketknife and scraping salt and residue off the copper. Then he tries to work out which wire is supposed to attach to which, twists them together and winds insulation tape around them.

He's wearing a thick parka and windproof trousers because the weather has been getting steadily colder over the past few days. His fingers are red and stiff with cold, but Sæli is so engrossed in his task that he hardly notices.

However, when a black shadow falls on the roof of the wheelhouse he loses his concentration, looks up and –

'CHRIST ALMIGHTY!'

Sæli is so startled that he almost loses his balance, but a moment before the soles of his shoes slip off the slick metal he comes to this senses and throws his arms around the radar mast like a little child running to his mother's embrace.

What should he do? The shadow moves over the ship and suddenly the sun disappears behind –

He has to warn the captain! He has to –

Sæli moves along the mast, stretches out his right arm and uses the blade of the knife to force open the lid of a break-out box on the outside of the mast, just above his head.

Which wire is …? And which ones are live?

There is a blow to the ship as the bottom collides with –

Boom, boom, boom …

Hurry!

He loosens two blue wires and two yellow ones, using the point of his knife as a screwdriver, then he switches the wires and screws them back on.

Suddenly the foghorn wails.

MBAHHHHHHH!!

The noise is so deep and so loud that the mast vibrates like a gigantic brass instrument.

* * *

Saturday, 1 December 2001

Every day is like the day before, never-ending, empty and boring, and that's how time is going to pass or stand still forever, right?

Until the last of them succumbs to starvation or an accident, right?

And then they would sail on and on and on as phantoms in a ghost ship until the curse was lifted from them, right?

Until the curse was lifted from *him*, that is, right?

As in *The Rime of the Ancient Mariner* by that eighteenth-century Englishman Samuel Taylor Coleridge.

Right?

Jónas is sitting on the edge of his bed in his starboard cabin on E-deck, staring at nothing, with his rosary between his fingers.

The curse …

No, he hadn't killed an albatross, lucky bird of seafarers, like the sailor in the poem; rather, he struck his wife in the head with a hammer and buried her body on the beach before joining the ship.

She who had been the mainstay of his life, if not the ship itself …

The ship.

What should he do? Nothing? Take his own life? Or wait for a sign from above?

'The Lord is my shepherd, my strength, my light,' he murmurs.

My light …

He is wearing nothing but a brown bathrobe; his hair is dirty and unkempt, and his eyes are cloudy and swollen after several days without sleep. His left wrist is bandaged. It's still quite sore after his fall, but the broken bone has healed.

But what does the condition of your body matter, when your soul is writhing in the fires of hell?

'The fires of hell,' mutters Jónas, blinking his tear-filled eyes. He rubs the black beads of the rosary, which are beginning to lose their colour, and watches it swing back and forth.

Where is it all going to end? And when? Will the ship sink before they die of disease or hunger or will divine providence direct it …

Boom, boom, boom …

What was that?

Jónas straightens his back and listens.

Silence.

Is he imagining things or is it getting colder in –

MBAHHHHHHH!!

Jónas clenches the fingers of his right hand around the rosary and crawls on his knees onto the bed.

The foghorn!

He pulls the curtains aside and puts his ghostly face against the icy glass. What he sees is so dreadful and at the same time so beautiful that he doesn't know whether to despair or rejoice.

'Oh my God,' whispers the second mate, crossing himself with trembling fingers. 'It's happening!'

The Almighty is watching him. Of course He's watching him! He's been called to meet Him …

★ ★ ★

13:31

The captain wakes in his chair when the bottom of the ship hits something.

Boom, boom, boom …

'What was that?' Guðmundur Berndsen wonders aloud. He sits up straighter in the chair, shakes off the chill of his catnap and yawns as he rubs the sleep from his bloodshot eyes.

Did the ship just …?

MBAHHHHHHH!!

When he hears the foghorn the captain comes to life with such a jolt that he almost loses that life at the same moment.

His mind goes empty, his eyes bulge and his heart contracts into a hard knot.

He looks out the salt-covered windows and sees white.

'HOLY MARY!'

The captain turns on the bow thruster, then he turns the ship to port and just barely manages to avoid a collision with an iceberg the size of an eight-storey building.

★ ★ ★

13:45

He has turned off the foghorn and climbed down from the radar mast.

Silence.

Sæli stands at the front of the wheelhouse roof and looks across the Weddell Sea, which is covered with broken ice as far as he can see. The ocean is dark blue and so cold it moves like syrup. There are a few dozen metres between the icebergs, but that space gets narrower as they get closer to Antarctica. The wind is picking up out of the north-west. There's a whirlwind in the offing.

Antarctica!

'Shit!'

The distance is overwhelming and unendingly white and its breath is cold …

XXXIV

Tuesday, 11 December 2001

Per se stranded two days ago in the Weddell Sea in east Antarctica, not far from the rocky coast and just under a hundred kilometres north of the double-peaked granite mountains that are part of the massive mountain range that towers over the awe-inspiring landscape. The approximate position of ship and crew, plus or minus two degrees, is:

72°S 16°W

Since east Antarctica is the largest part of the continent, as well as the part that few have explored, the survivors might just has well have been marooned on the planet Pluto. There is virtually no likelihood of running across other sentient beings in this largest ice desert on earth.

A month without a gale or a year without a whirlwind exist only as statistical possibilities in Antarctica. Along the Princess Martha Coast the average temperature is minus 20°C in winter and minus 2°C in the summer.

The atmospheric pressure is always high and there's a gale wind every third day of the month; it snows two days out of three all year round; there are, on average, thirteen days of fog each month; heavy winds blow across the ice for up to 300 days a year, and life-threatening whirlwinds can hit any time.

Every once in a while, though, a kind of ring of light will

form around the sun or moon beyond the clouds, and this is a sign that the storms are about to abate. Then it won't be long before the spine-tingling calm, the bone-white ice and the awesome mountains interlock to form one vast frozen silence that both paralyses and enchants, terrifying and invincible …

The ship is surrounded by huge icefloes that move on top of the water and scrape against the dented steel day and night. According to the calendar it is the height of summer in Antarctica, but even the summer is winter on this continent of vastness and permafrost.

Above the waterline the rust-brown ship's hull is covered with a greyish ice, thin to windward and thick on the sheltered side. On the weather deck are snow drifts shaped by the wind, hard as concrete. From the railings and the radar mast hang huge icicles and other ice formations, while in the most sheltered spots delicate ice needles collect, looking like glass crystals or wild vegetation.

The situation on board the ship is bleak. Only one dynamo is working, and only at half speed, because there's not much left of the 70 000 litres of oil that filled the tanks when they set sail. The water heaters in the boiler room are first in line for what oil is left, since while they have something to burn there is hot water on board the ship. Without hot water they couldn't heat the cabins, besides which it keeps the oil warm, which would otherwise thicken and be unusable. And it prevents the crew's limited water supply from freezing. The generator produces electricity for lights and gives off a good deal of heat itself, which is why the doors to the engine room are open. They've turned off power to the cold larder, the laundry room and part of the kitchen. The cooker gets power for one hour a day and they make coffee once every twelve hours, but they've stopped using any other electrical appliances.

There's no cleaning going on. It's cold on board the ship, especially on the upper decks of the wheelhouse. The cabins are cold and damp, and in the corridors the temperature is near freezing. It's impossible to stay in the bridge for more than an hour at a time, but every two hours one of the crew goes up there to send an SOS over the radio. It seems to be functioning, though they can't actually hear anything but faint static.

Twice a day Captain Guðmundur holds a prayer meeting in the officers' mess; these precious moments break up the men's negativity and build up a sense of community among the survivors. The days are long and monotonous, making it is easy for hopelessness and fear to stifle the will and paralyse the spirit. The officers' mess is the warmest room in the ship and that's where the crew hangs out together more or less twenty-four hours a day, sharing coffee, silence and the occasional word. All except Satan, who keeps to himself, either in his cabin or elsewhere …

★ ★ ★

17 December

The captain is standing by the dynamo that's still functioning, awaiting the inevitable. According to their measurements, the diesel-fuel tanks ought to have been empty long ago. One would think the dynamo was running on the smell of oil alone. The burners in the boiler room have stopped firing, the hot water is beginning to cool, and it's cooling fast. The only fuel that's left is what's still in the pipes leading to the dynamo. When the dynamo goes off, the lights will go off.

Then the lights will go off.

If only he has it wrong! If only the meters are broken! If only the fuel would last a little longer! Even just …

'No, no! None of that!' says the captain when the dynamo starts to stutter. He kicks the dynamo and bangs on the fuel pipe, though he knows perfectly well that nothing he can do will prevent the engine from dying.

When the engine finally stops, the captain's heart seems to stop beating in his chest – the shock is so great despite the long lead-up. Seconds after the engine stops, the lights begin to dim.

After thirty seconds the only light left is the dying glow of the wires in the dirty lightbulbs.

Then everything goes black and the oil-soaked air in the engine room immediately starts to cool. Within a few hours it's going to be as cold inside the ship as outside it. At that point living aboard the *Per se* will hardly be an option.

'Now what do we do?' mutters the captain in the dark, which swallows his words and turns them into a metallic echo. He's still standing by the dynamo, holding his hands over it and feeling how the warmth is slowly disappearing.

He's distracted and automatically ignores a strange sound that his ears receive. It's a weak sound yet oddly clear, even piercing. Though it doesn't actually gain the captain's attention, it does ring some bell deep in his subconscious.

'Yes, okay,' says Guðmundur Berndsen with a sigh. 'All right, all right! Daddy's coming!'

Daddy's coming?

The captain is startled out of his deep thoughts about the ship and the fate of its crew and starts listening.

Did he hear some sound? Or …

Waaahaaa …

Yes, he heard a sound – and it's like a baby crying. A baby crying! Is he going crazy?

'Go! Get thee behind me, Satan!' says the captain out loud and he covers his ears with his hands. Then he strides across the metal floor, though he can't see a thing, and tries to find the door to the storeroom.

★ ★ ★

18 December

Sæli, wearing a parka and headphones, is sitting in front of the communications console on the port side of the bridge, calling into the radio.

'Mayday! Mayday! Echo, Lima, Whiskey, Q, 2! Mayday! Mayday! Echo, Lima, Whiskey, Q, 2! Mayday! Mayday!'

But there's no answer.

Nothing except the hum of static that tickles his ears and irritates him. His fingers are red with cold, his backside is numb and his breath freezes as he exhales.

One more time!

'Mayday! Mayday! Echo, Lima, Whiskey, Q, 2! Mayday! Mayday! Echo, Lima, Whiskey, Q, 2! Mayday! Mayday!'

Sæli listens intently. At first he hears only static and hum, hum and static, and then detects a fitful tune and broken, stuttered song about words of music and lights. He tears off his headphones and throws them aside.

What was that? The Doors? On the ship's radio? Is he going crazy or …?

'That's enough for today,' he says, turning off the radio. He's not going near this contraption again. No way! The others can send out a distress signal if they feel like it. Or just not bother. It doesn't make any difference! Nobody's answering anyway!

Sæli leaves the bridge and makes his way down the stairs, which are covered with ice and very dangerous. It's dark in the ship but outside reddish-pink sunlight penetrates the clouds. He puts his hands on the icy-cold railings and walks carefully from one step to the next.

His mind turns home, to Lára and young Egill. What might they be doing now? Do they know the ship is lost? Has Lara developed a bulge? Of course she has a bulge! She's — what? — six months along. Which means she's only got three …

'I have to get home,' says Sæli, stopping on the stairs between E- and D-decks. He stares into the darkness and listens to his own heartbeat.

Home.

If only he —

Waaahaaa …

'Daddy's coming!' says Sæli and he starts back down the stairs. Then he stops suddenly.

Daddy's coming?

He holds onto the railing and listens intently.

A baby crying? Had he heard a baby crying? Was that possible? But there's no baby on board the –

Waaahaaa …

'I'M COMING! I'M COMING!' Sæli calls out and goes down the slippery stairs as fast as he can.

Is he going crazy? Doesn't matter! Crazy or not crazy, he can't listen to a baby crying without doing something about it!

'I'M COMING! I'M COMING!'

Down on C-deck he runs right into the arms of the captain.

'Christ, you startled me!' says Sæli, blinking at Guðmundur, who is studying the crewman's face, as if to assure himself that Sæli is a man of flesh and blood and not something else.

'What's going on here?' asks the captain, letting go of the breathless crewman. 'Have you lost your mind, boy?'

'Didn't you hear? Didn't you hear? says Sæli, catching his breath as he thinks back and tries to remember what he thought he had heard. 'Didn't you hear … a noise?'

'I heard you shouting!' says the captain, clearing his throat. 'I thought something … that something had happened!'

'I'm going crazy!' says Sæli, staring desperately into the captain's eyes. 'That's what's happened – I've lost my mind!'

'No,' says the captain with a sigh. 'You've not gone crazy. Not yet, at least.'

'But I heard …'

'Don't listen with your mind, Sæli, lad, because your mind is tired and confused and can't tell the difference between right and wrong,' says Guðmundur, clapping the seaman on the back in the dark corridor. 'Listen with your heart, rather, because it knows the difference between truth and a lie!'

★ ★ ★

19 December

Jónas is lying under his doona and three woollen blankets in the bed in his E-deck cabin, mumbling something incomprehensible in his troubled sleep. The cabin is dark and frozen, and the second mate's breath sticks to the air and turns into ice needles that, little by little, become small icicles.

Waaahaaa …

Jónas twitches, blinks his eyes and lifts his deathly pale head off the ice cold pillow.

Waaahaaa …

'Yes, okay,' he murmurs, crawling out from under his doona and blankets. 'Daddy's coming.'

He gets up and stands unsteadily in his long underwear, jumper and woollen socks. Then he sets off like a robot: four steps forwards then five to the left, straight into the wall by the door. He hits it hard, which wakes him from his half sleep. He puts his right hand to his face and feels around in the dark with his left.

Waaahaaa …

'María love! María!' Jónas calls as he feels around the cheekbone and jawbone on the right side of his face. 'Our daughter's awake! Can you …'

María?

But María's dead. I'm not at home …

The ship!

Waaahaaa …

'Hello! What? Where?' says Jónas and crosses like a drunk man to the door, where he turns the light switch up and down to no avail.

No electricity!

What's that noise? Who's crying? Is there a baby on board? Of course there's no baby on board. Is he going crazy?

Waaahaaa …

'Shut up! Shut up! Shut up!' says Jónas, walking in circles in the dark and scratching at his ears until the blood runs down into the neck of his sweater. 'Leave me alone! Do you hear me? Leave me alone!'

★ ★ ★

20 December

It's ten to six in the afternoon and a prayer meeting is about to start in the officers' mess. Captain Guðmundur is sitting at the end of the table away from the door, Sæli to his right and Jónas to his left.

'Dear friends, let us pray,' says the captain. He folds his hands and lowers his head. 'Our Father, who art in Heaven, hallowed be thy name, thy kingdom come, thy will be done, on earth as it is in Heaven. Give us this day our daily bread, and forgive us our trespasses, as we forgive those who trespass against us. Lead us not into temptation, but deliver us from —'

Waaahaaa …

The captain stops in the middle of the prayer when the bloody crying starts to sound deep in his head.

Not now! Not now!

'And lead us not into temptation,' he says with a cough, 'but deliver us from —'

Waaahaaa …

The captain opens his eyes and looks at his companions, who look back at him above their folded hands.

'Do you hear?' asks Sæli hesitantly, attempting to still his trembling lips.

'I hear,' says Jónas hoarsely, looking at Sæli with eyes heavy with sleeplessness and despair.

'What is it?' asks Sæli, with a terrified look at the captain.

'I don't know,' murmurs the captain, closing the Bible on the table in front of him. 'I've searched everywhere.'

'Down in the engine room too?' asks Jónas.

'Down in the engine room too.'

'And?' says Sæli hopefully.

'Nothing,' says the captain. 'Actually, Skuggi wouldn't go down there with me, but I didn't find anything. It's as if the sounds were coming from somewhere outside.'

'From outside?' asks Sæli, his bloodshot eyes widening.

'Yes,' says Guðmundur, rubbing his temples. 'Or from inside. What do I know?'

'From inside?' Jónas says and tries to swallow, but his mouth is utterly dry.

Waaahaaa …

'I can't stand it!' says the captain, standing up. 'Let's go outside for a bit.'

★ ★ ★

18:05

They stand close together in the stern of the ship, turn their backs to the wind and say the Lord's Prayer together, the captain in the middle with the crewman and the second mate one on each side.

'… the power and the glory for ever and ever, Amen!' says Guðmundur, making the sign of the cross before lifting his head and opening his eyes.

Silence.

'But what about that crying?' asks Sæli, sticking his hands in the pockets of his parka.

'Could it maybe be an evil spirit?' Jónas asks and pulls his woollen cap down over his ears.

'I've been thinking,' says the captain, holding his Bible tightly with both hands and pressing it to his abdomen, 'maybe it's God's way of answering our prayers?'

'How's that?' says Sæli doubtfully.

'We need a miracle if we're going to get away from here,' says the captain. 'But miracles don't happen every day. It may be God can't save us.'

'God is all powerful!' says Jónas, giving Guðmundur a dirty look.

'Of course!' says the captain with a faint smile. 'But isn't it asking too much to expect him to stretch down here and steer us clear of this —'

'Hell?' Sæli completes the thought and chews his frostbitten lips.

'The crying we hear may be the crying of the saviour,' says the captain, straightening up. 'The Christ child himself whom God gave to mankind. All we need to do is make the child welcome. "Suffer the little children to come unto me for of such is the kingdom of God", said Jesus. I say: receive Christ in the form of a little child and we are saved!'

'But there is no child,' says Jónas, irritated.

'The child is here,' says the captain, pointing at the second mate's chest. 'Receive the Christ child and you are saved! Your body will die but it is dust alone! God says: "Receive my son and I will receive your soul".'

Silence.

'I'd say you're losing it,' mutters Jónas, giving the captain a sideways look.

'No, Jónas. If anything, I've never been healthier than I am right now –'

'Look! There's a man there!' shouts Sæli, pointing over the gunwale on the port side and along the ship, where a dark shape comes walking out of the fog.

'Who?' says the captain, shading his eyes.

'The gangplank is down!' says Jónas, pointing to port, where the top of the gangplank is sticking in through the gate in the railing. 'It must be Satan.'

'Yep,' says Sæli as the being becomes more clearly defined. 'That's Satan.'

★ ★ ★

18:31

'Where have you been?' asks Guðmundur when Satan steps off the gangplank onto the stern of the ship.

'I made it to land,' says Satan, scratching his beard, which is covered in ice up to his nose and out to his ears. 'You can walk over the icefloes. When the fog lifts, we set off.'

'Off to where?' asks the captain.

'I'll show you after. There's a map up in the bridge,' says Satan, unwinding a white cloth from his neck; it's a sheet he cut a strip off to use as a scarf. 'What are you girls doing outside, anyway?'

Silence.

'There's crying,' says Sæli, sniffing. 'A baby crying.'

'A baby crying?' repeats Satan, brushing snow and ice off his parka.

'It's the Christ child,' says the captain, smiling the smile of one who has blind faith in one thing while refusing to face everything else.

'Or some devil,' says Jónas with a shudder. 'Let's not forget that there are two powers competing for the souls of men!'

'Anyway. It seems to come from below, this crying,' says Sæli. 'From the engine room.'

'There's nothing down in the engine room,' says Guðmundur, still smiling, though his smile is now a bit tired. 'I've looked high and low and found nothing. The only place we still haven't looked is in the hearts of us men!'

'But before we start digging in them, I'll just have a look down there,' says Satan with a grin.

'Very well,' says the captain, rising onto his toes. 'But remember that what the heart can hear isn't always understood by the mind!'

'You've lost it, man,' says Satan, shaking his head as he disappears into the wheelhouse.

★ ★ ★

18:59

It's cold in the engine room, colder even than out on the ice, and the silence that fills the dark and surrounds the engines is more troubling than the sound that disturbs it off and on.

Waaahaaa …

It can't be a baby crying because there's no baby on board the ship. Like everything else, this crying will have its natural explanation. Satan believes in neither ghosts nor any other supernatural beings. At any rate, he fears nothing that isn't flesh and blood. Only flesh and blood can conquer flesh and blood. Guys who lose their cool just because of mental pain or imagination aren't sane – that's all there is to it.

Satan walks slowly across the metal floor, hands outstretched, until he finds the railing above and behind the main engine.

Waaahaaa …

He ignites his gas lighter, which weakly illuminates the floor and down into the bottom of the ship, where the main engine is standing, cold and silent. The moment he lit the flame the crying stopped, which means its source is in the vocal cords of some form of life that is aware of his presence.

'Where are you, you crybaby?' says Satan, leaning over the railing and looking searchingly into the darkness. When nothing happens he takes to jumping up and down on the metal floor so that it shudders from end to end and produces a fearful rumbling.

And then the creature leaves its hiding place and rushes noisily across the floor behind the main engine. What Satan sees in the weak light of the flame is something white that scoots across like …

'What the fuck was that?' mutters Satan, staring into the dark, but when the flame burns his fingers he lets go of the lighter, closing off the gas so the flame dies.

Waaahaaa …

Satan creeps down the stairs to the main engine, waiting to ignite the lighter again until he's near the place where he thinks he last saw the creature. The ship must leak somewhere, because there's a couple of centimetres of ice on the floor of the engine room. Satan squats by the portside hull and reaches out his right hand with the lighter in it.

'Right. One, two and …' he whispers and takes a deep breath before thumbing the wheel on the lighter.

As the spark from the flint lights the gas, the creature shoots out of its new hiding place.

Satan sees something white that spreads itself out right in front of him. Its eyes are tiny and coal black, its yellow mouth opens wide and its red tongue sticks out like a poison dart.

★ ★ ★

19:07

'Here's your Jesus,' says Satan as he walks out the door to the back of the wheelhouse and returns to the stern of the ship.

Guðmundur, Sæli and Jónas stare at the creature he's holding out to them by its neck. It's a large bird, ruffled and covered in oil.

'It's a seagull,' says Sæli and he looks at Jónas, who lights a cigarette with trembling fingers.

'Are you sure that's …' says Guðmundur, but stops talking in mid sentence when the exhausted seagull gives a cry.

Waaahaaa …

'Any more questions?' says Satan, looking at the three men in turn like a parent who has just proven that there's no monster in the closet.

Silence.

'Then we'll just put this foolishness behind us,' says Satan coldly and smashes the head of the seagull hard against the iron wall of the stern.

The other three jump as if at a gunshot and watch, horrified, as the seagull's eyes turn red and the blood flows out of its open beak.

'Anybody want to eat it? asks Satan, holding the bird out to the three men, who retreat a couple of steps and stare at the bloody carcass, which is jerking and beating its filthy wings.

Silence.

'Just asking,' says Satan and he tosses the bird overboard.

'How did it get in the engine room, anyway?' asks Sæli as he looks over the railing to the ice, where the seagull lies on its back, head to one side and wings spread.

'What does it matter?' says Satan, looking at Sæli as if he were an idiot. 'Come with me up to the bridge. I want to show you the map I found.'

★ ★ ★

19:43

'This X here shows the position of the ship, according to the captain's calculations,' says Satan, who's standing by the table in the map room in the bridge pointing at an X on a small map of Antarctica, dated 1979.

'You know my calculations aren't exact,' says Guðmundur, looking at the map, which is in the scale 1: 40 000 000.

'They're all we have to go on,' says Satan, tapping his pen on the map. 'May I continue?'

'Go ahead,' mutters the captain.

'Look at this, and this,' says Satan, pointing with the pen at two black triangles on the map. 'Those are research stations, as far as I understand it. The one that's west or south of us is British, called Halley Bay, and the one more to the east is South African, called Sanae. If I've measured it right we're 600 kilometres from the British one and 400 from the African one.'

'Four hundred kilometres,' says Sæli, looking at the captain. 'That's not so terribly far.'

'Yes and no,' says the captain with a sigh. 'But that map is both old and tiny. Those stations aren't necessarily still there, besides which it's hard to measure distances on such a small map.'

'It's the only map we've got,' says Jónas with a shrug. 'Don't we just have to make do with it?'

'There's nothing wrong with this map!' says Satan, banging his pen against the table. 'One centimetre on the map is 400 kilometres on the surface of the earth. It's one centimetre to Sanae and one and a half to Halley Bay. Is that complicated?'

'No,' says Jónas, bending over the map. 'It's quite straightforward.'

'Gummi?' queries Sæli, looking at the captain.

'All right – it's not as if we have any choice,' the captain answers. He sighs. 'But I recommend we head for the British station, not the African one.'

'Why?' demands Satan, throwing up his arms. 'Do you want to walk an extra 200 kilometres? Or are you afraid of black people?'

'We can't just look at the kilometres,' says Guðmundur calmly, pointing at the map. 'Have you forgotten the mountain range? I'd rather take the longer route and get where I'm headed than lose my life struggling to cross these mountains. They're over 2000 metres high!'

'That's a good point,' says Sæli, looking at Jónas, who shrugs and looks at Satan.

'We won't necessarily have to cross the mountains,' says Satan. 'We can probably go around them, on the ice. There's bound to be a pass somewhere.'

'Bound to be?' says the captain then shakes his head. 'We can walk on ice all the way to Halley Bay, straight ahead. I'm not wasting precious time looking for a route across the mountains when I can just walk directly over the ice. And a route that may not exist, what's more.'

'The captain's right,' says Sæli, nodding.

'I don't agree,' Satan says, tapping his forefinger on the Sanae station on the map. 'In a frost-bound hell like this, the only sensible thing is to choose the shorter route. Besides which, out on the ice there's no shelter to be had if there's a sudden storm or whirlwind.'

'That's true,' says Jónas. 'I think it would be better to aim for the African station.'

'Out of the question!' says the captain, raising his voice. 'We head for Halley Bay and we leave at dawn tomorrow! There's no sense in waiting.'

'I'll be ready in the morning, captain,' says Sæli giving his superior a slap on the back.

'I'm not going,' says Satan, folding the map. 'I'm going across the mountains. And I'm not leaving in the morning. Actually, I wouldn't recommend anyone do that.'

'Why not, if I may ask?' says the captain, red-faced with fury.

'I'd wait until the wind changed direction,' says Satan. 'The north wind always brings fog, which is always treacherous, especially when you're walking on ice. I'm going to wait for a south wind and clear skies. True, south winds have only lasted a couple of days at a time over the past weeks, but we can make good use of two clear days.'

'Do what you like!' Guðmundur pulls his hood over his head as he walks towards the door to the corridor. 'The rest of us are leaving at dawn.'

'Captain!' says Jónas. Guðmundur stops and turns around.

'Yes?'

'If you don't mind, I'd rather go with the deckhand,' says Jónas, clearing his throat.

'I do mind, Jónas, my friend,' says the captain. 'But if that's what you'd rather do, I'm not going to stop you.'

'Okay, then,' says Jónas, nodding to Guðmundur, who turns on his heel and leaves the bridge for the last time.

★ ★ ★

23:21

Sæli is sitting at the table in his cabin, packing for the great march he and Captain Guðmundur are about to set off on. Six hundred kilometres – like walking all the way from Reykjavík to Akureyri.

There's a candle on the table which shines a soft light over the bits and pieces he is either taking along or wondering whether he should take along. He's going to take needle and thread, in case he has to repair any clothing on the way, but he's not certain whether or not he needs to have a knife. He reckons Vaseline could be useful – to prevent sunburn and chapped lips, for instance – but he's not as sure about disinfectant and rubbing alcohol. He's already packed all necessary clothing, as well as dried and canned foods meant to last for at least a week, even ten days.

All these things he has stuffed into a gym bag with a shoulder strap. The bag is already pretty heavy, possibly as heavy as eight kilograms, so if he's meant to be able to carry it all that distance he mustn't add much to its weight. They can't take water but plan to eat snow to quench their thirst.

Sæli sighs and his bitter breath becomes a frosty cloud.

He picks up a crumpled photo of Lára and Egill, who smile at him from a world so distant and hazy that it's almost nonexistent, kisses the photo and sticks it down through the neck of his parka and into his shirt pocket.

Then he blows out the candle. He has to go to sleep. He's got to rest up before the great march.

★ ★ ★

23:54

Captain Guðmundur has made shoulder straps for his suitcase out of two leather belts that he fastened to the bottom of the case with screws. He has packed the only camping stove on board the ship, along with two extra gas canisters. Earlier in the evening he cut a swatch of sailcloth and folded it to fit in the lid of the suitcase. This sailcloth he plans to wrap over and under himself and Sæli when they bury themselves in snow overnight. By lying in the sailcloth they'll avoid getting wet when the heat from their bodies melts the snow.

Like Sæli three decks below, the captain is completing his travel preparations by candlelight in his cabin. There are only two things he has left to do before he blows out the candle and goes to sleep. First, he says a short prayer and kisses his Bible before placing it in his case, which he then closes. The Bible admittedly weighs half a kilogram, but to his way of thinking the spiritual strength its presence will give the captain outweighs the calories this extra weight will cost him. Then he takes off his parka, winds Hrafnhildur's black dress around his middle, squeezes into a cotton T-shirt over the dress, puts his parka back on and zips it up to his chin.

★ ★ ★

21 December

Satan and Jónas are standing in the stern watching the other two walk out onto the ice: Guðmundur Berndsen with his suitcase on his back and Ársæll Egilsson with his gym bag under his left arm.

They turn to wave and Satan and Jónas wave back, while Skuggi circles and whines.

Every once in a while the ship shudders convulsively as it shifts on the skerrie on which it ran aground and sinks slowly into the sea under the ice.

When the walkers are out of sight in the fog the ship's dog barks loudly, as if to express his displeasure or warn the men of something

'*Shut up!*' yells Satan. Then the dog lies down on its belly and growls softly.

'Do you think they'll make it?' asks Jónas, beating his arms to keep warm in the temperature of minus five degrees.

'That depends,' says Satan. He lights a cigarette, his fifth from last.

'On what?'

'It doesn't matter where you're heading,' says Satan, blowing smoke through his nose. 'What matters is what you take with you.'

'Eh?' says Jónas, snuffling icy snot up his nose. 'What should you take with you?'

'What you had with you at the start of the journey,' says Satan, opening his left fist where a copper-coloured bullet rolled to and fro.

The captain had handed him the bullet when he said goodbye, without further explanation.

'"At the start of your journey" – what do you mean by that?' Jónas says and clenches his teeth when they start to chatter.

'Come on!' says Satan walking towards the wheelhouse. 'The wind could turn at any moment. We have work to do!'

XXXV

22 December

Satan and Jónas are walking along the shore over the creaking ice, wearing sunglasses and dragging the ship's stretcher behind them. On the stretcher — which is moulded out of fibre-reinforced plastic and resembles a sled or shallow boat — is all their luggage: clothing, coverings, fuel, instruments and provisions. It is generally easier for walkers to carry their burdens rather than drag them behind, but when you're walking over ice and snow it's better to spread the weight to reduce the danger of sinking into the surface over which you're travelling.

The two of them walk side by side a metre apart, wearing life vests over their parkas. Three-metre-long nylon ropes attached to the back of each vest come together in a hole in the 'bow' of the stretcher. They leave a trail winding across the uneven ice behind them, all the way back to the ship: a sporadic double stripe from the runners under the stretcher, the shallow tracks of rough-soled work boots either side of the stripes and Skuggi's paw prints all around. But the snow blows eternally over the ice, which means their tracks will disappear within an hour.

In the distance the ship is only a black stripe on top of the white ice and under the white sky.

Or is it the other way around?

Jónas looks over his shoulder to take a last look at the ship before it disappears from view forever. This automatically slows his walking, which in turn moves all the weight onto Satan's rope.

'None of that!' says Satan, punching Jónas's left shoulder with his right fist. 'Forget the fucking ship. It can look after itself.'

'No need to get steamed up,' mutters Jónas. He speeds up to keep pace with Satan, who's storming ahead like a hungry polar bear. The second mate already feels tired and anxious. He's thirsty, confused and dispirited. His back aches, his legs ache and his left shoulder aches. Most of all he wants to turn back and just hole up in the ship, but he knows he can't do that. He has no faith in this enterprise. What was he thinking when he turned his back on the captain?

Shit!

Now he's stuck with this madman!

Jónas deeply regrets not having listened to the voice of reason and headed south with Sæli and Guðmundur Berndsen.

23 December

They're sitting on their backsides, on a hard snowdrift facing each other, Jónas with the smaller pot and Satan with the larger. They've been walking for a total of fourteen hours and this is their third stop. It's evening, the sun is hidden by clouds, there's a strong breeze from the south-east and the temperature is about minus twelve degrees.

Jónas fills the smaller pot almost to the rim with snow. Then he measures out two plastic glasses of oatmeal and two of sugar from two plastic canisters and empties them into the snow.

Satan pulls five strips of thin cotton out of an overfull plastic bag and packs them into the bottom of the larger pot. Then he unscrews the cap of a two-litre Coke bottle wound round with cotton and aluminium foil, and pours about half a litre of petrol into the pot.

'I'm ready,' says Satan and Jónas places the smaller pot into the larger one.

Satan lights a match in the shelter of Jónas's hands and lets it fall down the space between the two pots. They hear a soft explosion; the red fire lights up their faces and black smoke rises into the night. After one minute all the snow has melted; after two the water in the smaller pot is boiling, and after three minutes the fire has gone out and the porridge is ready.

'Here,' says Satan and hands Jónas the spoon they brought with them. Jónas takes the spoon and fills it twice before handing it back, and they continue taking turns until they finish the porridge.

'It tastes of petrol,' says Jónas, retching.

'If you puke, I'll make you eat your puke!' says Satan, shovelling down two spoonfuls before handing the spoon back to Jónas.

'I can't eat any more,' Jónas says, leaning back so he won't have to breathe in the stink of hot petrol. 'You just finish it.'

'Okay,' says Satan and he carries on eating the sickly sweet, petrol-polluted concoction. 'But if you give up when we're walking, I'll leave you behind.'

'I don't doubt it,' mutters Jónas, lying down on his side in the snowdrift and closing his eyes.

'Don't fall asleep!' says Satan, kicking the second mate. 'If you fall asleep you'll never wake up again.'

'So what?' Jónas sits back up. The warmth of the cooling pot is nice but the thought of ice-cold eternal sleep is even better.

'You've got four minutes to recharge your batteries,' says Satan. He licks the spoon before he sticks it in his pocket. 'We set off again the minute the pots have cooled down.'

Skuggi whines and Satan lets him lick the scrapings out of the pot.

'I just want to sleep,' murmurs Jónas and he closes his eyes.

Or are they open? It's hard to keep your eyes open when the darkness outside them is as deep as the darkness within.

★ ★ ★

24 December

They are walking up a slope that appears to be as endless as the heavens. The snow seems set aflame by the sun that shines directly in their faces whether they look up or down; the headwind is as strong as it is cold; the snow is hard on top and soft underneath; the sled pulls at the ropes like a stubborn horse and their feet sink up to mid calf at every step.

The skin of their faces is red, swollen and cracked by the sun, frost and wind, their arms are stiff as planks, their legs burn with fatigue and tendonitis, red winds blow in their heads, nausea comes and goes and their stomachs burn like cauldrons full of petrol …

'Look!' says Satan when they finally crest the hill.

'I don't see anything,' says Jónas and he stops moving, then it's as if his body becomes weightless and rises off the ground. He lifts his arms very slowly, as if they were huge construction cranes, and shades his eyes, which are swollen and sore and full of yellow secretions and clear mucus.

The mountains! Millions of megatonnes of prehistoric granite surrounded by a whole Black Sea of dark-blue glacier. Here time is not measured in minutes and days – not even in years or centuries. Here a million years is one day, a thousand million days one year, and eternity is not simply a concept in this world of delirium and death. Eternity is a regular breathing beyond time, space and human understanding.

'We've come almost halfway,' says Satan clapping Jónas on the back. 'Not bad, comrade!'

In front of them are about fifty kilometres of snowdrifts, fissures and firn, then the enormous mountain range stretches halfway to the sky, far inland and way out on the ice to the north. The two peaks loom like a gigantic granite-and-ice cathedral and between them lies a shadow that looks not a centimetre smaller than Denmark.

'If all goes well we should reach shelter before dark,' says Satan. He signals the second mate to keep walking.

'Shouldn't we rest a moment?' asks Jónas, pulling his numb feet out of the snow. They've been walking steadily for fifty hours and have covered an equal number of kilometres. Every single kilometre has been utter hell, every single hour unbearable and every single moment laden with hopelessness, exhaustion and a death wish.

'We'll eat after two hours,' says Satan, striding off.

'Aren't we going to skirt the mountains?' Jónas points north to where the ice on the Weddell Sea stretches to the limits of their vision.

'No,' says Satan. He heads straight for the shadow between the peaks. 'I'm certain there's a pass through the mountains.'

'Up to you,' says Jónas under his breath. He can't be bothered to argue with this pig-headed halfwit. He doesn't have the energy. And why argue about something it's pointless to argue about. They're dead either way.

XXXVI

24 December

'And it came to pass in those days that there went out a decree from Caesar Augustus …' says Captain Guðmundur, attempting to turn the pages of the frozen Bible, his fingers black with cold. 'And it came to pass in those days …'

'Don't,' says Sæli, curling himself up as tightly as possible. 'I don't want to think about home. I can't bear it.'

They're sitting side by side on a hard snowdrift with the sailcloth spread over them and their backs to the growing wind. There's a storm coming, clouds are piling up in front of the sun and it's fast growing dark. They have had neither warm food nor water since they left the ship because they have still not managed to light the camping stove. After struggling for two days they decided to rid themselves of half their burden to make walking easier. Even so, they sink up to mid calf in every step.

'I can't go on,' says Sæli, closing his eyes.

'We can rest while the storm blows over,' says Guðmundur, putting his Bible aside. 'Then we'll carry on.'

'Yeah.' Sæli rolls over on his hands and knees and then stands up. 'I've just got to go piss first.'

'I understand,' says the Captain with a nod to the young man. He's pretty sure he'll never see Sæli again, but decides to say nothing.

He knows that this will be his own last night. There's no chance he'll wake up from the sleep that is about to conquer the dregs of his consciousness. He's too tired for that to happen.

Guðmundur unzips his parka and unwinds the black dress from his cold torso. Can he stand up? Yes, he can stand up. The moment the captain stands up from the sailcloth the wind tears it away and sweeps it like a leaf into the dim distance.

Why die lying down if you have the option of dying dancing?

Guðmundur embraces the dress and attempts to dance but he is so stiff, and the wind so cruel, that he can hardly keep his balance.

Dance into death! Has he gone mad?

Mad or not mad, what difference does it make? It's not as if anyone can see him!

Guðmundur Berndsen tries to lift the stiff, frozen dress to his lips but he loses his hold on it and it flies off like the sailcloth.

'*Sweetheart,*' the captain gasps, taking one step forwards, then he falls on his face in the hard snow.

★ ★ ★

Sæli shields his eyes from the icy wind and tries to find the sun before it disappears beyond clouds. It's almost completely dark but Sæli catches sight of a pink streak in the distance. Then he turns away and heads north.

Iceland is to the north.

Sæli walks homewards until he collapses.

XXXVII

25 December

Whirlwind, dark, cruel frost ...

'ARE YOU THERE?' screams Satan into the suffocating snowstorm.

First their sled overturned and was blown onto Skuggi, killing him before Satan was able to cut the ropes. Their supplies were spread all over the hard firn and lost in an instant, while the sled shot up like an orange sweet wrapper into the black sky, where the air pressure shattered it.

'I'M ...'

Jónas is lying on his face on the firn only two metres away from Satan, but in a blizzard like this you can't see your hand in front of your face. The snow is so fine and the strength of the wind so overpowering that you can hardly breathe; your eyes are blinded, your lips bleed and your nostrils close.

They had only half a kilometre left to reach the foothills of the mountain when the storm hit, like the shadow of some evil harpy that suddenly shuts out the sun.

A truly devil-inspired storm ...

'COME OVER HERE! THERE'S A CAVE UP THERE!' yells Satan, starting to crawl up along a fissure in the glacier. If his memory serves him, the fissure leads slantwise up to the foothills where he thought he saw the mouth of a cave under the sheer cliff. Maybe he had simply seen the shadow of the cliff, but that's not the main thing. Out on the snow there's nothing for them but a long, drawn-out death. Under the cliff there may be shelter – even a little cave.

Satan crawls on hands and knees when the wind lets up a little but on his belly when the gusts are most savage. Each minute is a whole life's supply of oxygen deprivation, and each and every metre is an almost insurmountable task. The snow slips in under his clothing and his flesh grows cold, blue, stiff and …

But he's getting there, he's getting …
Silence.
And he plummets into a pitch-black emptiness.

★ ★ ★

'Are you there?'
Silence.
'Who's asking?'
'Jónas.'

Satan opens his eyes but sees only blackness. He remembers having grasped at nothing, then …

'I saw you just disappear,' says Jónas as he comes crawling in the dark. 'You were right – we're in a cave of some kind.'

'Can we get back out?' Satan asks, sitting up on the ice-covered floor of the cave. His clothes are frozen through, hard like an eggshell.

'No. Not the same way. The mouth is somewhere above us. Can't you hear the wind?'

'Yeah.' Satan hears the wind and wonders at the same time why the sound isn't louder. Shouldn't the cave be full of snow and ferocious wind? But there's only a slight layer of snow on the floor and the air is hardly moving. If anything, what slight breeze there is seems to come from inside the cave, not down through the entrance. What's causing that?

'I'm falling asleep,' says Jónas, while quivering violently on the ground beside Satan.

'Try to hold on,' says Satan, inhaling through his frostbitten nose. He's dying to light a cigarette to get a bit of warmth, but he only has one left and he's not going to light that until the end of the road.

Suddenly something cold and wet hits Satan's right cheek. It's a drop of water that continues down the neck of his frozen parka.

'What'll we do?' asks Jónas sleepily.

'We'll carry on,' says Satan, getting stiffly to his feet. 'It's hardly freezing at all in here. Can't you feel the breeze? There's a breeze coming from inside the cave. Maybe there's geothermal heat under the mountain? Maybe there's another route out of the cave? We have to carry on!'

Silence.

'Jónas?'

'Give me a hand,' says Jónas and Satan feels around in the dark until he finds the second mate's stiff fingers.

★ ★ ★

'I can't keep on,' says Jónas an hour later, when they've walked through the winding passages without finding anything but cold stone walls and impenetrable darkness. They are now in some sort of underground chamber or vault so high and wide that every little sound echoes for a good while before finally dying out.

… keep on … keep on … keep on …

Satan says nothing. What should he say? He hears Jónas sit down on the icy stone floor but he is going to stand. If he sits down he may not be able to get up again. His hands, feet and face are all frostbitten. The pain is terrific and getting worse by the minute. His physical energy is dwindling; his heartbeat is getting weaker and weaker; fatigue, hunger, cold and damp – all have taken their toll. He knows and can feel that he's not got long to live, but he chooses to ignore that knowledge. Where there's life there's hope, where there's life …

Silence.

'It's Christmas,' says Jónas with a sigh. 'Where are my children?'

… my children? … my children? … my children? …

'I killed their mother. I killed my wife. Hit her in the head with a hammer.'

… with a hammer … a hammer … a hammer …

'I didn't want to go to prison. That's why I sabotaged the communications. I wanted to get away, get as far as possible from … from what I had done. I didn't want to be judged by men. I wanted to stand before God. God knows what I did and why I did it. He understands me. He's the one that should judge me.'

… judge me … judge me … judge me …

Silence.

'There is no God,' says Satan, his voice low.

… no God … no God … no God …

'That's not true,' Jónas murmurs, then there's the sound of wooden beads as he pulls his rosary out of the pocket of his frozen parka. 'God exists. He definitely exists. Otherwise the lifeboat wouldn't have drifted back to the ship. What I'm uncertain of, on the other hand, is his mercy. I'm not sure any more that I want him to judge me. I understand now what I did, but at the same time I don't understand why I did it. I must be sick. No – maybe I'm not sick. Maybe I'm just a human abomination.'

… abomination … -nation … -nation …

'There are no lies in an echo,' says Satan.

… echo … echo … echo …

Silence.

'I don't want to fall asleep any more,' says Jónas, breathing fast and unevenly. 'I don't want to sleep! I don't want to die! I can't —'

Slrrrrrghhhhh …

'What was that?' asks Jónas, flinching.

… was that? … was that? … was that? …

'I don't know,' says Satan, cocking an ear. 'It was like when water gets sucked down a drain. Maybe there's a stream or a spring deep in the cave?

… in the cave? … the cave? … the cave? …

'Water? That wasn't any water!' says Jónas, who's almost hyperventilating. 'That was some … some *creature*! One of those monsters Stoker worships in secret!'

… in secret! … secret! … secret!

'So you've visited Stoker too,' says Satan, taking a couple of steps forwards.

'Don't!'

Slrrrrrghhhhh …

'Don't leave me!' says Jónas and he tries to grab Satan, to no avail. 'For God's sake, don't leave me!'

… leave me! … leave me! … leave me! …

'Here, take this,' says Satan, holding something towards the place where Jónas is sitting. 'I guess I won't be using it any more.'

… any more … any more … any more …

'What is it?' says Jónas as he takes the cold, hard object. 'Is it a gun? Is it your gun? What should I do with a gun?'

… with a gun? … a gun? … a gun? …

'You can use it on those monsters of yours,' says Satan. 'But just remember: there's only one bullet.' He sets off deeper into the cave.

… one bullet … bullet … bullet …

'Satan! Don't! I …'

… I! … I! … I! …

But he stops talking when he realises he's alone in the dark.

★ ★ ★

Satan takes slow, painful steps into the pitch-black cave. The floor seems to slant down but he's not sure. His body is little by little going numb; the cold has almost paralysed his limbs; it's getting more and more difficult to breathe; his heart falters in his chest, and his thoughts are becoming more and more hazy.

Once he's been walking for a good while, he reaches a narrow cliff wall that divides the space in two. Should he go right or left? Left or …?

Slrrrrghhhhh …

The sound seems to be coming from the right, so –

Bang, bang, bang …

The shot echoes back and forth through the cave before it finally dies out.

Silence.

★ ★ ★

Has he been walking for hours or just a few minutes? He doesn't know.

Satan stares into the dark without seeing anything at all. He feels around with fingers that are blue and black and as dead as a withered tree. He has found two more cliff faces that split the space in two.

Or is it always the same one?

He keeps turning right, always right. That's how you're supposed to find your way out of a maze ….

No!

He can't believe this! The caves have been narrowing little by little and just lately he's been able to touch both walls by spreading his arms, and if he lifts them he can touch the ceiling.

But now …

In front of him is a wall. A smooth cliff face. An ice-cold surface. The journey is over. Or is it? To hell with it! He can't carry on …

Satan doesn't show it, but the minute he touches that cold

stone surface, the hope in his breast dies out like a candle's flame. And in the shadow of despair, evil wakes from its deep slumber and evil cares about neither life nor death. It feeds on itself and shoves everything else aside. It lives and behaves like a fire that grows and grows until it is so large and cruel that it swallows itself and perishes.

Evil takes possession of Jón Karl. It growls inside his head, pumps black poison into his blood, locks onto every nerve and has the one aim of thriving and budding and blossoming like a spirit from hell in the flesh that contains it, whatever the consequences.

Evil is by nature eternal and thus has nothing to lose and nothing to win.

Jón Karl's body is as stiff as a board and a fire rages in his head. He puts his hands against the wall and tries to pull his head back, but his neck is stuck. He tries to yell but his voice is useless.

RED! HE SEES RED!

Inside Satan's head there's another Satan who puts his hands against a red wall which is the inside of the skull of the Satan who is standing, as if petrified, in front of the granite wall at the end of the caves. This new Satan is shirtless, long haired, freshly shaved, wearing black leather trousers and surrounded by white-hot lava and spitting tongues of flame. He stretches his head back, strains his sweaty muscles, locks resolute eyes on the wall and looks right through the wall that, to his frantic mind, is nothing but a puny eggshell.

SATAN, DEVIL, LUCIFER!

He aims his forehead at a fiery red spot on the other side of the wall because *there is no fucking wall*! He roars like a wild animal, drives himself forwards at terrific speed and, with all his might, busts through the thin eggshell.

XXXVIII

It's very strange, travelling without a body. Pitching back and forth as if in a swing, only more slowly, but also with an uncomfortable sideways motion, and always this weird feeling that every swing down is longer and deeper than the swing up, as if the soul were falling over some final brink, shown in slow motion, like a replay on television, again and again. It's quite soothing in some hypnotic way, but above all there's this unending feeling of numbness, getting ever more unreal the longer you glide about in this ink-black emptiness that smells of tobacco smoke and is as large or as small as a man's mind, as deep as the echo of the slow beat of the bass drum in the band.

Boom, boom, boom ...

XXXIX

Heavy blues music, the clamour of voices and a cloud of bitter smoke are pierced by the loud peal of a bell, as if from a ship lost in fog near the shore of some strange land.

Déjà vu.

'Fifteen minutes to closing!' the bartender shouts, letting go of the cord that hangs from the clapper of the old brass bell that once served a Dutch freighter.

On the ground floor of the bar customers are smoking and drinking at the tables; some are playing chess or whist, others talking with their neighbours and others still are sitting alone at the bar, intent on their own wretchedness and the oblivion of drink.

Like the guy dressed in denim who looks glassy eyed at the last sip in a greasy beer glass and then at his watch, which tells him it's fifteen minutes to one in the morning on Tuesday.

00:45

He's on is way to work as a deckhand for the first and last time. He's going to work alongside his brother-in-law on a ship to Suriname, where he's going to buy a thousand dollars' worth of cocaine and smuggle it back home. Actually, he's not going to smuggle it himself – he's going to let one of the other deckhands do it, but without the deckhand realising who he's working for. That's precisely the reason he begged his brother-in-law Jónas for the job. He had heard about some wretched deckhand on the *Per se* who owed loads of money to the same gambling joint where he had himself lost all his savings.

Once he got the job he called the deckhand and said he was collecting on the debt. He told him his name was Satan because he knew that if the guy asked around about that name he'd be advised to do as the debt collector said, if he wanted to live. Then he got his mother to sell her flat and give her children their inheritance in advance. He was going to buy her a house, later.

He'd threatened to hurt the deckhand's family if he wouldn't fetch the package in Suriname and bring it to Iceland. Not a nice thing to do, but he couldn't take the risk of smuggling it himself, since he had a record and all. He's going to reward the lad later, once he's got the money for the coke and found a place to live in more southern climes. He's going to reward him for the task – he's determined to do that, since he's going to be so rich you can't imagine.

Money in the bank, man! Money in the bank!

Yes, he'd made his final call to the lad earlier this evening, just to put the finishing touches to the whole deal before he left port. Nothing left but to buy the coke over there and get it to the lad. He had phoned him and threatened him and stuff – ha! Since then he'd been in here boozing and floozing and schmoozing.

He's fuzzy headed from the drink, slouching over the bar, but then suddenly seems to remember something or get an idea. At any rate, he abruptly straightens his back and pulls a folded piece of paper from the pocket of his denim jacket, unfolds it and reads what's written on it in blue pen.

555-SKIP

He sticks the paper in his pocket, finishes the last of his beer, puts out his half-smoked cigarette and gets down off the high bar stool. Then he weaves his way over to a circular table, where five out of the nine-man crew of *Per se* sit drinking.

He claps the two nearest on the back, leans forward between Rúnar Hallgrímsson and Ársæll Egilsson, and smiles vacantly through his unkempt beard.

'D'you think you could lend me a ten-coin, lads?' he asks, clearing his throat. 'I haven't got any change and I have to make a call.'

'Leave us alone, man!' says Rúnar, poking his elbow in the drunk's stomach and pushing him away from the table.

The drunk takes two steps back then stops to gain his balance, freezes in that position and stares straight ahead, as though in a trance.

It's as if his soul has gone to sleep, as if his personality has abandoned the drunken body. His eyes go dark and sink into his head, his mouth gapes and for just a moment there is literally no sign of life in his deathly pale face, which is little more than a skin-covered skull. He is lifeless – he has turned into a ghost or a zombie – but only for that single moment.

Then it's as if a silent explosion takes place inside the man.

Boom, boom, boom ...

His lungs draw breath, his eyes re-emerge, his fingers twitch and from his mouth comes a long, eerie sucking sound, as if from the throat of a sea monster that is desperately trying to crawl ashore.

'*Slrrrghh* ... merge in me,' mutters the man inarticulately as he stares at nothing, his eyes more like the shiny black of a raven than any window on the soul of a civilised human being.

He twitches all over as if he's cold; the skin of his face stretches till his gums and the whites of his eyes stand out, then his expanded pupils fill his ghostly eyes, dark red blood drips from his nostrils and spit runs from his gaping mouth, down his chin and onto the floor.

Then he straightens his back, blinks his eyes and briefly looks around at the table of five.

'Five dead men,' he says in a soft bass voice, looking deep into Sæli's eyes, 'four of them in a ship.'

'What?'

The man regains his balance on the wooden floor, then turns around and crosses to the bar, where he takes the same bar stool and leans over the bar.

'So how about paying your bill now, pal?' says the bartender, wiping the bar with a damp cloth.

'Hold on,' mutters the man, patting all his pockets until he finds a crumpled pack containing one cigarette in his trouser pocket. 'Guess I'll have one more round. Double whiskey on the rocks and a glass of soda water. And a pack of cigarettes – Princes.'

The man sticks the cigarette in his mouth and lights it with a match from a worn matchbook that's lying on the bar. On the front of the matchbook there's a grainy black-and-white photo of an old passenger ship afloat under a full moon. The ship's name is *Noon*. Inside the matchbook cover some barfly has written in blue ink:

That which sleeps forever is not dead.

'Here you go. Anything else?' asks the bartender as he serves the drinks.

'No,' says the man, sticking the matchbook in his pocket before drinking the ice-cold whiskey in one gulp.

'That'll be twelve hundred,' says the barman, wiping sweat from his forehead as he thumbs through his notebook till he finds 'Slot-machine Kalli'. 'Which brings the bill to nine thousand one hundred.'

The man pats the front of his jacket and checks under the left side, where he feels something thick underneath. He sees a thick wad of bills but shows no reaction. In his hip pocket he finds a thin wallet, which he opens and inspects.

'I seem to be broke for the moment,' says the man with a smile, after searching through his wallet and finding only 1500 crowns.

'Can't you pay your bill?' asks the bartender, irritated, staring into the infinite deep of the man's eyes.

'Just chalk it up,' says the man with a bearded grin, taking a sip of his soda. 'Open an account or something. I'll pay tomorrow.'

'You don't have credit here, as you're perfectly aware,' says the bartender, shaking his head. 'Either you pay up or I get the doorman to —'

The bartender stops talking when the man takes him by the throat and pulls him halfway over the bar. The bartender's feet leave the ground and the veins at his temples swell and darken.

'You chalk it up or I kill you! Understood?' says the man, tightening his grip on the bartender, who is going bright red and blue round his nose and eyes, and nods as best he can.

'And your full name?' asks the bartender, gasping for breath as he takes out an account book and pen.

'Satan,' says the man, knocking the ash off his cigarette as he grabs the pack of Princes and gets down off the bar stool.

'Satan?' says the bartender, looking up, but the man is halfway out the door.

Outside the bar is a little garden. The sky over the city is dark and the air is cool and bracing. Under a tree sits a black dog of doubtful parentage who looks at Satan with its brown eyes and wags its tail.

'Come here, boy!' says Satan, slapping his left leg, and the dog trots up to him.

Satan bends down, a cigarette hanging from the corner of his mouth and scratches the dog behind its ears, then they stroll together into the night.

XL

He's standing on a curved balcony looking over a brightly lit assembly room the size of a ship's hold. If this hall has a name it must be 'The Golden Gallery'. The walls are covered with golden squares from floor to ceiling. In front of the squares are smaller squares and, between them, lights that flicker on the smooth gold like fire in a dream. From the ceiling hang cylindrical chandeliers the size of ships' funnels, made up of crystal threads. The chandeliers are two-layered, the inner cylinders reaching below the outer ones. Inside them shines a light that refracts, creating thousands of lights that give the impression of stars in the sky or diamonds in water.

In the distance is the sound of old-fashioned jazz, though there is no band to be seen.

He walks down the broad, curved staircase to the assembly room. As he steps out on the polished wooden floor he sees a similar staircase on the port side. Above him is the balcony, but there's no-one there now.

He walks through the middle of the room. There are formally decked tables to each side. First he passes tables set for two and four but then he comes to long tables for eight, sixteen and thirty-two. There are white tablecloths and heavy silver cutlery, linen napkins in silver napkin rings, handpainted porcelain dishes and cut-crystal glasses arranged on them.

Very good, he thinks, as though he is responsible for it all, that things are exactly as he requested, that nothing in the assembly room disappoints the guests or upsets them.

Off and on the room seems to fill with the sound of chatter, light laughter and the clink of glasses, then he turns around and looks at first one table then another. But the moment he looks over his shoulder the voices are silenced and the clinking of glasses dies out between the echoing walls.

Or was it the screech of metal and rattling of chains?

At the front of the assembly room is a cognac lounge. Heavy leather chairs around uncovered round tables of dark wood, a thick carpet on the floor and the aroma of cigar smoke, although no-one is smoking. Stoker walks up a broad staircase leading to a doorway with heavy wooden double doors opening into the bright room. He pulls a rusty key from the pocket of his tailcoat, sticks it in the lock and turns it counter-clockwise three times.

Beyond the door is another room: a vast, stinking space – dark, cold and empty. At first he can see nothing – it's as if the bottomless dark absorbs all light – but little by little he sees a slow movement in the dark, as though a huge, formless fish were crawling ashore out of a black lake. A huge fish that makes a long, drawn-out, terrifying noise:

Slrrrrghhhhh ...

'Master!' says Stoker, as he bows low and opens the door wide.